MIN'DARRAN TALES

by

Steve Rouse

Edited by Karen T. Newman

Copyright © 2021 Left Hand Publishers, LLC
5753 Hwy 85 North #6092 Crestview, FL 32536
All rights reserved.   ISBN: 9781949241297

https://LeftHandPublishers.com
Twitter.com/LeftHandPublish
Facebook.com/LeftHandPublishers
editor@LeftHandPublishers.com
Cover design by Paul Metheney, pmetheney@gmail.com

Author's Dedication

It is with a mere string of words that characters, events, even worlds are created. Upon the writer's musings, we discover who these people are meant to be and who they become through what they face. What the consequences are of their choices and how that shapes their lives and lays bare the very fabric of their souls are the goals of writing.

Countless individuals have influenced my life and therefore my writing. A nod in appreciation goes to the colleagues and students from my teaching days, and friends who endured this writing process.

Special thanks and all my love goes to my wife Jeannie, our children, their spouses and our five grandchildren, to Vicki Steger and Christine Verstraete and the Kenosha Writers' Group. Lastly and most significantly, to my mentors and good friends, the fabled authors Jean Rabe and Stephen D. Sullivan, without whom this tale would forever exist only in some alternate reality.

Table of Contents

I. ORIGINS

The Uncle

"He's coming," Bu'ka said, moving from the window past his son. "Remember what we've said."

At long last, Min'darr too, could see his uncle crossing the Shat'su Expanse heading into town. He could never have suspected that this relative stranger would bring him into an unimaginable world. A world that would end his uncle's life before his very eyes. A world in which Min'darr would happily spend the rest of his life.

Despite the intense whispering of his parents, he understood the need to comply with clan traditions. The eldest male would take a youth at age ten to train him for a year. The same happened with the eldest woman and the girls. The boys had to learn the way of things beyond town, in the mountains.

Min'darr turned ten five days ago. His Uncle Taf'nar was late.

According to the tradition, that was enough to both break the bond of the training. It also meant the elder could not get the Ma'har, the gifts from the clan for taking on the youth for the year. The baskets holding the Ma'har sat covered in the town's central plaza. The mules to carry them waited at the stable.

The morning's crisp autumn air added to the brightness of the trees as they gave up their greens, revealing the yellows, reds, and oranges of the season. That cooler air kept sounds closer to the ground. Min'darr's ears told him that others had recognized Taf'nar's arrival. Word spread rapidly among the people who were already filling the plaza.

Within a quarter hour, Uncle Taf'nar thundered into Min'darr's world, invading the family home, filling it with the incredible stench of an overworked man desperately in need of a bath.

"Bu'ka! How is my brother?" he bellowed, swallowing his shorter brother in a bear hug.

Gasping for air as much from the stink as the smothering hug, Min'darr's father huffed his hello. "All is well, Taf'nar. Where have you been?"

"Give me a moment, brother." Taf'nar turned to face Kir'ni. He advanced a step, dropped to one knee, then took her hand to his lips. "Forgive me, my sister-in-marriage for being late. My deepest desire rests on soothing your heart.

"Please forgive my delinquency. A rockslide from Mount Peka blocked my intended path. I had to seek another route, so I could not keep to my plan. That detour set me back days. I hope, in your graciousness, you can accept my apology. I am desperate to take your son into my care and teach him my world. I promise you he will learn things known to no one other than myself." He stayed, prompting her by continually kissing her hand until she relented.

"Of course, brother-in-marriage," Min'darr's mother said with a sigh. "Your reason is understandable. But it, ahh ... it does present a problem as the strict traditions of the Ma'har are most specific. I am sorry that you struggled so to come all this way, but I cannot let you take Min'darr. Traditions, you know?"

"I can only hope to convince you and the clan otherwise," he said in a more distant voice as he rose, leaving to fetch his belongings.

Min'darr spent the next hour fetching heated bath water for his uncle who reminded the boy of a dead tree. His tall uncle was colorless, skinny to a fault. His keen eyes kept the boy's attention. During that time, they spoke only once. He asked, "Min'darr, given the choice, would you want to come with me?"

Min'darr had considered many possibilities in the days before his birthday. If his uncle had failed to show within the month, he would have been assigned to another elder, completing his training with them. Taf'nar was his first choice. His personality alone had a reputation that attracted the boy, making the prospect of the upcoming year more than enticing.

Since their home was smaller with rare occurrences of actual privacy, many of his parents' conversations were easy to overhear. Min'darr had made it a point to always listen. Their content about Taf'nar painted a picture of an independent, daring man, who was brave to a fault. "Dangerous ... reckless," they'd said. Their criticisms heralded a year of adventure on his horizon, as long as he was allowed to go with him.

"Yes, Uncle, I do," he responded.

Taf'nar smiled. "Good. Gather your belongings. Be ready to go quickly then."

*

"I never liked your brother! Too odd. Who lives alone above the tree line?" Min'darr's mother muttered to the boy's father as the three walked to the plaza.

Bu'ka stopped to face her, bumping Min'darr from between them. He kept his voice low. "You know I am not happy with this any more than you. He has always been impertinent, willing to do things his own way, then expecting others to just accept it. I will do what I can. Go stand with Koo'bla until we are done here."

Min'darr watched her stand tall, chin quivering. "If he has to go, my son shall survive his year. I may not." She joined the women gathered behind the Ma'har, next to her daughter, Koo'bla, with their new grandson.

*

Min'darr stood on a small dais next to the clan's matriarch. Looking out, he guessed the gathering numbered at about a hundred. All the women were talking. Most of the men stood with arms folded, occasionally nodding to each other. No one smiled. He thought this odd as the Ma'har was generally a happy occasion. It was for the ones he'd seen before. It was a chance to celebrate growth.

Taf'nar was escorted into the plaza by Min'darr's father. The ceremony would charge his uncle with the boy's education and care. His bath had begun a remarkable transformation. He walked taller, wrapped in bear furs adorned with white fox tails. His long, grey hair pulled back into a single tail. A ram's horn hung from one shoulder, a full quiver of arrows with his bow on the other.

4

From his woven leather belt hung a great sheathed sword, a large, blue gemstone embedded in its pommel. His narrow eyes never wavered from looking straight ahead, yet Min'darr doubted anything escaped his attention.

Min'darr's father spoke when they reached the dais. "Milady, I would speak first as Min'darr's father."

Shin'Davi, the clan's matriarch, gestured her approval with her cane.

"Taf'nar is my older brother, the eldest male of our family. As such the Ma'har is his. He was, however, absent for the tenth marking of my son's birth. As such, by tradition, his mother and I demand that he relinquish the right to the Ma'har." He stepped back avoiding eye contact with Taf'nar.

Min'darr's uncle nodded with pursed lips as Shin'Davi's cane pointed at him.

His voice sounded as if it came from the frozen rocks of where he called home. "I hear what you are saying, my brother. To you, to his mother, to Min'darr, and to the clan, I stand guilty by circumstance. I was delayed by a landslide that blocked my way, forced to then go around Mount Peka which added days to my journey. Otherwise, I would have been here to properly celebrate Min'darr's moving from child to youth."

Taf'nar turned to Min'darr, bowing. "My deepest apologies to you, young Min'darr.

"To amend for my delinquency, I do hereby relinquish any claim to the Ma'har's supplies." The collective gasp of those gathered took Min'darr by surprise. To his knowledge, no one had ever done this before.

In the history of the training, the Ma'har had become a necessity. Taking on another mouth, another body for a year, was not without its burden, especially in the sparser Dreklidal Mountain region where they lived. Min'darr would be heading into its upper reaches to live with his uncle.

"That is not acceptable." The feebler voice of Shin'Davi, at least in her nineties, barely could be heard. "As leader of this clan, I remind you that the Ma'har is known to be the difference between life and death. It cannot be refused. But we must first decide if the boy remains yours to take."

"My lady, I have refused it. I am honor-bound to keep my word." Taf'nar had moved to stand next to Min'darr.

"It cannot be refused." She added a sharp rap of her cane to the dias to accent her statement. She looked at Min'darr. "What is your choice, young Min'darr?"

He glanced quickly around, spotting both his parents' faces filled with concern. One thought entered his mind. The question he'd avoided. What would his option be if he stayed? The only other choice available would deal with learning the finer points of how to clean the stables for a living.

"To be trained by my Uncle Taf'nar, my lady."

She nodded, speaking louder for everyone to hear. "Min'darr has accepted his training. His parents' objections are moot. I accept the reason given by Taf'nar for his absence. It is excused. Take it with you, Eldest Taf'nar. The Ma'har, the boy, along with the mules, all are yours. We cannot celebrate as if you had been here on his birthdate, so you may leave whenever you are so inclined. On behalf of the clan, I bid Min'darr goodbye and wish him a year of good growth." She turned her back on them, a sign of dismissal.

"No! I must not take the Ma'har. I cannot!" Taf'nar yelled. He stepped forward, dropping his furs, standing shirtless. "You force my hand. We must leave this up to the Creator." He stepped to the four baskets of the Ma'har and squatted, arms held over them. Before any objections were heard, he called out loudly, invoking the Creator.

"Most Gracious Creator, I humbly thank ye for all you have provided me. I failed in my obligation to my nephew. I am filled with remorse. Allow me my penance!" he screamed. "I must be made to do without." He paused, glancing around.

Raising his arms to the sky, he continued with a louder voice. "What then, O Wise One, must be done with these? We give them to you! They are yours, my Creator. I bid Thee, take them." Taf'nar lowered his hands, palms down, resting them on the baskets a bit more than shoulder width apart.

Min'darr stared intently, expecting ... something. The crowd too, stood silent in unspoken anticipation.

Two small glows flickered directly beneath his palms. Twin wisps of smoke rose skyward. It took a moment for some to see it. The flames, however, rose quicker than their shouts. The gathered folks gasped aloud, expressing disbelief. Some stepped back, others moved closer in the hopes of seeing more. Some mumbled, one cried. The effect was not wasted on his uncle. Min'darr saw his eyes widen and the corners of his mouth turn up for just a second.

He stood, again raising his arms, encircled by the wind-driven smoke. "O Creator! Thank you for blessing us by accepting our sacrifice to you." Taf'nar gathered his cloak, then strode to Min'darr. "Gather the mules for us. Don't forget your saddle. Be at the house quickly. I fear this town, always have."

Min'darr nodded. He ran toward the stables, veering to avoid the now fully engulfed Ma'har. A score of men gaped at the fire, though none moved to put it out. One eyed him suspiciously as he ran by them, yelling after him, "You'll die if you go with that demon."

Min'darr ran on, unsure how his uncle could be seen as a demon. He arrived at the stables, and ten minutes later, rode out on a mule while leading a second one. After bypassing the town's center, he arrived at his house. His parents were standing in the main room. Uncle Taf'nar's mules stood out front, fully packed.

His mother stopped when she saw him. She sobbed as she spoke. "Why would you choose him over us ... over me?"

"Now Kir'ni, the boy ..." Bu'ka tried consoling his wife.

"You shush! You're a man. You know nothing about the heart of a mother. Min'darr is my baby, my treasure. How could he leave me?" She draped her arms across his shoulders.

Min'darr hugged her and cupped her face in his hands. "Mama—uh, I mean Mother, you know that I love you, yes?"

She nodded, tears streaking her cheeks.

"Good, I know you love me." Min'darr felt calm as he worked to pacify this woman who'd provided his every need since birth. He knew her stories, retold to the point he could tell them himself. "You have raised me well, so well that I am ready to take my next steps in becoming a man. You always told me, 'Face what must be done and realize…'"

"… 'that you are the one to do it,'" she finished his quoting her. "Oh, my darling. How I wish you would stay, and yes, I know you must go, even if it is with him," she said, tossing her head aside in Taf'nar's direction. "It is so hard to say goodbye. A whole year …"

But she dried her cheeks and became more focused, instantly stronger. "You are my Min'darr. I am so very proud of you. You will survive this year in spite of the man you must learn from."

Taf'nar emerged from Min'darr's room with two bundles. Seeing the boy, he tossed one of the bundles to him. "Any problems at the stable?"

"No. I got both mules," the boy said.

"Only two?" Taf'nar asked. "So be it," he said gruffly. Then added, "Get these secured onto your mount." He handed the other bundle to Min'darr as well, then glanced out the doorway. "That little fire isn't going to keep them occupied for too long," he muttered.

Kir'ni eyed Taf'nar suspiciously. "How did you start that fire?"

"I didn't. The Creator did," Taf'nar said, following Min'darr out the door.

A minute later, Min'darr rushed back into the house. "Mom, where's Dad? I need a dagger. Taf'nar said I have to have one, maybe two."

Bu'ka came into the room from the back carrying a gift. "I have Min'darr's coming-of-age gift."

Taf'nar appeared in the doorway. "We must go now."

Kir'ni objected. "But why the rush? I thought you'd leave in the morning. We haven't had dinner! Min'darr has to open his gift."

Taf'nar visibly calmed himself. "I do apologize … again. You know this town isn't going to let the burning of the Ma'har go without some kind of retribution, even if they meant to give it to us. I am not welcomed here, lest you forget. I don't wish to be put through another trial for something they could never understand.

"We must leave immediately, Bu'ka. Help me get Min'darr to the safety of the hills, beyond Nordana Pass. Only then will all be well, I promise," Taf'nar pleaded. "His future depends on it."

Min'darr's father stood mute for a second. "All right, Taf. I don't know why, but I trust your senses." He thrust the wrapped package into Min'darr's hands. "Here. A bow, arrows, a short sword, and dagger."

His father grasped Min'darr by the shoulders. "May the blessings of our Creator, the clan, our whole family be upon you forever, my son. Go with our love, our hopes for health, growth, and wisdom," Bu'ka said solemnly. "Go!"

Min'darr stood, mouth agape as his father seldom referred to the Creator. He paused to hug his parents together. "Goodbye! I love you both! See you in a year," he managed to say as he disappeared through the doorway. Half a minute later, their mules produced a dust cloud as they headed out at a run.

*

They reached the midpoint across the Shat'su Expanse, a three-mile-wide plain before their trail narrowed drastically at Nordana Pass. So narrow, it would barely allow four riders abreast to pass. Min'darr glanced to see a dust cloud from riders behind them.

"They're following us," he called to his uncle.

"I knew they would. That's why I am prepared. We will be safe once we enter the pass."

"How?"

"That's for you to discover. Drive your mule, nephew. Make him believe he's a steed!"

"Gerg is the best mule. If any mule can make this, he can!" Min'darr bragged.

"Gerg?" asked Taf'nar.

"It's a noise he makes when he sleeps," Min'darr explained.

Taf'nar and Min'darr dug their heels into their mounts' ribs, urging them on. Their pack mules also responded to the need to run as hard as possible. Min'darr knew that mules were masters of climbing. On the other hand, they were a sad excuse for an open-field run. A good horse could have covered the expanse in a

9

fraction of the time they'd spent. He hoped those following were on mules, not horses. Still, he was stymied by not knowing why Taf'nar felt the need to flee or what whoever was chasing them needed.

Even at his young age, Nordana Pass was well known to him. It was the only pass within a two days' ride into the higher mountains to their east. As they approached, Min'darr's brow furled. "What's going on at the pass? It doesn't look right."

Taf'nar's breathing matched his mule's. "Wait ... surprise they'll get. Almost there."

The pursuing cloud was closer, yet not quite a threat. Min'darr guessed they'd reach the pass easily before them. He didn't understand how it would be so safe, as Taf'nar suggested, once into it. He looked ahead again.

The granite walls rose ten times higher than the trees, steep and impassible. A mere crack compared to that long rampart of mountain, was the lone throughway to the higher elevations beyond. Calstara, Min'darr's hometown, flourished as the first point of civilization west of the pass.

As Min'darr had seen, the pass looked different. Huge, dark masses seemed to cling against its inner walls. As they rode closer, he could see individual trunks of dozens of pine trees in each of the bundles. None showed any hint of green.

A minute later, they entered the pass. Min'darr had seen it correctly. Dozens of dead trees were raised, lashed to the sides of the pass. They slowed their mounts and Taf'nar dropped from his mule, its lungs heaving from their run.

"Stay in your saddle. Take them up by that second rise. Keep 'em steady," his uncle instructed.

When Min'darr had the mules in position, he looked back. Taf'nar was cutting through heavy, knotted ropes wedged into various crevices. A loud rasping filled the narrow canyon as the trees fell into the pass's opening, sealing it.

"Uncle!" Why are you closing the pass?"

"The clan pursues us to punish me for destroying the Ma'har," he said kneeling next to the fallen debris.

"This won't stop them, Uncle. Maybe slow them down a bit ..." Min'darr observed, "... won't they simply pull it out of the way?"

Taf'nar looked at him, grinning. "You and I will do well together. Yes, they could pull it out of the way, if it wasn't an inferno!"

Min'darr's uncle knelt solemnly as he'd done in town, keeping his shirt on this time. Again, flames flared from under his palms. He stood, then ran to the mules as the crackling of a very large fire filled his ears. Its quickly building heat warmed Min'darr's face.

"Uncle, tell me what this is about." Min'darr hoped for some explanation for his uncle's extreme behavior.

"As I told your father, we had to reach this pass to be truly safe. This fire will burn for three hours at least, plenty of time to make our escape.

"I will explain it to you when we reach my cabin. From there, in time, I have been told to take you to meet one who is of great importance to your future."

"What? Who? Someone knows about me?"

Taf'nar glanced back at his inferno and clucked his mule to walk. "All in good time, nephew."

At the Cabin

Min'darr and Uncle Taf—that's what he said he preferred being called—climbed their mules along some very steeply inclined, narrow ledges. They'd left the main trail far below after following it for about four miles. During that time, the smoke from the timber fire soared high along the escarpment, dissipating with the winds.

While resting the mules later, Min'darr huddled against a boulder to shield himself from the wind. He munched on a portion of trail mix.

"Uncle Taf, I need to know about the trees at the pass."

"Of course you do. I would, too. It took me about two months to collect them, then another to tie and hoist them. I've actually done little else in these past weeks but to prepare for today."

"So you weren't detoured by a slide like you claimed?" he asked.

"Oh, nephew, I truly hate that our year together started with a lie, however it did. I promise you two things. One is that I promise to never lie to you again. Two, you will come to understand why it was necessary for me to do what I did. Come, we should be off."

"Not until you tell me." Min'darr stayed curled up against the rock.

Taf'nar stood, a look of concentration flashed across his face, but was quickly replaced by a sparkling-eyed laugh. "We'll talk as we ride." He gathered his reins. He had to pause because the boy had not moved. "Min'darr, now."

"I need to know, Uncle. We have a year together. Why did you lie to us? ... to your own brother?" Min'darr said, still sitting.

Taf walked to Min'darr, grabbed his coat's collar, dragging him across the hard ground to his mount.

"This is not how it is supposed to be, Uncle!" Min'darr yelled. He wrapped his arms around the mule's leg.

Taf squatted next to his nephew. "You are so right, my boy. But I am your elder. Since you are to learn from me, it would be best for you to start listening to me.

"You may seldom agree with what I tell you. Rest assured that I'll tell you everything you need to know to survive. You will regret defying me. You don't want to get me angry, or I may, well ... watch. It will pay for you to learn this." He brought the rein of Min'darr's mule over its head, then held it between his finger and thumb in front of the boy.

"What do you see here?" he asked.

"My rein," he said after giving his uncle a look like the man was mad.

"Watch," his uncle ordered. As he held it, he mumbled something. A thin wisp of smoke rose a heartbeat before it ignited.

Min'darr held his breath, then blurted out, "I knew it! It was you! In town, you burned the Ma'har, not the Creator as you claimed! You got magic?" Despite the excitement in his voice, that last was more question than statement.

Taf extinguished the flame, then he held out his hand. Min'darr reached up and took his hand. Taf'nar effortlessly hoisted him to his feet. "This is something that is never, I repeat, never to be told to anyone. Understand?" Taf said with his nose an inch from his nephew's.

"Yes, Uncle Taf," he replied.

"Enough. We will talk of this when we are home, not before. Two days." He mounted his mule. Min'darr did the same. They rode, Taf ahead with two supply mules. Min'darr brought his supply mule behind him, alone with a million questions.

*

About midday on the second day, they arrived at Taf'nar's cabin. It had snowed the night before, only six or so inches. The wind had done its work in making drifts in areas after blowing the passes clean. The going was none the worse.

Min'darr had silently formed low expectations for his uncle's cabin, expecting a rough hovel with cracks in the walls, a leaky roof, rough-hewn furniture, and maybe an outhouse. He found a cabin that exceeded everything he'd imagined.

From the outside, it appeared frugal, yet sound. Situated on a slope, the rear was dug into the hillside. A covered porch spanned the length of the front. The thatched roof had a chimney slightly off center. A fenced corral was to the right, leading directly into what appeared to be a stable at the side of the building furthest to the angle of their approach.

Taf led the way into the corral. The two of them set to unloading the mules. The side doors opened to a cozy barn with six stalls. Hay, feed, blankets, and saddles were stored on shelving. They stayed in the barn until after they'd brushed and fed the mules. Min'darr used the barn's pump to fill a trough with fresh well water. A loud thump sounded against the door to the house. Taf's two mules brayed as if in response.

Taf looked at Min'darr. "Okay, I'm going in now. You have to wait here. You'll be meeting Hilda in a minute or so." With that, he pushed open the door just a crack, enough to squeeze through. Min'darr heard scuffling noises before Taf closed the massive door.

A few minutes later, the door opened. Standing on the other side was Taf, straining against a leash attached to a collared goat ... a gigantic goat by Min'darr's standards with prodigious horns, at least as wide for the doorway. It snorted, spit, frantically pawing the floor in an effort to enter the barn. Again the mules brayed. It seemed like a greeting to Min'darr. The goat looked only at him, bleating loudly and pawing the floor.

"Min'darr, meet Hilda. She is the best home security money can buy. Take off your shirt so she can get a smell of you." Taf said.

Min'darr furled his brow as he began unbuttoning his shirt. Taf struggled to hold Hilda at bay.

"Quickly!" Taf urged, struggling to hold the goat.

Min'darr complied, throwing the shirt to Taf. Hilda jumped, catching it. She snorted, biting and shaking the shirt. Within seconds, with the help of her hoofs, she'd shredded the shirt into ribbons of cloth. Then she bent, gnawing the remains.

All this while, neither Taf nor Min'darr said anything. Taf out of familiar expectations, Min'darr out of shock and sheer disbelief. "I liked that shirt," Min'darr said glumly.

"You ain't done yet, nephew. She has to know she can't push you around. Let her know you're the boss. I'm going to let her go in three, two, one ..."

"Geez, Uncle, what am I supposed to do?" Min'darr yelled.

"Dominate her. If she wins, you won't get a minute's peace living here. Don't let her butt ya! Now!" He let her go. Hilda's collar relaxed against her. She shook her head, then bolted into the stable area, straight for Min'darr.

He hadn't had too much experience with goats. He knew they were fiercely loyal, but possessed an overall nasty disposition. Not much help. She came at him head down. He grabbed her horns and was immediately pushed back against the wall. Keeping as low as he could, Min'darr used his leverage with the wall to push back. Hilda lacked traction against the wooden floor, so Min'darr gained some leverage.

"This is one strong goat, Uncle Taf. What does she like?"

"Beating up people she doesn't know." He stood leaning against the door jamb, grinning.

Min'darr twisted Hilda's head to one side. She resisted. He quickly reversed direction. She flopped down. He leaped on her, refusing to let go of her horns. "I don't like wrestling a goat, Uncle Taf. I never liked it when my sister wrestled me. She always won, too. I hated being tickled!"

Taf laughed. "I've wrestled Hilda. She never tickled me, although she came close to poking my eye out once or twice. Oh, she spits, too."

15

"I know," he said. Spittle ran down his left cheek. Min'darr was already thinking about possible tickle spots on the goat. He tried behind her front legs, nope ... base of the tail, also nope ... behind the ears, she leaned into it a little for a minute, then nope. Finally, Hilda stopped thrashing when he scratched behind and below her jaw. Yep, that worked. Just at the base of her throat.

After a few minutes of that, Hilda the attack-goat became Hilda the keep-scratching-me-goat. Standing now, she nuzzled into him, begging for more. Min'darr's smile beamed up at Uncle Taf.

"Well, it looks like you won, Min'darr. Now, let's see how long you gotta keep up the scratching. C'mon in."

He followed with Hilda right behind him, butting his backside if he stopped too quickly. Min'darr was more concerned that she'd be more likely to nip his buttocks. He grabbed some of the remnants of his favorite shirt to offer Hilda in case she got too demanding.

They stood in a mud room—a room used to hold outside clothing like boots, snowshoes, and skis. A sink with a water pump was in the corner. They changed into house slippers, then went into the house proper, again through a very heavy wooden door, about two feet thick.

The sitting room was next, complete with a fireplace, a stove, table, and chairs. An upper sleeping loft extended out a good eight feet. On the left side of the hearth was a set of shelves holding kitchen utensils as well as some books.

On the other side of the hearth stood a large cabinet, floor to ceiling. Taf, as part of his tour, opened it, showing Min'darr a store of clothing and supplies. Strapped to the inside of its single door was a good assortment of swords, daggers, bows, pikes, and axes. "The arrows are kept here," he said. He moved the lantern from the top off of a barrel in the corner, rotating the top to open it. Min'darr saw scores of arrows jamming the confines of their container.

"By the Creator, Uncle! You could fend off an army with all of this," Min'darr spoke as he withdrew one shaft, delicately feathered, tipped with a twin-bladed metal broadhead. "This is beautiful, Taf. Did you make them yourself?"

"I did, nephew. One of the jobs I had in town before I left. One of the few skills I use to this day," Taf said as Min'darr reinserted the arrow into the barrel. Taf reset the cover, then put the lantern back that set upon it.

"Now, to the lower levels," Taf announced. He reached into the floor of the cabinet, lifting the bottom plank out. A dark hole stared back at Min'darr, barely big enough to fit through.

"I'll go first to light the way after I take the chill out of the air." He leaned across and, with his special magical touch, lit the fireplace. He grinned then squeezed into the hole.

Within seconds, Min'darr saw a glow in the chamber beneath him. Taf's voice beckoned him. Following Taf's example, he sat dangling his legs, then twisted to face into the room. His feet found a ladder rung. He lowered himself into a surprisingly large chamber, the same size as the upper chamber combined with the mud room. A sconce on each wall lit the chamber.

Min'darr scanned the contents and found it to be a cold storage room. Shelving filled with jars of vegetables or fruit lined two walls. Wooden casks marked VENISON, FOWL, and OTHER were stacked in one corner. The floor around the casks was strewn with salt granules. Sacks of grain rested on wooden pallets. Spices and some salt blocks filled another set of shelves.

"This is so very impressive, Uncle. Way more than I would ever have expected. You have an amazing place here. Amazing!" Min'darr said, gawking around the chamber.

"So, could there be any more to show you? Is there anything that stands out as another passageway? Look around. What do ya think?" Taf asked, sitting on a cask.

"Of course there is," Min'darr said and looked more closely around the room. He moved, too, testing various structures until he stopped next to his uncle. "Get up, please."

Taf moved aside. Min'darr tried to rock the cask, slide it and lift it, nothing worked. "I give up. Where is it?" he finally asked.

"Are you sure there is one?"

"Yes."

"Why?" Taf asked.

"Well, you're missing a workshop. The stable has leather, shoes, but no workbench. Neither is there one upstairs or here. You can't have bought all this, it looks too new. You also need a lathe for the arrow shafts and a smelter for the arrowheads. Also, no bag of feathers for the vanes."

"Pretty good for a ten-year-old. The entrance to the last level is behind the spice shelf. Here," he pointed to the unit. "To unlock it, lift the end jar to the left on the top shelf." He demonstrated. They both heard a clunking sound. Taf then swung the shelf out exposing a narrow, short doorway. They stepped in and Taf again magically lit another sconce. Everything Min'darr had mentioned was there in the smaller room, along with a deep trough of running water. The pipe from the mud room pump immersed in it.

"Artesian well," Taf said. "Best water ever. It's the reason I built the cabin in this spot.

Here, Min'darr, is everything you said I needed that you didn't see. I'm impressed. You weren't guessing, you knew. Nicely done."

They spent an hour or so in both rooms of the lower level, Taf showing his pride in everything he'd included in his home.

"Have you ever had to use these hiding places?" Min'darr asked.

"I've been working on this place for about six years. Twice I've been overrun by people who thought it would be nice to live here. One trio, one group of five. None survived. The group of five took me three days to kill."

"Wow! I had no idea. Were you hurt at all?" Min'darr asked.

"I got a stab wound in my side. See?" He lifted his shirt to show the scar. Min'darr recalled seeing it during his uncle's bath. "And no, no one knows about it. Keep it that way, eh? The law is sparse around here, but they'd frown on so many being dead."

"Self-defense? You had no choice."

Taf stood and blew out the sconces. "Sounds good to me. Let's get some grub."

*

After their meal and the cleanup, they sat before the fire. Hilda rested on a mat at Taf's side. Min'darr said, "Time, Uncle Taf. Two stories. You promised to tell me about the trees and about your magic."

Taf sighed. "The magic story has to wait. Remember that you will be visiting those who gave me the magic to light fires. This spring, so be patient.

"The tree story goes a long way back. What have your parents told you about me?"

"Not much really. You've been gone from town all of your adult life. And, they said people don't like you too much."

"So, why would you choose to come with me?"

"No, Uncle. You owe me the story, no more distractions," Min'darr insisted.

"All right. When I was ten, I had to be trained by my grandfather, the town drunk. He had spent time in the kingdom's army as an armorer. Weapons. So, he owned a shop where he sold weapons that he'd made. He also fixed them for others. That's where I learned. I kept working for him well into my teens. He was a skilled tradesman. I learned much.

"But I also got to see him at his worst. That would have been most any night at the local pubs. I got into many fights defending his honor. I didn't lose any of those fights. Then one morning I went to open the shop and found him there dead. No injuries, just dead. Despite his public drunkenness, some of those I had fought claimed they heard us arguing the night before—so not true. It never pays to argue with a drunk.

"Anyway, it was three against one. I was arrested and tried for his murder. The doctor was my only defense. He confirmed that Grandfather hadn't died from any injuries. The trial ended with my acquittal. I stayed, trying to make the business work. From then on no one would come in. So I left, taking the inventory to sell elsewhere. Some of the stuff in this cabinet," he added, pointing, "were part of that.

"I came back twice over the years. Each time someone would bring up the past, wanting to belittle him or fight me. The last time, I couldn't avoid it. I fought two men. One of them fell after

19

I punched him, hitting his head. He died. There were witnesses who said I'd tried to avoid the fight. The sheriff told me it would be best if I'd leave and never come back.

"I expected trouble when I came for you. So I came prepared for the worst. No one there knows where I live. I like it that way. Note that I told the clan that I had to go around an avalanche on Mount Peka?"

"Yes, but ..."

"Go on."

"Mount Peka is two days' ride from the pass to the north. We turned south coming off the pass."

"And in so saying, we gain a whopping big four days if anyone wanted to try to find me ... rather, us. Come, it's late. You'll sleep here by the fireplace," he said. He climbed up to his loft, threw down a thick mat along with a few blankets for Min'darr to use.

"Thanks, Uncle Taf. I should be plenty warm with all these. Do you have enough?" Min'darr asked.

"Oh sure. Not to worry about me. I've plenty. You'll have one more thing to consider as you try to get comfortable. Good night."

Min'darr furled his brow wondering what that meant as he set up his bedding.

The lights were extinguished. Min'darr settled in. He closed his eyes and was almost instantly crushed. Hilda sidled in next to him, plunking down between him and the fire.

"Hilda! C'mon, move over," Min'darr complained while thumping against her side. She didn't move.

Min'darr felt the goat's breathing on his face as his uncle chuckled from his loft.

Ogre

As well stocked as Taf's pantry was, they needed to hunt to replenish what they'd used. It was nice to occasionally have fresh meat. Four months after Min'darr's arrival was one of those times.

Winter had been cold and long. The two established a routine of tending to chores, then working together on Min'darr's training. Taf proved to be a capable tutor while Min'darr soaked in what his uncle showed him about making weapons, also in preserving foods. He memorized all that he'd been shown. They both slept well after long days of schooling. Taf learned some things as well, especially in being able to communicate with a ten-year old.

Mountain snows had blocked most movements, so it got to the point where supplies were running short. Spring was in full bloom in the lower elevations while the snows were only a week gone at Taf's cabin. Time for the hunt.

*

The ram had moved very little from the floor of the ravine.

Taf'nar and Min'darr first saw the animal from atop the ridge, too far for a sure shot. The terrain with the surrounding scrub prevented a clean shot. Because he had younger legs, Min'darr ran farther along the ridge, then worked his way down to the gully floor with the intent to drive the ram up toward his uncle's hiding spot. The mountain sheep grazed unaware.

As they'd planned, Min'darr began thrashing the bushes. It worked beautifully. The ram bolted, heading up the bluff directly toward Taf'nar. Stopping about two-thirds of the way up, it glanced back down. Taf'nar notched an arrow bringing the bow to his eye. The ram was within range. He steadied himself by

21

controlling his breathing. He loosed his arrow just as a huge hairy beast streaked in and seized the ram. Taf's arrow drove deep into the thing's back.

Min'darr's feet moved before his mind told them to.

The creature's roar filled his ears as did the straining of his lungs as he raced up the bluff. The great beast writhed, roaring in pain. It finally dropped the still-struggling ram and, reaching back, yanked the arrow free. It looked after the fleeing ram. It then saw the approaching boy. It snarled, then whirled to face the arrow's source, Taf'nar, who'd already notched another arrow.

Never in his young life had he seen anything move so quickly. In a scant two heartbeats, the creature flashed across the hundred-foot distance to reach Taf'nar. Min'darr saw his uncle's second arrow fly. He watched his uncle hoisted into the air by the throat, bow sailing one direction, the quiver in another. The creature dangled him some five feet off the ground, then simply stood there, cocked its head to stare at him. Both of Taf'nar's hands were wrapped around the beast's thick wrist, fighting to breathe.

Min'darr charged, screaming and making as much noise as possible, notching his own arrow as he ran. It was at least nine feet tall, *An easy target. This thing has to be an ogre,* he thought. At least it fit the basic description according to Taf's stories.

Min'darr's arrow took flight, heading straight at the beast. It stood, watching him. He reached for a second arrow as the first arched toward its target. His shot was true. Just before it pierced the creature's chest, in a move that defied the eye, the beast's free hand snagged the arrow inches from its heart. In another heartbeat, splinters of it dropped to the ground at its feet. *Probably the same fate as Taf's second arrow,* he realized.

Mindless of the danger, the boy blindly continued his charge at the monster, drawing his hunting knife.

It leaped at him, again with incomprehensible speed. While holding his uncle, the creature lunged at Min'darr, grasping the boy mid-step by its free hand. In a single motion, it whirled him around, slamming Min'darr against its side, pinning him. Min'darr screamed mightily as the knife he held was jostled and embedded itself into the front of his thigh.

After tucking Taf'nar to its other side, the creature bolted down the hillside at break-neck speed. Amidst the bumping and thrashing about, Min'darr's senses were assailed by the creature's horrific, greasy stench. Pain from his leg shot through him with every movement. Finally, his reality dulled from the repeated thumping. He fell out of consciousness.

*

Min'darr woke to fiery pain. He felt the throbbing of his leg wound in his teeth with every step the creature took. His side and chest ached from being crushed against the beast's side. His leg was awash in searing anguish. Straining, yet unable to move, he found himself trussed in the grip of this monster. Everything hurt; even breathing was agony.

Why would the Creator think of making such a stench? He wished he didn't have to breathe such foul-smelling air.

The creature dropped them onto a cold, rocky floor, triggering Min'darr's pain yet again. He clutched his thigh, fearful of what injury he might find. His hand came back bloodied. The knife, however, was gone. Overcome by dizziness, he concentrated on the sound of Uncle Taf's voice.

*

His leg throbbed badly despite the fact that it had been wrapped. *Thanks, Uncle Taf.* He was lying next to a rock wall. Dim firelight flickered from around a corner, a different room.

That same odor permeated the room he was in ... a dominant, heavy, sickeningly oversweet musk. To Min'darr, it seemed a rancid combination of wet silage, bad meat, and sulfur. His eyes burned, his mouth dry from its intensity. It took everything he had do to keep from retching.

Min'darr calmed himself as best he could in order to take in his surroundings. The uneven rock suggested he was in a cave. An oily haze hung in the air. A lone candled sconce burned near him, its flame struggling to burn. Tendrils of its thin smoke filled the chamber.

He was in a dark corner looking toward a wall reflecting the light of a small fire. *This might be the ogre's cave,* he thought. It cast shadows that danced across the wall as the flames dipped and

23

flared. Two shadowy figures—one enormous, the other minute in comparison—shown on that wall.

Their voices reached his ears. A large, gravelly voice rumbled throughout the chamber's interior. Min'darr knew it had to be the ogre's, though he'd never suspected them of having speech. The other voice calmed him instantly. Uncle Taf! His voice was steady, his words deliberate. There was an intensity to it, matching what he'd heard once before in the town plaza. This time, though, he wasn't sure what caused his uncle's angst. As the two spoke, Min'darr stared intently at their shadows to glean some context to their words.

"No!" it said.

"Why not?"

"No abuse my cave, human. Me no bargain." The beast raised a great hand, seeming to point at his uncle. "I could eat you up on hillside."

"And, for that, you have our eternal gratitude, Lord Golreg. If I may, what purpose would it serve now? He's too scrawny."

"Humans fatty meat. Boy make good stew and he has no magic. If you make Golreg mad, I forget you have magic. I eat you too. Where you get magic?"

Uncle Taf'nar didn't hesitate. "I don't know what you're talking about."

"Golreg not stupid, human ..."

"For the tenth time, my name is Taf'nar."

"Golreg not care. You are human."

"He is, too!" Taf's shadow showed that he'd raised his arm to point in Min'darr's direction.

"He is food, like ram. You make Golreg loose ram. You owe me. How you get magic?" The ogre sounded agitated.

"What makes you think I have magic?"

"Golreg have magic. Magic knows magic, like I feel in you."

"That's how you move so fast. I knew it!

"See! Golreg right! You hide truth. You have no honor." A scraping sound of a large chair pushed over the rocky floor accompanied the ogre's shadow standing up, pointing a finger in a jerking motion at Taf. "Golreg knew you had magic when hand touched throat. I kill you then, but magic say 'No! Human has magic.' So Golreg stop. Then boy attack. Golreg bring you here. Now Golreg might end you both. You, Taf'nar ... you watch boy end first. You move, you die first."

The ogre's shadow changed shape and got smaller. Min'darr heard its movements sounding closer. Too anguished from the pain in his leg, the boy could only squirm as the ogre rounded the corner, blocking the light from the other room.

If it had seemed gigantic before, the presence that now loomed over him in the confines of this small rocky place was overwhelming. The ogre reached down, grabbing the boy around the chest causing his ribs to move oddly. Min'darr grimaced from the discomfort. One cracked, giving in to the pressure under the ogre's thumb. Min'darr grunted from the pain.

Golreg brought him into the lighted room. It was by a small fire in a floor pit. Its light flickered on the walls of the room, showing Uncle Taf in a chair on the opposite side of a massive wooden table.

Golreg slammed Min'darr onto the table, his head lopping over the edge. Again, pain washed out across his body in pulsating waves. His scream reverberated in the chamber. Lying on his back, Min'darr could feel the modest heat from the fire on the back of his head.

His uncle spoke. "Golreg, perhaps we could work for you, help you."

"No want human help."

"We have skills. We can help."

Min'darr added, breathing shallow, "Uncle Taf has been training me to help him. I'd be glad to help you too."

"You help. You be stew. That help Golreg best." The beast chuckled. "Help lots."

"Lord Golreg, he's a boy. How can you so brutally murder a child?" Uncle Taf's voice revealed his desperation.

"Young have tender meat," Golreg said. "No more talk." The beast kicked a large blood-stained bucket so it rested under Min'darr's head. The ogre took Min'darr's head in both hands, as if ready to twist it off.

Min'darr felt its greasy grasp. "Wait!" he yelled. "Wait! I have to say the prayers of the Mahar, of Death and Dying. "Uncle, I need you here to pray with me." Min'darr braced himself in case the ogre ignored him, but the pressure eased.

"What prayer?" the ogre asked.

Min'darr continued. "It is a final prayer to our Creator to take our soul when we die. If we can't say the prayer, our spirit drifts to haunt the one who killed us. Anyone who has honor is bound by the magic of life to allow the prayer." He was hopeful the beast would give him a chance to whisper to Uncle Taf an idea. If not, this is where he would die.

"Oh, by the Creator, yes," Taf'nar added as the creature stared at them in disbelief. "It should be done or his spirit will haunt you until your own death, great ogre."

"Golreg have honor. Why you not tell me? You want his spirit to haunt Golreg? That how you want to win?" The ogre's head jerked back and forth, pursing his lips as he considered this.

"You would fool Golreg. Golreg have honor, not want to be haunted. Say your prayer, human. I give you one minute." The ogre took a step back, then pushed Uncle Taf next to him, keeping his hand grasped around Min'darr's neck.

"This is a solemn prayer, Golreg. We must use solemn voices, quieter voices." Taf said as he lowered his face to within inches of his nephew's. "Pray, good Min'darr, what is it you have been gifted to see?" Taf spoke using emphasized words to confuse the ogre.

Min'darr did likewise. "Favored uncle, the magic of life ... it must burn within you as it did the Mahar and your trees when our journey began. I pray that you can light that same magical fire on our rancid host that he may know its power and that I may never haunt him."

"Good insights, my nephew. I pray that the Creator will immediately grant your desires," Taf'nar whispered. He reached out to touch the ogre.

It flinched back. "Why human touch Golreg?"

Taf reassured the beast. "We must be joined so our Creator will be satisfied that my nephew has died well, and that you have honor in his death." Taf touched its arm again. This time, it stayed.

Min'darr heard his uncle whispering loud enough to keep the ogre's attention. He quickly added, "Sorry about this, nephew, I have to get you out of the way."

Suddenly, the ogre roared. Uncle Taf shoved the table away from the ogre, tipping it onto its side, spilling Min'darr onto the floor. Pain seared through his body as the table toppled toward him. He managed to roll away as the edge of the table slammed against the floor inches from his shoulder.

Deafening roars from the ogre filled the cave. The room seemed brighter. As it moved through Min'darr's field of vision, it flailed wildly, its arm, the back of its head and upper body were aflame. It seemed to run aimlessly, bouncing off of walls while beating itself, trying to snuff the flames fed by its greasy fur. A putrid smoke filled the room. Taf dove in next to him.

Very quickly the ogre was fully engulfed. The sound of the fire's roar drowned out any noise it may have been making. The image of the giant, burning as readily as a marshmallow would if held too close to a fire, would forever remain in Min'darr's memory. Golreg, a sooty inferno, stumbled down a passage into the depths of the cave, never to return.

The stench remained. Taf climbed over the table to help his nephew.

As Taf helped Min'darr to stand, an icy blue flickering crystal the size of a fist floated into the room. It hovered over Taf's head. Min'darr reached to flick it away. Taf said, "No, it's okay. Something tells me this means that Golreg is dead."

The crystal rested on his head, then dissolved into him. Taf's skin flashed blue.

"What was that?"

"I'm not sure," Taf said. "But it looked familiar."

*

Resting in the cool night air on the rocky ledge near the cave's opening, Min'darr's lungs finally agreed to fill without coughing. Moonlight lit the hills while a dense fog filled the lowlands below them, giving the scene an ethereal look. Min'darr shuddered from the chill. An involuntary moan accompanied the grimace of pain that swept through the boy.

"I hope I never see another ogre as long as I live. It was a demon, living to kill. Us or other animals, it makes no difference."

"It was only being what it was. You can never expect anything else, Min'darr. Every living thing has to be true to its own nature whether it's a bug, a tree, a bear, an ogre, or a human."

"That is one lesson I'm glad to learn." Min'darr remarked.

"Why?"

"It means I lived through it. We survived this one."

"Speaking of surviving, are you ready?" his uncle asked. "I think I can heal you."

"You can just light fires. You said so yourself." The youth sighed. "At least we weren't burned up."

"Ah, speak for yourself." Taf'nar walked a few steps to retrieve his badly burned coat. Dropping it in front of his nephew, he said, "I was wearing it at the time."

"Uncle! I'm sorry. Were you burned? Are you hurt? I've been so caught up in my own pain. Please, forgive me."

"I'm fine now. Remember that blue crystal we saw? That had to be the magic from our charred ogre friend. I went back into the cave. I found his carcass. Definitely dead."

"How is that from the ogre?" asked Min'darr.

"He didn't need magic anymore, so it came into me. I guess, maybe because I already had some? It's made me stronger in using magic. Here, see?" He showed him his arm and back where his coat had burned. "I healed my own burns. Since I know how to use it, I can heal you, too."

Min'darr lay quietly, facing the stars as his uncle accessed the magic within him. He saw something odd as the man bent over him. "Uncle?" he whispered.

Taf'nar turned his head. His eyes glowed blue, bluer than a noontime sky. Min'darr decided to say nothing about it.

"Umm ... go ahead. I guess I'm ready," Min'darr said and closed his eyes.

Within a few breaths, he felt a warmth. Instead of soaking in as he'd imagined, this sensation began from within him. It continued for a few moments. Then the stab wound in his leg seemed to vibrate like the purr of a kitten. His injuries rapidly got intensely cold. He could feel a tingling sensation in his leg and by his rib. Then it stopped quickly, just short of being painful. That relaxed him to the point of sleep.

*

He opened his eyes and panicked, realizing he was back at the cave's entrance. Clouds and rain replaced the stars from before.

Uncle Taf walked to him from within the cave. "Good afternoon, sleepy. I found a few things inside we can use ... rounded up our mules, too. How are you feeling?"

Min'darr tested his level of discomfort, finding none. He stood, testing his leg. "Perfect! You're good. You should set up an office in town."

Taf'nar gave him a sideways glare. "Me? In town? Have you not learned anything about me yet?"

"I'm kidding, Uncle Taf. I gotta tell you I would love to learn this magic stuff. Comes in pretty handy, eh?" He chuckled as he spoke. "Do you have any idea where we are?"

"Three valleys over from where we saw the ram. If we set out now, we should be at the cabin by dusk."

They did, arriving home half an hour after sunset, soaked from the all-day rain.

After greeting a happy Hilda, they changed clothes, burning the ones they had on in the ogre's cave. At dinner, Taf said, "I think it's about time we made that special trip to see that magical someone I've mentioned."

Within the Cave

The month of May began with ample sunshine, chirping birds, even a few bugs. Hilda had been outside for most of the prior month. Taf had commented that the house smelled better because of it.

For most of the winter, as well as so far this spring, Taf had taught him skills in woodworking, canning, skinning, and had worked diligently in building weaponry skills. Making arrows was one thing, shooting them was another. So a good part of Min'darr's training involved becoming proficient with the weapons they had on hand.

He loved the bow, soon becoming so accurate, he could put an arrow within a square foot from a hundred feet. He could throw a blade half that distance, although he had yet to perfect its rotations. He avoided the hatchet at all costs. "It doesn't like me," he would say. Taf merely shook his head.

By the time most of the snows had melted, Min'darr could hunt anything using most of Taf's weapons.

Within that first week of May, with sporadic clumps of snow lingering, Min'darr was out repairing the corral fencing. A corner post had split, causing the cross members to drop. One of the two ponies brought from town had gotten out. They'd found its carcass several hundred yards from the house a day earlier. Taf said, "Mountain lion, it looks like." Then he added, "Some of the neighborhood wolves probably feasted well, too. You can tell by the difference in the chewing patterns. Cats are more meticulous nibblers like you can see here. Wolves, as you can see here," he said pointing, "rip it out, then eat."

Min'darr hated losing the mule. "They have such unique personalities," he'd said. Taf's one regret was that the wild animals had eaten so well.

"Once fed, they'll stay near in the chance of killing another. They're not dumb. They know where the mules live. We'll have to keep a good eye on them when they're out. Get that fence fixed right away. Hey, then I'll show you some good night hunting techniques as well."

Taf began walking away when he abruptly stopped. Min'darr saw him standing there, like a statue. Although he was tempted to call out, instead he scanned around them, thinking Taf had seen something, maybe a mountain lion, and froze to avoid detection. Min'darr could see nothing, nor did he hear or smell anything out of the ordinary. He gripped his hatchet a little tighter and held his breath. "Uncle Taf?" he finally whispered.

Half a minute passed before Taf moved. He stood upright, then turned to face Min'darr. His eyes shone blue, like they did in the ogre's cave when he used his magic. When he spoke, his voice sounded strange. It was his own, but at the same time it seemed somehow not. Perhaps stiffer. "Make your journey to the place mentioned. Your time is nigh."

Then he almost fell over, everything going limp. He caught himself, staggering, then looked around, unsure. "What happened, Min'darr?" he asked.

He told his uncle what he'd seen and heard. "Are you all right, Uncle Taf? That was ... well, that was scary. You said my time was nigh. Then, your eyes, they ... they glowed blue."

"Okay," Taf said with a sigh like he had to catch his breath. "They want to see you now. So we go now. Finish the post. We'll leave at dawn." Taf went into the stable.

Min'darr returned his attention to his task. Experience had shown him that Taf wasn't much of a talker. He said what he needed to say. Min'darr knew this was important, since he had mentioned it more than once since they came together. The timing couldn't be that much of a surprise. Taf had mentioned spring for this to happen at least once before, too.

An hour later, Min'darr came into the house after storing his tools. Taf had started dinner. It smelled of cinnamon-sugared quail, one of Taf's favorites. A root stew bubbled quietly on the stove. Taf called down from the loft. "You'll need to pack for a week ... layers of thick stuff, too. The nights can get pretty cold yet."

They spent the rest of that evening packing. Hilda acted funny, sensing that they'd be leaving. She spent as much time demanding Min'darr's attention getting scratched as she did when he'd first arrived. After they'd settled in for the night, Min'darr's curiosity broke through his self-control. "Uncle Taf? Is there anything you can tell me about who we are going to see that will help me understand what might be happening?"

Min'darr heard a chuckle through the thick darkness of their loft. "That, my boy, was one of the best phrased questions anyone has ever asked me. In answer, I can tell you that there is no way you can prepare for this. There is nothing in your experience to draw upon that will help you. Except for maybe this. Look up here."

Above him, laying in his loft, Min'darr saw a small flame illuminate his uncle's face. That same face with blue eyes slightly glowing.

There was one thought that stuck in Min'darr's mind that struck a chord of terror in his heart, yet brought a smile to his face. *Magic!*

*

They left early the next morning and headed northeast toward the snowcapped ranges. For three days they rode up into the farthest ridges of the mountains. Days were tedious always going uphill. The nights were cold in the thinner air so far above the tree line. Breathing it slowed the mules down, too.

Midafternoon on the third day they stopped without any warning on a sloped plain below a bowl-shaped outcropping in the side of a rocky escarpment. "We're here," Taf announced, dismounting.

"Here? Where? There's nothing here," Min'darr observed sarcastically. "How can we arrive at nothing?"

"Get down. Mind your manners," Taf said. He dug into his pack and took out a tied bag the size of a loaf of bread. "Offer this to them. It's kind of a welcoming gift. You know, when you're invited into someone's home, it's polite to bring something."

"Where is this 'home'?"

Taf pointed to the ridge. "Up there. Follow this line along its face," he said as he pointed at a smoother area of rock leading up to a lip about twenty feet above them. "Go down into the bowl and enter the cave. They are waiting to greet you."

"C'mon, Uncle! Who will be waiting? You're scaring me!"

Taf grabbed his collar roughly, pulling him in close. "Just do as I've told you. You'll be all right, I promise. This is too different from anything you've been through. Painless. Easy. Different. Go!" He turned, mounted his mule, and headed down the slope with the animals. He hollered over his shoulder, "Get going! They told me to come back for you at dawn."

"Wonderful!" Min'darr called after him. He muttered to himself as he climbed the rocky face. "Now I get to find out who wants to meet me. This is so weird! By the Creator, how could anyone living way out here know anything about me? Well, I can hope that this might have something to do with getting magic stuff like Uncle Taf has. I'd love that!"

He reached the lip, looked down into the hollow and saw a small hole, too small for anyone larger than he. "Here goes nothin'." He slid down into the bowl's shade.

*

Alone in the cave, Min'darr remained alert. The cold, damp air penetrated his clothes, leaving him shaking uncontrollably. No one had come out to meet him. Somehow, he knew he'd best stay. He silently cursed his uncle for leaving him without the courtesy of a fire. His eyes failed him, as the darkness of the cave was complete from the setting of the sun. Slowly, subtly, his young ears picked up a growing sound. He questioned if he'd actually been aware of it for some time, just now having it reach his conscious mind.

It was distant, rhythmic, and growing. Soon it filled the cave, seeming to emanate from its depths. *No*, he thought, *closer. From this chamber he was in?* He couldn't be certain. It seemed as loud in any direction he faced. As his interest in it increased, so did its volume. A pattern became evident. A beat, like chanting. *Voices? Finally! I've been waiting here for hours!*

With that thought came anticipation. His breathing sped up and his heartbeat thundered in his ears. He cried out, "I'm here!" The sound ceased abruptly.

For the better part of another hour, Min'darr heard only his own breathing, felt nothing other than the finger-aching cold. He tightened his coat around his shoulders, burrowing his hands under his shirt. Sitting on a hard, raised ledge, he rested his weary head on his knees. Finally, fatigued from fighting the cold, the boy faded into a restless sleep.

Pulsating from within, his conscious mind swam up, out of the dullness of sleep. The sound had returned, in time with his own breathing, in time with his heartbeat. His ears clearly heard its cadence and now his eyes, too, could see it. Min'darr sensed movement. He brought himself fully awake. A dim luminescence saturated the cave's interior with the blue of twilight's shadow. The walls, floor, and ceiling of the entire cave glowed in this singular hue, diminishing the cave's depth.

Along its surfaces came a liquid-like shifting of the color, flowing closer toward his ledge. He quickly twisted around to see behind, but his ledge and the wall behind him remained untouched by the glow.

All the while, the cave's sound became more dominant. *Definitely voices*, he thought. Like the glow, it, too, seemed to come from everywhere.

With more control than before, he spoke, "Who's there?" His call did not echo, as he'd expect. Instead, it seemed to be absorbed by the cave. This time, instead of stopping, there came a response.

The throbbing of the voices sped up, noticeably louder. Despite this, the sound seemed muffled, fuzzy, unintelligible. The flow of the light also increased. Min'darr slid back the few inches he had to be flush against the wall. The color flowed toward him, centered on the base of his ledge and, as he watched dumbfounded, began piling up on itself, building a mound. As it formed, waves of more intense colors, particularly greens and yellows, rippled up from the bowels of the cavern into the mound, soon a foot below the level of his ledge. As the surges continued, the rest of the cave dimmed. The color abandoned the cave's depths to collect within the mound. The chanting seemed to emanate from it as well. Ancient words, mysterious, menacing, yet melodic came from the edifice.

Too awed to be bothered by the cold, Min'darr stood with his back pressed against the wall, mouth agape. The mound was reshaping itself with the passing of every pulse. It stretched, flexing into a tower that loomed over him, then shortened to his eye level, finally taking form. Most of it was unrefined, but the face, as large as the boy's five-foot height, showed the smallest details of lips, teeth, beard, and skin features. Recognizable, yet not quite human.

Its eyes glowed, holding Min'darr's attention. He could not take his own from them. They burned a bright orange, with an intensity of the hottest smithy's fire, looking deeper than any water or sky he'd ever seen. Then, the thing's lips parted. It spoke.

"Min'darr, son of Bu'ka and Kir'ni, nephew of Taf'nar. What is your purpose here?" The voice was harmonic, as if it were of both genders, speaking in synchronized speech. As it spoke, its coloration, again with darker blues, yellows and greens, vibrated with its speaking, spreading out from its mouth. The effect was hypnotic.

"M-m-my uncle brought me here at your bidding," he said.

"Is that all? He said nothing else?"

"Only that I should not be afraid."

"And are you?"

Min'darr paused, catching his breath. He felt he should be afraid, but, without any particular rationale, he felt he wasn't in any danger.

"No, I am not."

The glowing visage before him smiled. "Good. You speak from your heart. You have passed the first test. What have you brought for us?"

"Oh, I'm sorry. A gift from my uncle. A thank you for allowing us to come." He held out the tied bag Taf had given him.

It floated out of his hand directly into the mouth of the face. "We appreciate the gift. Do you know what it was, Min'darr?"

"No, I don't."

The face quickly blurred, breathing a tremendous stench which caused Min'darr to recoil. "Oh, that's like the ... oh, no!" It was the ogre that faced him now. It smelled as bad too. Helpless to fight back, he vomited.

"It was the heart of the charred ogre you both killed. You destroyed a creature of magic. Do you know the penalty for that?" The ogre shape's arm swung at him. "Do you?"

He murmured, "No," ducking away, expecting to be struck. Nothing happened. He looked back to see that the face of the magical creature had returned.

"There is no penalty. Magic is a tool, a force, like the wind or the sun. Both good and bad can be done through its use. Now for your second test," it said.

The creature's colors immediately surged into a blinding light.

Instinctively, Min'darr covered his face with his arms. With his eyes covered, he was not able to see the creature surge out toward him. Its liquid blueness reached Min'darr, quickly spreading out over his lower body. Feeling that pressure, Min'darr squirmed against the rock wall, trying to sweep it away with his hands, panic showing in his widened eyes. As he flailed, it swiftly enveloped him in a blue luminescence. He could not pull free from it. It swam over his skin, upward, across his chest, back, and head. Within seconds, he was completely engulfed, unable to move. Min'darr was drawn in toward the creature. Within moments, the two forms merged. The cave plunged into perfect blackness, perfect silence.

*

Within the mass, Min'darr's consciousness was aware only of the color blue, the same color as his uncle's eyes, the floating crystal from the ogre's cave, and these very walls. He was devoid of any other sensations. He found he did not need to breathe.

His capture by the creature startled him in its swiftness. Despite the creature's aggression, he was unharmed. Min'darr felt no danger.

"Min'darr, remember." The voice dominated his mind.

As its words reverberated in his mind, Min'darr was aware of events of his recent past running in reverse. He saw himself and his uncle riding to the cave, then back in his cabin. The hunting they'd done days before, their encounter with the ogre, and the burning trees of the pass. His own history ran quickly before him as his images grew ever younger; until he knew his own birth.

Then, he saw himself as an infant gazing out the window. His awareness rose above their home, high into the sky he went, higher than the pass, above the clouds. He flew so high he saw the shimmer of the ocean to the south and the curved surface of the horizon.

The lands of his forefathers, the oceans and the lands on the other side of those seas basked beneath him in the light of the sun. He found he could look right at it and not blink or hurt his eyes. He continued higher until everything below him was gone, except the stars.

Then he fell. He swiftly hurtled toward the rapidly rising earth, its waters beneath him. He felt no wind, so he knew he was not truly falling. He watched intently as his descent splashed him into the waters, passing creatures there that were larger than his house.

Then there was the waters' blueness. Then just the color blue.

"Would you like to know more?" the harmonic voice whispered in his consciousness.

"Oh, yes," he answered.

Min'darr felt the creature's collective sense of approval. Its presence withdrew.

"Wait!" he called out.

"Wait," came its response. "You are beginning a journey, young Min'darr. A journey of knowledge and of skill with magic, yet more, of understanding. You have access now to controlling energies few have ever imagined. It is a part of you now.

"We will be watching you. You will be summoned when you show readiness." His mind went totally blank.

*

Min'darr found himself standing on the lip of the rocky cup just above the cave's entrance. Better than halfway across the meadow, Uncle Taf trudged with the mules toward the cave. The new day's sunlight touched the peaks around him.

He slid back down to the cavern's mouth. He looked in, seeing its deep darkness. "Thank you," he called out. His own voice echoed back. The cave remained silent. Min'darr felt something different stir within him, undefined. Looking at his hands, he somehow expected to see them changed. Not so. He nodded with the thought that he would return here soon, then he climbed back out into the light of a new day to greet his uncle.

Using Magic

After three minutes in the saddle, Taf asked, "Well?"

Min'darr was riding next to his uncle. He took a minute to find an answer. "I don't know. You were right," he said. "Nothing could have prepared me for any of that."

"I know!" Taf said. "By the Creator, I've dreamt so often of my own magical baptism."

"Why don't you tell me about it? I mean, now that I've been through it too."

They rode as Taf talked. "I was up here hunting a wolf pack I'd been tracking. I spent the day sitting on the lip of that bowl, looking out across that meadow, watching for trail patterns. Every once in a while I thought I'd hear my name being called. 'I must be nuts,' I told myself I must be nuts. I looked into the opening, wondering if it came from there. I mean, maybe someone I knew was in there playing games with me.

"I decided to camp in the bowl and couldn't get my campfire lit. So, I ate cold food, then hunkered down to sleep. I thought I was dreaming at first. A small, blue flame came floating out of the cave, landed on my firewood, igniting my fire. Nice light, warm too. It had blue flames, not regular yellow or orange flames.

"I yelled 'thank you' kind of as a joke, then I distinctly heard someone inside say 'You are welcome, Taf'nar. Please, come in.'

"I was shocked. I wondered who could it be? How would whoever it was know my name?" I went in and was greeted by— now remember, I promised I would never lie to you—a big elk stag, completely blue, glowing like my blue campfire. Except it had orange glowing eyes. Creepy! Then it spoke. A blue elk, talking to me! Anyway, it asked me if I would like to make fire whenever I wanted to. Of course I said yes.

"It came close to lick my hand. I could feel its tongue on the back of my hand. It kind of burned. I mean, it was really hot, not at all what I expected.

"It told me two special words to say. With that, I could make fire whenever I wanted to. I could never tell those words to anyone, though, ever. 'One more thing,' it said. 'Bring your nephew here when he is yours. Be warned! Do not allow the Ma'har.' Then it walked into the rock wall of the cave! Passed through it like it was a cloud or a waterfall.

"I've been able to light fires ever since. That was two winters before I came for you. Your turn. Did you see the stag?"

Min'darr paused. His own experience was so much more involved than his uncle's. He knew enough about Taf's ego to realize that telling it exactly as it had happened might upset him. So, Min'darr decided to be a bit sparse with the description.

"No, I didn't meet a stag. There was a lot of blue luminescence in the cave. I got to speak with a huge talking head, at least as big as me."

"What did it say?" Taf asked.

"Say? It didn't really say much. It shoved me into its mouth! I remember seeing things from my past, when I was a little kid. Then it took me way high into the sky, so high I could see the oceans and the lands on the other side of them."

"That is amazing. What next?" Taf asked.

"It said I had to wait, that I would be summoned when it felt I was ready."

"Ready for what?" Taf asked.

All Min'darr could do was to shrug his shoulders. "No clue, Uncle."

Taf shook his head. "I was so excited for you, too. I hoped you'd be able to do ... well, something magical. I mean, we're a pretty good team right now. That would have been really special.

"I wonder why they didn't do that to me, too," Taf mused aloud.

Min'darr sensed his uncle's growing jealousy of his own experience. So he quickly added, "You know, there were other things ... I don't remember what exactly. Things they told me I would not be allowed to remember. Maybe they did that to you too?"

Taf paused while they rode a few minutes in silence. He then announced, "You know, I had forgotten that part. There are some things I don't recall, so you are right. There probably was much more to my experience than I consciously remember. I mean, it has been over two years since it happened. Thanks, Min'darr. I appreciate your insights and honesty. I wonder if you even have magic. They didn't tell you that you did."

Min'darr silently breathed a sigh of relief.

They eventually stopped to camp for the night. Taf set up the campfire, refraining from lighting it with his magic. "Your turn. See if you can make fire."

Min'darr thought. "I don't think so. Like I said, the memories of what happened in there are really fuzzy," he said. "I feel different ... I don't know. Nothing was said about doing any kind of magic."

The matter was again dropped. Taf cooked dinner while Min'darr set up the tent, then attended to the mules.

Sometime during the night, the mules began braying loudly, agitated about something. They both hurried out. The mules were rearing and kicking out at a cougar. Taf dove back into the tent for his bow. Min'darr stood there, yelling at it. The big cat crouched, offering a low growl. It leapt right at him.

Taf heard the predator's deep growl, then yip repeatedly. He ran out, an arrow notched. He saw the cat caught in midleap, tumbling in the air about three feet off the ground. Min'darr stood before it, palm extended.

Taf lowered the bow, walking up to his nephew. "You got magic, boy," he said patting the boy's shoulder. "Let me see your eyes."

Min'darr looked at him.

"Yep. Both of them bright blue," Taf said. He raised the bow and drew back the arrow.

"No," Min'darr said. "We don't have to kill it, do we?"

"If you let it go, it will follow the mules' scent. We'll have the same problem tomorrow night." Taf said, aiming his shaft at the still-spinning wildcat.

"No," repeated Min'darr as Taf's arrow shot out. It stopped just short of the cat, floating in midair.

"Are you doing that?" Taf shouted. "Stop it."

"I don't know how this is happening, Taf. I'm sorry, but killing it is wrong." Min'darr stepped closer to the still-gnarling cougar and said, "Go away. Leave us alone." The cat fell to the ground and scampered away. Walking back to Taf, Min'darr plucked his arrow out of the air, then handed it to Taf as he walked past him.

"It will be back," Taf warned.

"Somehow, I don't think so," Min'darr said, shaking his head. He walked back to the tent staring at his hands.

*

All the way back to the cabin, Taf kept asking Min'darr to try to do more magic. Min'darr kept saying no, that it didn't feel right, he didn't know how to, or he didn't know if he could do magic ... every excuse in the book.

"Look," Taf said to reassure him. "I went through the same thing. It was so totally weird to be able to do this one little thing."

"Did you try different things?" Min'darr asked.

"Of course I did. But, nah, nothing worked."

"... until you got the ogre's magic, right?" Min'darr asked enthusiastically.

"That's right. I was able to heal us. I wonder why. I remember really hurting and wishing I wasn't burned."

"Maybe the ogre was trying to heal itself when it died," Min'darr suggested. "So, it was on its mind. The magic was maybe kind of ready. Since you got its magic right then, you could use it. Maybe?"

"Well, that does make sense. I remember how the spell works, too. It worked for you. So, if we get hurt, I could use it again. Nice to know. But remember your eyes ... they showed that same blue glow you told me about mine. So, I knew you had magic. Last night, we found out what you could do.

"We did. But, hey ... I got one more question. Remember how fast the ogre was? Can you do that?

Taf sat a moment, then dismounted his mule. "Let's see." He took a deep breath and ran. After about twenty steps, he became a blur, racing within a few seconds to the distant tree line. In a flash, he was back, hardly breathing heavy. "I like this," he said. "I like this a lot!"

*

Beginning the morning following their return to the house, Uncle Taf showed an increased obsession with magic, both his own and his nephew's.

They went out for target practice with their bows. He presented Min'darr with a brand-new bow that he'd made for him. Min'darr was very grateful. Excited to try it, he notched an arrow, took aim at the target and loosed the shaft.

Taf took off after it, running with his magically enhanced speed. He was a second behind the arrow. He plucked it out of the target, then magically ran back to Min'darr. "Not bad for a first try, eh? Let's try it again. This time, aim to the left so I can catch it. I want to see how close I can get."

For an hour, Taf chased arrows. High shots, lobs, straight targeted shots. All were chased. All were retrieved.

"Taf, I love the bow, but my fingers are getting blistered," he said.

"Maybe you could use your magic to help. Wait! I could use the healing spell. Yeah, let's do that. This is too much fun."

"No. I'm done," Min'darr said, walking back to the cabin with his equipment in hand.

Seconds later, his bow and quiver left his hand by force as Taf ran past him, snatching the equipment. "All right, your turn. Use your magic to deflect the arrows." Taf nocked a shaft and pulled back. He was aiming at his nephew.

"What are you doing, Taf? Cut it out!" Min'darr cried out.

Taf loosed the arrow.

43

Min'darr saw it approaching, dropped to the ground and rolled to his left. The arrow sped past exactly where he'd been standing.

"What are you doing? C'mon, that's not fun. Use your magic," Taf yelled. He fired another arrow.

"I don't want to do this!" Min'darr hollered back. He waved his arms as he spoke and the arrow immediately drove straight down into the dirt about twenty feet in front of him.

"Better! See? You can do this. One more," Taf said as he loosed a third arrow.

Min'darr's vision suddenly shaded blue. Everything was tinted the same blue as the inside of the cave. Everything seemed to have slowed down, too. Fascinated at the effect, Min'darr watched the scene with a sense of wonder. Distracted, he lost sight of the arrow until it dug into his shoulder. The rush of pain banished the effect.

Taf, as apologetic as he could be, spent considerable time using the healing spell to repair the damage caused by the arrowhead. He concluded that having magic didn't safeguard anyone. Like anything else, someone with magic had to know how to use it.

He asked Min'darr once the healing had been done, "Why did you just stand there?"

Min'darr decided to keep what actually happened to himself. "I guess I couldn't believe that you were trying to shoot me for the third time after I'd said no."

"Well, we won't do that again, at least until we're sure about what kind of magic you can do, eh? One of those kinds of things, I guess. Something no one else needs to know about, eh?"

Min'darr stared at him. He'd already learned that guilt was his uncle's weakness.

One night, a little more than a month after the cave, Hilda started snorting around the house. Taf was in the lower level preserving some venison they'd killed earlier in the day. She was very upset about something, even Min'darr's scratching didn't help. He followed her to the stable doorway. She was insistent, pawing, then butting the door. Min'darr couldn't hear anything and opened it to show the goat that everything was fine.

It wasn't.

He swung the thick door about halfway open when it flew open, throwing him back against the wall. A body fell through the doorway, landing at Hilda's feet. She immediately dropped her head, ramming into the man, who instantly began screaming and bleeding. Hilda had caught the man's nose with her horn.

Min'darr scrambled to his feet as Hilda pushed the man back out into the stable. Min'darr yanked his dagger from the sheath on his belt, screamed for Taf, while running into the stable. He then noticed that the stalls were empty. The outer door was open. One mule was being led out of the stable by a second man, who was paying more attention to his partner's dilemma with the goat than the mule he was stealing. His attention swung to the doorway when Min'darr had called for Taf.

Hilda had the man prone, covering his face, while she worked at cracking some of his ribs. The man with the mule panicked, abandoning the mule. Instinctively, Min'darr extended his arm. The man lost his footing, rising up a foot or so above the ground, screaming loudly.

Taf rushed up behind Min'darr, sword in one hand, bow and arrows in the other. He quickly started laughing. Walking up behind the still-butting Hilda, he gave a sharp whistle. The goat backed off, still snorting. The man on the ground pushed himself up, spitting blood as well as a tooth. Blood ran freely from his obviously broken nose.

"Get up real slow or I'm ready to end your stupidity," Taf said with the point of his sword at the man's chest. The man sat back on his haunches, held his hands up, locking them behind his head.

Min'darr's perception changed. Things were covered in that same blue veil as had happened to him earlier. Voices became reduced to low slurs. The movements of Taf, Hilda, and the bleeding man were slowed to a snail's pace.

He looked in awe, wondering what prompted it until his attention was drawn to the floating man. He continued floating due to Min'darr's magic, yet somehow managed to throw a knife toward him which was merely ten feet away, spinning on a dangerous trajectory directly at him. Min'darr gestured, his fingers somehow knowing what mystical dance to do.

The knife stopped, then reversed its flight and, as fast as an arrow, drove into the floating man's chest. His gurgling scream ended the blue veil. Everything returned to normal as the dead man dropped into the corral's mud.

The man with the broken nose hollered, "Korbin!" He glared at Min'darr. "You killed my brother!" He rose quicker than Min'darr thought he could, just not as fast as Taf's sword. A second later, he too lay dead.

"Great. Look at this mess we have to clean. Hilda, mules!" The goat took off, running out into the night to find the mules. Taf turned to Min'darr with a cocked eyebrow. "You want to explain what happened here?"

"I'm not sure I can. Uncle Taf ... I'm scared. I, umm, I killed him, didn't I?"

"No, I think your magic killed him. Let's get the mules. I think you deserve a mug o' mead." They went out to help Hilda round up the mules.

*

The next night, the two bodies were draped across the mules as they headed to the hollow where they had found the dead mule's carcass a month or so ago. Taf and Min'darr rode the horses left behind by the thieves.

"I prefer to burn them. Less for anyone to accidently come across later. And," he emphasized, "there's little to no chance that they can be identified. Both were killed in self-defense, so we bear no guilt. I want you to understand that." Taf said.

Min'darr rode next him, a mix of emotions. The initial shock of the deaths of these robbers was wearing off. They attacked him. They were stealing the mules.

It was how they died. Not by blades either, but by the magic Min'darr had that virtually acted on its own to protect him. "I didn't have any control over this magic. It reacted. It killed him, not me."

The Mulu said that magic was a tool. How can this tool act on its own? It's a part of me now, they said. Maybe it interacts with me, keeps me safe? Is that part of what this tool is all about? I guess I'll learn more, as they said, 'when I'm ready.'

"Let's just get this done," Min'darr muttered as they dismounted at the hollow.

"You do it," Taf said, after they'd put the bodies on the ground next to what was left of the mule carcass.

"What? I don't know how to make fire."

His uncle persisted. "You didn't know you could do that knife throwing thing either. Try."

The ten-and-a-half-year-old boy closed his eyes. He relaxed himself, thinking, *fire*. His mind instantly returned to the cave. Consciously, Min'darr knew the color blue, despite the fact that it seemed different. It moved oddly. He felt something was happening and opened his eyes. He watched in amazement as a torrent of fire leap from his out-stretched hand. It struck the bodies, engulfing them. Within a single minute, there was no smoke coming from the ash. No clothes, metal, or bone could be identified within the pile of ash.

Taf kicked at the ash for a moment, mounted his horse and gathered the reins of the other horse and one of the mules. Without saying a word, he spurred his horse and galloped off. Min'darr stood there dumbstruck. The moon set an hour later, his eyes still glowing blue in the dark mountain night.

Confrontation

Stranded by his uncle, he spent a restless night tossing and walking about. The absolute finality of what he'd done bore into his heart. *How could I so easily obliterate the bodies of those two men? Taf killed one who attacked us. I killed the other man. What is wrong with me?*

He sat back down, then rekindled the campfire. The words from the cave haunted him. "Magic is a tool." Had he done good or bad with his magic? He could not decide. He focused his mind to think of those in the cave. He asked them, *Good or bad?*

A few seconds had gone by when he felt an answer. *Neither or both. Decide this based on why you acted. Or allow it simply to be without a need to render judgement.*

He also recalled his own words to Uncle Taf about the men who had attacked him in his own home, "self-defense." Now this. There was no difference. Min'darr's magic let him defend himself. Taf then saved Min'darr's life. Self-defense.

Getting rid of the bodies saved them both from having to lie to the law. Min'darr felt better about it all. He was satisfied that they had done what had to be done to protect themselves. He covered back up in a blanket from his mule, Gerg, and fell asleep.

He woke in the morning to a pain in his gut. "I'm hungry," he mumbled, unconsciously looking to the ridge crest leading to the cabin. *Would he come?* Min'darr wondered. Uncertainty dominated the way he felt. *Exactly why would he run off like that?* That answer he did know. Jealous rage.

The whole idea of that was based on the extent of the magic that Min'darr had. "I have no idea what I can do. Some stuff, yeah ... lifting, repelling objects, and fire. Fire ... not a little flame like Uncle Taf has. Nooo, I have to have fire as hot as a smithy's forge. Makes his look like a toy. No wonder he got upset.

"What can I do?" he asked. His mule, Gerg, ignored him. "Let's find out." He stretched his arm out, fingers spread wide, then said, "Lift."

Gerg brayed as his hooves left the ground so high that Min'darr could walk under the mule. He set his mule down and then had to comfort the beast. It was making the 'gerg' sound with its rapid breathing.

With a sly grin, Min'darr gestured at his own feet. He rose up far enough to get a glimpse over the top of the nearest tree. It felt uncomfortable ... weird, so he lowered himself.

Then it was Gerg's turn again. Min'darr concentrated. The mule faded away. Min'darr then walked over to where he had been. He bumped into him, found the mule's jowls, and gave him a good scratching. He continued that until he made Gerg fully visible again.

By dinnertime, Min'darr had experimented with at least two dozen different "tricks." He then remembered he was famished. The budding magician loved rabbit stew. He closed his eyes, thinking hard. When he opened his eyes, a rabbit was nibbling at the grasses next to him. He shook his head and thought again. This time he focused more on a bowl of steaming rabbit stew. Fifteen minutes later, he sat at his rekindled campfire with a full stomach.

He remained there, sifting through the thoughts in his mind that weren't the least familiar. Some were in languages he had never experienced before. He realized, as he settled down for the night, that this magic stuff would not be easy to manage.

*

Min'darr stirred. Something caused him to wake. He forced his eyes open. The distant peaks were just signaling the arrival of the new day. It was his second dawn at the fire pit. Uncle Taf's flight from him the other night continued to bother him. He'd rather be angry at him, however, from his nearly eleven-year-old perspective, he almost understood his uncle's ire.

Taf had never turned away from him before. He'd always been there with some lesson, some point for him to learn. Min'darr had learned to deal with his sarcasm, his loathing of other people, even his frequent self-pity. Of late, he seemed particularly sensitive to Min'darr's new magic.

Not that he had magic, but it surpassed Taf's own. Taf used his magic as a badge. He wasn't condescending, though he managed to comment regularly about how he felt it set him apart from others. His magical use of fire had made his life so much easier. So his reaction when Min'darr so successfully cremated those robbers—their dust had already been blown off the mountains—Min'darr was sure that it would make his uncle's arcane skill look like a charlatan's trick.

It made the young learner nervous about facing him. Using any more of his magic might incur his uncle's wrath. So, it was a good thing that Min'darr had been able to test the extent of his skills with magic yesterday, without his uncle to see.

He reminded himself that Taf'nar had inherited the ogre's healing and speed magic. So, hopefully, that would fill Taf's need for superiority for a while. As long as Min'darr used his head to not show him up with whatever the cave had given him.

All these thoughts whirled in his mind as he stretched, poking his way out from his blanket. He faced Gerg, standing against the trees, nervously pawing the dirt. "What's the matter? You hungry?" he asked. He walked to him and patted his jaw. The mule jerked his head into the boy.

Nudged enough to face him in another direction, Min'darr looked out, seeing an amazing sight. About the size of a turkey, a blue orb floated in the meadow, about an arrow's flight from him. More awesome to him were the myriad animals surrounding it. An elk, deer, wolf, cougar, bear, rabbits, mountain sheep, and at least a dozen different birds ranging from a tiny hummingbird to a massive eagle.

Each one faced the orb, seemingly oblivious to each other or anything else. He startled when a voice from behind him spoke.

"By the Creator! What is that? Did your magic do that?" It was Taf.

Min'darr spun to face him. "Whoa! I didn't hear you. No, not my magic. I just saw it." He glanced behind his uncle. "No horse? Did you walk here?"

"Ran. I really like this magic stuff. You okay? It's been two nights. I got worried."

Min'darr smiled, inwardly relaxing. "I had to try to put some things into ... ah ... oh, what's that word ... Mom loved it. The one that means how you see something?"

"Perspective?" Taf answered.

"That's the one! Hey, uhm, thanks for coming back. I missed you."

Taf smiled back, then looked out over his nephew's shoulder. "So, you sure you didn't conjure this thing?"

"I didn't. I woke up and saw it a few seconds before you scared the breath out of me. Look at 'em all. Totally taken in by that ball. The color's right. It has to be from the cave."

Taf nodded. "I'm with ya there." He watched it for a minute. "What do you think it's for?"

Before Min'darr could answer, a blue veil again fell across his world. Nothing had changed. Taf remained still, as if frozen. Then the voice from the cave filled his mind. *"When you feel you are ready, Min'darr, return to us. Discovery awaits."* Then everything became real again.

Taf'nar's hand was on his shoulder. "Hey! You doing okay?"

"Please tell me you heard that. That voice just now?" Min'darr pleaded.

Taf's eyes narrowed. "Oh, so it's speaking to you?" He stepped ahead of Min'darr yelling at the orb. "What's wrong with me? Did I do something to piss you off? Am I not good enough anymore?"

He whirled, taking Min'darr by the shoulders. "I am your mentor, your Ma'hara. I am the one training you, not them. Whatever they offer, I will train you. I will see to your well-being. Do you understand?" Taf's eyes narrowed, his breathing quick and shallow.

"Yes, Uncle. Of course. What are we to do about that?" Min'darr ask pointing to the orb.

"I'll deal with that," he said and ran toward it, using his magic.

The orb spoke in Min'darr's mind. *"Do not allow Taf'nar to interfere. You are the prize, he is a means to you. There will be a price to be paid for his insolence."*

Min'darr cried out to him. "Uncle Taf! Stop!" He saw his uncle reach the orb. The animals reacted to his being there. Most ran or flew away. The elk, with the eagle on its back, stayed, as did the bear. The elk snorted, pawing the ground. The eagle flapped its wings, kreeing. The bear stood on its hind legs, snarling.

Taf's attention stayed on the orb. He created fire, throwing a ball of it toward the animals. The elk ran while the eagle soared to the east. The bear dropped to all fours, still growling. It positioned itself between Taf and the orb.

Min'darr decided on his course of action. Knowing Taf might be angry, but wanting only to keep him alive, he called on his magic to lift Taf up, preventing him from attacking the orb or the bear. He felt the magic in a wash of blue. It stirred within him. Taf rose, losing his balance, as the bear lunged.

The two connected. Taf spun within the spell's confines. Min'darr reacted with an arcane push, sending the bear toppling away. The bear rose, turned, and ran. Min'darr was already running toward his uncle. He couldn't tell if Taf had been hurt.

Once there, he slowed the effects of his magic, lowering Taf gently to the ground. Taf cradled his arm, some blood seeping between his fingers as he grasped his upper arm.

"Uncle Taf, oh Uncle, I'm so sorry. They warned me. They said you'd get hurt if you did anything to the orb or the animals. They sounded mad. What can I do?" Min'darr bent low next to his injured uncle.

"Nothing. Do nothing, ever!" Taf said as he sat up, grimacing. "You used your magic against me, didn't you?" Taf was yelling at him now. "You lifted me so I couldn't defend myself against that bear! Damn you! What did you think was going to happen?"

Min'darr started to tear, voice quavering. "They warned me! Uncle, they told me you'd get hurt if ..."

"Well, they were right about that, weren't they? Here, look, see my arm?" He took his hand away. Min'darr glimpsed torn shirt fabric with blood seeping from a large gash. "Thanks to you I get to use my healing magic. This hurts and it's your fault. If you'd have left me alone, I'd have scared the bear away and sent that orb back, too. Where is the thing, anyway?" he asked turning around.

Min'darr looked, too, finding it floating high above them. "Right above us," he said.

"Good. Probably watching us too. Well, they can rot in their stinking cave." He screamed aloud, "You can all rot!"

Min'darr reached out. "Here, let me ..."

"No!" Taf yelled, kicking out at him, but missing. "Don't touch me. You did this. You let that bear attack me. Go away! Get outta here! Get outta my life!

"We're done! No more Ma'har. Go home, little boy. You failed your Ma'har ... damn near got me killed. Don't you dare go back to the cabin. That's mine! You're not welcome there anymore. I'm going to have a huge bonfire tonight ... everything that's yours is going up in smoke. I disown you, Min'darr, son of no one!"

Taf stood, spitting at Min'darr's feet. Using his magic, Taf ran over the far ridge in seconds.

Min'darr stood silent, empty. He should be crying. He should be angry. He should ...

"Come to us." The orb was behind him, at his eye level when he turned around.

"Why?" he asked.

"You know the answer to that already," the orb responded. It then disappeared.

Min'darr looked north, then began trudging to the fire pit, back to Gerg. As he approached, he saw that the mule had company. The elk, cougar, eagle, and the bear waited with him. Gerg pawed at the ground, nickering, looking more than a bit nervous.

Fateful Return

Reluctantly, Min'darr dismounted Gerg at a copse of smaller elms and pine, the last shielded camp sites he'd have. He wished he was at the cave already. The next two camps would be amidst cliffs with only a few scattered boulders. He'd spent most of his day after leaving the fire pit in a dismal mood.

Depressed by his uncle's betrayal, he plodded north with his animal entourage. The initial novelty of being escorted by these creatures amused him. Soon, though, he worried if they were meant more for protection. *Against whom? Taf? Someone else, like another ogre?* His constant checking around them with his magic failed to justify his apprehensions. By nightfall, the animals wandered off, Min'darr presumed, to hunt. He had watched throughout the day as the bear and elk kept pace with Gerg.

Then he was alone.

Despite it being one of the early summer months, the mountain air chilled him. He doused the fire, choosing instead to wrap up in his two blankets. He hadn't an opportunity to retrieve a tent, so he, along with whatever Nature pleasured, would pass the night together. He shook with the cold wishing the fire could burn through the night without the danger of burning everything around him in the process. Sleep eventually found him.

He woke facing east to the sound of the eagle's kree. The sun was not yet in his eyes, though it shown on the trees around him. Next to him the scent of an animal's musty fur filled his nose and kept him warm. *Gerg.* He patted the mule's back, stretched and sat up. The eagle sat atop a nearby pine. Min'darr spotted Gerg standing close within the trees, chewing on some of the lower foliage. *So what was next to me?* A closer look showed that it was the bear curled next to him, slumbering.

With that he grinned. No way would a wild mountain bear stay with a human all day, then sleep next to him at night. Somehow, he thought, these animals must be able to feel his magic. That was what they were responding to. Through it, they were his friends.

As he moved around the bear, it stirred and yawned. Min'darr had never looked into the mouth of a bear before, especially from within reach. *Those teeth!* He found some mangled plants laden with berries heaped together on the ground. Blueberries, strawberries, and gooseberries rested at the fire site. Min'darr sat to eat them. He realized it had to have been the bear who had gathered them. Before that first berry passed his lips, the bear was sitting at his side. Feeling a touch guilty, he decided to share the fruit with the beast, to stay on its good side. It was a nice way to thank the animal for procuring it and sharing it with him. He'd never hand-fed a bear before. It was surprisingly delicate using its lips only. It made Min'darr chuckle. Such a dainty gesture for such a massive creature.

They set out, making good progress throughout the day, pacing themselves so they would not have to stop to rest. Min'darr sensed that they might have been affected by some magic, too. He'd have to remember to thank the ... whatever it was from the cave when they got there.

That night, both the eagle and the cougar provided dinner. The eagle arrived after a brief absence carrying a huge fish. Min'darr assumed it came from a mountain lake or stream. It left, returning twice more giving each to the bear. The cougar brought a rabbit. Min'darr cleaned the fish and the rabbit. He then set up the night's fire.

Min'darr searched for the matches he'd used the night before but could not find them. He chuckled, looking at his hands. The thought of his fire-making ability flashed across his mind. He stepped back, saying the words his memory gave him. A thin fire stream extended from his palm. Doing so caused him to think of Uncle Taf. He felt sad—no, miffed that their relationship had dissolved on such a circumstance of Taf's greedy anger that Min'darr's magic was bigger and better than his own.

Both the rabbit and the fish cooked well, although he wished he had some salt for seasoning.

Wedged in against the cliff face with some scrub brush, Min'darr settled in to sleep, tucked between the elk and Gerg. He quickly decided he'd best ignore their smells, drifting off to a dreamless sleep.

When he awoke, only the mule remained. He got up and patted Gerg's flank. He pulled his hand back in surprise. Gerg was cold and hard. He looked intently at it. It was stone. Every aspect of the mule was perfectly preserved as rock. The reins, harness, and saddle that he'd taken off of Gerg when they made camp were off to the side, still leather.

How? Could this have happened from his own magic? Something he thought of in his sleep? He thought hard, not coming up with any recollections of doing this, nor could he know any kind of spell to reverse it. His mule was a statue ... a rock.

Min'darr began to panic. Not because he was alone, but that he was without transportation and two days' ride away from the cave. He looked around to orient himself. There was no sign of the other animals.

He knew he had to follow this cliff line to reach the cave. He scanned the precipice not able to tell how far he had yet to go. He didn't notice any landmark from which to judge. He thought about twenty miles or so. Min'darr sighed, collected his blankets and slung Gerg's saddlebags over his shoulder. With his first step, his world was yet again, covered in a blue haze.

What danger was there? He stood, staring in every direction, intently looking for danger, for some source of harm, for some sense of other magic. Nothing. He hesitated, then, since nothing presented itself, he again began to walk.

With each step he took, the ground beneath streaked behind him. The rock face beside him rushed by, like he was running, only he wasn't. It mattered not if the ground was flat or if he walked up or down hillsides. His pace never wavered. The sun had not reached its zenith when Min'darr arrived at the base of the bowl.

About two months had passed since he'd first been brought here by Taf'nar. The drifts of snow that had draped the upper elevations were gone, replaced with tall grasses that wafted in the breeze. Though he could not see the cave's entrance, he felt it. His proximity to this place seemed to strengthen his arcane awareness. The blue haze dissolved. While there was no physical sound to hear, his mind echoed with the invitation to return to the cavern's depths, to continue his eldritch experiences as a part of his magical education. He climbed the base of the bowl, quickly slipping out of sight of the rest of the world.

It took his eyes no time to adjust to the utter lack of daylight. As he entered, the surfaces within the cave shown the same blue as before. He took his same spot on the raised ledge. Speaking as softly as he could, he said simply, "I am here."

Without missing a heartbeat, the cave creature—what else could he call it?—once again began building on itself until it towered from the cave's floor to inches above Min'darr's eye level.

"We are pleased you have returned, Min'darr, son of Bu'ka with Kir'ni. Tell us what you have learned."

"I have learned that your magic cannot be left to my world," he stated without hesitation.

"More," it prompted.

"You want more? Sure. I may be a little kid without years of experience, but even I can see that having magic can change a person, ruin them. It will allow them to become so powerful that they can then get anything they want. It can make them a demon. It should have no place in my world."

"Are you a demon, then, since you possess the power to do magic?" the voice asked.

"I don't know, maybe I am. I killed a man using magic. I destroyed two men's bodies with that same power. It has cost me my uncle. He is jealous of the abilities you have given me.

"Why? I knew nothing of any of this before I came to you, at your request. Why would you play with my life? Why?" Min'darr hadn't realized he was screaming.

"Min'darr, your anger and fear are refreshing. We are Mulu, the fountainhead of the energies of this place, this planet. The Universe of which it is a part is vast, so intricately interconnected that it surpasses the understanding of those with mortal lives. We tap into the energies of our own perpetual existence to further our understanding. In so doing, we have learned how those energies can be diffused, how they can be focused, how they can be manipulated. Doing so is what you call magic.

"Nature has given you a sensitivity to these energies. You felt them outside. We know. We have felt your presence since your conception. We have waited throughout your lifetime to train you in these skills. If you are successful, you will control more power than any human before you.

"It is essential to this existence that magic should dwell among your kind. That is beyond anything we can do ourselves. It is up to you to wander among your fellow men to influence their lives with your understanding.

"But mark us, young human. You will be watched to see how you deal with magic. We will not let it or you get out of control. As you said, mankind will abuse this power as they abuse everything else. You must guard your abilities carefully. Fail and it will be your end, hopefully not the end of your world.

"But come. It is time to further your understanding," it said while tendrils of blue magic reached for the boy. He willingly surrendered to them, not resisting. In fact, he felt very much at home.

He found solace in the comforting sensation of the blueness enveloping his body. Once within, there was no hunger or any senses of pressure or temperature or even time, just a calming existence without physical sensation or distraction. Though he'd experienced this once before, he felt he could stay this way forever, comfortable with this separation from reality.

And then it began. His mind was deluged with the history of the human race, the formation of the very planet upon which they lived. He marveled with the same sense of awe as he understood both living cells and atoms of the air. The encyclopedic stream of information formed a network from which he could understand those forces involved in forming all that he experienced. The energies with which he was coexisting helped him know them, how they came to be. He saw how they worked individually or in network with others.

Soon enough, magic was self-explanatory, no longer the amazing, wondrous mystery he'd once perceived it to be.

Then a blemish occurred. A disturbance that affected the flow of the energies in which he was submerged. It withdrew from him. He felt himself being pulled out, back to his physical self. Min'darr knew enough to ride the currents of the energies. Fighting them would be useless, in fact, dangerous.

And so, Min'darr returned. The blue receded from him. His own eyes opened, seeing the familiar blue of the cave. His ears were barraged by sounds, human noises. He recognized both the sounds and the sight of its source. Uncle Taf'nar hung in the center of the cave, each limb strung by blue tendrils of magic attached to opposite corners of the cavern. He looked like a big fly caught in a bigger web.

Taf'nar screamed about being released, about reclaiming his nephew. He also threatened to burn down the cave. Incoherent ramblings followed about being Min'darr's mentor, his savior, and then something about mastering the village to rule its people. Finally, Taf'nar ranted about revenge, about burning the mountains and everything within them if his words were not heeded.

He didn't act like he saw Min'darr standing there, his cloak of blue magic withdrawn. Within his mind, the Mulu told him Taf'nar had burst into the cave, despite it being sealed, as only a creature of magic could do. They told him that stripping Taf of his magic would kill him.

"*Eldritch energies combine with the body's life force in such a complete way as to make them one,*" they told him. "*Even using our magic to change his mind's perspective will drive him further from reality.*

"*I know,*" he thought back to them. "*The man has a profound jealousy of others with magic deeper than his own. He loves his isolation. His words here show he could be a danger to the village he wants to control. His thoughts about destroying life within the mountains cannot be dismissed nor forgiven."*

The Mulu paused. Min'darr suspected a conversation deeper than he could hear. Then the Mulu posed their question. *"What should be done with him? He is your uncle."*

Min'darr's thoughts flooded him. *A test. Am I ready? I am not the boy he delivered here, nor am I the boy who came here on my own. My understanding of this world surpasses his. He is like a primitive savage with the sophistication of magic. That cannot possibly work, he'd be ... be just like the ogre.*

Min'darr was resolved. He said simply, *"He cannot be released. Can he remain here in your care, sealed within this place?"*

"That is not possible for we are not here in the same sense as you are here."

"Well, you made him into what he is. Is that not your responsibility?" Min'darr asked.

Another pause in the conversation. During which Taf'nar ranted, bellowing obscure statements. Min'darr noted he wore shabby clothing. His hair and beard had grown considerably—at least a year's worth. Both were equally disheveled.

The Mulu responded. *"All we can account for is his energies. Remember, his magic has become one with his life force."*

"Since he can no longer control himself, he cannot be returned to his world. Too much evil will happen to too many." Min'darr said. He understood the consequences of his statement. Taf's energies, both magic and life, would be returned to the flow. The biological man would end.

The Mulu said, *"So shall it be."* The blue tendrils holding Taf got brighter, quickly advancing on him, climbing onto his trunk, his chest, finally covering his head. As it did, his shouts of anger became screams of fear, until the blue essence covered him completely.

Silence filled the cave, save for a background susurrus like a distant stream. Each strand pulsed once, thinned, then retreated back into the wall from which it was attached. Nothing remained.

Min'darr's arcane awareness noted the passing of a soft bolt of energy back into the flow of countless other energies. He experienced a twinge of sadness, noting to himself to be sure to tell his father about Uncle Taf's passing.

"May I return to my training?" he asked aloud. He sensed the Mulu's collective approval. Min'darr allowed the tendrils to take him into the blue magic again. The cave's complete darkness returned. Min'darr had no need for light. Immersed within the eldritch flow, the energies of life and magic coursed through him. With every touch, he was granted insight into the human condition.

He also saw how the Mulu had influenced those who had come before him. Not magician candidates as he was, but through their perspectives and "discoveries" that he found had been planted by the Mulu ... just to see what would happen.

He realized that he too was to be one of their experiments. It didn't matter, though. He had magic.

Reality Beckons

Awareness returned. Self-awareness balked, not willing to become himself again just yet. His existence within the eldritch flow pleased him. No needs to be met, no distractions to stay the fulfillment of experiencing the energies of creation and life. At one point during this journey, Min'darr felt drawn to some of it. It felt familiar so he flowed with it for a while.

Now, his time within the flow was at an end. Like any child, a good part of him wished to remain. Yet, his understanding surpassed that simple yearning. Out of necessity, he capitulated, allowing the blue essence to withdraw from him.

He stood on uncertain legs, stretching, relearning the sensations of his physical existence. Once again, Min'darr used muscles, felt hunger, knew darkness and cold. The oddity of being confined within his body did not agree with him. His mind, too, was so limited in what he could actively remember compared to before when he'd been within the eldritch flow.

A blue light filled the cavern. Min'darr turned to see a glowing orb like the one from the fire pit. This one, however, was about as large as he was. He recognized it as Mulu. It spoke.

"Welcome back to the physical world, Min'darr. It will take some time for you to be comfortable in your body. We have nurtured it in the years while you experienced the eldritch existence.

"You will retain your command and understanding of magic, but, as you can already tell, your physical mind cannot grasp all its intricacies. Allow yourself meditation so that much of what you have learned will again be accessible to you. Your ability to call upon magic will also seem limited because of this. Still, you will be a powerful magician, able to conjure miracles in the eyes of your fellow humans."

"Thank you for what you have done for me. My mind is abuzz with words in languages I don't know. How can I keep these to use?" Min'darr asked.

"They are forever yours. Your inner self will search them out as you need them. They will come. Any other questions?"

"How did the ogre have magic?" Min'darr asked.

"The beast slept here some time ago. We were interested to see how such a primitive creature would deal with having magic."

"And ...?" Min'darr prompted.

"As we thought. It used its magic for itself, despite many opportunities to help others. We sent it near you and your uncle so it would die."

"You knew we'd kill it?"

"We would have been surprised if you hadn't. We knew its own tendencies. We also knew that the two of you would be clever enough to find a way to defeat it. Remember, Min'darr, magic is a tool. Know that it can be used to build or to destroy. You have shown yourself to be our strongest learner yet."

"Yet? There are others? Any I can ..."

"Do well, Min'darr, master of magic."

He felt himself thinning until he was no longer standing where he had been.

Min'darr stood outside the cave, blinded by the harsh daylight and assaulted by the winter winds that whipped across his body. The cold shocked him. He instantly shook. *Fire! I need fire.* He looked yet saw nothing to burn as he stood midthigh in new snow.

An eagle kreed high above him. His mind reached out to it. He felt its hunger, its primal need to survive. A thought struck him. *They last throughout the seasons without coats. I need to be like an eagle.*

His mind centered on the words that rushed to his consciousness. A flash of blue washed over him. His skin tingled as it sprouted feathers. He legs got quickly shorter. His arms stretched out, becoming wings. His eyesight changed, so different, so perfect. He opened his mouth to shout for joy, now only able to kree. Min'darr flapped his wings and took to the air, letting the winds that had worked to freeze him lift him up, beyond the heights of the leafless trees.

He knew to head south. The winds blew him that way. *Where shall I go?* he thought. The answer that came was his before he asked the question. He'd go to Taf'nar's cabin, the last home he knew.

*

The impact of the recent weather had lessened as Min'darr swooped down, settling onto the cabin's roof. A thin trail of smoke came from the chimney next to him. *Taf'nar is dead. Who would be here now?*

Since people were in there, he kept the eagle's form. No tracks were in the snow. The shaded windows showed no light coming from within.

He needed a plan. To get the people outside, he had to make the inside uncomfortable. The eagle Min'darr waved a wing across the chimney causing the smoke to stop rising, covering it with a magical spell that would force them out.

Three minutes later, the stable door opened. Smoke billowed out. Two people followed, coughing. They struggled to breathe while they worked to get coats on that they had grabbed on their way out.

The man's voice said, "Must be some snow fell down the stack, blocking it.

The woman's voice said, "But wouldn't it melt from the fire?"

"Depends on how much. This cooking fire isn't up to temperature yet. You didn't want to char the rabbits, remember?" he said.

"So how long do we have to stay out here? I'm freezing."

"Let's go back in the stable. I'll go get the windows open to air the place out." That said, the two moved back toward the doorway.

Min'darr spread his wings, diving down on them, screeching, fluttering his wings in the man's face, getting between them and the doorway. The man waved his arms at the large bird, but

Min'darr stayed back far enough to avoid being struck. He landed in the doorway, then removed his magical spell to stand before them as a human. "This is my home!" he hollered. "What are you doing in my home?"

The man eyes rolled up. He fainted, collapsing into the snow. The woman, grasping a long knife she'd been using preparing dinner, dropped it from the shock of what she had witnessed. Her eyes glared. "Wha ... what, umm, I unh ... who, umm, who are you?" she finally managed to say.

"I am Min'darr. This place is mine. Leave!" Despite the cold, Min'darr maintained his composure.

"You ... I mean, how can this be your home! We've lived here for nigh onto two years. We found it abandoned. Well, there was an old goat that died the day we got here."

"You killed Hilda?" Min'darr asked, his mind racing with fond memories of tickling the goat.

"Hilda? You mean the goat? No. No, sir. We spent the night in the stable 'cause she wouldn't let us in. In the morning, though, we tried again without any problem. We found her dead by the fireplace. We buried her in the yard," she said, pointing to the corner of the corral.

"We shall go inside. Come," he said. As he turned to go in, the woman said, "Hey, magician? Can I get a little help here?" she asked, struggling to prop up the still-unconscious man. Min'darr gestured, causing the man to rise and float behind him as they entered the stable, scattering a dozen or more chickens in the process.

Within the first minute of being inside, Min'darr worked two spells. He removed the spell from the chimney top and swept the stinky smoke out of the cabin. He finally produced clean clothes for himself ... pants, a loose shirt with a sash of a very familiar shade of blue.

As the woman tended a fire in the stove, she drew water to prepare a tea mix. "My name is Sar'ti. His name," as she pointed to the unconscious pile of clothes on the main floor, "is Kar'tum. Did, umm, did you do anything to him? I mean, you know, magic-wise? He should have woken up by now."

"No. Does he do this often?" Min'darr asked.

"Whenever he gets surprised." She went to him. Kneeling next to him, she prodded gently. He did not respond. She slapped him across the face. Nothing. "Oh, by the Creator ... no!" Lifting her head from his chest, she cried, "No heartbeat!" Her eyes teared as she cradled the man's head. "Please."

Min'darr came to them. With his hand on Kar'tum's chest, he sent his magic within the man. He found energy, weak, but present. "He's barely alive." He looked at her. "I have never done this before."

"Whatever you can! Please?" She cried openly. "He is my life."

Min'darr realized the man's energies were ebbing. He would die. "I cannot share either of our life forces with him." He thought a moment. "Bring me two birds from the stable."

"I'll bring a knife, too." She rose and ran to the mud room.

"No! Alive." He shouted after her.

Thirty seconds after raucous clucking from the stable, Sar'ti returned, cradling two still-clucking chickens. Min'darr reached out, touching both birds. They became instantly silent.

He allowed the magic to rise within him, the words calling the forces came easily. He looked with eyes that could see the magic and watched the lighter blue life forces of the birds rise to his hands where they combined into one. This he placed onto Kar'tum's chest. It quickly sunk into him. Min'darr laid his hand on the same location and sent a spark of magic into him.

"Slap him," he told her. "This should help his weak heart be stronger."

She did, as hard as she could muster.

Kar'tum gasped. His jerked awake, continuing to breathe heavily for a bit. He then worked on peeling Sar'ti's form off of him. He sat up and asked, "What's wrong?" He looked behind her and saw Min'darr, who had backed up to stand next to the fireplace.

"What the ...? Who are you? What's going on here? Sar'ti, you alright?" He struggled to stand, managing only when he allowed her to help him.

Sar'ti sat him down in the chair near the fireplace. "You, umm, you fainted when Min'darr showed up, sweetheart. He's a magician. He used to live here. It's his home." Kar'tum glanced between Sar'ti and Min'darr, then nodded in understanding.

"We will talk about this place later," Min'darr told them. "Are you feeling better?"

Kar'tum nodded. "Of course. I feel fine." He looked around suddenly. "Did you clear out the chimney? We had lots of smoke in here before. Probably some snow fell in. Thanks. By the way, sweetheart, we got anything ready for dinner?"

"How about chicken?" she said, holding out the dead birds.

"Two?" he asked.

"Of course. We have a guest. We can cook the rabbit you snared tomorrow." She looked at Min'darr, grinning. She went into the kitchen.

Kar'tum remarked. "By the gods, two chickens dead? Just like that damn goat when we first got here. Animals shouldn't go dying off like this ... or do they?" Kar'tum mumbled.

"All things happen for a reason. We simply can try to understand," Min'darr said.

"I don't mean to be disrespectful, however, you are kind of an odd one, eh? How old are you?"

Min'darr thought a second and then asked, "How old do you think I am?" Min'darr knew that much time had elapsed while he'd been within the cave. The Mulu said they'd nurtured his body while he was within the eldritch flow. In addition to the limitations he had to get used to when rejoining his body, he realized that it felt different from when he'd left it. He had no idea how he appeared to these strangers.

"Judging from your height ... the scruff on your chin, I'd say maybe fifteen years. I'm not that far from there. Celebrated my twenty-fourth a month ago."

Min'darr smiled. "Happy birthday, then."

*

Following dinner, the three sat by the fireplace. The snows had moved on, leaving them with a clear, frigid sky. Despite the fire, the cold worked to saturate their bones.

"Tell me about finding this cabin," Min'darr said. He regretted it after the first half hour of their rambling, yet detailed oration.

They shared the responsibility of telling their guest everything, frequently correcting each other as well as filling in specifics the other had missed. Min'darr understood that they had come from south of his hometown of Calstara, seeking a mountain home. They'd wandered for the better part of a year, stumbling upon the cabin by sheer happenstance. The stable doors were wide open. No animals were to be found. Their knocking on the inner door resulted only in repeated thumping from its other side. Despite their efforts, they got no other response.

When they finally tried to enter the house, a goat with massive horns kept them at bay by repeatedly butting the thick door closed. They ended up sleeping in the stable with their own mules that night. The next morning, they managed to enter the cabin unchallenged. They found the floor littered with poop pellets. The goat lay dead next to the fireplace. She was very old from what they could tell. Out of respect, they buried her in the corral, dubbing the cabin "Goat's Crest." That happened two years ago by Kar'tum's reckoning, twenty-one months by Sar'ti's.

At bedtime, Sar'ti offered Min'darr their bed. He politely refused, intent on going to the lower level, but without telling them. He bid them good night, settling in in front of the fireplace with a collection of thick blankets.

Min'darr recalled the extensive cellar of the cabin, replete with all manner of saved foods, weapons, and a shop full of tools. His uncle had spent six years building and stocking the cabin. Min'darr suspected its current residents were unaware of the cellar.

He overheard very little from them. Kar'tum asked about events while he'd fainted, Sar'ti gave him a huge hug saying that she and the young magician spoke about the cabin's past. Min'darr appreciated her discretion concerning his healing the man. They soon were asleep in the loft.

Min'darr stealthily moved the cabinet bottom, slipped down the ladder, closing the access behind him so they wouldn't know he was down there.

After lighting the sconces, it was easy to see that no one had visited here for some time. *There's dust everywhere!* he observed. He examined the preserved foods. Each had a date when Taf had canned it. "I need to know how old these are to know if they're safe."

He went to the weapons area to select a long dagger, bow and quiver. He also chose a staff with metal ends, intent on taking these with him. Sitting at Taf's old workbench, Min'darr drifted off to sleep.

*

He climbed up the ladder that next morning, opening the cabinet and crawling out into the living room. Kar'tum and Sar'ti stood motionless at the kitchen sink, mouths agape. Min'darr laughed, quickly whispering, "Surprise!"

"What ... where?" Kar'tum managed to say. "We thought you'd left."

"Follow me. You'll be surprised what you've been living on top of all this time."

They followed him to the lower level. Kar'tum was amazed by the rooms, the tools, and weapons. When Sar'ti saw the canned goods, she was at first thrilled, then, after looking at them, declared them unsafe, too old.

"How old is this? It's marked '52." Min'darr asked.

Sar'ti tsked when she saw it. "All this work ... what a shame. That's at least six years old. I wouldn't trust eating it anymore." Then she added, "Wait ... you can add and subtract, yes?"

"Yes, I can," Min'darr admitted. "But I've been gone for a very long time. Sadly, I have no idea how many years."

"Okay, this is '58. When were you born?" Sar'ti asked, a maternal tone tinged her voice.

"In '43," he replied.

"You're fifteen. Does that make sense?" she asked.

"It does. More importantly, it also means I have to return to my parents' home. I have been gone from there far too long, much longer than I had anticipated.

"This cabin was built by my Uncle Taf'nar," he continued. "All of the foods, weapons, and tools were his. He died some time

69

ago. As his heir, I give this to you, with the exception of what I will take with me."

Within an hour, Min'darr said his goodbyes. Kar'tum gave him his own coat, a monstrously heavy fur-lined piece with a full hood. Sar'ti donated some food and a pair of snowshoes she'd recently finished making. He had at first refused, reminding them of his magic.

Sar'ti wouldn't hear of it. "You can't use magic all the time," she lectured. "You will have to act like a normal man soon enough. Keep in mind, normal men do not walk about in winter without coats."

Min'darr smiled with them, appreciating their caring. "You are both very kind."

So, with the gifts, the weapons he'd selected, and a full belly, Min'darr left to make his way back to the village of Calstara, to his parents' home.

He found that his walking fast magic worked well on snow. He did so without once thinking of the ogre, which first demonstrated that spell. He'd progressed far enough in his magical training to not remain entrenched in his human memories.

By sunset, he stood atop the fire-charred walls of Nordana Pass. Overlooking the Shat'su Expanse, he saw the undeveloped plain with mixed feelings. Something within him stirred. It didn't feel right. He dismissed his reaction to the guilt he felt for being gone so long. He regained the trail, but his exhaustion prompted him to camp near the crest.

Unable to fall sleep, Min'darr once again became an eagle. He took the time to pay attention to the process, enjoying each sensation of his shifting form and the growth of all the feathers. Spreading his wings, he leaped off the top, then soared along the Nordana Pass. He was surprised to find that a gate blocked the entry to the pass. Next to it stood a gatehouse. He sensed people within. He couldn't help wondering how many or who they might be.

He next soared across the expanse toward a very dark Calstara. The dark line that surrounded his hometown looked ominous in the depths of a cold winter's night. People were moving about near it. *I'll have to be prepared for almost anything tomorrow.*

He returned to his campsite, his mind filled with burning questions about what lay below. That would wait for the morrow when he'd also face his parents and his sister, four years overdue.

He finally fell asleep not sure how he would be able to explain who he'd become.

A Different Calstara

Shortly after dawn, Min'darr set his feet within the Nordana Pass. He stashed his gear near the gatehouse, then snuck into it as a mouse. He wasn't the first one, either. There were lots of mice scurrying about, plus a cat busy with the rodents elsewhere. Eight soldiers were starting their day. They spoke Kordalian, the language from the neighboring country to the south. Each man was armed. Min'darr understood enough of the language to know they expected a caravan to come through the next day from the north.

Min'darr tucked himself into a corner to think. *Do I deal with them now, or just continue on home? Three miles. So close. I don't know why they're here or how this came to be, so I'll concentrate on going home. I'll deal with this later. Let's see, I think a strong wind is what I'll need to get away without being seen.*

Back in human form outside the gatehouse, he used his magic to summon a strong wind to sweep through the pass. Snow blew to the point that it rattled the doors of the gatehouse. It swirled, clapping the shutters open, then closed. Min'darr concealed himself within the blowing snows so sneaking past the gatehouse was easy. The snow quickly filled in his footprints as he walked.

The shadow of a trail was exposed by the morning's light, slanting in low across the eastern ridges. He trudged on, allowing the stormy winds to remain around the entrance to the pass, lest he be spotted and pursued. "Three miles," he reminded himself aloud. "No more magic, or I'll have to explain myself to the law. Superstitious lot, this town. Bunch of folk with wide-open mouths and closed minds." His memories of the town refreshed with each step he took. One of the reasons he'd left with Uncle Taf was that, although he loved his family dearly, he didn't care too much for the rest of Calstara. Too stodgy, too buried in the past.

Still, the existence of the gatehouse meant one of two things. War had broken out because they did seem like soldiers, or some foreign company was charging tolls to use it. Neither option was necessarily a good thing.

Even as a boy, a year with his uncle had shone brightly to him as a way out, something he'd never allowed himself to realize, let alone tell anyone. Now, his experiences with Uncle Taf, as well as his own exposure to magic and the existences beyond human reality, Min'darr was more than comfortable with his leaving home. Well worth the trauma.

"Certainly not for this long, though," he said, wondering how he'd explain his absence. His one-year term with his uncle turned into five times its original plan. Had they searched? Had he been given up for lost ... or dead?

He'd reached about halfway across the expanse to the town. Looking ahead, he saw again how things had changed. It appeared to him that the town was encircled by a wall, like a fortress would be. A higher area was centered at the point where the road passed into town. It was gated, a closed gate. *What is going on here?* he wondered. A strange sense of foreboding filled him. He consciously felt that his weaponry, a bow with a quiver of arrows and his dagger, were conveniently positioned. The walking staff was already an old friend, used throughout his journey home.

A smattering of remorse went through him that he'd not been more successful in his training with Taf'nar. They'd spent weeks on each type of weapon, hours at a time with Taf pushing Min'darr's skills, strength, duration, and accuracy. He'd never felt good with a sword or an axe, but loved working the long hickory stave. He'd done well as an archer, too. While he hadn't progressed too far in his training with daggers, he felt having a poking or cutting weapon would be advisable, should the need arise. He'd enjoyed learning to throw them at fenceposts, a fun game with fairly reasonable gains once he'd figured out the rotation part.

He huddled into his hooded great coat to keep the winds from interfering with his comfort as he continued to trudge toward home.

*

He was challenged before his staff struck the closed wooden gate.

"Who goes there?" a gruff voice called out from behind the wall.

Either an angry man or one extremely cold. "I am Min'darr, son of Bu'ka. I return after five long years of travels. I bid you open this gate so I may greet my family."

A shutter in the gate opened. A bearded man Min'darr did not recognize glared at him. "You claim relation to Bu'ka the Traitor? Bu'ka who was executed after he tried to assassinate his lordship, Magama the Conqueror?"

Min'darr stared at the man while his insides twisted and churned from his words. "When did these events take place, good sir?" he asked.

"If you are from here, boy, you have been gone a long time! Two years since Magama declared his lordship over the town of Calstara, now known as Magamara."

"This is the rogue general from Kordal that you speak of?" Min'darr asked, remembering overhearing conversations of the old men in town about some in-fighting within Kordal's military.

The gate opened. Three soldiers came out brandishing spears that they leveled at Min'darr. The same soldier who'd spoken through the window came out to poke at him with his sword. "So, son of a traitor, let's see if your blood is the same color as your father's."

Min'darr sighed and summoned his magic. The four soldiers saw his eyes shine blue a heartbeat before their world changed. They became mice, like Min'darr had been in the gatehouse, except not of their own volition. Min'darr kicked at them as they scampered off. "How rude. They left without saying thank you." He strode through the gate intent on finding his family, pausing to lock the gate behind him should anyone come by.

*

The fourth door closed in his face. No one would speak to him. No one acted as if they'd recognized him either. He'd sensed enough to know to ask for his sister's husband, Jal'oot. No one answered his question. He'd knocked on nine or ten doors yet only four had opened.

Pausing in his quest, he saw a young face in an upper window peering out at him. Just in time, a woman whisked the child back. He saw his sister's face as she took a quick look out, saw his form, then closed the curtain. Though she looked older, he'd seen those eyes too many times to not recognize them. She would not have been able to see his face with his hood up, so he knew his work lay ahead of him.

His first stop had been to his parents' home. It was no longer there. Some smaller debris lay buried under the snow, so he couldn't tell what it might have been. He sensed a fire. His heart sunk, haunted by the words of the gate guard. No one near it answered his knock.

*

He stood at the upper door to the apartment he'd seen the boy. The outer door had been locked, but it wasn't magic-proof. Koo'bla and he had had many name-calling sessions as kids. The one name he called her that always caused her to react was Bisha. It was a word that meant stinky. He tapped lightly on the door, whispering, "Hey, Bisha, it's me."

Silence reigned for a full minute. He tapped again. The door cracked open a finger-width. The eye he saw was three feet from the floor. A little voice whispered, "You Bisha nakka."

Min'darr smiled at the response. "You stinky, not me." He responded, "Bisha nakka go'laga." Words from their childhood condemning the other one to be forever stinky, thanks to a grandfather who devoutly stuck to his own native tongue. The eye backed away. The door opened. He quickly stepped in.

A woman's hands cupped his face. "Oh, thank the Creator, it is you." She hugged him tightly, then pulled away and punched him, already sobbing. "Where were you all this time? One year. One year you'd be with Taf'nar in the mountains. Where, by the

Creator have you been? Didn't you hear of our downfall? The war? Anything?"

As she cried to him, she continued hitting him, pummeling his shoulders. The little boy too, joining in his momma's attack, was busy kicking his legs.

"All right! Stop! I'll tell you everything, just stop."

Koo'bla ceased her barrage to hug her little boy. They sat themselves on a chair by the doorway into the next room. Wiping the tears from her eyes, she said simply, "Well?"

"Taf'nar is dead," he began.

"So are our parents," she retorted.

He hid the shock of her words, confirming his fears. "Do you want to go first?" he asked.

She shook her head. "Sorry. No, you tell me. I truly need to know."

"Taf'nar had gotten some magic from an entity in a cave in the high ranges. It's how he burned the Ma'har. He took me there in the spring. They gave me some too. He got really jealous when mine was stronger than his. The entity killed him when he attacked it in the cave." He paused. She remained placid. He continued.

"Then the entity—the Mulu it's called—exposed me to more magic. I was in some kind of trance for ... I don't know, a couple or more years, I guess. Just over four years in all."

"So you, my little brother, have magic?"

In response, he gestured with his fingers. The chair, with both of them on it, floated up toward the ceiling. Koo'bla's eyes widened. The boy's eyes were closed tightly.

"No fly. No like flying," he whimpered.

Min'darr lowered them to the floor. "I do," he said.

She turned her son to face her. "Mah'zan, this is your Uncle Min'darr. He may be able to help us."

*

A while later, after Mah'zan went down for a nap, Koo'bla and Min'darr spoke softly. She told him that teams of searchers had looked for him and Taf'nar for two months after he was more than a month late returning home. His parents were angry, grief-stricken, assuming the worst.

"Three years ago," she continued, "some riders from the capitol arrived to say that the king had been murdered by invaders from Kordal, the renegade Magama. We were at war.

"Two years ago, his army showed up here, killing so many. In no time they'd taken over the town. They forced us to build the wall. That's when ..." She began to sob. "... that's when they killed my beloved Jal'oot. They caught him rigging a part of the wall to allow people to escape. They executed him in the square with five others.

"Dad tried to kill Magama a month later by shooting him with an arrow. He hit and killed a man who walked between them. He was—oh my goodness, Min'darr. They executed him too, after a week's worth of torture. I found Mom that night dead on the kitchen floor, a knife ..."

Min'darr winced, continuing to wipe the tears from his eyes.

"Oh, Min'darr, I hated you so much! You weren't here to help. You weren't even here to know what was happening." She clung to him weeping. He cried too.

They spent their day reminiscing. Min'darr played with five-year-old Mah'zan, beginning his role as an uncle.

*

A knock at the door—more like hammering—woke Min'darr up the next morning. Koo'bla was feeding Mah'zan. She looked frightened. Before either could move, the door burst open, splintering the frame. Three men surged in, armed with drawn swords. Min'darr recognized the uniform they wore as the same the men at the gate and the gatehouse were wearing.

"That's him! Arrest him," one of them shouted. The other had grabbed Koo'bla and her crying child.

"Why do you need to threaten them? Neither can hurt you," Min'darr said calmly.

"Shut up." The man sheathed his sword, then added, "Bring them." They were ushered down the stairs, out into the cold. A hundred eyes watched through thin draperies as they were marched to the town's center and the office used by the occupiers.

Arcane Revenge

They were each locked in different cells, Min'darr between them. Koo'bla did her best to quiet her crying son, straining through the cell's bars to reach his mama. She did her best for quite a while, then the stress broke her will. She slumped to the floor, racked with sobs. At one point she gulped, managing to ask, "Can't you do anything? You know, with your ..."

"Shh. Never ..." he said, managing to quiet her before she finished her thought. "I will do everything I can to stop this," he said softly, kneeling at the bars facing her. "Neither you nor Mah'zan will be hurt. I think I have an idea, but I must speak to Magama's regent here."

"You can speak directly to me, whelp." The renegade tyrant Magama, a tall, fat man in full military regalia, had entered the room, followed by about a dozen soldiers. He walked directly to Koo'bla's cell, eyeing her like a vulture would its prey. He calmly said, "Kill the boy. Let her watch." He turned to leave.

"You are too weak, General. There's nothing noble in slaughtering a child," Min'darr said. "In front of your men, I challenge you to a fight. You may use any weapon. You may choose any for me."

He looked at Min'darr and spat. "And what if I'm not interested in getting your blood on my shoes?"

"Then I will fight your entire force that you have here," Min'darr answered.

The man eyed the young man in the cell thoughtfully. "Are you so skilled, so brave or are you just stupid?" Magama asked with a laugh.

"All at the same time," Min'darr replied.

Magama pressed closer to Min'darr's cell. "And who are you that you would boast so wildly of your own death?"

"I am Min'darr, son of Bu'ka, the archer who missed."

Magama's eyes widened. A sneer twisted his face. "Then it will be a pleasure to see you die as it was to see your pitiful father die for his failure. And why wait? We will do this now." He turned to one of his officers, muttering quick instructions to arm and assemble his troops. The man left as did the rogue general.

Min'darr swallowed, hoping his plan would come together. He closed his eyes to hide their blue glow as he magically sent the suggestion of a torch to the officer charged with Magama's task.

"What are you doing?" Koo'bla wailed. "Now I'll lose you too."

Min'darr suggested to their guard, with a bit of a magical boost, that he could put the boy in the same cell as his mom, making the jail so much quieter. He agreed. Min'darr then looked at his sister. "I am so very sorry for the pain that you have endured. I hope that we can talk more tonight. I hope I am right about what I can do here. If I fail in this, know that I love you. Now, I need to prepare." He sat on the floor neither moving nor speaking until they came for him ten minutes later.

*

Min'darr was escorted out into the town's center, brought to stand on the same dais he did the day of his Mahar. Magama joined him there and waved an arm. In a rush of marching boots, the center filled with nearly two hundred archers. In concentric circles, they faced the dais, arrows nocked.

Magama raised his voice to speak to the townspeople who had gathered behind the soldiers, on their decks and at their windows.

"It gives me great pleasure to introduce to you, Min'darr, son of the traitor Bu'ka, executed for treason in attempting to assassinate me. This whelp has returned to challenge me and my army to a duel. Him against all of us." The crowds of soldiers laughed as did some of the residents.

"He has been so noble as to allow me to fight him, or he would fight my army. He has also given me the choice of weapons. Am I right, Min'darr?"

"You speak the truth, Magama," Min'darr said.

"As you can see, I am partial to the bow. Fitting, yes? For Min'darr, I have chosen a special weapon. He will face my warriors ... with a torch, so that he can see each shaft fly to poke holes in him to drain his life's blood, just like his failure of a father.

"But know that I am above the senseless execution of a boy, even if his father did try to murder me. So Min'darr, I charge and find you guilty of murder. Four of my guardsmen are missing, presumed dead. Your death will come as payment for their lives as I am certain it is no coincidence that your arrival here prompted their deaths."

He walked down the dais steps, passing his troops. One soldier came up, handing Min'darr a lit torch. "Nock your arrows," Magama screamed. "On my mark ... Three ..."

Min'darr's closed his blue eyes, filling his mind with the magic spells he conceived for this encounter.

"... Two ..."

He turned in a quick circle to take in everyone around him and felt the power of his essence ready to burst, to surge out.

"... One ..."

He could magically see each arrow tip, the bows, the brows and fingers of every soldier who was a moment away from killing him.

"... FIRE!" screamed Magama.

Arrows from every bow streaked out toward the lone figure of a fifteen-year-old youth. Each travelled only a few feet when bolts of fire streaked from Min'darr's torch, simultaneously incinerating each arrow.

The stunned silence was broken by the hissing sound of another volley of fire from that same torch. This time, the soldiers were struck. Fire so hot and fierce that none had time to react or feel pain as it seared through to their bones. Within a few seconds, each was merely a smoldering pile of ash, save for Magama.

Min'darr whirled to face him, holding out his hands. In another instant, Min'darr levitated the renegade general, who then was spinning and screaming, and floated him onto the dais.

"And now, oh great Magama, for the souls of all those you have hurt, I sentence you to die. Your crimes against humanity condemn you. Feel the pain you have inflicted on others." He threw the torch at the still-floating renegade leader, instantly igniting him into a rotating ball of fire. His dying screams echoed off the face of the nearby mountains.

*

Later that afternoon, a delegation of townspeople came with Min'darr as witnesses to watch a huge part of the Nordana Pass cliff face give way and crash down onto the gatehouse, burying it forever. The pass itself remained unblocked.

Stray soldiers were quickly found, then killed by the rest of the townspeople, emboldened by Min'darr's success to fight on their own behalf. Riders were sent to spread the news.

A dinner was organized for the next night to both celebrate their freedom and to honor Min'darr as the vanquisher of their captors. At first he refused, then he realized that a message needed to be delivered.

He was seated at the head table with his sister, his nephew, along with a collection of elders who were going to lead Calstara.

A man named Ilk'bari stood after the meal, welcoming all. He went on about how he had always liked Min'darr as a boy, had respected Bu'ka, both before the invasion and for what he tried to do to save the town. He acknowledged Min'darr's bravery, declaring that they genuinely respected the boy turned magician.

"It is my distinct honor," he said, "to offer Min'darr a permanent seat on our council. I also name Min'darr to lead us in battle to bring down any of Magama's remaining forces."

When it was Min'darr's turn, the great hall fell silent. Min'darr felt it was more out of fear than any sense of reverence or respect. "Thank you for this welcome. I am glad things have come to pass as they have. But too many have already died. Since I prefer to not kill, I must reject your offer.

"I worked very hard to save this town, to save all of you. But to be blunt, I'm not sure it will be worth it." Those at the gathering gasped. "Magama was successful because only some of the people feared him. Some others cowered. Maybe those were the smart people. There also were those who worked against him. They had that kind of courage. They never gave up, despite the risks. So many of them paid with their lives. They are the ones to be honored. The ones I fear are those who did nothing or those who helped him."

"No one ever helped him, Min'darr," shouted a person from the gathering.

"Wrong. I came into town yesterday after an absence of five years. Everything had changed. I knocked on doors to ask after my parents, my sister. Yet, no one would speak to me. But one of you or more spoke to them about me. How do I know this? They knew where to find me." He looked out over the crowd. Some watched him, others looked down.

"I have no interest in Calstara any longer. My past has been paid. I have no desire for a future here. Hence, I will leave you to your own ends. The magic I have will not help you any further. You must be the makers of your own fate. Follow those worthy of leading. Fight for what is worth fighting for, despite the cost. Live your lives with pride so those you know will gladly say they are your friends and kinsmen. I wash my hands of you." He left the silent gathering.

*

That night, after Mah'zan was in bed, Min'darr and Koo'bla sat, sipping some ale. "Are you truly leaving, Min'darr? Do you want us to come with you?" she asked.

"I won't stay here. Too many people will want me to work for their ends, to use my magic to solve their problems. They may threaten both of you to force my hand. You are not safe here. It's good that you're considering leaving. But, no, as much as I love you, my path will take me into the wilderness, not a place for a child.

"Please, though, consider moving to another town, for your own safety."

Koo'bla smiled. "To be honest, I've already spoken to my friend Sha'dabi. Her family will be leaving in a week to go to the port city Vila'Borin on the southwestern peninsula. Would you

82

consider coming with us?" She asked her question with a hopeful hint of voice.

"I am not the boy I was, Koo'bla. The Mulu from the cave, the magic ... the eldritch energy has changed me into something I don't recognize." He gazed at his hand. "Am I even human at this point? I don't know. Magician, mage, wizard, any of it, I don't know. I have to go back to find out or I fear it will cost me my mind!" He sighed, feeling very weak.

Koo'bla patted his leg, then hugged her little brother. "So much has happened that has changed us both. You have to go, as I know I have to."

She kissed him on the forehead. "What you did today was amazing. It was also horrible. To have to kill so many in such a way. There's a part of me that is afraid for you, and a part that is afraid of you. How can one person harbor so much power? Why would you want to go back to get more?"

"I have to go back so I can better understand, so I can be a better vessel to hold this. If I must wield this kind of power, I have to know ... I, umm ... I have to know everything I can, to understand as much as I can. I feel as if my own life's energies are entwined with these magical energies. We are one. I will not live without them. So, I have no choice. I have to work to be better able to understand them. That's why I have to go back there.

"In this short time I've been out among people, I've learned too much to be able to trust them in general. Part of my charge is to help humanity. I have the feeling, though, that most will not accept that help.

"If there is any way, my sister, I hope I can come find you again. Please be safe."

"I will if you will, Bisha," she said, smiling.

They hugged and said good night. Koo'bla checked on her son, then went to her room.

Min'darr waited for the gentle sounds of sleep to reach his ears. He tiptoed into Mah'zan's room to spend a few minutes drinking in the sight of his sleeping nephew. He held out his hand, muttering some ancient words. A blue spark formed at his fingertips. At his gesture, it drifted down to the boy, disappearing into his chest, next to his heart. He then did the same for his sister.

"With these markers, I will be able to know you are well and to find you if need be." He paused in the doorway, whispering. "Not good night, dear sister, it is time for goodbye."

The moon was the sole witness to the young magician's departure as he, once again, pointed himself toward Nordana Pass. A certain cave in the high northern mountains held his fate. He would journey there again in his quest to master it.

The Mulu

Min'darr stood at the edge of the clearing below Taf'nar's cabin. He recalled the first time he'd seen it, how impressed he'd been. He thought of what he'd learned here, thanks to his uncle. He'd also learned to expect the worst from people, based on what he'd experienced both here and in Calstara.

Those events and their reactions helped him grow cautious. To avoid bumping into others on the trail, he projected an aura around him that would alert him to someone approaching. It worked for animals, too.

He'd managed to surprise a few wild animals on this trek, too. His magic acted as a great buffer, stifling his noises that they would normally hear and warn them of his approach. They never attacked, thanks, he believed, to that same magic.

He'd refrained from using the fast-walking spell to hurry on his way since leaving Calstara. His mind appreciated being in the midst of Nature, away from people. Nature's energies were plentiful and calming. He enjoyed being alone with his thoughts. The sensations that picked at his magic-attuned awareness as he walked along the trail were intriguing. He enjoyed the sounds of the wind, the calling of birds, snow falling from branches, and the trickle of water in the mountain streams when not frozen. This kind of tranquility would prepare him to re-enter the eldritch stream to further his understanding of magical energies and how to use them for the benefit of such a stubborn people.

So, as nice as it would be to sleep in warmth with a full stomach in the comforts of the cabin, Min'darr opted to forego visiting Sar'ti and Kar'tum and continue on his way. It had been a month since he'd left them. He enjoyed their company but saw no reason to disrupt his chosen solitude. He kept to the tree line, bypassing the cabin, again heading northeast.

He camped a few hours later near dusk. Hungry for some real food instead of conjuring things onto his fire, he transformed into an owl, his magic once again allowing his skin to sprout feathers to take him into the winds. There was something bewildering about the physical sensations of morphing into a different kind of creature. Nothing painful, neither hot nor cold, just a series of odd shivers that compacted some of his shape or stretching that elongated others.

Within half a minute, Min'darr the owl was airborne, using his fantastic owl-vision to locate prey amidst the snowy forest. Tree after tree served as a perch, however nothing was moving that would be an owl-sized meal. Fully dark with no moon now, even his owl's eyes had to strain to see.

He flew toward a spot of light that turned out to be a campfire. He landed to scan for anything worth eating. Two covered wagons, six horses, and three men made up the camp. Then he saw it ... a huge, meaty mouse moving beneath the horses. He watched its path, anticipated its movements, then launched himself as the rodent cleared a horse's rear legs. With talons outstretched, Min'darr thumped into the snow atop his prey. He instantly took flight with his dinner tightly gripped.

The horses were spooked by the owl's swooping in, neighing loudly and rearing up. Their anchor line pulled free. The animals bolted. The three men instantly rose, screaming for the horses, as if they'd return when called. They didn't. The men had no choice but to run off after them.

Min'darr had been perched in a neighboring tree, already working on his dinner. Then he heard something. An anxious sounding woman's voice, then a man's voice, both coming from one of the wagons. He looked. The men had not yet returned. So, who was talking?

Min'darr listened and realized the answer. He recognized those voices! He dropped the remnants of the mouse's carcass and flew down to the wagon. He transformed back into his human shape and peeked into the rear of the wagon. Kar'tum and Sar'ti were tied back to back.

"Well, hello there," he whispered. They stared at him, staying quiet as he held his finger up to his lips. "I'll take care of these three. You stay here."

They both nodded. Min'darr heard one man returning. Shivering for lack of a thick coat, he opted for some magic to keep from being too cold.

Within ten minutes, the horses were back and retied. The men warmed themselves at the fire. Min'darr knew it was time to act when he heard some lewd suggestions about how the men should be dealing with their prisoners. He heard them mention "that woman" a few times. They began trudging toward the wagon, laughing. Min'darr had to protect his friends. Magically, he became an ogre.

His immense form, snarling loudly, burst from the trees directly in front of the men. Two of them fell backwards, scampering back toward their fire. The third man held his ground, pulling his knife. Yelling loudly, he ran right at Min'darr's version of the stinking beast. The horses reared, pulling loose again.

As the two men reached the fire to grab their weapons, the body of the third man crashed down next to them. His neck was broken. His impact dislodged a log onto one of the other two, catching his coat on fire. The second man held a bow and was nocking an arrow when Min'darr, as the ogre, reached him and snapped the bow in two. The man continued to fight, punching and hitting him. Min'darr caught both his arms in one hand, yanking them high above his head, dislocating both his shoulders. Min'darr quickly wrapped the bow string around his wrists, tying his arms together. He tossed him to the ground near his dead friend.

The man with his coat ablaze had shucked it off. He could only stare at what was happening to his friend. The ogre jumped, grabbing him quickly, both hands easily encircling his chest.

The ogre carried him to the wagon and shoved him in, saying, "Untie" in his best beastly voice. The man quickly freed his two captives, who somewhat reluctantly squirmed out past Min'darr.

The man scooted himself to the front of the wagon to be out of reach of the ogre. With his freed friends standing near him, Min'darr the ogre shoved the wagon, sending it wheeling downhill toward some distant trees.

They returned to the fire. As they approached, the man with his arms tied together managed to stand. Seeing the ogre again, he ran after the wagon.

Min'darr looked at his friends.

Sar'ti wrinkled her nose and looked at him cautiously. "Min'darr?"

He nodded, then ended his spell, rapidly regaining his human form. "Okay, let's warm up by the fire." He used his magic for that as well as for large, thick blankets for each of them.

He then used a spell to call the horses back. Only five came, but that would be enough.

Two hours later they'd put some miles between them and what was left of the robbers. Sar'ti felt there would be danger should they simply followed their tracks back. Min'darr nodded, then gestured behind them. Their tracks disappeared. Neither did the horses nor the wagon make any more tracks.

While they traveled, Kar'tum told him that the men had pulled up to the cabin during a bad storm, asking to sleep in the stable."

"We fed them," Sar'ti complained.

"As we were settling in for the night, I checked on them to see if they needed anything. They said no, then wished us a good night. I was closing the inner stable door when they attacked, forcing it open. One of them held us at knife point while the other two ransacked the cabin. That was two days ago. We expected to be killed about any time. It was lucky we didn't freeze to death."

Min'darr said nothing of what he feared they were planning to do when he had become the ogre to stop them.

They reached the cabin without further incident. Min'darr stayed, spending three days helping them repair things. On the fourth morning, he called them out to the edge of their meadow. He told them to look back at the cabin. As they did, Min'darr called upon his eldritch energies, surrounding the cabin and meadow with a spell. The two watched as their home changed into a large outcropping of granite.

"What did you do?" Kar'tum wailed.

"I cast a true illusion," he said laughing. He reached out, touching both their eyes. They saw it as it always had been. "I have placed a spell on the space around the cabin. It will always be visible to you. To all others, it will look like a rock outcropping. Even your tracks and the smoke from your chimney will be hidden. You will be safe here. It will also be the same for your children and their children." He patted Sar'ti's tummy, winking.

"How could you know?" Sar'ti whispered.

Min'darr merely shrugged.

"We can't thank you enough, Min'darr," Kar'tum said. "If there is anything ..."

Without waiting for him to finish, he transformed himself into an owl again, bolting into the sky. He circled, swooping in on them, screeching. He then rode the wind, flying off toward his last campsite.

*

Two days later he stood before the bowl in the cliff face. He had gotten no response from the Mulu when he first called to them. The cave entrance was gone, sealed as if it never existed. Everything appeared solid. Min'darr used several spells to gain access, but none worked.

He grew frustrated, feeling cheated, but refused to get angry. He recalled that the Mulu said Uncle Taf had burst into the sealed cave as only a creature of magic could. He'd died because of it. "I don't want to break in!" he called out. "I'm ready for more understanding. How can I use magic to help make things better? Please allow me entrance."

No response.

A night and a day passed. He never left the bowl, continuing working to convince the Mulu to allow him to enter. "I know you're listening," he repeated a thousand times.

Toward dusk of the second day, Min'darr sat back, exhausted. He mused that so much magic existed within this rock. It should not be closed off to him.

He bolted upright. "That's got to be it! The magic I carry is nothing compared to the magic within. If I could access that magic ..." He repositioned himself to face where he knew the entrance to be. He began a spell he didn't know, the blue aura surfacing within him, calling to its kindred energies within the cave. A minute or so was all it took. He felt it coming to him, migrating through the granite walls. The snow within the bowl melted, the grass greened and small flowers bloomed.

He continued concentrating on the doorway, asking the magic to open it from within. He poured every effort into that thought. Ancient words of a language no longer spoken filtered through his mind. He broke into a sweat, panting from the pure effort of summoning the magic.

Soon, however, trickles of blue energy surfaced on the rock. It puddled at his feet, leaching into him. Then, the rock surface in the shape of the opening shimmered, its surface seeming to thin and peel back. Then it was there ... the hole just like before.

Before he could move, a surge of blue magical energy erupted from the entrance, washing over him, through him. Amidst the tumult, he heard the Mulu screaming, "You are not welcome here."

Min'darr was completely submerged in the swirling blue energies. It soaked into him. He stood, invigorated, and entered the cave. He called out, "I seek the eldritch stream. I want to know more so I will be able to make a better world."

"Go! You are not to be here. It is not your time." The Mulu sounded frantic.

The force that the Mulu exerted against him was beyond words. He felt himself being pushed back toward the entrance. Each physical step forward he took required more magic. His muscle was useless here. Tendrils of magic struck out from the walls. He had to focus on each to intercept them, knowing they could possibly end him, as they did his uncle.

Then flashes he'd not experienced before filled the cave. He closed his eyes so not to be blinded. They made him shiver as his magic reacted, foiling whatever the Mulu were sending to fight him. He felt like a shell was enclosing him, a skin too thick to allow for movement. He envisioned an eruption, a mountaintop blowing into countless pieces. His magic responded. He felt the thud, then could move again. The flashing stopped.

Silence. A great nothing filled the space in which he stood. So calming, so effortless. Yet, he knew it to be dangerous. Min'darr collapsed his magic into a dynamic core of energy. For the first time since he had magic, he pushed it outward at the speed of thought.

The cave's walls buckled. Debris fell from the chamber's roof. The cave was filled with an amazing light. Min'darr looked to find its source, then realized it was him that glowed.

He then heard the Mulu speaking to each other, not to him. *"He is too powerful. Magic seeks itself and his draws from us all that we have left. Make him leave else we will perish. Must escape."* These came as bits of conversation with the Mulu itself. *Not one, but many*, he noted. His powers were now able to access them directly instead of waiting to be addressed by them.

"I will not harm you, my brothers. I seek understanding, not power. I beg you, teach me." Min'darr knew he'd been heard, he felt their reactions. They'd never encountered his like before.

One voice reached his mind. *"You must know this, or be driven to insanity. Your life is forever altered. The magic that changes you is you. You will physically age one year to every five that pass. After five hundred, you will be called to the eldritch stream for eternity. That cannot be altered. We must leave you forever. We are not allowed to face what we have created in you."*

He felt them withdraw.

But then Min'darr felt the magical flow of the eldritch stream beneath him. *They must have been shielding it from me.* He reached out, not able to achieve it. The magic within him surged, summoning the stream, wanting to be one with it. Without his knowing how, the magic created a hole in the cave's floor. At the bottom of that crater, Min'darr's magic found the blue eldritch flow. He sighed in relief, *Finally*, he thought. He slipped down into it, physically lying within the river of magical energy. A bliss overcame him. His senses were overwhelmed as the magical energies enveloped him. He knew he was home.

A New Magician

Soft sounds breached his consciousness. He became aware of some bear cubs laying on him, playing with one another. Min'darr would have played with them, if not for feeling momma bear's presence. He knew she would not like that. He wished he was somewhere else.

Instantly, bright sunlight shone on him. He sat on a large rock next to a high precipice. Birds chirped, insects buzzed about. The air felt hot. *Summer.* The clothes he wore were tight, uncomfortable. He realized they were his childhood clothes. *I've got to get some clothes that fit.* In thinking about it, he instantly found himself wearing some.

"Wow, this magic works well!" he mused.

He took a moment to examine himself. Untanned skin, a full beard with a head of rich black hair were what he discovered. He stood stretching for several minutes. *Something seems missing,* he thought. "Oh, I know. No one is in these mountains without a staff and at least some weapons for protection. At least that's what Koo'bla told me. He remembered his pike, dagger, and archery things. He also knew that his magic made conventional weapons archaic. Still, he would stand out, drawing unwanted attention without them. Closing his eyes, Min'darr envisioned each of them from his last camp. He called for them. When he opened his eyes, they lay at his feet.

He donned those, then looked about to get his bearing. The cliffs seemed somewhat familiar. The southern ridge of some mountain range. The high trees below were tall enough to block his view of the lands to the south. He then looked closer to where he stood.

The rock he'd sat upon ... an odd configuration. He moved around it, curious. It appeared to be the perfect shape of a sleeping mule. *Could it be? Gerg!* He recalled waking up sometime in his past to find his animal escort gone, his mule turned into a boulder. "Yes!" he hollered, inexplicably excited. His eyes shaded blue. He put his hand on it, calling its name.

The rock, already warm from the sun, softened and became furry. He detected a pulse, then some movement. It stood, shook itself off and nickered. Seeing Min'darr, Gerg nudged his hand with its muzzle, begging to be scratched. Min'darr complied.

He sensed the mule's happiness to be with him again, even though he was not the boy he'd been when they were together last. Min'darr liked that. Pure acceptance. That would be a great thing for the world to realize.

To test himself, he used his magic to lift the mule. But he put Gerg down quickly when the mule's braying showed he still didn't like being levitated after all these years.

He knew that they were about twelve miles west of the cave. He had no interest in going near it again, at least for now. A part of his mind wondered what he'd find if he did go back.

He was in no hurry. He felt his body was now about twenty to twenty-five years of age. A man. The memories from this latest excursion into the magical energy flow remained, not dulled or forgotten. These made his arcane potential almost unlimited. He would need to use his understanding of humanity to temper his use of the magic. Right now, he still felt more like a boy. He needed to gain experience, to dwell among them, these people, despite his distrust.

"From what I can gather, about ten years have passed since I went into the cave. Let's go see what has become of mankind since then.

Min'darr paused, putting one hand on his heart and holding his other up before him, quietly listening to ... something. "Ahh, I feel you both," he whispered.

"Come, Gerg, it's a long walk. I'd like to introduce you to my sister and nephew.

"We'll go west, then south. The walk will do us both good. A little exercise, a chance to learn about people, maybe help some of them become more accepting of others. Don't let on that I'm a magician. At least not yet. We'll keep ourselves busy making this a better world."

Min'darr and Gerg began their journey, a new magician and his mule.

II. DEALING WITH PEOPLE

Finding Family

The new magician Min'darr still wasn't used to walking alone. For the past month he'd been by himself. A farmer in the village of Tre'altu at the base of the foothills had made a good case to leave his mule, Gerg, with him and his other mules. He'd spoken about the miserable conditions in the city for mules. Sadly, it made sense.

Min'darr then magically asked Gerg. The mule's response had been very positive, yet touched with a bit of sadness. Mules aren't known for being diplomatic or sentimental, and yet Gerg seemed hesitant to let his magician friend go. He was excited at the prospect of spending his days with fellow mules. Thankfully, Gerg didn't know about the receipt of money to Min'darr from the farmer. Like most mules, he would never consider himself as property.

Min'darr hadn't either, though he knew he'd need money in his dealings with people. The farmer assured him this was a fair amount. So, the sale was finalized. The farmer allowed them to say goodbye, not able to hide the grin on his face. Min'darr then purchased a hooded robe, sandals, pants with a travel bag in that same town. He kept his weapons, slinging them across his back.

En route to the port city of Vila'Borin, he'd been accosted twice. The first robber he turned into a snake. The second turned out to be more interesting. While holding Min'darr at bay with his own staff, he'd commented on its weight and the fact that such a skinny man shouldn't have it for he couldn't wield it properly. The robber offered to take care of it until Min'darr got stronger.

With that suggestion, he did so, magically. Min'darr then picked up the robber and threw him against a tree. The man got up and limped off, soundly defeated. Min'darr then allowed his magic to give him a more muscular build to be a physically threatening presence, so as not to be as tempting a target to the next would-be robber.

Now approaching the port city of Vila'Borin to find his family after a five-month trek from the mountains, Min'darr realized the wisdom of his decision to allow Gerg to stay back in the hills. The traffic was horrid. So many people with so many goods moving both into and out of the city, horses aplenty with riders claiming more of the road than they were entitled. Wagons of every size creaked along at paces from spirited to crawling. Gerg would not have fared well, being as free-thinking as he was. Min'darr was pretty sure someone would have gotten kicked if they'd gotten too close.

Then there was the language. Far from anything Min'darr had ever used, the words firing from their mouths were as vulgar as anything he could imagine. Min'darr could understand several languages, thanks to his time in the eldritch stream, so he was unlucky enough to understand most everything he heard. In addition to that, the heat, humidity, the dusty roads, as well as the smells that came along with all these people and livestock, overloaded his senses.

In order to clear his mind, he focused on his goal of finding his sister, Koo'bla, and her son, Mah'zan. One of the last things he did before he left that night nearly eleven years ago was to lay a spell upon them. More accurately, he placed a small piece of magical energy within each of them. It would help to protect them in addition to allowing Min'darr to find them.

As he'd descended from the mountains, he called upon that magic. Acting as an arcane compass, he knew the direction he needed to go to get to them. It pointed him toward the coastal port city, the same city Koo'bla had mentioned before they'd parted in Calstara. Now, mere miles from the edge of that city, Min'darr had a sense of only one of them being near.

He could not tell whose magic he sensed, even though he was getting closer to it by the hour. He hoped to be able to find this one by the close of the day. And, with much trepidation, find out why he could sense just one. What had happened to the other?

His introspection stopped with the traffic. For the third time that day, angry shouts could be heard ahead. He had the advantage of being a lone traveler. As such, he could more easily sidestep any of these repeating obstacles. Working his way through the crowd, he came upon a broken cart, its axle snapped. Its contents, cages of chickens, had spilled onto the roadway. Two men argued loudly. One, an elderly man was demanding help, the other ready to brawl for being delayed.

Min'darr sensed a real danger to the older man. "Gentlemen, gentlemen," he said approaching the two. "How is this noise helping solve the problem?"

The older man spoke first. "At last, someone with reason! Tell this loudmouth here that I cannot go on with a broken cart. I need help to move it before I'm expected to restack my hens."

The other man laughed at him. "You old fool! You don't get nothing for free. Demanding that we help you for free means you know nothing. My muscles are worth more than your smelly cages."

"I can help you." Min'darr said. "Stand back, please," he said to the braggart. "I wouldn't want you to hurt yourself."

"Another fool," he said, backing away from the broken cart anyway, as did everyone else.

Min'darr gripped the cart. His eyes flashed blue as he effortlessly hoisted the cart to an upright position. He then repositioned the wheel. The crowd gasped. The old man clicked to his mule to move the cart as Min'darr guided it off to the edge of the roadway. Several others had gathered the man's chicken cages, putting them next to the wagon.

The braggart stepped up to Min'darr, poking him on his chest. "How did you do that? What are you, mister?"

Min'darr smiled. "I'm a nicer person than you. Kindness will allow you to work miracles, too."

"You're just lucky ... this time. Don't get in my way doing your good deeds, or I'll run you down." He spat at the ground then walked off toward his horses and wagon.

Min'darr turned his attention to the old man who was crawling out from under his cart, almost in tears. "What can be so wrong that you should be this distressed?"

"Oh, good sir, thank you so much for your kind help. I fear, though, I am done. The cart is old. The axle broken. I have no recourse but to go home. I have no money to fix things." He slumped to the ground, cradling his head in his palms. He cried out in a mournful voice, "Chickens for sale!"

"I have some experience with fixing things. May I try?" Min'darr asked.

The old man whisked his hand toward the cart, saying, "Chickens for sale."

Min'darr crawled under it and saw the broken axle. It was shattered, nothing short of a new one would do. Unless ... he crawled closer, hitting it to make noise. As he did, his blue eyes flashed. Pushing the two pieces into position, his blue aura spread across the axle. It creaked as it regrew together, rejoining at the break site, becoming one again, stronger than ever.

"There," he proclaimed. "Good as new." He clambered out and dusted himself off.

"What?" the old man asked. "Are you mad? It is worthless, I say."

"Look for yourself, sir." Min'darr stepped aside.

The old man crawled over to inspect it. He guffawed. "Ha! What is this? Fixed it is! How have you done this? I've never seen repairs done better in all my days!" He came out and hugged Min'darr tightly, dampening Min'darr's robe with his tears. "However you have done this, you have saved my life today. I am in your debt, sir."

"No, sir, you are not. I did for you as I would any other who could use my help. I wish you well, sir. I would ask, should you encounter any who are in need, please help them as I've helped you." Min'darr patted the man's shoulder, nodded, then blended into the crowded roadway.

"Thank you, thank you. May the Creator bless you, my friend," the old man shouted after him.

99

The young magician smiled as he walked on. *This is how people should be toward one another.* The smell of the city continued assaulting his nose. He was nearer.

*

The blue waters sparkled as the sunlight reflected off the Western Ocean beyond the harbor. A salty tinge rode the winds that tousled his hair. *Very near.* The signal was strong enough to touch. He'd circled a block very near the wharf twice, making certain. Finally, his magic singled out a café. The building from which the aroma of food wafted with a sign announcing rooms on the upper floors were housing either his nephew or his sister. As he entered, a bell above the door tinkled his arrival.

Chakula Café held a dozen tables, seven of them with customers. A girl, maybe fourteen years of age, carried serving platters of steaming meats and stews. She smiled at him. "Please take a seat at that third table, sir. I'll be right with you."

Min'darr sat at the table she'd indicated next to an open stairway leading to the upper floors. His attention was drawn to that area.

"What can I get for you?" The girl stood at his side, waiting.

He startled, not hearing her approach. "I'm sorry," he said, "I, umm, what do you serve?"

"Well," she sounded a bit perturbed. "We serve food. We serve our customers. The menu is up on the wall," she added as she pointed to the wall opposite the stairway.

"My apologies, young lady." He scanned the offerings, quickly choosing. "May I have a bowl of the spiced sausage stew, please."

"All right. That will cost you four steels." She waited a moment. "Now, sir. You eat after you pay." She waited while he produced the required coins. "Thank you." She headed back to the kitchen.

Min'darr continued glancing around the room, finding several signs posted about paying before the meal, not wearing weapons at the tables, and no fighting in the café. There was also a sign indicating that rooms were available upstairs at a cost of a copper for a night per person, or a week for five coppers. A meal a day was included with a room.

Within the café, one table had four eating from the same dish at the center of the table. Another had an old woman gingerly slurping some broth or soup. He couldn't see enough of the other tables.

Again his attention seemed unnaturally drawn to the upper floors. He closed his eyes to focus. The magic he sensed was definitely up there. Without thinking, he stood, intent on going up there.

"Hey, don't you want your stew?" The girl stood next to his table with his dinner centered on her tray.

He quickly sat back down, like a schoolboy caught in some mischief. "Oh, yes. Thank you," he said as she put the bowl in front of him. "Could you tell me what's upstairs?"

She looked over at the stairway, then back at him. "Pretty much just what it says. Rooms for rent. You need one?"

"Perhaps," he said. "Could you tell me who's up there?"

"No." Her response was pert.

"I'm sorry. I'm looking for someone, two people actually. Would a woman named Koo'bla be here? Or, maybe a young man, about your age, Mah'zan?"

Her gaze at him intensified, glaring through him if she could. In a very controlled voice she said, "I'm not certain. Let me go check. Please enjoy your stew." She left quickly for the kitchen, walking past a customer calling for a glass of ale.

He sampled a spoonful of stew. Spicy, tingling his mouth. "Pretty good," he said aloud. His eyes had followed the girl into the kitchen area. Within a second, two faces peered out at him, then quickly retreated. One had been the girl's. The other was a woman's he didn't recognize.

After a minute, the same woman came out, crossing the café, heading toward him. She greeted several customers along the way. "Hello, thanks for coming in," she said. When she got to Min'darr, she said, "Hello, sir. I'm the owner here. Our server said you were looking for someone. Maybe I can help?"

Min'darr set down his spoon. "This stew is amazingly good. The best I've ever had. I am looking for Koo'bla and her son, Mah'zan ..." he paused, then added, "my family."

Her eyebrow raised. "And your name is?"

He smiled, leaning back in his chair. "You already know that, don't you? Are they well?"

"We don't give out information that easily on the wharf. Too many people carry grudges, too many people disappear. I know who you seek. I need your name to know they would want to see you. Your timing is suspect."

Min'darr closed his eyes as they flashed blue. "Go into your kitchen, then go tell her what you see. I'll wait here."

The owner hesitated. A screech sounded from the kitchen. The waitress who'd taken his order burst from the kitchen screaming. "I'm done! I quit, I ain't working in a haunted café." Everyone watched her run out the door, flinging her apron behind her in the process. The woman turned to eye Min'darr, then rushed into the kitchen.

Another minute passed before Koo'bla came running out from the kitchen. Min'darr stood. She paused a moment until she locked eyes on her brother. She then dashed into his arms, shoving the table several feet and upsetting his bowl.

"Only you could make the pots in Ram'ili's kitchen float in midair," Koo'bla said laughing. "You look good, my brother. You are well?"

"I am," he said. "I'd ask about you, but I think someone is a bit upset."

Koo'bla turned as the owner of the café reached the two of them. Koo'bla wrapped her arms around the woman, kissing her on the cheek. "Min'darr, my brother, I'd like you to meet my partner, Ram'ili. She owns the café. "I run the inn upstairs. The Chakula Café and Inn, Vila'Borin's finest ... well, along the wharf anyway."

"A pleasure to meet you, Ram'ili. Did I put your kitchen back properly?" Min'darr asked.

Ram'ili stared at him. "Koo'bla told me back when we met that her brother was a magician. She's also told me of how you managed to rid your town of General Magama.

"Now you are here, rearranging my cookware." Ram'ili paused, then thrust out her hand. "A pleasure to finally meet you. Don't ever touch my kitchen again. Understood?"

"Yes, ma'am," Min'darr said.

Koo'bla squeezed her brother's arm. "Ram'ili, if everything down here is where it belongs, we're going upstairs to catch up."

Ram'ili waved them on and returned to checking on the guests who had remained in the café.

*

What of Mah'zan? I have not found his magic yet."

Min'darr's sister said, "I don't know where he is, exactly. He's out on a ship. He worked here for Ram'ili serving in the café and helping me with the roomers. He longed for more. He signed on as a cook for the shipping company. Many of their sailors ate here. He loved talking with them about their voyages. He's been out on his first voyage for the last nine weeks. They are due back any day now. But, if you can't sense him, maybe he's too far away. How far can you sense?"

Min'darr shrugged. "I don't really know. I haven't any practice. You two are the only ones I've done this with. I couldn't tell which of you I felt. I did have a general sense of direction from up in the mountains, though, so I knew I was getting closer.

"So, tell me of your move." Min'darr sat back on the chair in the sitting room upstairs of the café. The setting sun's light streamed through the window as a gentle breeze flipped the edges of the curtain.

Koo'bla sighed. "A boring trip, really. We left home within the week after you left, making our way down the Nordana Highway to Ooston. When the town board heard I was leaving, they were upset. I heard that they felt if I was gone, you'd never come help them again if they needed it, exactly like you said they would."

"Let them fret. The last thing I told them was that I'd washed my hands of Calstara." Min'darr shook his head as he spoke.

"That's exactly what I reminded them of," she said. "Anyway, Sha'dabi's family changed their minds, wanting to stay in Ooston. They found that the stable was for sale with fifteen horses. I had my mind set, so Mah'zan and I kept going south. It took two months for us to make it all the way."

"And that's when we met," Ram'ili interjected as she came into the room. "As long as I have your attention, I've some news to share before I can't get a word in edgewise." She turned toward Koo'bla. "I spoke to a friend of mine. They've heard nothing so far other than the ship Mah'zan is sailing on, the *OuterWada,* sailed from Prarnafta a day late. It's a three-week voyage back, with good winds. So, she's only two days late. He'll be back before you know it."

Before Koo'bla could say anything, Min'darr stood abruptly, knocking back his chair, and staggered toward the wall. His eyes were wide, and blue.

Koo'bla also stood. "Min'darr, what's wrong?"

"I am thinking something has happened ... no, is happening. Mah'zan is in trouble. I feel it. My magic is a link to him. He might need my help. I don't know any specifics, but his ship and crew are in danger."

Finding Mah'zan

Min'darr had to find a way to prioritize his magical energies. Using his arcane powers this way was new to him. He had to be sure he had it right, for his nephew's sake. They showed him to a quiet inner room, Mah'zan's bedroom. He sat on the edge of the bed, allowing his magic to well up within him. It warmed him as it took over his consciousness. His increasing awareness connected him to the rest of the world.

When he'd been within the cave, he lacked physical sensations when the stream took him. Here, he discovered that he had to make the progress happen while blocking out so many of the natural sensations that acted to distract him. *Like the difference of floating on a tree-lined river to floating in the middle of a calm lake.*

Once he had his own senses dulled, he could concentrate his energies outward to find that one distant speck of magic he could identify as coming from his nephew. It had reached out to him, warning of danger. He had to find it now.

As his awareness spread, he was surprised and marveled at the many, softer eldritch energies he witnessed. Magic in nature existed in abundance ... some in people, but more in the sparser areas where people didn't live. What could be there that harbored an eldritch energy? The possibilities might be endless!

No! Not what I'm to be doing. Focus!

After scolding himself for allowing his mind to wander, he became calmer, more aware of what he was to do, and better able to overlook the magic he'd found, promising himself to investigate it some other time. None of these other things mattered right now. He pushed those energies into the background. Mah'zan was the one he should be concerned about right now. He continued his search.

Frustrating silence. Darkness. "Where are you, nephew?" he finally muttered. Then something! In the distance, an eldritch spark brightened for an instant. He'd called and it answered. His mind, linked to the magical connection called out again, "Mah'zan!"

Like a distant candle, his nephew's magic once again shown brighter, drawing from Min'darr's own connectedness. Utilizing those powers bestowed through the Mulu, his consciousness traversed the distance to him. The boy was lying within a shallow wooded niche. Covered with brush, a stream trickled under him out onto a narrow rocky beach. He lay still, shallow breathing, a cut in his leg causing him significant pain. Min'darr's awareness spoke to the sleeping form. *"Stay,"* he commanded. *"I'll be there soon."*

Somehow, he knew a deeper part of Mah'zan had heard him.

*

"I know where he is," Min'darr announced entering the women's room after rapping on the door frame. They lay on the bed, Ram'ili comforting Koo'bla. "He is ashore, up the coast about a hundred miles from here. He is hurt, but not in any danger because of it."

"How are we to get to him?" Koo'bla asked, scrambling to her feet and smoothing her hair.

"It would take days via ship or horse." Ram'ili said. "This is impossible." She looked at Min'darr, eyes narrowing. "All right, wizard, can you get him safely home?"

"I'll find a way," he said. "Look for us tomorrow night." He turned and left.

*

Even before he'd reached the street, he knew he'd have to fly there. The limitations were daunting. Fast would mean either a gyrfalcon or eagle. Neither would allow him to bring Mah'zan home, not big enough to carry a man. Or, if he would be well enough to fly, Min'darr could transform him into a bird. *All too early to tell.* Lastly, he couldn't know if flying to him, then getting him home via horse and wagon would be viable with his injury either, unless Min'darr could heal him first. Too many unknowns to be able to decide right now!

Only one thing would work given the factors he had to consider. He'd encountered it only during his time within the eldritch stream.

Min'darr walked away from town, away from people. He made his way toward a dark hill covered with brush with a few trees. No homes or buildings near enough to be of concern.

Once certain he was alone, he called upon his magic to shape himself into a creature of magic. The flow of energies came from deep within, coursing through him. His size swelled. His shape altered, growing a long neck, powerful legs, a tail, and leathery wings. His complete transformation took a handful of seconds.

He stood tall, stretching his neck and wings. *This feels so good!* he thought. As much as he wanted to, he knew breathing his own plume of fire just would not be a good idea at this moment. At least he'd conjured a dragon with dark scales to be stealthy, blending better into the night.

Thank the Creator it's a moonless night, he thought, gliding mere feet above the waves. Dragons are such powerful beings, able to fly so fast for long distances. He used another layer of his magic to enable his dragon form to fly even faster, like the walking spell he'd first encountered with the ogre. As a dragon, his senses were a hundred times finer than any other creature's, so he easily avoided getting too close to the coastline, islands, or any ships, while seeing them clearly. As he flew, specks of magic blinked at him, some from the waters beneath him, others from the distant shoreline. He had a deep sense that they were somehow aware he was passing by. *These are the same arcane flecks I felt before. Most curious.*

Nearly two hours passed before Min'darr finally saw the magical illumination he sought. As he came in toward shore, he flew over the sunken hulk of a ship, surrounded by debris. The beach near Mah'zan's hiding place was also littered with flotsam ... papers, boxes, and clothing appearing to be from the ship. Min'darr landed in the surf, then waded in to shore in his human form.

*

He stopped to scan the shoreline. A narrow copse of trees and a trickling brook proved to be Mah'zan's hiding place. The child he remembered had grown into a strapping youth.

Right after getting there, Min'darr induced a spell to keep him sleeping, then worked to heal the cut in his thigh. *From a cutlass, it looks like.* He also had several cracked ribs and a cut scalp. The magic worked on all of his injuries while both slept. As Min'darr drifted off to sleep, he realized how exhausted he felt. *Haven't been this tired since ... I can't think of a time.* He cast a concealment spell so they wouldn't be seen or heard while they slept.

Dawn found the wizard sitting in the day's new shadows next to his nephew. As the sun lit the eastern sky, he spent a few minutes gazing out across the calm waters, small waves lapped at the shore. Min'darr was hungry but knew there could be no campfire. About a mile off the coast, a two-masted ship flying a pirate's banner sailed toward them. He checked to be sure the concealment spell was working. Mah'zan stirred, then awoke. He was unaware of any of the goings-on of the night just ended.

He startled to see Min'darr within reach, then narrowed his eyes, glaring at the man sitting so near to him while his hand groped beside him, presumably for a weapon.

Min'darr smiled with a quick nod. "A pleasure to see you again, nephew.

A glimmer of recognition shown on the boy's face. "Uncle ... ah, Min'darr?"

Min'darr nodded. "We have company," he said, pointing at the approaching vessel.

Mah'zan turned to look and gasped. "It's them! The pirates ... the ones what raided our ship yesterday. By the Creator! How are they back? What could they want?"

"Tell me what you remember," Min'darr said.

His nephew, obviously distraught, fought to regain some composure. "It was past eighteen bells. I was cleaning pots in the galley when I heard about an approaching ship. The crew were talkin', always talkin' about what was happening on deck to those of us stuck below.

"I poked my head out the nearest porthole n' saw this two-master quartering toward us, big yellow face takin' up its prow. See?" He pointed at the approaching ship.

Min'darr nodded.

"Well, the captain was on deck. Since no warnings came down, it must be good. I'm down on the fore third deck in front of the cargo hold. All of a sudden, as they came aside, I hear shouts n' clashing steel. Never heard any warning. We's being boarded!

"The cook rushes in grabbin' knives n' tells me to do the same, then to follow him. We go to the midship hatch to climb up. He's half out the main hatch, me below him. Without warning, he drops down onto me, knocking me down. He's bleedin' from a huge gash across the side of his neck. He dies on top o' me. I'm covered in blood when the pirates rush down the hatch. One looks at me while I'm holdin' my breath, tryin', ya know, to look dead. He kicks me head and runs on.

"I don't know how long I laid there. Didn't dare move whilst they be running the gangway. Well, at least until I hear them call to abandon ship, sayin' the explosives they set in the hold after they transferred our cargo was lit. That's what my crew told me during our voyage that they does. I think 'I'm gonna die lest I get out.'

"So I moved as quick as I could to climb the ladder. One pirate was standin' between me 'n the gunwale. He had a sword, I had one kitchen knife. I ran right at him, managed to block his slash while I drove my knife into his chest. As we fell, he got me in the leg, bad. I managed to jump overboard anyway n' headed to shore.

"About a minute later, the ship blew. I just kept swimmin', never looked back 'til I could stand. By then, she was two-thirds under. I crawled into this creek bed, prayin' they'd leave me be. They never did come. I didn't feel safe until after dark. I did what I could to wrap my leg. Hey, what the ... My leg! It's ... it's healed! Did you ... oh, yeah ... you're magic." He rubbed the slightly visible pinking scar line, all that remained of the original gaping wound.

"Oh, Uncle Min'darr, thank you so much. How did you find me? How could you have known?"

"Years ago, when I left you and your mom in Calstara, I put a sprinkle of magic within both of you. Kind of a way I could keep in touch with you, especially in the case that I wanted to find you. I used it to find your mom. I got into town yesterday. Last night I felt your magic call out, right about sunset. I knew you needed help. I used magic to find you here. We need to get back to your mother tonight."

Min'darr gazed out at the approaching ship. "What would bring that ship back?" He looked at Mah'zan. "Could they have forgotten something of value? A coin chest? Something else?"

"I can't help you, Uncle. I spent eighteen hours a day cooking, then cleaning the galley n' every pot ever made. I know nothing of our cargo. I made a mistake signing on to work for the Wada fleet. It was nothing like they said it would be."

Min'darr furled his brow. "Who said?"

"The sailors ... the ones who ate at the inn. They're the ones who talked me into signing on. Said it was a manly way to live. Adventures, foreign ports, exotic people."

They fell silent, both of them watched the ship maneuver alongside the wreck of the Wada cargo ship. Mah'zan detailed the way the ship had sunk, so the pirate ship lined up astern. It dropped anchor. A small skiff with four men aboard was lowered too. The skiff rowed to the Wada ship, then three of the men jumped into the water. A few minutes later two climbed back aboard and started tugging on a rope. Pretty quickly, a chest or box was hauled aboard. The skiff returned to the pirate vessel. There was no sign of that fourth man. Shortly after that, the pirate vessel hoisted its mainsail, quartered to the southwest, heading out to sea.

About midmorning, when the pirate ship was a distant blip on the horizon, Min'darr changed into a hawk to find out more about the area they were in, also to find some food. Mah'zan watched dumbfounded at Min'darr's transformation, shrinking back when the wizard-hawk spread his wings to take flight.

He flew inland a mile or so before finding a cluster of four homes centered on a farm. The people were working in the fields. Their crops were coming along nicely, nowhere near ready to harvest. He did smell something ... something cooking in one of the homes. He flew lower, landing on the barn roof. His hawk eyes enabled him to see some pies resting on a kitchen table. He flew around the home several times, seeing only an old dog on the front porch.

Within a few minutes, the human-shaped wizard cradled a still-warm meat pie as he entered the woods behind the house. He grinned at the thought of the farm's matriarch wondering why there were only five pies, not the six she'd prepared. She'd also have a time explaining the five copper pieces stacked on the table where the missing pie had been.

Min'darr was also thankful that animals seemed to accept him and his magic. Otherwise, that dog would have bitten him for sure and not sniffed him while wagging his tail.

*

"I *really* think I should go to that farmhouse to get her recipe," Mah'zan insisted as he licked his fingertips.

"Again, no," replied Min'darr. "You and Ram'ili can work on it tomorrow. You can tell her how delicious it was and concoct your own version."

"But how will we get back in one night? Are you going to use more magic? I'd love to become a hawk like you did. Can we?"

Min'darr was tempted to agree. But a flood of memories came back to him about using magic without understanding its consequences. His own uncle, Taf'nar, had been given some magic by the Mulu. It warped his perspective and proved to be his undoing.

His nephew would revel in the experience to the extent that he wouldn't be able to refrain from telling about it. Should the wrong person hear, he would be in such danger that Min'darr may not be able to help him. *I have to keep him safe. How?*

"I think we can make that decision when it gets dark," Min'darr said. "We can't be seen, or you may be in deeper trouble than some pirate's sword can cause you. For right now, I'd like you to get some rest. The healing magic can only do so much to help your wounds." As he spoke, he cast a sleeping spell on his nephew.

Leaving his nephew to his dreams, Min'darr walked across the narrow beach to the water's edge. Troubled by the missing fourth man, he dove in and became a dolphin. He quickly swam to the sunken ship, having no trouble seeing the gaping hole in its hull. The damage from the pirate's explosion was extensive. He swam across its deck, noting the empty cargo hold. Many bodies drifted within the ship. The last place he swam to was the aft window, traditionally the captain's chambers, the ship's office. He noticed the rope markings on the window's framing made by the chest he saw them take. He also found the fourth man afloat within the cabin, the hilt of a knife protruding from his upper back. Based on the uniform he wore, he had been the ship's captain.

*

Min'darr waited until the darkness was complete. Mah'zan slept. *Better to carry him asleep in my claws than to have him remembering things he shouldn't be talking about anyway.*

He called upon his magic, feeling the warmth as the eldritch energies rose within him, altering his form again. With his nephew firmly held within his talons, the dragon wizard lifted off the beach, flew out over the waters, heading to deliver him safely to his mother.

As he flew, Min'darr pondered the piracy, their return for the chest, and the murder of the ship's captain. He felt the need to get some answers. Right now, though, he wasn't certain what the right questions were or even whom to ask.

People of Vila'Borin

"You can't talk about what you don't remember. That's why," Mah'zan's mom said. "He saved your life. Why would you want to risk it all over again by talking about magic in front of superstitious sailors?" She returned to the sink. "Perhaps, Min'darr, you could cast a spell on him so he remembers nothing. Then you could do another one to make him appreciative, then a third to make him polite, then ..."

"All right, Mother. I get the idea," Mah'zan said loudly. A second later he added, "It's such an amazing thing."

"Nephew, it is a tool, nothing more. Not many can wield it, just like the wondrous foods Ram'ili makes. Like any expert, those trained can use their skills effectively, safely too. You understand?" Min'darr asked as his eyes maintained a light blue glaze.

"Of course. I've seen some sailors do amazing things with a sabre, with harpoons, tying special knots, or the way they dance along the rigging in high winds. You have a different skill, that's all. No big deal, right?" Mah'zan said it very matter-of-factly, like a lesson from school.

"Good. Why don't you get a few hours' sleep?" his uncle suggested.

"Great idea. Get out of that smelly uniform, too," she instructed.

His nephew yawned, went into his room, and closed the door behind him.

"I'm sorry, Koo'bla. I hadn't thought his excitement about magic would get in the way. The magic he was involved in was getting his leg healed and seeing me become a falcon. At least he doesn't remember the flight home. He'll be fine, maybe a strange dream or two, that's it. If you want, I can seal his memories?"

"No, he'll be better off dealing with this. I have to admit that he does have some growing up to do," Koo'bla said. "Who's going to believe him anyway?"

Ram'ili chuckled. "Just about anyone around these parts. Superstitious bastards. Most'll do or believe anything."

"I suppose." Min'darr sighed. "Makes me sad. The first thing I need to do is to find out about this Wada Shipping he's sailing for. I have some very unsettling thoughts about them."

Ram'ili spoke, "The company has been around for about twenty, twenty-five years. Until about ten years ago, they had a spotless record, losing one ship to a storm. Now, they've become a preferred target for pirates, it seems. This sinking is the sixth in about four years. Still, they're the only shipper in port, so, if businesses around here want to send their goods abroad or get supplies or other goods to sell, Wada is their one choice. Either that or send their goods by land to Kim'stwa. More expensive and so much slower that way, though."

He nodded. "How have they covered their losses?"

"Insurance," Koo'bla said.

"What's that?" he asked.

"Some kind of business contract," she said. "They pay for coverage to protect their investment. When the ship arrives, they have paid a little bit to the insurance company. If the ship is raided or sinks, the insurance company pays for the lost cargo and for the ship."

"Strange," Min'darr said as he yawned.

Koo'bla rubbed his head. "Maybe someone else needs to get some sleep. Maybe being a dragon and flying a hundred miles takes more out of you than you imagined."

Min'darr nodded. When he stood up, she hugged him until he hugged her back as hard. "I can't begin to thank you for bringing him back to me in one piece. I love you. This is the second time you've just shown up to save the day."

"Magical, isn't it?" he said sarcastically. "Love you too, sis. It's going to be a busy day tomorrow. G'night, ladies." He made his

way to a makeshift bed in the corner and was asleep within
minutes.

*

They decided that Mah'zan should stay out of sight for a few
days. It wouldn't make sense if he showed himself too soon since
his ship had sunk so far away. He spent his next few days washing
dishes, changing bed linens, or anything else that would be
needed, being certain to stay out of sight.

Min'darr had awoken midmorning and immediately left to
wander the wharf area in the hopes of learning anything about the
attack on the ship or the Wada company. As he wandered, he
watched as harbor workers strained against ropes that lashed
crates or steadied pallets of goods being moved. They hollered at
each other in language less than pure, their rough voices rivaling
the caws of the harbor birds circling above the piers.

It was a busy place with at least five ships either loading or
unloading. Four of them flew the Wada banner, a triangular
pennant with a circled yellow "W" on a field of dark green. It
looked nicer this way than it had on the sunken ship he'd seen
yesterday. The Wada ships were docked at a large pier that looked
fairly new. The other ship, identified by a dock worker as a light
frigate, a naval ship flying the orange, green, and blue national
colors of Rougahn, was docked at an older, obviously lesser
quality pier off to the side of the regular wharf area.

When Min'darr asked why it was off on its own, the sailor
grimaced. "They be thar cause they ain't gotta pay no docking
fees. Government ship, ya know ... the navy."

Min'darr decided to get closer to the Wada ships so he could
talk with the crew members. He walked from the wharf, past the
Wada office, out onto the pier. Within twenty paces he was
approached by two men. The taller of the two held out his hand
and said, "Stop." What business do you have here?"

Min'darr stopped, studying the men. Each had a sash with
three knives plus a sword hanging from another belt. The tall man
spoke again. "State your business. Otherwise, turn and go. This is
private property."

115

"I come to seek information about your missing ship, the *OuterWada*. My nephew is aboard."

"The *OuterWada*? She's only a few days late, certainly not missing. What makes you think that?" he asked.

"His mother is gifted and had a dream. She feels the ship has been sunk by pirates. I promised her I would come here to see after any news." Min'darr stood in front of them. The second man, younger with barely a beard, gripped the pommel of his blade.

"Tell her to rest easy, my friend. We expect the *OuterWada* to sail in by sunset today, tomorrow at the latest." They stood their ground, keeping Min'darr from any access to the pier.

"I will tell her that," Min'darr said. "Thank you—eh ... who may I say told me this?"

"I am Mok'sni, chief of security and port sheriff. And you are ...?"

"Min'darr." He paused. "Tell your young friend here to relax. No swordplay is required to deal with me today." He left with a sour taste on his tongue. Nothing that man said was true, and he knew it. His magic tinged during their encounter. He took it as a sign the man lied. Min'darr quickened his pace, determined to learn more. Then he stopped short, next to the entrance to the Wada Shipping office. He went in.

After talking with three people behind various counters and getting the same story from each, Min'darr left frustrated that they obviously either didn't know the fate of their ship or repeated the same dribble as this Mok'sni did. As he stepped through the doorway out onto the dock, the same younger security man stepped in front of him.

"Y'all getting the same info from the folks inside, mister? We don't like strangers poking around our docks asking questions. Ya best git back home, or I'll decide if'n I need to vent your hide with my steel."

Min'darr glared at him, debating with himself over the fate of this upstart. He then merely grinned. "Thank you for your concern," he said. He walked past him toward town, aware that his every step was being watched, at least until he'd put a building or two between them.

Entering a blind alleyway, Min'darr moved between some boxes. A few seconds later, a gull with blue eyes took wing from the same spot. It flew over the building that housed the Wada offices, the one he'd just left. He settled onto a pier pylon, right next to the open window of an office. The tall sheriff sat facing an older man with his back to the window.

"... was alone?" he heard the older man ask.

"Yep. Nothing to him really, didn't even carry a blade," Mok'sni said.

"No blade that you saw," he corrected the sheriff. "Nobody around here walks unarmed.

"I got word from Gur'ata late last night. The ship went down off Grimari Point, about halfway between here and Kim'stwa. She'd sailed from the capitol three days ago, heading back from the Eastern Peninsula. He didn't report any trouble."

"What about the insurance, Mr. Wada?" the sheriff asked.

"None of your concern, Mok'sni. You'll get paid the same as always. Don't worry about this man. He's a concerned family member. We'll see him at the memorial service, no doubt. Then we can be all sympathetic at the death of his nephew along with everyone else from the ship. Its replacement has already set sail, should be here in a week's time. Too bad we lost the captain, though. He was one of us." The older man stood, dismissing the sheriff.

The gull stood silently. Min'darr hadn't guessed that this was some kind of scam. He took off to figure things out.

*

He meandered through the crowded plaza next to the wharf to help clear his mind. Vendors hawking their wares combined with various musicians filled the air ... the sounds of commerce. A young boy attracted his attention. He would stand next to people, suddenly bolting away. He watched the boy do this several times until he saw the boy tuck a purse into his pocket before running off. *He's stealing from these people!*

Min'darr followed the boy and decided he must be taught a lesson. *What if his fingers didn't work?* He summoned his magic and gestured at the boy. The boy screamed as the person he'd picked to rob spun around, snatching his arm.

"What are you doing, boy?" the man growled. "Pickpocket!" He looked at the boy's hand, seeing he had no fingers. "Begone, varmint!" the man said, pushing the boy to the ground before stomping off, while retying his own purse strings.

The boy sat, glaring at his hands without fingers. He screamed loudly, rubbing them together and in the dirt. "My fingers! My fingers!" he yelled, running off through the crowd, bouncing off of passersby.

Min'darr followed. Not a difficult thing to do given the amount of noise he made. Not in pain, just afraid, he knew. In the process of following the waif, he fell behind due to the crowd. Clusters of shoppers blocked his way. He turned and squeezed between two displays. Using another quick magical spell, he dropped into the form of a rat and scooted along the edges of the walkway toward the boy's wailing. As he went, he developed a plan.

He finally caught up to the boy who sat sobbing, rocking on his haunches in what appeared to be his own tent, a makeshift collection of linens and towels sewn together.

Min'darr the rat spoke, using his magic to give his voice a mysterious quality. "You have angered the Creator."

"What? Who's there?" the boy sobbed.

"Names matter not. I am the consequences of your stealing." He stepped out so the boy could see him.

"You're ... you're a rat!"

"And you have no fingers, thief. Your soul is dark for you steal."

"No! I take to eat ... to live."

"You steal what others have earned. It is wrong to steal. To pay for what you have done, I have stolen your fingers."

"How am I to live?" he wailed.

"Have you tried to earn money? Be honest, for I know the answer."

"I, uh, I ... no. I was raised by thieves to be a thief."

"The Creator can forgive you, if you promise to never steal again."

"How will I live, Creator Rat?"

"For each day you go without stealing, you will wake the next day to find a copper piece next to you. If you steal, it will disappear along with anything you have bought. Doesn't matter how long ... a month or a year, steal once, and everything you've been given will disappear. All of it! Understand?"

"Yes, Creator Rat. What, umm, what of my fingers?"

"Earn them back. A finger a day to start. But, beware! If you are not faithful to this, they may wander off again. There are many of us who would find them tasty." Min'darr smacked his rat lips and scampered away. He quickly returned to be himself again. He paused to conjure the spell on the boy to fulfill what he had said would happen. Now, to find his way out of this marketplace.

Min'darr wandered amidst a throng of shoppers. He'd not before been so deep within this maze of vendors. Before he could orient himself, a carnival barker's chant caught his attention. "Magic lives! Come witness the arcane skills of the greatest magician of our time."

He couldn't help himself and walked in the direction of the voice. A woman wearing very little other than a tall hat and matching cape stood within the crowd, directing passersby to stop to watch the magical performances of her "wizard" associate, another woman, older, probably her mother.

Min'darr approached then, using his magic to scan them, found no magic within either of them, as he expected. Magic acted like a lantern, highly visible to other magic. He recalled the ogre's cave and how the beast's magic floated to his uncle after it died. These two were charlatans, fakers. *That doesn't make them bad or evil. It's all for show ... a way to make a living.*

So, he watched them. They performed well together. Their "magic," however, was clearly sleight of hand. He watched them make a playing card "change" into a different one, burning the original with a flash of "flame." The ring of spectators was kept back a good seven to eight feet, so as to not get too close a look.

He applauded their show when it ended with a "floating" ball. He saw the guy wire, but the showmanship was well choreographed within their allotted space. He had an idea, so he milled around as the rest of the crowd dispersed.

"Ah, excuse me, please," he said approaching the women.

"So sorry, sir, we've finished for the morning. Our next act begins at two. We don't do fortune telling if that's what you are interested in. Madam Tru'lant is up the street a ways ..."

Min'darr interrupted by magically making their floating ball truly float. The women gaped at the sight, not knowing what it meant. He drew it to him allowing it to come to rest on his outstretched palm. "I have not enjoyed a magic act like yours in a long time." He lied to them, having never seen a magic act in his life. "But this ball ..." he added.

"How are you doing that, sir? It is ours," the older woman said. She snatched at it, but her hand passed through it and his own hand.

It split, becoming two, then four. Min'darr made all of them float up and rotate in a vertical circle, a loop of four magic balls right above Min'darr's hand. He moved his hand from beneath them. They froze in place. He said, "To me," and they disappeared.

"Where is my ball?" the woman demanded. The daughter put her hand on the woman's shoulder.

"Good sir, could you teach us this trick?"

Min'darr smiled. "It is no trick, my dear woman." He reached out with an empty palm up, covered it with his other hand for a moment. When he quickly moved both his hands away, the ball floated there. The older woman grabbed it, eyeing the ball, as if looking for damage.

"It is yours. It will do whatever you wish it to do. However, if you use it for anything other than your magic act, its magic will forever be gone," Min'darr said, smiling back at the younger woman. *About my age, I'd guess.*

"And how much will you charge us for this, my good wizard. At least, I assume you to be one," the older one snapped.

Min'darr touched the corner of his eye, carrying a small, shining sparkle of blue light on his fingertip. He reached out to touch the younger woman's temple. The sparkle stayed on her a moment, then dissolved into her skin. Her eyes flashed blue.

He addressed her. "You, my dear young lady, have paid for this by your trust." He turned to the older woman. "You should learn from your daughter to believe. This will not work for those who don't believe."

For nothing other than effect, Min'darr instantly became an owl, fluttering before them, then rising above the marketplace, flying away.

That was a fun diversion. Now, I have yet to deal with this man Wada, his sheriff, and a mysterious pirate.

Ma'hana Wada

It had been a long day for everyone. Finally, after the dinner hour rush in the café, plus getting rooms rented, the four had their first chance to sit down. Since Mah'zan had to stay out of sight behind the kitchen doors, Ram'ili worked as server in her café. With her help, he'd done a fine job cooking, He surprised her with a new meat pie recipe she'd not made before.

He couldn't tell her where the idea came from until Min'darr reminded him that they'd bought a similar one from a farm near where he'd come ashore. With a little modification from Ram'ili, it was to be added to the café's menu. Not as many sailors as usual came in today, she'd reported, although business had been brisk. "Maybe they'd heard about the fate of the *OuterWada*. They wouldn't want to face us concerning Mah'zan's fate," Min'darr suggested.

Koo'bla, with Mah'zan's help in cleaning rooms and changing sheets, had rented out every room. She expressed some concerns about the night's customers. "We've got three rooms with some real ruffians in them. One of them patted my butt as he entered his room, then said I would be welcome to join him." She saw Min'darr bristle. She added, "Oh, don't worry, I've dealt with so many of that kind, I've pretty much come to expect it from most of them. This one stood out from the others, though, when he offered to pay me 'extra.'"

"What did you do to him?" Mah'zan asked. "I'd be happy to slit his throat for you if he tries it again."

She looked at him with surprise. "You're not on a ship. Stop talking like a thug. Remember your manners. You ignore them. If I was in any danger, I know how to hurt a man. One of the last

122

things your father did was to train both of us how to fight, remember?"

The youth nodded. "Why do people have to be so selfish?"

No one offered a response.

"Did you find out anything about Wada today?" Koo'bla asked.

Min'darr recounted his experiences, both as a human and as a gull. He left the rest out of his retelling. "It is very clear to me that something very wrong, probably illegal, is going on at Wada's Shipping Company. They have tight security on the wharf. Wada's comments to his own sheriff show he's not being open about things, probably not honest either."

A loud banging was heard from the street. A muffled yell reached them upstairs, "Open up! We's hungry!"

Ram'ili opened the front upper window, then hollered down, "We're closed. Come back tomorrow."

The racket continued until the crash of broken glass reached them. Everyone stood. Ram'ili went to the door. She held up her hand to stop Min'darr when he followed. "This is my café, my job. I don't need some man coming to my rescue." She went into the hall, closing the door behind her.

Min'darr and Koo'bla exchanged glances. "You worried, too?" he asked.

"I am. She's strong, but not as invincible as she thinks she is," Koo'bla said, blinking back tears. "Protect her, please?"

He nodded. Voices below raised to a shouting match that could be clearly heard upstairs. Clearly, Ram'ili was outnumbered. Min'darr opened the door, running to the stairs followed by Mah'zan.

Min'darr came down the stairs. Within the café, one man stood at the bottom of the stairway. Two others stood blocking the smashed door.

The man at the base of the stairs faced him brandishing a sword. "Bug off, matey. Nothing for you here. We's just getting a bite to eat."

"No, you're not," Min'darr said, never breaking stride. His eyes flashed blue. He gestured. The man's sword burst into flames. He dropped it screeching, cradling his scorched hand. Min'darr grabbed his collar and swung him into the other two. The three hoodlums fell together into a clump in the doorway. He then heard Ram'ili scream from the kitchen.

Approaching the kitchen, he swept his arms back. The room's furniture obeyed, sliding across the floor, blocking the entrance while pinning the ruffians in the doorway. Min'darr pushed through the kitchen doors into the heart of the café.

Ram'ili stood with her back to the iron stove, brandishing her own knife toward the brigand. He stood facing her, pointing his sword's tip at her face. She bled from a cut on her forearm, the blood dripping onto the floor. She saw Min'darr and yelled, "No! Get out! He's mine. I don't need your help."

"That's it, me feisty girlie," he said as he peered over his shoulder toward Min'darr. "Keep back, matey, or you'll be burying her later today," he sneered, sounding thoroughly drunk.

Min'darr paused. It would be so simple to end this. But, for Ram'ili's sake, he had to be careful. He wanted to respect her pride. It would be so easy to drop one of her pots on his head. Instead, he asked, "Do you mind if I watch?"

He turned. "Wha ...?" came out of his mouth.

Ram'ili lunged, knocking his blade away from her and thrust hers into her attacker's stomach. "Here," she said as he dropped to the floor. "Eat this."

*

Sheriff Mok'sni sat at Koo'bla's kitchen table. He'd responded to a neighbor's report of a fight at the café. As head of security for Wada, as well as being the port's sheriff, he was the law enforcement for this part of town. He took their statements about the attack as his crew took them to the jail.

He paused when talking to Min'darr about the fight. "I remember you. Down at the docks earlier today, eh?"

"I was. What does that have to do with this?" Min'darr asked.

"Nothing." He faced Koo'bla. "You must be the sailor's mom, the one with the dreams."

She shot a glare at Min'darr. "Must be," she said.

"Wait, why the glance, then? Something I need to know?" he asked.

"She doesn't like people knowing she has psychic dreams, that's all. Sorry, Koo'bla. He needed to know why I was asking after the *OuterWada* at the docks," Min'darr explained.

"You're forgiven," she managed to say, keeping both the stern tone and the look.

A muffled sneeze came from the adjacent room.

"Who else is here? I thought it was just the three of you." He walked into the next room, looked around and saw no one. He walked to the closed door, glanced back out into the kitchen. All eyes were on him.

Mok'sni knocked on the door. No answer. He tried the knob. It was locked. Stepping back, he kicked the door open. It swung violently, cracking the wood of the door frame. He stepped in. A second later, he reappeared holding Mah'zan by the back of the neck and sat him at the table.

"So, who are you?" he asked.

Mah'zan looked frantically between his mom and uncle. Min'darr nodded to him. "Tell him."

"I am Mah'zan, former galley cook of the *OuterWada* that was sunk by pirates three days ago."

"Sunk by pirates, you say?" Mok'sni asked. "When?"

Mah'zan said, "Around dusk three days ago."

"How many of the crew survived?" the sheriff continued his questions.

"Just me. At least that I know of." Mah'zan said.

"Were you hurt," he asked.

"Oh, yeah, I got a cut on my leg from one of their swords," Mah'zan told him.

"Tell me how it happened."

Mah'zan took a deep breath and spoke. "The cook and I were making our way topside to help fight the pirates. He was killed on a ladder and fell back, pinning me to the floor. When I heard the pirates yelling about setting off an explosive, I went topside and ran toward the gunwale. One pirate tried to stop me. I stabbed him with the knife I had. He cut me during our fight."

"How did you get back here?" Mok'sni asked with an intense glare at Mah'zan.

Min'darr interrupted while massaging his eyebrows to hide the blue glow in his eyes. "Sheriff? Don't you think we should be talking with Mr. Wada about all this?"

The sheriff paused, seeming a bit unsure. "Absolutely," he finally said. "Mah'zan and his mother have to report to the shipping offices by ten o'clock tomorrow morning." He then abruptly left.

In the silence that followed, Min'darr spoke softly, "Now we have time to plan."

*

At the appointed time, Mah'zan and Koo'bla sat in the entry room of Wada Shipping. They said nothing to each other until Koo'bla patted his once-wounded leg. "Ow, that hurts," he said.

The sheriff emerged and signaled for them to come in.

The office was huge, festooned with a ceiling of sailcloth and rigging to mimic being aboard a ship. Wooden ships in glass cases lined the walls. Above them, framed nautical maps of coastlines with at least a dozen pieces of shipping paraphernalia with the name "Wada" incorporated into them were scattered throughout the room.

Wada, a short, balding, older man, sat at a massive desk. A portrait of him hung strategically centered on the wall opposite the entry. One could not help seeing it when entering.

"Come in, come in. Welcome to my lair," he said chuckling. A large cigar poked from his clenched jaw, jutting sideways. Its smoke filled the room, despite an open window. Two wooden chairs were available in front of the desk. Three cushioned easy chairs of rich dark leather were situated in a corner of the office.

"Come, sit here," he directed them to the two wooden chairs. "This shouldn't take long at all." He harrumphed, making a great deal about positioning himself in his overstuffed leather chair behind his desk. "There. Now, are we comfy?

Without waiting for a reply, he continued. "I'd first like to congratulate you on surviving such a horrific attack. It is a miracle that you were not killed with the rest of your crew. Alas, the poor captain and his crew! I heard what you told Sheriff Mok'sni last night. A remarkable tale! I am so very glad you are not seriously injured. I mean, it says here you were cut. May I see the wound, please?

Mah'zan's eyes widened. "Wh ... why?"

"Well, in your employment contract it says that you are to receive two gold shillings if you are wounded defending the ship and survive. I need to see the wound for you to collect."

Mah'zan said, "That's not necessary, sir. I don't want to claim the money."

"Nonsense, my boy. Please. There is no need to be embarrassed."

"It's fine, son," Koo'bla said.

He made a face showing his angst to his mom.

She seemed distracted, then nodded, saying, "Show him your leg."

He sighed, stood, dropping his trousers.

"Ah, a good-sized gash, I'd say. Turn a bit, please. Appears to be healing properly. That's good."

Mah'zan stared down at his own leg. He saw a gash about halfway across his thigh, with different shades of light red and pink. He stared at his mom, saying nothing.

"He continues to suffer some significant pain. The muscles were cut, too. The doctor said he's going to have a slight limp because of this," Koo'bla added as she watched Wada place two gold coins on his desk.

"Yes, yes, of course. An honest injury. One you'll be able to tell about on future voyages, I'm sure. But there is one thing I must address. It says in your statement to Sheriff Mok'sni, that you were running to the starboard gunwale when you encountered the pirate who gave you that cut. Yes?"

"Aye, sir." Mah'zan answered.

"By that, I am understanding that you were abandoning the ship at the time of your injury. Is that correct, sir?"

"Well, yeah. They had planted explosive charges in the hold. They were leaving the ship too 'cause it was about to blow. The pirate I fought was running toward his ship, sir, for that same reason," he said.

"Well then, young Mah'zan, I am afraid I cannot reward your injury. The contract clearly states that you must be 'defending the ship' at the time of your injury. You were clearly running to save your own hide, obviously not in the process of defending the ship. Am I right?" Wada picked up the coins, waving them in front of Mah'zan and Koo'bla. "Am I right?" he repeated.

"But I did kill the pirate, sir. For what it's worth."

"A matter of coincidence. I'd say he was unfortunate in that he got in your way as you were busy fleeing the ship. Right?" Wada asked.

Mah'zan sighed. "You are right, sir."

Wada smiled wide, clenching his cigar between his yellowing teeth. He puffed a large billow of smoke from his grinning face as he pocketed the coins. "You will be assigned a new ship in a month to give your leg time to properly heal. Since you are not working during that time, you, of course, will not be paid. Stop at the quartermaster's office to receive your pay voucher for the time you served on the *OuterWada*.

"I don't know if you're interested, there is a memorial service planned for the rest of your crew in two days at noon. We are done here."

Sheriff Mok'sni appeared at the door to usher them out.

Wada spoke again. "Oh, I forgot. Ms. Koo'bla, you have psychic dreams, yes?"

She stopped. "I do," she responded with a sigh.

"What are these usually about, if I may ask?"

"You may not, sir. They are of a deeply personal nature. I choose not to share them with you, or anyone."

"I see. Are they random things or do they have a pattern to them?" he continued.

Koo'bla stood erect. She answered in a soft, yet firm voice. "I choose to not share them with you, sir."

"I understand, ma'am. The reason for my asking is that I am always searching for a way to avoid bad weather. Now, too, I must also work to avoid pirates, it would seem. Would it be possible that your ..."

"Good day, Mr. Wada," she said, and exited the room.

*

When Mah'zan and Koo'bla came into their own kitchen, Mah'zan surprisingly found his mother sitting at the table. "Oh, thank the Creator you're back! How did things go?"

He stared at her in disbelief. Turning hard to his left, he also saw his mother standing next to him chuckling. She then began to look fuzzy, out of focus, then transformed into his Uncle Min'darr. "What the ...?"

"You didn't tell him? Min'darr! How could you?" She stood and hugged her son. 'Zanny, I am so sorry. Your uncle thought it would be safer if he became me for this meeting."

"It worked out," Mah'zan said. "Sure explains how I got that scar on my leg. That old bastard—sorry, Mom—managed to find a way to not pay me for it. Still," he said as he held up a bag of coins, "I got paid for the time I was onboard the *OuterWada*!"

"Be smart, don't spend it all, okay? Get used to saving some for later," Koo'bla told him.

"That sounds smart, Mom, thanks," Mah'zan said. "I'm going to head out for a while." He left the bag at home, taking some of the money to get a few items he'd been wanting.

Koo'bla and Min'darr sat down to talk. "Good that he's gone. Most of the things I have to tell you are for adult ears," he told her. "The things I overheard while waiting for our meeting with Wada and as we were leaving will chill your heart. Ram'ili's too. I have to find a way to prove that Wada is way more than a mere thief."

"What do you mean?" she asked.

"I used magic to listen in to a few conversations. The four who attacked last night? Three of them were there in one of the offices with Sheriff Mok'sni! The fourth one ... the one Ram'ili stabbed, died last night. Turns out that they were part of the pirate crew that sunk Mah'zan's ship. It appears that they work for Wada, too."

Koo'bla's Advice

"They were—get this, they were in another office across the hall with the port's sheriff! Mok'sni was biding his time until Wada was done with us, just chatting with the very same thugs who attacked us!" Min'darr began pacing the room. "Mok'sni is the law here. They were the law breakers. Those guys should be in a locked jail cell. Am I right? How is this close to being right?"

Koo'bla said, "Min'darr, calm down. What were they talking about?"

"Calm down? I don't think so. But, okay, let's see … Mok'sni was first telling them how stupid they were for being drunk, breaking down the café's door, then wanting to fight us. Then he told them they were lucky, because they'd accidentally stumbled across where the one sailor lived who'd survived their attack on the *OuterWada*.

"One of them said he'd seen 'that one sailor running to the far gunwales when Varko got in his way. He killed ol' Varko.' The pirate claimed he had wanted to chase him down, but the explosives had already been lit. They let him go figuring the blast or a shark, because of his cut leg, would finish him off.

"Then he told them that, after they spoke to Wada, he'd escort them back to a sloop that would take them back to their ship. They couldn't show their faces in town anymore. It was all I could do to hold back. I should have turned every one of them into bug, I've never been so angry!"

Koo'bla patted his chair. "Min'darr, please, sit down." When he had, she continued. "I keep forgetting your history, how truly unaware you are."

"What do you mean unaware? Why I can ..." Min'darr sputtered.

"Yes, yes, yes. I know," she interrupted. "With your magic you can do virtually everything. Except for one thing that actually is a pretty big deal," she added.

"You will never be able to change people, they're too set in their ways. They will continue to be whoever they were born to be. Some are kind and happy. Some are cruel. Some are selfish. Some are caring, while others would think nothing of slitting your throat to watch you die.

"Min'darr, my sweet little brother ... you know so much about so many things. Of course there will be some people that you can influence, but not all of them. Certainly not enough of them to make a difference. The time you spent learning in your 'eldritch stream,' as you've called it, gave you historical insights. You don't know people yet. They tend to be self-serving ... greedy. They may want money or things or love or to be happy or just to be fed. The degree and the manner in which they will go to achieve each of those tells you everything about who they truly are.

"A man like Wada ... well, he'll do anything to make money, obviously, even kill for it. We have proof of that. A man like our Uncle Taf'nar ... what would he have wanted most?"

Without hesitation, Min'darr said, "Power in influencing others. He couldn't deal with the fact that I had more magic than he did." Min'darr recalled how his uncle, who was supposed to guide him for a year for his Ma'har at age ten, had abandoned him when he saw that Min'darr's magic was more powerful than his own.

Koo'bla continued. "So perhaps Wada and Uncle Taf'nar were very much alike. Consider that there are hundreds of thousands of people, each with a different way of seeing things, understanding them, reacting to them.

"Yes, what you overheard at Wada's offices is disturbing. It is wrong, no question about that. Sadly though, it doesn't surprise me. I have been here dealing with these people for too long to not understand this. It is something you have to learn if you are going to get by in your life so you won't be taken advantage of or endangered by others. I'd be willing to bet that all the magic in the world will not 'fix them.'

"Hold on to us ... to me, to Mah'zan. And ... well, maybe this isn't the best time... then again maybe it is. I want you to hold on to Ram'ili, too. She is special to me, as special as you and Mah'zan are. We share a deep love for each other."

"Like the sister you wish I had been for you?" Min'darr winked, remembering their childhood spats.

Koo'bla allowed the corners of her mouth to curl up. "No, my Bisha, more. She means as much to me as Jal'oot, Mah'zan's father, ever did, ever could. I love her. She is my partner. We share ..." she paused as she looked deeper into his eyes. "... we share everything any two people could share."

He stared, then nodded as her true meaning dawned on him. "You are lovers in every sense. How can I not accept this? My dearest Koo'bla, as long as you are happy, I couldn't possibly object. Love, happiness ... both are rare quantities. They have to be celebrated."

They stood and shared a massive hug.

"Thank you for being so amazing. I think I have to go out into the throng, experience more of these people you spoke of," Min'darr said. "I've dealt with a few. Now, with your insights to aid me, I want to understand more. Tomorrow will be a most interesting day, I hope. Good night, my Bisha, and thank you for loving me, too."

Koo'bla grinned. "Have a restful night, my dear brother," she added.

*

Min'darr rose early to wander the marketplace before many of the vendors had lifted their tarps. His intent was on watching human interactions. He remembered the two men arguing when he'd first come to town ... the old man with the broken cart axle and the loud man demanding he get out of the way while refusing to help him.

Without using his magic, he hoped to experience a plethora of emotions of those he encountered. He was not prepared for the wide range of assorted reactions to the events of their days. One was tired and angry. It seems someone he relied on to be working with him was sick so wouldn't be there to work today. He was frustrated at the prospect of spending the entire day doing everything.

Half an hour later Min'darr came across another lone worker. She seemed upset, sad. She thanked him for the concern he expressed to her. She told him her partner was ill. Min'darr sensed from her a deep concern for her co-worker's well-being. *Koo'bla was so right. Here's the exact same situation and these two people had very different reactions. One was concerned for himself; the second, for the other person.*

As shoppers arrived to buy, he quickly heard one of them arguing about the prices of items that were for sale with the owner. "No, please, my friends, this is not worth fighting over," he pleaded with them.

The shopper, an older man, pointed at the vendor. "See! See what I tell you! You are robbing us blind. No one should have to pay this much."

The vendor balked at the accusation. "What do you know? Do you know how much I have to pay for these? Am I not entitled to be able to afford to put bread on my own plate?"

Min'darr put his arms out between the two. "See, you are talking about it. That is good, yes?"

The shopper turned to see him with a skewed face. "What? Are you new to this world? You know nothing about buying and selling? We are ... er, we are negotiating a price. It is what we do ... what we all do."

The vendor added, "Go away. Why don't you go feed the gulls, something more useful than bothering people earning a living."

Much to learn. He left, unsure. *It sounded like arguing, and they wanted to? How does that make sense?*

As he continued along, a vendor's table some thirty feet ahead of him tipped, spilling various fruits that rolled off in every direction. He watched, pleasantly surprised, as the vendor's neighbors stopped their own work to help. Two assisted in propping up the table, resetting the leg that slipped, while the rest gathered up the fallen fruit. The whole thing took less than a minute.

He approached them. "Excuse me. I have a question. Each of you compete for shoppers' money, yet you stopped your own work to help a competitor. Why?"

They exchanged a glance. A cloth vendor, sorting his products said, "My goodness, man, are you daft? If someone can use your help, for any reason, would you not help them?"

The other chimed in as well. "Were it not for others, I could not be here. It takes many people working together to get things accomplished."

"I understand that," Min'darr said. "But you both are competitors, yes?"

The second vendor answered. "That doesn't matter. If his booth is in shambles, buyers will avoid it and us since we are next to him. That doesn't help anyone. And, since we do not sell the same thing, it is possible that those who look at his cloth, may also be interested in buying my precious metals or gemstones. The same for the fruit seller.

"Lastly, if some tragedy hit one of us, would we not hope that others could help us in our time of need? Haven't you ever needed anyone's help?"

Min'darr thought. *Not since before my Ma'har did I need help. My parents helped me, then Uncle Taf. Since magic, I have done for others, but haven't needed anything from anyone else.* "Of course I have," he said believing that to be the expected answer.

"Then, do not waste our time with childish questions," the cloth vendor said and he returned to readying his booth.

The gem seller smiled sheepishly at Min'darr adding, "It's just the right thing to do."

"Thank you, sir." Min'darr left. He fought the urge to use his magic to give the vendor more success today.

In the process of his wanderings he stopped to watch the magician pair, especially the part of their act with the magic ball. He was impressed. *The girl has most definitely been practicing,* he thought. It brought a smile to his face, having been able to help the daughter and her mother. He thought of what Koo'bla had said, the vendors, too. It applied to him. *Magic was my help. A part of me that allows me to help both myself and others. I have the benefit that I don't have to rely on others.* That thought caused him to pause. The idea of never needing anyone's help may be a boon, or it may merely be keeping him apart from the rest of humanity.

A few minutes later, he noticed a heavily robed man moving quickly through the now-crowded avenues. He followed him, suspicious of his clothing in the rising heat of the day. His behaviors were very odd, as well. He stopped near a vendor's booth that sold leather goods. He picked up a pouch, inspected it, then dropped it back onto the counter. He turned the corner and then stopped. Min'darr then saw the pouch virtually leap off the pile, round the corner, and land in the man's hand.

Min'darr, sensing no magic in the man, quickly approached him. The thief noticed, then scurried into the crowd. Min'darr blurted to the vendor what happened, that he was going to pursue the thief. As he kept pace with the robber, Min'darr saw the young man who had been with Mok'sni when they'd confronted him on the Wada part of the wharf.

He veered to him. "Quick, come with me. A man has robbed a leather vendor. I'm after him." The young man nodded, moving to follow. Min'darr could no longer see the robber, but kept on in the direction he'd gone. As he went, he cast a spell to locate the man. Things around him faded into a thin, smoky veil. Through it, he saw the man as the sole solid object. Min'darr called behind him, "Hurry, over there," he said, pointing in the thief's general direction.

Two turns later, he caught him at a corner of the pier's decking. "Stop!" he demanded, putting out his arms.

The robber glanced quickly around, seeking an escape. The young deputy ran up at that point. "Good morning, Snake Eyes. Having a busy day already, eh?"

The robber dropped his shoulders, recognizing the lawman.

Defeated! Min'darr thought. Then the robber lunged at Min'darr. A glint of sunlight shone off the blade of the knife he held, intent on putting it into Min'darr's chest. His magic surged to protect him. The man froze in his tracks, no longer able to move.

Realizing this could expose him as a magician to the lawman, Min'darr stepped into the robber, taking the blade to the side of his stomach. Pain coursed through him as his blood stained his shirt. *Shut off the pain. I have to make this look real.* He winced and grasped the robber's tunic under his throat to force him back off the pier.

The man dangled in Min'darr's grasp, dropping the knife into the water beneath him.

"Let me go, damn you!" the robber growled.

Right into my plan, Min'darr thought. *Your stolen goods are worked into this robe, I see them.* Min'darr quickly worked two spells. The first allowed the robber to slip out of his cloak. He screamed as he dropped into the cold water. The second spell transformed him into a fish ... a tiny, helpless fish, at the mercy of those bigger fish that loved to hunt in the waters beneath the piers of the wharf.

The lawman ran to the nearest ladder and slid down, intent on seeing where the robber surfaced. After watching for a good fifteen minutes, he returned topside of the pier. "He never came up," the man said "Too bad, a fitting end. I've dealt with him before."

Min'darr sat cradling his side.

"How badly are you hurt?" he asked Min'darr as he looked at the red stain.

Min'darr had already emptied the two dozen pockets of the robber's robe while the lawman searched the waters beneath him. "I'll be all right. He poked a hole in my fat. Look at this stuff he's stolen. Uh, what's your name?"

The lawman had squatted to see the collection of stolen goods. The leather pouch was there, along with eleven rings, seven necklaces, a silk cloth with embroidered trim, and an empty sheath, presumably for the dagger used to stab Min'darr. He glanced again at the blood stain on Min'darr's shirt, then he answered. "I'm Gor'und, Mok'sni's second in command. You're umm ..."

"Min'darr," he said. "I am uncle to Mah'zan, the sailor who survived the *OuterWada* attack."

"I remember you. They busted up your sister's café too, eh?"

"Some drunkards did. They were pirates?" Min'darr challenged, taking advantage of his apparent slip.

"Wha ...? Umm, no ... I mean, uh, don't know who did that. Just heard that your place got busted up. I got no idea who did it. Mok'sni handled that. I was busy elsewhere on another matter." He recovered quickly, staring at Min'darr from then on. "You want to see a doctor?"

"No, I'll head home for now. My sister's good at this kind of thing. You want help taking that stuff back to the vendors?"

"No. Gotta inventory it all and file a report. Ol' Snake-Eyes might get caught the next time, if he survived ... no, he probably did. I'm not that lucky. We'll let a judge add this to his list of crimes when he finally gets brought to trial. He'll slip up and we'll nab him." Gor'und continued eyeing Min'darr as he gathered up the stolen items. "You want help getting home?"

"I'll be fine. Glad I ran into you. Thanks for your help." Min'darr shook his hand before turning to go back to Koo'bla's. *Ol Snake-Eyes ain't going to rob anyone else. He's probably being digested in a bigger fish's gut by now. You go ahead and file your report.*

It hurt to walk, so he cast a healing spell on his stab wound. He felt the magic repairing the cut flesh and could very quickly walk normally.

Min'darr stopped watching people as he made his way home. Looking back, it had been a busy and confusing morning. One day he was happy to end early.

The Affront

Wada's "request" for them to meet with him immediately was delivered by Mok'sni himself, so they knew it was a serious issue. Ram'ili would not be left behind. She shooed the few customers from her café after reimbursing the cost of each meal. She left a hurried note stuck to their new door that she would return soon. Mok'sni, aided by four of his deputies, then escorted the group to the Wada offices.

*

"Come in, come in. So glad you could spare the time for this ... uh, little talk, eh?" Wada said, then prattled on about common goals, mutual benefits, etcetera. He eyed Ram'ili. "Oh yes," he said with a smirk on his face, "You are the café owner, eh? Or should I say, the killer?"

"Now wait a minute," Min'darr said.

"No!" Ram'ili yelled out. "I do not need any man, anyone, to speak on my behalf. I will speak for myself."

"You killed a man in your kitchen. Yes?" Wada asked.

"I defended myself from the man's attack." Ram'ili stated with her arms folded.

"And he is dead by your hand, yes?" Wada asked.

"What is this? Am I on trial here?" she asked. "By you?"

Mok'sni interrupted. "You will be respectful, woman. Master Wada is the duly appointed magistrate for the harbor district of the city of Vila'Borin." He stood, grabbing a sheaf of papers and put them before Wada who had lit one of his cigars. "These documents represent my investigation into a break-in at the Chakula Café three nights ago.

"By their own testimony, the deceased, a sailor by the name of Jas'atu, was drunk. I propose that he was then unable to properly defend himself when she stabbed him."

"He attacked me, cutting my arm, damn you. His sword didn't care if he was drunk or not. I have the right to protect myself!" Ram'ili screamed. "Here! I hear you like to see wounds," she fumed, ripping the bandage from her cut arm revealing the wound she refused Min'darr's magic to heal. She bared her teeth as well. "See! You see the wound I suffered in his attack? I can't show you the handprints he left on my blouse, the filthy, drunken bastard, nor his foul breath as he forced his tongue into my mouth.

"No," she continued. "He deserved everything he got." She spat on the top of Wada's desk. "How dare you pretend that that scum was some kind of victim."

Wada looked calm. Min'darr had the impression that all this played into his plans.

"Well, well, well. Powerful testimony to be sure." He waved his hand at Ram'ili's spittle. An aide wiped it up. "I will consider that in determining whether charges should be filed against you. Until our investigation is complete, you will be held overnight. I should have my findings ready by tomorrow. If not, oh well ... Sheriff, would you please escort her to a holding cell. Oh, please be sure to be gentle with her wounded arm."

Mok'sni placed his hand on her lower back to guide her. She slapped it away. She was two steps ahead of him as they left the room.

Koo'bla was about to say something when Wada held his hand out to her. "We are still in session, ma'am. I do not like to be interrupted."

"Master Mah'zan, step forward." He did.

Wada continued. "You are a sailor in the employ of Wada Shipping, yes?"

Mah'zan looked around, uncertain. "Yes, sir, I am."

"And you were aboard the *OuterWada* when she was attacked?"

"Yes. We already talked about all that ... umm, sir," the youth responded.

"How did you get back to Vila'Borin so quickly?"

"I ... uh, I don't know, sir. I have a vague memory of lying in a wagon, rocking along the roadway."

"Whose wagon?" Wada asked.

"I have no idea. I was pretty delirious from the attack and my wound. The one thing I remember was an older woman with an amazing meat pie," Mah'zan said.

Wada scrunched his lips, spending an inordinate amount of time smoothing the ash from the tip of his cigar. He finally continued. "Your new ship is anchored in the harbor, the *WesterWada*. You are assigned to her as the bilge tender." Wada rang a bell and two sailors entered. "Gentlemen, Master Mah'zan will accompany you to the *WesterWada*. You will be sailing in two weeks to establish a new trade route with the Tan'diali Islands people. I would expect you to return within the next eight to ten months. Go. May the Creator sail with you."

The sailors each took Mah'zan by an arm, marching him toward the door. He managed a "Goodbye, I love you," to his mom, twisting his head around as he was forcibly escorted through the doorway. Mok'sni returned and closed the office door.

It was now the four of them. Wada and Mok'sni, Min'darr and Koo'bla. Her breathing was rapid, despite her efforts to remain calm. She was the one who spoke first. "How can you be so flippant, so cold? You rearrange people's lives with that god-awful smirk on your face as easily as if you were sorting buttons. Know this, my son will survive your hate. I don't know why you are punishing him ..."

"Punishing him? My dear woman, I am employing him. He works for me. I will treat him exactly like any other employee. He is assigned to further his experience to make him a better qualified sailor. He has to know the ship he's on.

"Perhaps, though, I might be willing to give him a safer position. If you were to reconsider my offer to share your dreams ... any information that comes to you that make things less costly, less risky ... you know."

"No chance in hell." Koo'bla stated, glaring at Wada. "You are as vile as they come."

"We can discuss that aspect of things if you need to. But I can help sway your decision. Stay a night or two in my guest suite. Work with me, and it can be yours. No need to wash filthy sheets anymore. You would be employed by Wada Shipping as a special advisor. Believe me, the fringe benefits are ... ahh, shall I say, quite substantial."

"No. No dreams, no job. The sheets on my filthiest bed are much cleaner than the way you do business. I'll have none of it." As Koo'bla finished her statement, Mok'sni stood and opened the office door. Four men entered the office, surrounding and quickly overpowering her.

She screamed, "Min'darr! Do something!"

Min'darr had stood quickly, eyes aglow with his hands extended, ready to turn them both into butterflies, or fish, or anything.

Half a heartbeat later, Wada also stood, pointing at Min'darr and screamed, "Do anything, magician, and I swear to you that this will be the last you see any of them. You might be able to save one, but the other two will certainly die if you lift a finger against me. Do you understand?"

His tirade worked to slow Min'darr's reactions, allowing his threat to take hold.

"And who do you think I am?" Min'darr asked.

"Give me some credit, my good man. The blue glow coming from your eyes tells me everything I need to know. I don't accuse just anyone of being a magician ... at least not without proof. Deputy Gor'und has provided me with enough information. You slipped up when you gave him your real name, assuming you were intent on not letting me know who I was up against. I mean, considering the fact that you don't walk or sit like a man with a knife wound to your gut."

"All right, Wada. I am Min'darr. I have been honest with you from the start. I never tried to hide who I am. I deplore your practices, sir. You are a cheat, a crook, and a fraud. You are responsible for the deaths of your own sailors. What is to stop me from turning you into something I can step on?"

"Oh, I must say, I am insulted by your affront. How dare you sit in my own office and so blatantly accuse me of things of which you have no proof? I am a businessman. You are the criminal, murdering how many foreign soldiers, sending a poor pickpocket to his watery grave? Who knows what other crimes you've magically committed?

"Now when it comes to stopping you, I probably have little to offer." He sat back down. "But then, I really don't think I have to. Like I said, if anything happens to me, my associates have orders to ... ahh, attend to your family.

"Actually, I am honored to have you here, Min'darr the Magician. You have become an historic enigma. We suffered from the onslaught of that Kordahlian madman, Magama. He set up his forces, then took a small contingent into the mountains because he heard about a mountain pass that he could control, making millions charging tolls on the trade caravans using the Nordana Pass.

"The next thing we hear is some fantastic tale of a young magician who killed all his soldiers in one fell swoop, then burned Magama in the town square for everyone to see. Two days later, he disappeared.

"Until now." Wada leaned back in his chair. "And I control him." He actually spun in a circle on the chair. "Imagine that. Me!"

He then sat up, elbows on the desk's edge. "You will use your magic at my direction to make Wada Shipping invincible! You'll make the weather perfect for sailing, keep pirates away, and see to it that our cargo is sold high while the imports we buy will be at rock-bottom prices."

Min'darr stood in a stupor. He had to consider how best to defeat Wada. *He has my sister, her partner, and my nephew. There is no law to turn to. Wada owns everyone. I have to be careful ... there must be some way I can take him, his system, his whole empire down. And it will have to look real, not a sign of magic. If it does look suspicious, he'll know it was me, then I may not be able to prevent his hurting the others, or worse.*

"Understand that magic has limitations. It cannot do everything," Min'darr finally said.

"As long as it does what I need it to do, your people will live," Wada said.

Min'darr looked across at Mok'sni. "How does this fit into your perspective, Sheriff?" He emphasized that last word.

The man sat back, grinning. "The law is meant to keep the masses in line. Those with the means will always be able to influence how the law is enforced. You'd be a fool, magician, to believe anything else."

"Then I will take the woman, Ram'ili, and be on my way."

Wada shook his head. "No. She will stay with me."

"She comes with me or there is no deal, Wada. I am not your pawn. I want the woman. She comes with me. Now." Min'darr said. "I promise you, Magama never saw it coming."

"She is an attractive thing, eh? If you like her kind, I have access to others who can offer you so much more. Something to keep in mind."

"Her. Ram'ili. No one else will do," Min'darr stated. "And I grow impatient, Wada."

"Remember what's at stake, magician." Wada glared at him.

"You are the one who has forged this partnership, Ma'hana Wada. Do you want to back out of it now?" As Min'darr spoke, Mok'sni, who had stood a moment earlier, palming his dagger, shot up into the air, banging against the ceiling, and then clung to it like a fly on flypaper. His weapons had dropped to the floor.

Wada was startled at first, then chuckled to see his righthand man stuck on the ceiling as helpless as a fly caught in a web. "I may have underestimated your resourcefulness, magician. So be it, take the woman. I will act on the fact that by doing so, you are agreeing to be in my service. Just remember what—or rather who else is at stake."

*

Sitting at the kitchen table with Min'darr, Ram'ili broke the uncomfortable silence. "Why? Your family was taken hostage by that monster. Why bargain for me?"

Min'darr looked at her dark hair, mostly disheveled despite her combing at it with her fingers. Her face was drawn. Clearly she'd been crying. Still, no matter his prompting earlier, she refused to reveal anything that had happened to her after she'd been taken out of the office.

"I'm able to find both of them when that need arises. I couldn't be sure I'd be able to find you. Koo'bla would never forgive me if I allowed anything to happen to you."

"Thank you, Min'darr. Look, since she and I are one in our hearts, I ask if I may consider you my brother also."

Min'darr smiled. "I am honored. I am happy that Koo'bla has your love in her life." He squeezed her hand. "Thank you, my sister-in-heart, for loving her, as well as Mah'zan, even if he is a teen."

"He is tolerable, for a boy, I mean," she said.

"There is a cost to you for joining my family," he said as he took her hand.

She raised her eyebrows, her interest nudged. "What would that be?"

He smiled and said, "Your arm."

Ram'ili scrunched her face. "What? What about my ... she started to say, then looked at her arm. The cut had healed.

"I get to take care of the ones I love," he said in a whisper.

She smiled back and nodded.

He paused, stretching out his magic. "There are three men watching us, Wada's, I would assume. Two are below with one more on the roof across from us. We must be quick and quiet in what we do," he said.

"And what will we do?" she asked.

"Well, Wada conceded to releasing you to me assuming I wanted you. So, I guess we should go to the bedroom," Min'darr told her.

"What? Wait ..." she blurted.

"Shh, I said he assumed, right? I would never do such a thing. He doesn't know that, though. We should make it look good."

She stood, took his hand, and led him toward the next room. She lowered the shade of the window as they passed.

With the window shades down, they could not be seen. Min'darr reached out to touch her neckline. A blue spark from his finger rested on her skin and slowly sank in. She lowered her chin against her chest, straining to see what he had done.

"There. Now I'll be able to find you, too. I'm afraid the things we have to do will require more refined magic than I have had to call upon before. You may not be able to help much."

"No." She winced as she said it. "I mean, yes, I understand that, but I'm not the kind of person to just sit back. I need to be fully involved."

"I got that impression, a few times. Okay, I have an idea that might be right down your alley." They sat closer to whisper, in case the wrong ears were somehow straining to listen.

*

Min'darr then sat for a long time, calling upon the magic he would need, spells he'd never considered using before. All very complex.

He finally sighed, opening his glowing blue eyes. "Ready, Ram'ili?"

"All set, my brother," she said, her blue eyes glowing back at him.

Magic to the Rescue

"I'm one hundred percent certain Wada has his minions warned to watch for anything unusual. So, we go carefully. No mistakes. Lay down, please, under the covers," Min'darr directed, then cast his spell over Ram'ili as she lay in bed. "All right, take a look," he said.

Ram'ili got up, gawking at the magical image of herself laying in the bed. "Eww," she murmured.

Min'darr climbed in next to her form, applying the same spell to himself, then he too got up to look. There, in the bed, were the two of them curled up next to each other. Min'darr said, "For a quick peek, I think it'll work."

They left the room. Ram'ili walking behind him. She looked back, seeing them as if they were asleep in bed. "I can almost see myself breathing," she said. "Creepy."

"But effective in case they decide to check in on us. This is what they'd expect to see." Minutes later they stood in the kitchen after being sure the doors were locked. Min'darr drew her to him like a hug, muttered some weird sounding words she could barely hear. The chest she pressed her face against vanished.

She felt it as firm as before, however could no longer see it. She moved her hand to scratch her nose and found she couldn't see her hand. "I'm invisible, too?"

"Of course you are." Min'darr pulled away slightly to inspect his work. "I've only done this spell once before on a mule. Pretty cool, eh?" She felt his hand in hers pull slightly. She followed and they moved together toward the kitchen light. She watched the flame flicker as it went out. They then moved to the kitchen window, left open an inch or two deliberately for this next phase of Min'darr's plan.

"Okay, this is the scary part. I practiced this before. I have to admit, it feels strange. We are going to become vapor ... a cloud. You'll move with your mind. Your body will have changed too much so it won't work the way you think it should, the way you're used to. All right?"

"I guess," she whispered uncertainly.

"It worked best for me when I thought of myself like a clump of cloud. I have to layer the magic we're using. We are vaporizing our invisible forms. I've practiced this on my own, so though I've never done it with two people before, it should work. I feel confident. Stay focused on the pressure of my hand in yours. Ready?"

"Can you do it already? You're scaring the crap out of me," she retorted.

He responded by murmuring more unintelligible words. Min'darr felt wet and knew she would too. Not quite the dripping kind, sort of warm and tingly. It left him feeling itchy. They could feel, but no longer see or hear. He was aware of the sensation of her hand as he moved them along.

In a few moments, things became more familiar. The itchiness dissipated. They could see again. They were no longer in their kitchen, but on the sidewalk below. She felt Min'darr squeeze her hand. She squeezed back. She faced the wall directly beneath the window they'd come through as vapor.

"Are we still ..."

"Shh," he whispered, pulling her along the walkway. "Let's go," he said softly. The two walked hand in hand, passing a man tucked into a crevice between buildings watching their now-dark window. They headed toward Wada's offices. "Koo'bla needs rescuing," she whispered. Min'darr squeezed her hand.

As they walked, Min'darr said, "When we get to Wada's, we'll have to find Koo'bla first. Then we'll know how to get to her. I was thinking of sending you in to her with some renewed magic to share with her, so you can make her invisible, then you both could sneak out."

"That won't work, Min'darr. There will be too many doors, locked and guarded probably."

"I thought of that. Also, there's the possibility you could become a vapor to get the two of you out that way."

She turned to face where she believed he would be if she could see him. "You're nuts!"

"Shh, not so loud," he cautioned.

"I can't do that stuff!" She pushed a whisper to its limit. "How am I supposed to know how to do magic? You just said it was difficult for you. Feeling or doing it once doesn't mean anything. I can taste a dish. That doesn't mean I can recreate it. And I've no clue how this magic of yours works, let alone do some myself."

"No, I guess not. Damn! Okay. We'll have to rethink this."

"Why in the world would I have to do it alone? Where would you be?" she asked.

"I was thinking of heading out to rescue Mah'zan as quickly as possible. They must have some kind of signal worked out. Wada said I'd have trouble rescuing everyone. So he must have something planned."

"If we can find Koo'bla and get her out, where are we supposed to go while you do that?" Ram'ili asked. "And don't say home. That's the first place they'll look for us."

Min'darr stood silent for a few moments. "I'm sorry, Ram'ili. I've focused so much on how to do the magic we need to use, that I overlooked so much of the practical side. Thank you for pointing this out. I'd have gotten her killed, both of them probably. What do you think?"

"First of all, she's going to be well guarded. Most likely in an interior room ... harder to get in and out of. I think once we're there as vapor, we should stay that way until we find her. Can we do that?"

"Yep. We do have to stay connected or the vapor spell for you may end."

"Wonderful," she quipped sarcastically.

"Sorry, I'm not used to plotting out every detail. We know what we have to do, even if there are too many things we can't anticipate. No way we can plan against everything that may happen. Let's play it by ear ... be ready for anything."

"All right. But don't forget," Ram'ili said, "we have to get out, too. So, don't burn the place down, okay?"

"I'll be as careful as I can but, no promises," Min'darr responded.

*

A broken window in a storeroom allowed them access to the inside. Slipping under locked doors as vapor wasn't a problem either. Their invisible cloud-like form was impossible to see against the wooden floor in the dimly lit halls. Ram'ili's expectations had been exact. Armed guards stood on alternate sides of the corridor spaced about every twenty feet. She could sense them, so she knew Min'darr could as well. They'd passed seven of them before he stopped their progress at a doorway. There was a guard on each side of it.

Ram'ili felt Min'darr's excitement. Their shared physical state allowed her to know his awareness of Koo'bla's magical signal within the guarded room.

They slipped under the door effortlessly.

Once inside the room, they solidified in a corner behind some furniture, remaining invisible. Across the room from where they huddled, Koo'bla sat on the edge of a bed, handcuffed to the sideboard's framing. Mok'sni stood at its foot, facing Wada who sat in an easy chair to Ram'ili's right. Wada was speaking.

"... matter if you can't control the dreams. We can find a way to help you focus. Desperation can accomplish things mere pain cannot."

Min'darr noted his sister's forearm was bruised. She looked generally disheveled and uncomfortable. *Roughed up for certain. They will pay!*

He got distracted, sensing Ram'ili moving toward Koo'bla, but he saw no reaction from her. He had to stay intent on getting Wada and Mok'sni out of the room. Wada, of course, had his cigar, this time resting in a tray next to him.

What happened next was simple, way too easy. Wada reached for the smoldering Maduro without looking. Min'darr magically jostled the ashtray, allowing his hand to bump it, knocking it onto the carpet. Min'darr then magically encouraged it to ignite the shag carpeting as well as the chair Wada sat in. Wada jumped up.

"Damn! Mok'sni! Put this fire out."

That was not something Min'darr allowed, instead flaring the blaze up along the chair's backing with another arcane nudge. Billows of smoke quickly filled the room.

Mok'sni backed up from the sudden intensity of the fire, advancing along the carpeting. Flames crawled up the wall behind the chair.

"By the Creator, man. Put it out!" Wada screamed.

"With what? We need water." He jerked the door open, yelling, "Fire! Get some water!" to the guards stationed there.

"You deal with this. I need air." Wada ran from the room coughing.

The sheriff took a quick look around, muttered under his breath as he walked to the door. Pausing a moment, he said, "Sorry, lady. The smoke should get you before the flames do." He ran out, slamming the door behind him.

Koo'bla glared at the flames. "Hey, don't leave me here!" she screamed, yanking against her handcuffs. She stopped abruptly, looking beside her. "What? Who the ... Ram'ili? Is that you? Oh, thank the Creator! Min'darr? Are you here?"

He'd moved next to her. Ram'ili soothed her. "Relax, honey. We're here. Everything will be fine," she said patting her shoulder. "Min'darr? I told you not to burn the place down!"

"No promises, remember? Lots of movement in the hallways. They'll need to air out the building, so we can't vaporize, too much of a chance to lose each other. Koo'bla, hold Ram'ili's hand," he told her, "and stay against the wall. Do not let them know we are here." Koo'bla stood up and promptly vanished from sight.

They couldn't see his hands wave across the handcuffs. They did notice when the heavy metal cuffs dropped to the floor. "Let's go," he said.

Holding someone's hand, he suspected it was Ram'ili's, Min'darr led them out into the hallway which was also quickly filling with smoke. Two of Wada's men ran toward them, each carrying two buckets of water. The first turned into the room, the second followed, but one of his buckets hit the door frame, spilling and causing the man to sprawl across the floor.

Koo'bla's voice was heard by the other two. "Clumsy of me. Couldn't help it. Not sorry."

"Not now. Plenty of time for revenge later, sweetheart," Ram'ili whispered.

A man's voice from within the room said, "The woman's gone. Tell Mok'sni."

In a heartbeat the door slammed shut, Min'darr's magic locking it.

"Shh! More coming. Tuck in!" Min'darr whispered. They managed to press against the wall as three more ran past without incident. "Stay together."

Within another minute, they'd reached the main doors, which were locked. A guard stood coughing in front of them, blocking their way out. Wada could be heard calling out from the next room.

"Stay here, I'll be right back," Min'darr told them. He went to see what Wada was doing in his office. He was standing on his chair, leaning out the open window. The sound of approaching sirens reached Min'darr's ears. *Good! A way out.*

He heard glass breaking and returned quickly to the lobby. Rounding the corner, he saw that the guard was gone. The door swung wide open, its glass window shattered.

He went toward it, bumping into something.

"Min'darr?" Ram'ili's voice said.

"Here," he said. Her hand brushed across his arm, latching onto his hand. He was pulled away from the building at a run. They ducked between buildings as the oncoming fire wagon passed them.

"Did you break ..." he started asking.

Koo'bla interrupted. "The guard broke it open. He didn't like not being able to breathe, I guess."

"We have to get away from here. Too noisy coughing this smoke out of our lungs to make sense staying invisible."

"No, Min'darr," Koo'bla said. "Even in all this confusion someone may see us."

Min'darr muttered, "Where is it safe?"

Ram'ili pointed to the horizon away from Wada's. "There's the naval ... oh, my god! Another fire! Isn't that ... oh, no, it looks so close to the café ... the inn. C'mon." She took two steps when Koo'bla yanked her back.

"No, honey, no. Don't you see?" Koo'bla asked as she gathered her partner in her arms. "That's what they want. They want us to show up there. They'll kill us when we do."

Ram'ili calmed as the realization took hold. "Koo'bla, so you know ... we left images of ourselves asleep in bed. If they broke in, they may think they've already killed us."

Min'darr took in a quick breath. "Mah'zan! I have to get him. Stay away from the fires. Get over near the naval base. Find somewhere to hide. I'll find you." They then heard him running off into the darkness.

*

Every ship, when anchored in a harbor, used lanterns to help avoid collisions and to let skiffs find them. Min'darr transformed into a sea gull, then flew out over each of the dozen ships in the bay to see which was likely the one Mah'zan was on.

Min'darr's gull's eyes had no difficulty locating the newest ship in the harbor. Its painted name, *WesterWada,* virtually glowed from the lantern light shining on it. All of Wada's vessels had lanterns highlighting the ship's name.

He landed on its main spar, about twenty feet above the deck. Two sailors meandered below him as watchmen. Another sat in the crow's nest a good fifteen feet above him. A sudden burst of noise from the mizzen hatchway garnered everyone's attention.

Three sailors struggled to lift someone who was bound and gagged. The gash over his eye said he'd been beaten as well. He was being dragged. Despite the swelling of his face, with the help of his magical tracer, Min'darr instantly identified him as his nephew.

Anger rose within him. Min'darr's sea gull transformed into an osprey. Kreeing at the top of its lungs, the raptor swooped down, raking one sailor across the back of his head. He screamed, dropping to his knees, pawing at his wounds. The other two gawked about, not certain what had happened.

Min'darr dove in again, hitting the second of the sailors square in the middle of his back. He pecked and clawed at the sailor's shirt. His hit drove the sailor away from Mah'zan. The two watchmen ran to the aid of their injured brethren. The third sailor grabbed Mah'zan, spun him, flinging him through an open gateway in the gunwale. Mah'zan fell into the dark waters of the harbor.

Min'darr was a second behind him, changing into an octopus as he hit the water. Using his tentacles, Min'darr worked furiously to free his nephew. The bindings loosened a bit, but the tie covering his mouth refused to loosen. Mah'zan panicked, instinctively fighting off whatever was grabbing at him while feverishly trying to clear whatever was on his face.

Min'darr magically reached out to communicate to Mah'zan so he knew what was happening. He glowed blue and sent that same eldritch aura to surround his nephew. Mah'zan

became a salmon. His bonds fell off, freeing him. Min'darr then changed him again,

elongating him to become a large shark. Since they had physical contact, Min'darr could communicate with his nephew.

With Min'darr the octopus hanging on to his dorsal fin, Mah'zan the shark calmed and began swimming toward the piers. The light from two fires reflected in the waters around them. Wada's offices, adjacent to the wharf, flared wildly, fully engulfing the building as it belched smoke into the night sky. The café's fire burned bright, its brilliant orange and yellow flames dancing skyward.

Min'darr paused, seeking where Koo'bla and Ram'ili might be hiding. His magic showed them to be in a building on the military side of the harbor. He told Mah'zan. They swam in that direction.

When they reached shallower waters, they returned to their human forms so they could climb the ladder to the pier's decking, fully expecting the guards to stop them, which they did. "Must be my night to get tied up," Mah'zan joked as one guard yanked his bonds just a little tighter in response. "Hey," Mah'zan said, wincing. "Does it have to hurt?"

Min'darr and Mah'zan were presented to the watch commander, soaking wet with their hands tied behind their backs. "And what have we here, seaman?" the man asked.

The guard jerked to attention. "Sir, these men were apprehended when they climbed onto the pier from ladder five, sir."

"Excuse me, Commander, this will go much quicker if you could include the two women you have in the next room with our interrogation," Min'darr stated.

"Now, how would you know about them?" the commander asked.

"With all due respect, sir, I'm Min'darr the Magician. We have a serious issue that may need your help in being resolved."

Goat Island

"So, while we can't get involved in any civil matters with Master Wada's shenanigans, we will be most happy to do everything we can to thwart the piracy issue. The yellow-prowed ship you reported is well known. The *Scourge*, the flagship of the pirate Gur'ata's fleet. He's run the Tunor'Abal gang for at least nine years that we can figure.

"Now, you said it was sailing alone? Interesting ... perhaps a sign of a disagreement within their ranks." Commander Jak'enge stretched back in his desk chair, stifling a yawn.

"Sorry. First night back on duty in a week." He eyed the foursome. "Gotta tell ya, the last thing I expected to happen tonight would be this. Two ladies jumping the perimeter fence, then two drenched men climbing up from the harbor. And you ... the national hero," he said looking at Min'darr. "Did you, sir, think you wouldn't be honored for the heroics you'd performed to end the Magama invasion? As soon as word of his demise reached here, citizens fought back against his troops. They were demoralized, giving up relatively easily.

"The government of Kordahl has condemned his actions, officially apologizing. Their offer of reparations was declined by Rougahn's Grand Council, to foster better relations. Both countries have recognized you as a hero. Where have you been hiding all this time? Uh, if I may be so bold as to ask."

Min'darr hesitated, then said, "I have been in seclusion in the mountains, learning magic's finer points. I was a boy when that happened. I have no use for notoriety, Commander, especially given that my 'fame' comes from being an accomplished assassin.

"I do have a current purpose ... putting people like Wada and his pirate counterpart out of business. Seems like the majority of folk are decent. Unfortunately, they are like sheep to those who would shear them of everything of value. Even the so-called port's sheriff is a puppet of Wada's."

The commander nodded. "Understood. I can send word to the authorities in Vila'Borin. They will be happy to have an excuse to investigate Mok'sni, Wada, too, if what you say is close to half true. I'm sure they will be more than willing to speak with his insurance company as part of their investigation. They shall have a report from me by sundown. Rest assured, we will be more than willing to keep an eye on Wada's fleet. It will be, umm ... amusing to thwart their scheming." He stood. "Anything else?"

"I believe that covers it. Wada is most likely aware of our escape by now, so we will be moving, probably into Vila'Borin. Staying near the harbor may not be our safest choice. Thank you again, Commander." Min'darr stood to shake his hand.

"Umm, Master Min'darr ... uh, if I could ask ... sir, would there be some possibility that I, or umm, rather you could ... could leave a keepsake of your visit?" Commander Jak'enge asked.

Min'darr inhaled, glancing around the office. "Hand me that ornamental dagger."

"That's used to show guilt or innocence in court martial cases," Jak'enge said.

"Then we shall empower it to do just that," Min'darr said. He held the blade out, running its edge along his forearm as he muttered his spell. A thin trickle of his blood covered its edge. He passed his hand across it. The blood glowed red, then blue, and then disappeared. The cut on his arm vanished as well.

"It is done. Point the dagger at a person who is speaking. They will be able to utter only the truth. Observe." He pointed the weapon at the commander. "When was the last time you lied to your commanding officer?"

Jak'enge did not hesitate. "Three weeks ago when I told him our kitchen needed more beef cuts. I complained that we had too much fish." His eyes widened in surprise. "It works," he said.

"Impressive. Thank you, sir." He took the blade, carefully setting it back in its stand on his desk.

As the four were being escorted from Commander Jak'enge's office, Ram'ili darted back in. She grabbed the knife, then pointed it at the commander. "Are you in any way in league with Wada or any of his men?"

Her friends froze in step.

"I have met him. I assure you that I am not under his influence in any way," Jak'enge said, then paused. He then turned to Min'darr. "I'm not going to burst into flame if I lie, am I?"

"I'm not certain," Min'darr responded. "But, please, let me know if you do. I'll have to adjust the spell."

*

"This really seems pretty extreme. Are you sure we have to?" Koo'bla asked.

Min'darr couldn't answer aloud, being a dragon at that moment. He nodded, hoping that was sufficient. Mah'zan took it upon himself to prompt his mother to climb up onto her brother's back. "We talked it out, Mom. C'mon, get up there!" She frowned at his impertinence, reached up and took Ram'ili's hand. The eastern horizon had lightened enough to make their plan dangerous. They could be spotted, so word could possibly get back to Wada.

Their discussions had centered on finding a place to stay hidden from Wada, who would certainly spare no effort to seeing them dead. Mah'zan told them of a small island about six miles off the coast that he had passed when sailing on the *OuterWada*. It was too rocky for anything but some abandoned goats. It was there they were headed.

A heartbeat after climbing onto his uncle's back, Mah'zan slapped the side of his neck with an encouraging "Go."

They had found a deserted area just beyond the naval pier and the promontory on which their base was situated. They needed a deserted spot to make their getaway. There, out of sight of the harbor, Min'darr spread his leathery wings to rise a dozen feet above the waves.

157

Min'darr had warned them they'd have to hold on tightly. He paralleled the shore a bit, then rose quickly, turning to fly inland, back across the forest. His passengers did not hesitate to question his action, loudly.

"Do you want them to hear us?" Min'darr asked them via a telepathic connection now that they were touching. He sped up, flying north, away from the shore. Rising with the landscape, Min'darr gained altitude, soon lost in the clouds.

Exactly what he wanted to happen. *"Hang on, here's where it gets fun,"* he sent.

Concealed by the clouds to any casual eyes from below, a blue glow washed over them, eliciting another gasp from his passengers. The effect of flying invisible was uncomfortable for his family. Not for Ram'ili, however. Min'darr had come to appreciate her spirit. As a final insult to their expectations, Min'darr banked right, coming around to fly south, back toward the coast.

"What are you doing, Bisha?" Koo'bla asked.

"Patience, my sister, please," he thought to her.

Still invisible, they flew out over the ocean, east of the harbor. Smoke from Wada's office and the café's blazes continued to snake into the still morning air, far to their right. They dropped closer to the waves, skimming mere feet above them, quickly losing sight of the mainland.

Min'darr had to avoid two ships. He kept himself level, choosing to fly several hundred feet above them to make any accidental contacts less likely. At this point his still invisible passengers complained of being cold. He could sense warmer air above them, since dragons were adept at this, but continued on, having already spotted their destination. Within minutes, he landed on a meadow near its center. They became visible again. His passengers climbing down stiffly, rubbing their cold-numbed hands.

He became himself again, instantly collapsing, overwhelmed with fatigue. They tucked him into a tuft of vegetation near some boulders to sleep off his weariness. The rising sun cleared the lower hills to their east. It felt deliciously warm. Mah'zan quickly surveyed the island and declared it deserted ... no people, no buildings, but lots of goats. They found comfortable spots to rest. Sleep came quickly after such an adventurous night.

*

They decided a small fire would be able to happen after dark when its smoke wouldn't be visible and the flames' light would be deflected by the lower surrounding hills. The circumference of the isle was a bit more than a mile. They patrolled it hourly. A goat dinner was had. Following their dinner, they sat together to consider their options.

"I appreciate your efforts to confuse Wada's people, but you could have warned us about going the wrong way," Ram'ili said.

"And then the invisible part. That was too strange!" Koo'bla added.

"Sorry, I know it wasn't part of the original plan," Min'darr conceded. "I couldn't shake the feeling that we were being watched. There wasn't time to plan anything, so I made it up as we went. With us being seen heading inland, they won't readily look for us out here."

"So, c'mon ... we all got to experience what a bird feels when it flies. That was total freedom," Ram'ili said. "I enjoyed it."

Koo'bla wasn't fond of it. Mah'zan would rather be a bird than a passenger. "And that was your second time flying by dragon, nephew."

Mah'zan stood. "At least I'll remember it this time, Uncle. It's time for us to come up with a plan. I'm really tired of Wada calling the shots."

They all started speaking at once. Min'darr chose to listen for thirty minutes as the three debated how best to deal with Wada, his minions, and the law.

He finally asked for his turn. "I've listened to some foolishness as well as some clever ideas. My one question is this: how do you expect to make these schemes work with Wada expecting us. We are here hiding from him to avoid being hunted by his people and maybe even killed. If any of us show our faces, we could be dead. You can bet on that. And we don't know how many people he has looking for us or who they are. As much as I love you all, I cannot see any of you going back to Vila'Borin." He drew his hand across his face becoming an old man, then again showing himself as a young woman. "I'm the only one who can hide in the open. I'm not going to risk any of you.

"I'd rather take the lot of you down to Kim'stwa. The capital city is large enough to get lost in, to allow you to start over. I'd suggest that staying away from its harbor might be a good idea, though."

Ram'ili spoke. "Why should we let you decide for us. I hate it when some man starts dictating my life."

"Even when what is suggested will save your life? You are brave, spirited beyond measure. I have come to love you, too. You would surely waste your life going back against Wada now. Then what would come of Koo'bla?" Min'darr rose and walked away from the fire.

They can't help me ... risking their lives ... too dangerous for them! I'll be watching out for them ... not able to focus on catching Wada. By the Creator, I'm not even interested in showing myself back in town. He found himself unable to think clear enough to plot out any strategy, any series of events to trap Wada. There were too many unknowns. At least the navy commander might be able to force Wada's hand.

Hmmm, the navy ... maybe Wada isn't the one I need right now. Maybe that pirate ... what's his name? Gur'ata? He might be the weak link in Wada's chain. How can I convince this buzzard to betray Wada? His wandering took him to a rock outcropping. He saw the moon's reflection held a puddle of water amidst the rocks about belt high. *Water! Scrying!*

"That's it!" he screamed. "Hey, everybody! Over here!"

They made their way to him expeditiously, excited to see what he'd found. None of them understood until he demonstrated.

Passing his arm across the top of the water, it rippled, then clouded, seven equally spaced swirls forming within it. He said, "Show me Ma'hana Wada." The swirls converged at the center. The water bubbled up once, then calmed. They could see an image of Wada and Mok'sni walking between boxes in a large, darker room, dim light from small sconces along the wall in addition to a torch that Mok'sni carried.

"It looks like some kind of a warehouse," Koo'bla said.

"Shh! Listen," Min'darr whispered.

"I don't care about the navy right now," Wada said. "I want those people. I want them brought to me so I can personally see them die! Especially that magician.

"So the navy is offering to escort my ships to prevent them from being boarded, eh? Why would they get involved? Has to be Min'darr's doing.

"How is it possible that he ... that all of them got away?" He turned to face the sheriff. "How? I had it planned. I'll bet he had something, if not everything to do with that fire, too. Either I've got to learn magic or buy me one helluva good mage to thwart him."

"Your snitch at the navy yards ... what'd he tell you, again?" asked Mok'sni.

"The word was that this magician and his family were with the base commander for a time last night. That explains the commander's concern today about our pirate problem, eh? Then ... get this ... he said he saw a dragon take off just east of the base right about dawn. Three people were riding it, heading inland," he reported.

"No telling where they might be going. Good riddance, I say. It's a good thing you had your records in this building and not your offices, Hana," Mok'sni added.

Min'darr waved his hand, ending the scry. "So, we were being watched. I felt we were. So, we know where his records are. I'm not a lawyer, but I'd bet those would put him in jail for fraud for a lot of years."

"I know he's got a number of warehouses. If you want to do that scry-thingy again, I might be able to tell which one," Mah'zan said.

"Later," Min'darr sounded anxious. "I need to find this pirate, Gur'ata. I'm hoping we can convince him to change his allegiance and to help us turn Wada in."

"Do pirates keep records?" Ram'ili asked.

"I'd doubt it," Min'darr said.

"I guess we'll find out, won't we," Mah'zan said.

"It's late. We can sleep easier here. Pirate searching comes in the morning," Koo'bla said. Each nodded in agreement.

*

As the sun cleared the eastern highlands the next morning, Min'darr refocused on the pool, speaking his enchantment, finally adding, "Show me Gur'ata the pirate." The pool responded, showing a two-masted ship at sea, its infamous yellow prow dipping to slice into the waters ahead of it. The early morning light gave an eerie sheen to the ship's sails, wet rigging, and its bow spray.

At the base of the bowsprit stood Gur'ata. On its planking stood three people, one with a rope around his chest. The scry allowed them to hear their conversations.

"I didn't take it, Captain, honest!" the bound sailor cried out.

"Well, thar ya be. We's the means to find out. Ya gets to test the waters, so to speak. Jump in an' swim under the ship. If'n yor innocent, you'll be alive when we pull ya back aboard astern. If'n not, the ship'll kill ya fer stealin' then lyin' 'bout it."

"But Captain, I swear ..."

"Jump now, or I'll hang ya meself!" he bellowed back. He waved his arm. The two men holding the bound sailor gave him a shove. Min'darr and the others heard his scream until he disappeared in the ship's bow wave. The rope trailed behind him. After a second or two, Gur'ata looped the rope around a thole, jerking the line to a sudden stop. He turned to the gathered crew behind him.

"Never steal from each other or me. It'll mean your end, buckos." He looked back at the two sailors on the bowsprit's planking saying, "Cut 'im loose in about ten minutes. The sharks'll appreciate a snack."

"I think we've seen enough," Min'darr said. Instead of ending the scry, he gestured and the view of the pirate ship expanded. The ship got smaller and the view wider.

"They're sailing north," Mah'zan said.

"How do you know?" Ram'ili challenged.

"Look at the shadows," he said. Then he pointed to the sun. "Same sun, same angle. Nothing nautical about it."

Min'darr stifled a chuckle, pointing to the scry, now showing the nearest landmass. "It looks like they're actually coming closer to us. Here's the point where they got your ship, Mah'zan. That's where I found you."

Mah'zan agreed. "Looks like they're about a day away."

Koo'bla took a closer look at the pool. "So, they're coming here?" she asked wide-eyed.

"Not likely. They will come within a few miles probably," Mah'zan added.

"We will have to be very careful when they are close," Min'darr said. "We know we're dealing with cutthroat murderers in both Wada and Gur'ata, so there's no room for mistakes.

"I think ..." He gestured, ending the scry. "... I'll go pay him a visit, see if I can get him to come say hello. When I get back with him, you will need to be as fierce as he is. I apologize to have to put you through this. I see no other option right now. We will have to scare him to death if there's any chance of convincing him to betray Wada." Min'darr glowed with a blue aura and grew, once again spreading huge leathery wings. With a powerful jump, he beat his wings against the ocean breezes, soaring ever upward, out toward the western horizon.

Gur'ata

Min'darr flew above cloud level until he spotted the *Scourge*, Gur'ata's pirate ship. He'd figured correctly. Then, becoming invisible again, he dropped down to skim the wave tops as he approached the vessel. He knew this encounter would be difficult, requiring many layers of magic at once. Thankfully, the ocean's energies filled him.

He approached the ship from its left side, the port side, as his nephew had so frequently referenced. He veered ahead, coming up to stand on the bow sprit, not as a dragon, instead looking like the sailor they'd seen from their scrying who had been keel hauled. Min'darr gave himself a watery, luminescent sheen, very ghost-like. His presence could easily be seen against the ever-brightening morning spray.

And indeed he was seen. A shout went out "Ghost!" Also "Mic'raf is back to take us to Hell!" Min'darr stood unmoving, waiting for the captain to show himself. The magic he employed would give him a loud, hollow haunting voice, to allow anything to pass through him including hands, to repel or attract objects in order to scare the bejesus out of the crew and their captain. Finally, he could tap into his dragon fire if the need arose. Would Gur'ata have the courage to face this unknown, or would he cower as well?

The fore deck was barren near him, the crew crowding behind the foremast from gunwale to gunwale. All eyes stared wide. Some shouted warnings for him to return to the dead or pleaded for mercy based on their friendship.

Min'darr began his ghostly moaning. "Gur'ata! I did not steal ... oohh ... not steal from you." The crew cringed until one sailor approached with a drawn cutlass. His daring was instantly prompted by others, urging him to rid them of this spectre.

As he neared, slowly sliding his feet as he went, he called back. "I can see right through 'im. He's got to be a mirage, not real at all!" When close enough, he poked Min'darr with the tip of his cutlass.

Min'darr stopped wailing and locked eyes with him. "Would you kill me twice?" he sang. A flame, from his dragon spell, shot out from the ghost's mouth, catching the sailor on his chest. He flew back, screaming, clothing ablaze. His mates dragged him back, beating the flames out.

"Enough!" Gur'ata voice sounded from the midships. The crew parted, allowing the pirate to advance toward the "ghost." The pirate approached the vision of the dead sailor. "An' what have we 'ere?" He eyed Min'darr. "Archers! At your leave," he shouted, stepping back. Within seconds, a dozen archers were drawing their bows back, arrows nocked.

They counted and fired, each bolt flying through the image, then dropping into the ocean.

"Gur'ata!" Min'darr howled again. "Steal not from others or suffer a fate worse than mine."

"I don't steal, phantom, I borrow, permanently." He jested, turning to his crew to elicit their raucous response.

Louder still, Min'darr cried out. "Redeem your ways, felon, or pay with your life."

"No one threatens me, not even the dead. I'll be ... arggh"

Min'darr's figure had reached out, as did his magic. He took the pirate by the throat, lifting him as he clutched at his neck. Gur'ata kicking his legs as he rose. Min'darr floated the pirate out over the bow, dangling him above the ocean.

Min'darr then also rose, looking aft at the crew. "Suffer not to steal from others. Your duty is to help them. That is the single way can you buy back your souls," he howled. This call was followed by another flame, shot out from the ghost's mouth. It caught each sail, both masts, engulfing the ship's rigging in an intense, drenching fire. Burning pieces of sailcloth and rigging began raining onto the decking. The din of burning wood crackled in their ears. The crew instantly worked to fight the blaze.

Only a few saw the "ghost" drop into the sea, taking their captain with it.

*

Min'darr kept the unconscious Gur'ata within a magical seal, isolated from the world. It gave him time to recount to the others back on Goat Island the events that had unfolded along with the rest of his plan. Now, he was tired. Despite his ability to channel the eldritch energies through him, manipulating it to his wishes, the efforts took their toll on his physical body. He had his limits, just as the Mulu had warned. He drew more of those energies from the earth and sea, then took a nap, bidding them to wake him in an hour's time.

In the meanwhile, Koo'bla, Ram'ili, and Mah'zan discussed their parts in the magician's scheme. "I've never been a god before. How am I supposed to act?"

"I don't know about you, but I'm going to be indignant," Ram'ili said.

"So, like every other day, eh?" Mah'zan quipped. Koo'bla stifled a chuckle, then laughed aloud with her son. Ram'ili finally joined in, not able to contain her laughter.

"Just you wait, smart boy ... one day when you least expect it ... probably in a stew or soup, I'll exact my revenge."

"Anyway ..." Koo'bla shouted. "We're supposed to scare this pirate into thinking he's dead, yet he can 'buy his life back' if he testifies against Wada. How are we going to scare a pirate? This pirate especially?"

"Maybe we can be giants. That'll make him think seriously about it. What happens if he says no? What leverage do we have?" Mah'zan asked.

"Me," Min'darr said as he rejoined the group. "What have you got?"

"We need something to keep him scared. So ... we thought if we were giants, he'd be intimidated, more willing to listen," Mah'zan summarized.

"Not bad. It will be easier for me if he were shrunken. That way he would be so much smaller than the things around him ... the land. He wouldn't feel as prone to run for it, either. Truth be told, it's easier for me to shrink one pirate than to make the three of you giants. I'll make sure you look godly to him anyway."

"Three of us? What about you? What're you going to be doing?" Ram'ili asked brusquely.

"I'm the threat. I'll be behind him in the form of a dragon once I introduce him to you gods as the ghost of his sailor, Mic'raf. I really love being a dragon! Anyway, I can eat his soul. Then he'll suffer in my fires throughout eternity. That's as good a starting point as any.

"You can also threaten him with other things," Min'darr added. "Be reasonable, though, and I'll do my best to conjure up something he won't like. I also want you to laugh at him. Tell him his 'friend,' Wada, laughed when he'd heard about his death. I'll show him something like a scry to make him think Wada has betrayed his trust. Regardless, you have to be mean, or at least angry for the way he's wasted his life. Then offer him a chance for redemption, a way to, you know, make up for some of his evil deeds. Any questions? Fine. Let's go scare a pirate."

*

Gur'ata became aware of his own physical presence, blinking, yet not able to focus on any one thing. The pirate noticed and looked intently at the shimmering of his own skin. Mic'raf stood next to him, also with a ghostly shimmer.

"They will see you now. I wish you well. My task to bring you here is done. It is time for me to pay the price for my earthly choices." With that, Min'darr the spectre let out a mournful wail and disappeared.

Gur'ata stared out ahead of him. He saw a meadow between he and some massive hills in the distance. He stood on a flat rock above the ground. It seemed a long way down. In fact, everything seemed kind of big. He gawked around, checked out his hands, his legs ... everything about him looked ghostly, yet he couldn't say he could actually feel them.

"Look what we have here," a powerful voice resounded. "This abuser is finally dead to appear before us." It was Ram'ili, but due to Min'darr's magic, the shrunken Gur'ata saw a luminescent, robed figure ten times his size. Next to her stood two other godly figures. All three were monstrously tall, wrapped in some kind of glittering heavenly aura.

"What goes on here?" he asked, louder than normal to be certain he was heard.

Koo'bla laughed mightily, very exaggerated. "What is this? The little man questions us?"

Mah'zan answered. "My lords, do you not recognize this one? He was known as Gur'ata, a powerful pirate of the Southern Sea. He has killed more innocent souls in his time alive as have any twelve other rogues. He died this day after he killed yet another innocent, his sailor Mic'raf. I sent Mic'raf back to bring him to us, to end the terror he has caused.

"He has also made a fortune in stolen goods, selling on the black market the things he had stolen. That would not be the case for his co-conspirator, the cretin Ma'hana Wada. Gur'ata sold the goods he'd stolen from Wada, splitting the profit with the merchant, defrauding his customers."

"What? This idiot worked with Wada?" Ram'ili laughed. The others joined in.

Gur'ata stood dumbfounded as they spoke, his ire growing, not fully comprehending his status. "Explain yourselves, damn you!"

Ram'ili gestured to Min'darr, standing behind the pirate, to lift him. She held out her hand as Min'darr magically lifted Gur'ata to within a few feet of her. "You, little man, are dead. You drown at our bidding and you stand before us now, a marred, pitiful soul awaiting your sentencing for eternity."

"I do not believe a word of your story. I stand here just as alive as I when I woke this morning." He pounded on his chest. "See I am still here," he declared.

"How much of his arrogance need we suffer?" Mah'zan asked.

"This body you claim as yours is being kept alive for you for this meeting, to ease your transition to death. If you'd rather," Koo'bla asked, "we can be rid of it."

"Aye," he growled, "free me of my dead body."

Min'darr rolled his eyes, sending his magic out. Gur'ata began gasping for air, then went totally numb, unable to move or breathe. He collapsed into a pile before the "gods."

A quick, two-minute exchange of ideas between them, then Min'darr reversed the magic. Gur'ata's eyes fluttered open. He found himself floating above his body. He no longer shimmered and could feel nothing.

Min'darr's magic kept him numb, floating above an image of his own body. "Now do you believe?" Ram'ili asked.

"I want to see my face," he demanded.

Min'darr was growing weary managing so many spells at one time. He allowed his dragon form to speak from behind Gur'ata. "I am here to claim Gur'ata. His soul is mine. I will wait no more." His voice was both loud and gruff.

Gur'ata's eyes widened in terror as he saw the dragon. "What is this?" he gasped.

Koo'bla answered. "This is the Demon of Death. If a soul cannot remain based on the life it led, it is eaten by the Demon. It ends. There is no eternity, there is no suffering ... well, of course, not beyond being eaten ..."

"... and the one hundred years it takes to digest such a foul soul as his," Min'darr growled.

"But I feel nothing. How can it hurt, Dragon?"

"You dare to challenge me? Your impudence will be your undoing!" Min'darr the dragon shot a bolt of fire from his mouth. It grazed the pirate. He screamed. "The pain you have felt is a thousand time less than you will suffer for a century before I'll let you truly die."

He looked at the others. "Decide his fate. I grow weary of your tolerance for this fool."

Mah'zan's godly figure spoke. "Patience, Demon, for I would ask you if you would prefer to digest this one or would you like to digest Wada?"

"It matters not. I will digest them both. Wada will die and I will digest him then."

Koo'bla jumped in. "Perhaps the Gur'ata would be able to hasten Wada's death by admitting his deeds. They have a court in which they sentence criminals to death, do they not?"

Gur'ata hesitated. "They do."

"Would you tell a court of Wada's crimes, if we were to pardon you?"

"What?" screamed Min'darr's arcane dragon. "No, I do not approve. This one is mine!" Min'darr held out a glowing claw. Gur'ata screamed, cringing from pain as the dragon's magic washed through him. "I want his end! Now!" he growled fiercely.

Ram'ili yelled back. "And I want Wada's end first!"

Gur'ata called out, "Wait, please," until the dragon eased his pain. "If I do this, can I have me life back? Can I live again?"

"If we grant you your life, you must live it honestly. Merchant, shipper, lackey, it does not matter," Koo'bla said.

"But if you steal anything of any worth, you will immediately die. Your soul will go directly within the Demon," Mah'zan added.

"No chance to escape or to make a deal. Do you understand?" Ram'ili finished.

"Aye, I do. And I will. We have a deal," Gur'ata said without hesitation.

Immediately in front of the pirate as a flash of fire, Min'darr the dragon appeared the same size as Gur'ata. He pressed his claws against Gur'ata's chest. The pirate grimaced, screaming yet again. His flesh sizzled.

"You are marked, mortal. You are bonded to me through honesty. Break that bond and you will suffer as no human soul has suffered before." Min'darr the dragon disappeared. Gur'ata became like a statue, frozen in time.

*

Things returned to normal. The others ran to help Min'darr who'd dropped to his knees.

"Are you all right?" Koo'bla asked, kneeling next to him.

Min'darr looked very pale. Sunset was upon them. "Well done, everyone. I'm just tired. We'll let the commander know in the morning. Maybe they can round up Wada and his people ... in time for a tri ... trial." With that, he drifted off to sleep.

As he lay there, Ram'ili noticed something in the gathering dark. She stooped, pulling his shirt up. "Hey, look at this? Ever see anything like this before?"

They saw small blue particles coming up out of the ground where he lay, going into him. Koo'bla yanked Ram'ili's arm back as she reached toward them.

"What are you doing, Ram'ili? You don't know what that is? It might hurt you! Please, don't."

She smiled at her dear friend, then jammed her finger under Min'darr. Nothing happened. "They're like little lights," she said, "but they don't make any shadows, or light up anything as they pass. Most curious."

Mah'zan knelt to examine them as well. "Here, let me try. He gave us a tiny bit of magic years ago. It's how he found me," Mah'zan explained.

Ram'ili sat back on her haunches. "I know. He gave me some too."

Koo'bla looked at her with eyes wide. "Really?" She leaned across to her partner giving her a kiss and a hug.

"Yep," Ram'ili said. "He's like a brother to me now. He gave it to me before we came to rescue you from Wada's dream room." Koo'bla and Ram'ili spent a moment looking at each other. Then they settled in to sleep. Tomorrow promised to be another interesting day.

An Arcane Battle

The next morning Min'darr changed Gur'ata into something small and thin, then tucked him into his jacket's pocket. "I'll deliver him to Commander Jak'enge for safe keeping. I'll let him know where to find the *Scourge*.

"Thank you all for everything," he said to them. "You have helped me immensely keep focused on the tasks that need to be done. I remain hopeful that we'll to be able to capture Wada, too."

Koo'bla sighed. "So, you're just going to go off. What happens to us if something happens to you? Or are you that invincible?"

Min'darr thought a moment. "Good point. I'm sorry. I can fly you down to Kim'stwa if you'd like."

Koo'bla said, "We've talked. We're not interested in going anywhere until we know Wada's in jail."

"Fine, I'll go see Jak'enge first. I can let him know where you are. Do you want him to send a boat, or do you want to wait for me?

"When can we expect you?" Ram'ili asked, standing next to Koo'bla.

"Oh, I'm not sure. Maybe between lunch and tea time," he said sarcastically. "There's no schedule for something like this. That's ... that's ridiculous. I'll plan to be back or send you some kind of signal by dusk." He swirled his arms, vanishing.

"Well," Koo'bla huffed. "Kind of moody, don't ya think?"

Mah'zan said, "I don't think I can blame him."

"Of course not, you're a man," Ram'ili said.

"C'mon! He's not going to forget about us," Mah'zan sighed.

Koo'bla sighed back at him. "So you're fine with sitting here. Not knowing anything, at the mercy of whoever shows up? I'm really uncomfortable not knowing. And how are we supposed to get hold of him if something happens here?"

A blue light flashed next to them. Min'darr stood where he'd been standing before.

"So, now you're spying on us?" Koo'bla asked.

"No, Bisha, listening without being expected to explain things that have no explanation," Min'darr said. "Come over here, please" He led them to the nearby rocks.

"So you can follow along to mark my progress, I've awakened the scrying pool. The magic you each have should be enough to direct its view. If not, combine your magic by holding hands. Your efforts should succeed." He sent a blue spark into the scry pool. "If you need me, tell the pool to summon me.

"After I see Commander Jak'enge, I'm going to confront Wada and his fake sheriff. What the pirate told us yesterday is enough for me to justify changing them both into worms."

Min'darr looked up across the sky, noting the direction the clouds were drifting. His blue aura surrounded him as he changed, becoming wispy and cloud-like, losing his form. He drifted up with the breeze, floating out over the hills toward the distant shore.

The three checked the island's shores and met again at the scrying pool. The sun already warmed the air that the gulls rode out over a gentle surf.

*

"Really?" Min'darr said to the commander as they stood in the outer office of the naval base.

Jak'enge nodded, saying again, "Yes. We located the *Scourge* about fifteen miles south of here. One of my captains spotted a plume of smoke and went to render aid. He was shocked to see it was Gur'ata's flagship. His crew prepped for a battle," he told him.

"They got none. Every single sailor stood with their arms up, gave up willingly, begging to be taken off ship. To a man, they told the story of Gur'ata being shanghaied by the ghost of a crewman he'd killed earlier in the day. They searched. Gur'ata wasn't on board"

"Surely, Commander," Min'darr scoffed, "it sounds to me that it was too well-rehearsed to explain his absence perhaps?"

"Possible, Master Magician, quite possible. Please, I'm a terrible host. Come into my office. We can at least sit as we talk. I insist."

After settling in, Jak'enge closed his door. Min'darr said, "I have been less than honest with you, Commander. I apologize. It was I who dealt with Gur'ata."

"Tell me more," he said.

"I found his ship by a magical process known as scrying. I watched as he keel hauled one of his sailors. His name was Mic'raf. I decided he needed to be frightened into cooperating, so I visited his boat as Mic'raf's ghost."

"That pretty much sums up what I've heard. Well done. What's his status now?"

Min'darr produced the miniaturized pirate, assuring the commander that he would be a cooperative witness.

Commander Jak'enge was, to say the least, ecstatic accepting the magician's gift. He gestured to the enchanted dagger. "At least we have a failsafe."

"Never hurts to be prepared," he said in agreement.

"Besides what we know, it's been very satisfying having the charred *Scourge* chained up at our dock. I've already interviewed more than a dozen of the pirates. They've given me so much information, I could lock Gur'ata away for seven lifetimes. Thank you again for the enchantment, Min'darr. I'll put our friend here in safe keeping." He stood behind his desk to tuck Gur'ata's essence between two books on the bookshelf.

"The Admiralty has sent word that Judicial Advocate Sar'kat will be here to start hearings at noon tomorrow. She is a very tough judge, sending more than half coming before her to prison or to hang."

"Is there any chance, Commander, that Wada can be included in these proceedings?" Min'darr asked.

"I've actually checked into that. We are limited to charging him as an accessory to piracy. Other than that, his criminal charges would be civil violations for fraud, deception, and possibly a criminal charge for grand larceny."

"That's a good start. What about the murder of the crews of the ships that have been raided?" Min'darr asked.

"Well, if Gur'ata testifies that Wada instructed him to kill them, yes. Otherwise, those charges would be against the pirates. Wada's sheriff, Mok'sni, by the way, is being investigated by the city. He's been suspended pending that. It is coming together, but, of course, everything takes longer than it should."

"Thanks, Commander. I'll see you tomorrow morning."

Jak'enge shook his hand. "It would be best to have your family with you, too."

"That reminds me, we are camped out on Goat Island. If anything happens to me, please send a boat to bring them back."

"Guaranteed, my friend. Happy to." They shook hands.

Min'darr left the navy building unsure of exactly how to proceed. He wanted more than anything else to end Wada's reign of thievery. *How many lives has his greed cost? I need to find him.*

Walking toward the wharf, he sidestepped a large puddle. It reminded him of the others, probably watching him right this moment. He looked up waving to them.

"Argh, that's it!" he muttered to himself. He scanned the area to find a smaller puddle in a somewhat more secluded spot. *No sense attracting everyone's attention. This is wizard's business,* he thought. As he searched, he considered his statement.

"*Wizard,*" he repeated. "*More in the process of becoming one, I guess,* he mused. "*They are always wise. I've got a good deal to learn if I ever can say that I'm that. So, I'll stick with magician for now.*" He found a hollowed area behind a wall next to some crates brimming with puddles. *Perfect!*

Within a minute, Min'darr had awakened a pool to show him Wada's location. The image cleared on a room full of people. Wada and Mok'sni sat together behind a desk. It was considerably smaller than the one Min'darr had seen. *Probably burned in the fire.* Around the room, either sitting or standing, were five other men in very dignified clothing, surrounded by box after box of paper files.

He listened to their conversation. "... repeated claims for piracy. Fifteen, in fact, over the course of the past eleven years. That exceeds the international shipping average by three hundred seventy-eight percent, sir." The man speaking sat directly in front of Wada.

"We then have processed twenty-nine salary compensation claims for workers injured during the course of their labor during the past eighteen months. Did you know, sir, that we, as a matter of course in our investigations, contact those workers? None of them could ever be located, let alone interviewed to confirm their injuries."

An elderly man sitting to the side spoke. "It would appear, therefore, Master Wada, that you have become a bit of a pirate yourself, sir. Oh, ahh ... I should add, we continue to investigate this fire you recently suffered. Our decision of coverage and damages is still pending."

Wada sat silently, looking out at no one in particular. In a small voice, he asked, "Are you denying my claims, then?"

"We are, too suspicious they are. You have provided little verifiable evidence, have never reported any of the thefts to the authorities ..."

Mok'sni interrupted. "I have filed every report with your company, Master Gud'ida. Since I am the law for this port and for Master Wada's company, that constitutes notice. You are free to examine my reports here."

"No, Sheriff Mok'sni. You yourself are currently suspended, under investigation by your own department for fraud as well as ... umm, shall we call it 'other irregularities.' We will not be your victim yet again."

He looked at Wada. "Your policies are all cancelled, sir, effective immediately. We will see you in court to be reimbursed the monies we have paid out for your previous fraudulent theft claims." He threw some papers on the desk in front of Wada. "These are subpoenas to produce the entirety of your records within the week, sir. Good day."

The group left with their files. Neither Wada nor Mok'sni moved. After some moments, Wada said in a quiet voice, "I have no one to blame but the magician. All of this ... his fault. It is too coincidental that this should happen now."

He turned to Mok'sni. "Bring in our three guests."

*

"Three 'guests'? Damnation! He couldn't have found them, could he?" Min'darr thought.

Ten minutes later, Min'darr landed on the island, still in dragon form. Wada's comment almost stopped his heart. He'd ended the scry and transformed, in a single move, desperate to see Koo'bla, Mah'zan, and Ram'ili in front of him. *He said "our three guests"? Maybe I should have watched longer ... couldn't take that chance!*

"Uncle! What are you doing here?" Mah'zan asked before Min'darr had finished transforming back into his normal human form.

"Thank the Creator!" Min'darr gasped. "I thought Wada had ... I mean, I was scrying him when he ... oh, never mind." He stepped closer, hugging his nephew. "I feared the worst ... that Wada had the three of you. Where's your mom?"

"They went off someplace to 'talk.' You know, women stuff. They'd been talking about some of the things they wanted to do, you know, like where they might want to live since their jobs in town got burned up."

Min'darr nodded. "Good," he said. "They need to plan things out. What about you?"

"Yeah, ya know, I have to do that too. Can't live with Mom the rest of my life, eh?" Mah'zan said. "I'm not sure. I did love sailing, though, too bad it was for such a putz."

"Let's round them up," Min'darr said. "We have to talk."

*

Shortly, Min'darr had updated the others. They'd a plan, of sorts. It always depended on things going the way they expected, which so far wasn't what usually happened. They all were expected at the naval hearings tomorrow. Mah'zan would testify about his ordeal with the pirate raid of his ship.

177

"With Wada's insurance fraud out in the open, he's going to strike back. I'll work on some spells to protect you from anything he may try. He is a dangerous man now that he's cornered." Min'darr thought, then asked aloud, "Are people this inherently greedy ... this evil?"

Ram'ili shook her head. "Thankfully no. People like Wada are the exception, believing they're too smart to get caught. He thinks he's invincible. You're so right, though. He is a desperate man. He has to realize that he's losing his grip on things.

"You said he claims that it's your fault. Did you have anything to do with the insurance company showing up?" she asked.

"Nope. I had no idea who to contact or how. I figured that could be more punishment for him later," Min'darr responded. "I really ..." He stopped, then looked around with a distinct frown on his face. "What was that? Did you feel something?"

They looked at each other, shaking their heads. "Feel what?" Koo'bla asked.

"A twinge, along the back of your neck, like a shiver," he detailed.

"Well, yeah actually, I did ... just now." Koo'bla asked.

The other two nodded. "Yes. What does it mean?" Mah'zan asked.

"I'm not sure. Felt weird, though." He closed his eyes. "Like a magical wave washing over us. I don't know what it was, and I'm not comfortable with it." He paused a moment, then opened his eyes. "We have to go. Now. C'mon ... like we did before." He glowed blue and another dragon transformation began.

They quickly climbed onto the base of his neck. Min'darr finished morphing into a dragon and again made them invisible. In their minds, they heard his thoughts. "I'm making us magically invisible as well, more than just physically. Something about that wave ... I don't know. I can't shake the idea that we need to be completely invisible."

Min'darr rose into the sky, taking them south, high out over the ocean, so far that Goat Island was little more than a dot on the horizon. He finally turned north toward the mainland, some seven miles west of the island.

"Look! Something's on fire," Koo'bla yelled, pointing at a rising column of smoke in the distance. "Another pirate ship?"

Looks more like our island. It feels wrong, like that wave we felt. Bad magic, if that's possible. How else can you make a whole island burn?

"Can we get closer to get a better look?" Ram'ili asked.

No, better that we steer clear. My dragon eyes can see everything for quite a distance. I can see fourteen goat carcasses on the beach closest to us. Even the rocks are burning. Definitely magic. If I didn't know any better, I'd say it looks like Wada has hired himself a magician. A good one, too.

*

They landed in the navy's shipyard, staying invisible until safely within the building housing the cells. One was empty. The others were filled with Gur'ata's crew of pirates. Commander Jak'enge was surprised to see them, telling Min'darr that he had not heard about another magician but would stay vigilant.

Min'darr placed protection spells on his family and the commander. He laid spells on the grounds, the air, water, and finally the navy's ships in the harbor as well. "Done," he said to no one. "They are as protected as I can make them. Now, Ma'hana Wada, it is time to end your career."

Min'darr walked into the marketplace, seeing it differently somehow. Instead of enjoying conversations with the people there as he'd done so many times, his senses were finely tuned. His awareness took in every detail. He felt like a hunter, stalking a quarry he didn't know, ready to attack or be attacked at any moment.

There was obviously other magic afoot. There was no denying what happened to Goat Island. The question plaguing him was where would he strike next.

He froze in place, concentrating on the feelings of his magic, until a familiar voice seeped into his consciousness. "And now, ladies and gentlemen, for our final act, I would like you to pay attention to this little ball. This magical sphere that refuses to obey the laws of gravity."

Despite the dire situation, he smiled, remembering the women, their struggling magic act, and the ball he'd enchanted for

179

them. The younger one saw him and waved. He waved back but continued on his way, staying intent on his quest.

A magical trap sprung. The colorful canvas fronts of three vendors' booths sprang at him like hungry mountain lions. Min'darr was instantly covered in the heavy cloth, wrapped into a cocoon. It lifted into the air, sailing out over the water to splash into the harbor, plunging to its murky bottom.

Three men stood at the pier's edge, gazing into the wet darkness. "Are we ready to get rich by destroying this fool?" asked the short one in a red turban. The other two nodded. The three stretched their arms out over the waters, jeweled rings on their fingers glowed yellow.

*

His first reaction was to beat it back but couldn't as his arms were instantly pinned against him. His arcane self recognized the yellow magic. He'd been aware of it, yet hadn't anticipated how close it was because it was so different from his own. He knew it was the same magic he'd felt earlier on the island. *Seems this mage set a trap by exposing his magic like bait. Lesson learned.*

Being wrapped up so completely didn't help him think.

His next thought was to become a dragon to destroy the mage who did this to him. But, being on the marketplace pier, too many people could get hurt. Water started seeping in around him. He knew he was underwater. *Magic is his weapon, so he won't rely on water to finish me off.*

With a sense of urgency, Min'darr recalled the eldritch stream he'd experienced in the mountain cave of the Mulu. Its calm, its infinity. He brought himself to feel the same, to be the same. He visualized the stream of arcane energies in the waters surrounding him. The thousands of small patches of magic he'd sensed flying to get Mah'zan ... summoning all of them. They responded, flowing quickly toward him within the harbor's water, concentrating them within the confines of the canvas that enveloped him. They formed an eldritch stream. He joined it.

*

Leaving Min'darr underwater until they felt he would be unconscious, the mages raised the canvas from the harbor, its

180

dripping mass hovering at the level of the pier. Throngs of people behind them screamed, running at the sight of the men glowing yellow, levitating the soaking canvas surrounded with bands of shimmering yellow light projecting from their many jeweled rings.

Together they chanted. Their yellow magic undulating with the rhythm of their chorus. It pulsated with the emphasis of key syllables, glowing ever brighter. Finally, a blinding surge spread out from them, striking the dripping canvas bundle as they ended their enchantment.

It burst as bright as the sun, yet as silent as a winter's night. Glowing embers hung in midair until they, too, were merely ash. The mages congratulated each other for their success.

All at once, the mage in the middle was struck in the head. Something hit him so swiftly and with such power it cracked through his skull, bursting out the other side of his head. He dropped to the pier, his weight carrying him under the railing, splashing into the water below.

The other two mages, frantically huddled together, shielding themselves in a yellow, magical dome. A young woman in a performer's costume stepped forward from her vendor's tent, holding out her hand. She looked at it expectantly. Nothing happened. Panic gripped her face as she frantically scanned around her for something. She ran back to her performer's booth, into the waiting arms of an older woman.

The mages dropped their shield. They walked deliberately toward the women, anger evident on both their faces. After three steps, their feet fused to the planking of the pier. Struggle as they might, they could not move any further. The magic holding them began creeping up their legs, turning their flesh and bones into the same wood as the pier's decking.

Before them a fog formed, taking on the shape of a person without solidifying. From it a voice emerged.

"From whence doth come thy eldritch energies?"

Neither spoke, busy fussing about, yanking on their legs in vain attempts to free themselves. The first mage, a shorter man in a red turban, gestured magically at the fog shape. Nothing happened, despite his many tries. Their yellow magic also bounced ineffectively off their legs as they continued their efforts to stop turning into wood.

The women shuddered as they watched what the magic was doing to the men. The men's legs had mostly turned to wood. Whatever spell had been cast would consume them until they stood as wooden statues.

The fog's voice repeated its same question. "From whence doth come thy eldritch energies?"

The second mage spoke, quickly, with fear tainting his words. "We'll tell you all ... anything you want to know if you stop this ... this spell." His fear overtook him. He batted at his wooden transformation as it rose to his waist. "On Rac'ken, the enchanted isle of the Southern Sea," the same mage said, panting.

"You idiot!" the shorter mage screamed. "You've killed yourself and most likely me as well."

"Wha ...?" the second mage blithered.

The shorter one screamed, "What is the Fifth Rule?"

The mage froze in terror as some realization came to him, followed by a grimace that distorted his face. His upper body, the only part not wood, writhed in ways flesh and bone should not. A second later, he screamed fiercely. The lower wooden parts of him began to smolder, cracking. His skin blistered and split, his insides spilling out as they boiled away, staining the pier. The figure slumped, unmoving yet smoldering.

The fog form materialized into Min'darr. "Speak quickly or become a permanent fixture for gulls to soil," he demanded of the remaining mage.

The remaining mage was wood up to his neck. As the spell continued upward, he managed to say, "You'll have to go there to find out for yourself." He managed one more blink before the spell was complete.

The women ran out to Min'darr. They hugged him, crying from fear.

He twirled his fingers and a magic blue ball appeared. He handed it to the younger woman. "When I gave you the first ball, you had to use it for your act. Sending it against the mage violated that, ending its magic, yet I am so very thankful that you did. This one has no such limitation. Use it carefully."

"Thank you, kind magician. How could you survive that?" she asked, pointing out across the waters.

Min'darr thought better than telling the details of entering the eldritch stream to step from one physical place to another within this same plane of existence. He merely said, "I was able to use my magic to be somewhere else."

Finding Wada

Min'darr surrounded himself with an eldritch aura, protection against any weapon or attack Wada could throw at him. He was ready to drag the man all the way to the capital city of Kim'stwa, if need be, to turn him over to the law. However, the plan he hoped to follow was simpler. Commander Jak'enge said he would arrange temporary jail quarters until the civilian police took him. Since Wada's sheriff, Mok'sni, probably had connections with the city's police, Min'darr preferred the navy's facilities.

He stopped.

Looming before him was the burned-out husk of the Wada Shipping offices. *Not a good thing not knowing where Wada is! Where is he working from now?* The wharf was fairly extensive. In addition to the main piers and marketplace connecting it to the town, the wharf had an expansive warehouse section along its western edge. It covered at least as far as a man could walk in half an hour. Min'darr expected some sign or notice ... something indicating a location for their offices since the blaze. There was nothing. Any one of the three dozen warehouses could be the one Wada used ... or more.

He looked out at the ships anchored in the harbor. Five of them flew Wada's banner. He could be on any one of them, able to flee at a moment's notice. Time was critical. He couldn't scry the entire harbor effectively. He instead opted to see it from a different perspective.

Moments later, having become an osprey, Min'darr rose above the burned offices and flew toward the warehouse section. Becoming a bird of prey, he had the advantage of eyesight more acute than a mere seagull. He recalled scrying the shipping magnate before while he visited there with his sheriff, saying his real records were stored there. So, searching for him amidst the warehouses made sense.

As much as he wanted to confront Wada, he realized that no confrontations would be needed if he could find the records. *The police could collect the records and Wada would be as good as convicted. He's not a young man now. I'll bet he'll be a very old man when he gets out of jail, if he gets out.*

Min'darr flitted over the tops of the buildings, watching for any indication that Wada was there. Many people were working in the course of loading and unloading the ships using the port. They talked as they worked. By eavesdropping, Min'darr was able to understand that the majority of the dock workers were simply people earning a living.

Then he heard a voice he recognized, louder than the others. He landed at the roof's edge of the closest building, glancing down. He saw Mok'sni in his police blues, despite his suspension from the force, yelling at a laborer who was on his knees, scooping up papers. A box had fallen off the pile of boxes on a cart.

"Put your back to it, you miserable grunt," he growled. "Get those papers, all of them— over there, too," he added as a gust of wind shuffled some along the pier. "Put 'em back! Get this cart to the loading dock so they can get aboard by dusk. You understand me, grunt?"

"Ye ... ye ... yes, sir. I'm on it, sir. Sorry, sir. It slipped off when we turned, sir. Sorry." The man scrambled after the sheets of paper skiting across the dock by puffs of wind. Min'darr wasted no time. He leaned ahead with wings outstretched and, like the paper, caught the breeze. He circled the building to come at a distant piece of paper from the other direction, snatching the sheet furthest from the trio. He wheeled about, skimmed the top of the next building. Within a second, he was out of sight.

Ospreys were not a rare occurrence on the wharf. From what he could tell, he hadn't been noticed. He listened but heard no more bellowing. Peeking down, the men were finishing collecting the last of the wayward papers. No more sign of Mok'sni.

Before he took a moment to read the paper he'd snatched, he transformed back to himself, scooting back a distance so he could not be seen from below. He heard the heavily loaded cart with the papers pass by him, presumably on their way to the docks. *I should follow that cart to see which ship it goes to.*

Min'darr picked up the paper. It was a list of crate numbers followed by other numbers. At the top of the page it said, "From *AquaWada* 17". He stood, folded it, and was in the process of walking along the roof's crest, stuffing the paper into his vest when the roof behind him rose up, splintered, and knocked him forward with a deafening blast. The explosion sent a fireball bursting through the roof twenty or so feet from him. *Right where I'd just been sitting!*

Fiery debris rained down on the entire area threatening other buildings in addition to some of the nearer ships in the harbor. Smoke and flames blew through the hole, as it did from the doorway. *Mok'sni!*

Min'darr quickly slid to the building's edge, then slipped down a rainspout. Instead of leaving to keep himself safe, his concern was for the sheriff. What was his fate? Had he left after berating the laborer? Or had he gone back into the building?

If inside, was he the cause of the explosion or its victim? Many dock workers were charging to the area to fight the fires. Min'darr could not risk being discovered here. He could certainly be accused of the explosion.

In order to investigate, Min'darr secluded himself behind some empty crates and focused his eldritch energies to become invisible. He also cloaked himself from the fires, then went into the warehouse. People were already at the closest doors throwing buckets of water onto the inferno. He moved further within, working his way to the doorway he'd last seen Mok'sni near, intent on learning the fire's origin. A large area had been scorched. The crates that had been there were either destroyed or blown aside. He looked up. The hole blown through the roof was very large. *Right where I'd been sitting.*

He moved past the last of those crates to find an indentation in the dirt floor. *This would have been the spot the explosion occurred, directly under the hole.* From there, something caught his eye. *There, against the pillar of the main wall.* He moved closer and could clearly see a mass of stained blue clothing slumped on the floor against the wall. No longer recognizable, no longer alive.

Wada is desperate ... even Mok'sni was expendable. Probably because he knew too much.

Min'darr extended his magic, working to calm the blaze. Soon, the fire crews had advanced to the point that they were stirring ashes, making certain the hot spots were controlled. He saw the fire department's captain come in to examine the scene. An invisible Min'darr watched as Captain Mac'fers found the body. "Better contact the police," he said to his aide, pointing to the body. "Another Wada property up in smoke? I'll bet a month's pay that this is the one who set this fire. I'm thinking this would be Wada's go-fer, Mok'sni, based on what's left of the uniform."

It was nearing dusk when he returned to the navy yard. He had dinner with his family and the commander. The story he told of the fire kept them on the edge of their seats.

Mah'zan and Ram'ili were visibly happy with the news of the sheriff's demise. She said, "At least we don't have to worry about him anymore." The others nodded.

Commander Jak'enge said he'd ordered his naval ships to cordon off the harbor's entrance, allowing no ships to enter or leave. He then held up the paper Min'darr had snatched when he was an osprey. "Any chance any more of these survived, Master Min'darr?"

Min'darr thought. "Not too likely, Commander. The warehouse explosion probably was centered around the records he'd kept. You remember, the ones his insurance company said they wanted to see. He wasn't stupid. He was obviously moving some of them. Too bad I didn't have a chance to follow the ones on the cart to see which ship they'd been placed on."

"Too bad. I have to wonder…, are they destined to be saved for whatever purpose he wants them for, or to be 'lost at sea'? Mah'zan questioned aloud.

There was a pause in the conversation. "I have to confront him, now," Min'darr declared.

"Wada's not going anywhere," the commander added. "The harbor is closed. We'd expect him to leave by one of his ships. But with the fire investigation involving him, the police will be watching every road out of town for him or anything associated with him."

Koo'bla put her hand on her brother's arm. "How long can you keep going, Min'darr? You have been deeply involved in every aspect of this for days. You have to be exhausted."

Min'darr smiled at them. "True. I've been tested by this more than I thought I would be ... or could be. It's good. This magic I can channel invigorates me as I use it. When I stop, I am tired, more from use as opposed to wear ... just the opposite of muscles.

"I'm growing more familiar with how to use it, too. More and more, the power comes with a thought. I can use it without the need to recite magical words of an actual spell. It's more instinctive." *Much to the chagrin of the Mulu,* he thought.

"Look, I'm fine. Energized, driven to put this man in prison. Now, if you'll excuse me," he said, standing. "Are you ready for the hearings tomorrow?"

Jak'enge nodded, smiling. "More than ready, my friend. Tomorrow marks the last day Master Wada will enjoy any legal freedom. He will officially become a wanted man."

"All the more important that I see him tonight," Min'darr stated as he left the room.

"Please be careful, my brother. I love you." Koo'bla called after him.

*

Min'darr left the building as the sun set, pausing to appreciate the beauty of the orange-streaked sky and its reflection on the seas, the brighter clouds lit the harbor for many minutes. He loved the contrast he saw between the bright clouds and the deepening blue of the evening sky. The inevitable darkness crept down from the hills, spurring the ritual lighting of the streetlights.

He was well known on the base by now, so he felt comfortable asking one of the sailors if he could borrow the bucket they were using. They helped him, joking with him. He walked to the pier, filled it, then he settled down alone to scry.

He saw the shipping magnate sitting in a captain's cabin in front of a plate full of gnawed-on chicken bones. He obviously hadn't lost his appetite in the midst of the recent chaos. Min'darr adjusted the scrying view to see which ship he was on. It was the ship *Crest Spray,* a smaller, single-masted schooner anchored nearest the mouth of the harbor at its breakwater.

Not on one of his own named ships, that dog. At least not on one of his cargo fleet, flying his company's banners. Now, how to best nab him? Well, first things first. I'll have to fly out there to get a closer look.

He emptied the bucket into the harbor, then transformed into a gull. Min'darr enjoyed the magical freedom of becoming other kinds of creatures, especially dragons. But he knew that this was a time for stealth, something a dragon wouldn't be good at.

He found the ship and perched atop the masthead. He spent some time watching and listening. Members of the crew spoke of not having any idea when they expected to depart. One said he'd be in favor of running the navy barricade. The two others he was with called him dumb, saying they would be "run down within an hour, then jailed for the Creator knows how long."

Nothing else was gleaned, so Min'darr changed into a rat and scooted down the mast. He chose to hide in a corner near a hatchway. As soon as it opened, he dove through, dropping down the ladderway. He magically broke his fall, then scampered toward the ship's aft where the captain's cabin was usually located.

He crouched, waiting, wanting to use magic to open the door. Restraint, however, he felt was the better course of action here. From within, the door opened. Min'darr lurched through, misjudging his clearance and hit the foot of the man exiting. Stunned, he dropped to the deck. The man bent down and scooped him up.

In his tight grip, Min'darr could not move, not enough to bite or scratch him.

The cabin was filled with cigar smoke which, with the door open, escaped out the open cabin windows. Wada sat within. "What is it, Captain?" he asked when he noticed the man in the doorway.

"Nothing, sir, a scared little rat is all." He held Min'darr out for him to see.

"Where? Oh, I see. Well, break its neck and be done with it."

The captain strode to the porthole saying "I respect life more'n that, sir. I'll let 'im fight with the fish 'n the birds," tossing Min'darr out.

"Wait!" Wada screamed. "Its eyes ... are they blue?"

Min'darr the rat hit the water before he heard the captain's reply. *I'll thank him later for disposing of me as quickly as he did,* he thought. With a quick blue flash from just under the ship, Min'darr became a shark. *This way I don't have to worry about being eaten.*

He swam around the ship a few times, contemplating his next move. If this was the ship those records had been brought to, he had to save it from being destroyed. Then a thought crossed his mind. He wondered if sharks actually smile because he felt like he was.

Swimming beneath the ship, he changed into an enormous octopus. As such, he gripped its keel. It wasn't too soiled, some barnacles and algae grew across its wooden bottom. *Too bad it all has to go bad. Dirty rotten wood spreads quickly.*

Min'darr cast his spell. In the dark waters, a gray film fanned out from each of his tentacles until the entire keel of the vessel was infected with a grey rot. As he let go of it, he felt the wood had softened. He swam away and crawled up onto the breakwater, becoming an owl for its night vision because he wanted to be sure to watch.

The ship creaked, then listed. Shouts from the crew filled the night air. A dozen or so men appeared on the deck, running about, gawking over the sides. *As if there was anything to see,* he thought. Suddenly, a great geyser of water shot up from the deck hatchways as the *Crest Spray* sank into the harbor, first to the gunwales, then, with a pause, the harbor waters cascaded over its sides, swamping the ship. There was no time to man the lifeboat, so the sailors abandoned ship and swam toward the breakwater.

Hidden by the night, Min'darr fluttered onto another area. Within a few minutes, Wada's voice could be heard cussing and questioning what happened as he swam noisily to the nearby rocks. The top two yardarms of the ship's main mast was all that could be seen of Wada's ship.

Min'darr flew back to the navy base and, as himself, told the guards to round up the sailors making their way along the breakwater—as a security measure, of course. The sailors formed a line on the breakwater to escort some of the more reluctant sailors to the base.

When Wada came to shore, he saw Min'darr standing next to Commander Jak'enge and swore. "You! I should have known, damn you!"

The soggy shipping company head was led off to a nice, dry jail cell.

The Trial

"All rise."

The crew's cafeteria had been transformed into a courtroom. Judicial Advocate Sar'kat, a shorter, slender woman with just a touch of grey in her hair, entered the room and sat at a long table against the narrower wall. Her office's logo banner hung on the wall behind her. Paintings of naval ships had also been tacked to the walls. Her station included a stuffed leather chair, some law books, as well as volumes of naval regulations. To her right was the navy's flag. To her left was the national banner of Rougahn. A tall, crystal pitcher of water, some glasses, a gavel, and the naval dagger from Jak'enge's office completed the staging for the trial.

Commander Jak'enge stood next to the main table. Everyone stood until Sar'kat took her place at that table. "The case of the Government of Rougahn against the crew of the pirate Gur'ata is hereby convened. The Honorable Judge Sar'kat, Judicial Advocate of the Department of the Navy presiding." Jak'enge took his place at a side table with pen in hand, ready to take notes.

Judge Sar'kat cleared her throat as she paged through some papers. "We will be here for a month if we take each man's case individually, from the reading of the charges through testimony and findings."

She looked at the mob of chained sailors. "There are forty-three sailors here, all charged with petty theft, larceny, and piracy which is a capital offense. Would each of you please rise to take the oath?"

They rose and then swore to tell the truth, the whole truth, and nothing but the truth.

"Captain of the Guard," she continued, "please present each of the accused as I call their names.

"When you appear, please state your name for the record, then answer my questions directly. Understood? Let's us proceed." She reached out to turn the enchanted dagger so that it pointed to the spot each would stand.

The guards presented each sailor. Each one stated his name. Judge Sar'kat asked each in turn how they pled to the charges. Each pirate, in turn, responded with a "guilty" plea. They then were led back to their holding area.

Once the pirates were in place, Judge Sar'kat addressed the group. "Each of you have pled guilty of the charges read to you. I therefore find each of you guilty as charged. You are all hereby sentenced to ten years' hard labor in the national prison system. Your time will be effective as of today. Captain ..." she said to the Captain of the Guard, "please arrange transport as soon as practical for these convicts to the Kim'stwa Penitentiary for their intake, eventually being assigned to different project locations. Escort them back to their cells. We will take a ten-minute recess."

While the prisoners left the room, Jak'enge spoke quietly with Sar'kat, with Ram'ili and Koo'bla looking on. Koo'bla exhaled with a puff. "Wow, that woman doesn't mess around. One—two—three. Almost fifty pirates heading to prison in less than an hour."

"Yep," Min'darr said. "The commander said she has an awesome reputation. I can see why. Can't wait to see what she'll do to Gur'ata and Wada."

Mah'zan asked, "What was our jolly ol' pirate's reaction when you brought him back to reality?"

"Not bad, really. Remember, he was aware of nothing. So, when I brought him back, it was like a blink of the eye to him from when he was pleading with the 'gods.' I reminded him of his promise, which he acknowledged."

"What do you think will happen to him, Uncle Min'darr?" Mah'zan asked.

Before he could answer, Commander Jak'enge hit the tabletop several times with the gavel, calling out for order. "Court is back in session." They sat back down, ready to resume. Min'darr noted that the dagger was still pointed at the witness stand.

Judge Sar'kat said, "Bring in the prisoner."

The pirate Gur'ata was led into the room. He wore wrist chains that the guard secured to the witness stand. "State your name," Commander Jak'enge said.

"Seriously? Y'all know me well enough," Gur'ata retorted. The angry looks he got prompted him to comply. "All right, me name's Gur'ata."

Sar'kat peered at him. "Gur'ata, you are charged today with eighty-seven counts of piracy on the high seas and at least thirty-one murders of both your victims and members of your own crew. There is also a list of trade violations that would take an hour to read. Interestingly, you have refused to have legal counsel. How do you plead?"

Gur'ata smiled at the judge, bowing slightly before saying, "Guilty, me lady. Guilty as hell."

The judge stood, her chair scratching at the floor as it was pushed back. She moved around her table, taking the commander's dagger as she passed. Walking deliberately to the witness stand, she stopped inches in front of Gur'ata.

"Then I find you guilty. I sentence you to die." In a single motion, she pulled his beard out, tipping his head back, and drove the blade up through his throat into his brain. "This is for my sister."

Gur'ata collapsed with his eyes wide, quickly dying, soaked in his own blood.

The room, silent in its initial shock, erupted. Min'darr and the others stood, screaming warnings that the man was to be a prime witness in the next case. Commander Jak'enge rushed to the stand to render aid to the pirate, stopping short when he faced the point of Sar'kat's dripping blade.

"What have you done?" the commander begged.

"I have exacted justice," she sneered. "From the moment he pled guilty, he was convicted to die. There was no reason to delay things since I saw in this an opportunity for personal vengeance. Fifteen years ago, he raided a ship my sister was on to attend school in Kordahl.

They murdered everyone. Justice is served. Get your men to clean this up.

"Court is in recess for one hour." She announced and dropped the dagger as she walked from the room.

*

One hour later, to the minute, court resumed.

Judge Sar'kat called for the prisoner. Ma'hana Wada was placed in the very stand where his pirate cohort had just died. "Excuse me, Your Honor, is there any chance I could have a cigar while my case is heard? I haven't been allowed to smoke all day."

She glared at him. "No." He held out his opened hands with a slight shrug of his shoulders in response.

"You, sir, are charged with a plethora of crimes, most of these are under civil law. I have a letter here from the Port Authority remanding you to this court to be tried on these in conjunction with being party to piracy and fraud under the current import/export laws." She read through the lengthy list, finally asking him "How do you plead?"

"Not guilty, Your Honor. These charges are trumped up lies. There is no proof to any of them."

"We'll see, little man, we'll see." Sar'kat took a sip of water.

"And, hey! Where's my lawyer?" Wada asked.

"Your lawyer sent me a note saying he quit. Guess that means you have to represent yourself."

Turning to Jak'enge she said, "Commander, I understand you are the prosecutor for this matter."

"Yes, Your Honor," he said with an appropriate bow.

"Proceed."

A parade of witnesses were brought forth, including Capt. Mac'fers of the fire department, Min'darr, Mah'zan, Koo'bla, and Ram'ili. Each discussed the details of their dealings with Wada, highlighting how he cheated them, threatened them, and so forth.

Min'darr was also questioned about how his magic had allowed him to know things about Wada no one else could. He discussed, at length, his encounters with Mok'sni, whose loyalties lay with the shipping magnate. He finished with the discovery that the sheriff had died in the blast that destroyed Wada Shipping's warehouse.

"I assume you have some documentation ... some proof of your allegations?" she asked.

"That has been destroyed, Your Honor, by the fires in Wada's office complex and in the warehouse explosion. He has been most meticulous in his coverup, even the insurance company claims are in jeopardy without the paper trail he has worked so hard to eliminate," Min'darr stated.

Commander Jak'enge confirmed what Min'darr had said. He produced the one piece of paper rescued before the blast that Min'darr had snagged as an osprey. Judge Sar'kat examined it.

"What is its significance? It is a list of numbers ... a shipping form ... from a voyage perhaps? There is nothing here that proves it is a forgery, or fraudulent, or indicating any kind of crime. Is it coded, somehow?"

Jak'enge shook his head. "We have not been able to decipher any code in it, Your Honor."

"This is the extent of your proof, Commander?"

"At this time, Your Honor, yes. We have divers retrieving boxes containing records from the schooner Master Wada was occupying when it sank in the harbor last night."

"Really? Well, if this list is the extent of your proof," she said as she picked up another paper listing the charges against Wada, "you are sorely short of proving your case.

"Master Wada," she continued, looking at the man.

He was already smirking.

Judge Sar'kat sighed before she continued. "It would give me great pleasure to find you guilty of a few of these charges, if not all of them. I mean, there must be something generally scummy about you, sir. You have insurance companies filing suit against you. You have had two extremely suspicious fires destroy your offices and your warehouse and, therefore, all the records that would prove you to be everything these charges say you are. Your personal law enforcement officer, himself under investigation, is conveniently killed in an explosion causing the warehouse fire.

And the infamous pirate, Gur'ata, was allegedly ready to testify against you about your business dealings with him.

"I have no doubt, sir, that you are everything these people are asserting you to be ... a criminal, a conman, a thief, a crook ... basically the scum of the earth. Fortunate for you, they can offer no proof other than intangible testimony and a single piece of paper from your records which tells us nothing.

"Based on this, I cannot even hold you until their investigation of the records found within your sunken ship is finished. You are free to go. The charges against you are dismissed."

Min'darr sat in silent disbelief. His family joined in the cacophony of protests. Judge Sar'kat stood, obviously angered by the disrespect she saw in the protest. Commander Jak'enge stood next to her, banging on the tabletop, shouting for order.

After several minutes, things had calmed to the point that Sar'kat's voice could be heard again. "I would direct Min'darr to approach the bench."

They glanced at each other, uncertain about what this might mean. Min'darr stood and walked to the front, joining the judge.

"Master Min'darr," the judge said, "how did the ship Wada was on happen to sink?"

"Wada could not be allowed to escape, so I used magic to rot the ship's keel."

She nodded. "As a duly sworn officer of the court, I hereby place you under arrest for criminal damage to property." She pointed her finger under Min'darr's nose. "You have broken a law, Master Magician. Despite your national status, I expect you to face that law's consequence. Any magic on your part to escape will result in an immediate death penalty. Commander, confine him to a cell."

Captured

The entire wing was empty, except for him. The others were put in another section, "to avoid collusion" according to his guard. The meal had been tolerable. To idle the time, he fed a rat the leftovers from his dinner plate. He cast a spell on it allowing it to talk to him.

The rat told him little, except that the others ... the smoky man, the lady, and the big boss were together in another room where there was lots of food.

Odd that they'd all be together like that. His suspicions were enough to attempt to scry under the guard's nose. Min'darr tucked himself into the corner of his cell. Thus secluded, he poured the water from his dinner pitcher into the now-empty plate. He was forced to wait for the rat to drink its fill.

After his incantation, the water rippled, then showed the threesome sitting in the commander's office. What was more odd, the commander squatted to be face to face with the seated judge. A blank stare dominated her expression. Jak'enge spoke in whispers.

"... sister's murder. You are happy now that the pirate responsible is dead. Ecstatic because it was by your own hand. Sweet revenge. Done and proper. Grnatta Loy."

He turned toward Wada, who also had a very blank expression. "You will sail to the Tan'diali Islands. Once there, you will set up a new company without using your name. In fact, you will call yourself Myr'dal. Your company will be called Global Commodities. You know nothing about Wada Shipping. You remember nothing of your past life except for me. I will be your cousin.

"Follow the laws until I come to visit you. Then we will set up banking for me. I will transfer all our money there when I retire next year. Grnatta Loy."

Min'darr sat speechless. *I have searched this entire complex with my magic and found no other magic. At least not since the three yellow mages. How can he do this? He has no magic. What are those words 'Grnatta Loy'?* His magic knew no such words as part of an incantation. He stretched out his magic, again feeling no other magic, no abnormalities.

"Hey! What are you doing?" the guard spoke harshly.

"What? Nothing ..." he said. "Just thinking." He stood, stepping on the edge of the water bowl, making it look like a clumsy accident. "Oops. Sorry."

"I wanted you to know that the lights are going out for the night. And, umm ..."

Min'darr cocked his head to look at the guard who looked less threatening.

"I ... umm, I wanted to say that I'm sorry this went down as it did. I ... no, we've all heard about Wada. We know he's a crook. If there was some way I could help, I would. Others would, too."

"Quickly then, what kind of power does the commander possess to control others as readily as he does?" Min'darr asked in a whisper.

"Yeah, he kinda does, doesn't he? Gets us all to do anything, really. Kinda strange 'cause it goes beyond his rank. I don't know. I remember that one of the master boatswains said he saw stuff like that down in the Southern Sea. He said the commander served down there for a while, too. Look, I gotta go. Good luck, sir. I hope things go well for you." He left. The wing's lights went out immediately after the clunk of the closing lock resounded down the short hallway.

It took not quite a moment for him to decide. *I have to find out what Jak'enge is doing to control Wada, and apparently the judge, too.* Then another thought, more ominous than he could imagine took hold. *Could he do this to my family? Ram'ili?* Not understanding exactly what Jak'enge was able to do left him with no clue to form an answer. His pulse and his breathing quickened. "I have to protect them. I can't do that from here," he muttered to the rat, sitting next to the overturned plate. A blue flash filled the cell block for an instant. When darkness resumed, the rat sat alone.

*

He appeared next to the area where he'd felt Mah'zan. His magic told him that the women were together in a separate room down the hall. His nephew was alone, so Min'darr passed through the window and reformed in front of Mah'zan.

When he saw his uncle, Mah'zan sighed. "Thank the Creator! You got out! Can you untie me?"

Min'darr saw his hands laying across his lap. He looked and saw no ropes on his hands, arms, legs, or around the chair. "What are you talking about? You're not tied to anything. Come on, we have to get your mom and Ram'ili."

"Uncle Min'darr! You have to untie me. Can't you see the ropes? My ankles, my arms ... what's wrong with you?"

Min'darr stared at him. *He's been here,* he thought. "Mah'zan, did Commander Jak'enge come in to talk with you?"

"Yeah, he did. Why?"

Min'darr realized that he was subject to whatever the commander's influence was. Without knowing how to break it, he was powerless. He waved his hands in front of him, mimicking a spell gesture. "There, let's go."

Mah'zan flexed his fingers. "Thank you." He walked to his uncle and the two crept toward the door. Min'darr saw no presence in the hallway, so he looked back to say "Let's go find ..."

He didn't get a chance to finish the statement. The club Mah'zan wielded crunched against the side of his head.

*

He couldn't open his eyes, something was wrapped around his head. *Ow, my head! Pain! What happened?* He tried moving but couldn't. Everything seemed immobilized. *Pressure on my back ... back of my head. Lying down ... tied up really well!*

Allowing his magic to work, it swept through him relieving his pain. He focused his senses. No movement. No sounds, except for the distant goings on of a typical day. Waves. And ... he

200

listened harder, picking up heartbeats and breathing ... of a total of twelve people. He stilled his own breathing. *Who are they all?*

"He's awake."

A sudden jab of pain shot through his side. *I got kicked.* He turned his magic to protect himself. A second kick resulted in a moan from the person kicking him.

"Your magic is a remarkable thing," the familiar voice uttered. "I can't wait to learn it from you."

Min'darr recognized Jak'enge's voice. He let his magic see through whatever covered his eyes. The commander was standing next to him. *I'll pretend to be blinded. It might be the edge I'll need.* He used his eldritch powers to scan the room. Jak'enge, the judge, Wada, Mah'zan, Koo'bla, Ram'ili, and six armed guards.

"I'd be hard pressed to teach you a simple card trick," Min'darr said, allowing some of his anger to taint his words.

"Oh, sure you will, and happily, too. You, like everyone else, will simply do whatever I ask. Despite your magic, my friend, I will control you. You have no choice," Jak'enge said.

"But first, I have to say, this magic of yours is totally remarkable. It saved your life today, several times. I tried stabbing you and my knife's blade dissolved. My guard's sword did the same thing. We tried suffocating, choking, and finally burning you. Nothing worked. Nothing we did could penetrate that magical aura that surrounds you.

"So, since I can't get rid of you, I'll hypnotize you, too. That will make you the most powerful member of my entourage."

Min'darr heard what he needed. *Hypnotize!* His magic quickly brought to his consciousness what it was ... except nothing about how to fight it.

"This will work out so much the better. I learned how to do this from on old witchman in the southern archipelago of Conda'Strano. I saved him from some of my drunken crewmates and, as a thank you, he taught me his tricks. It's worked beautifully. I was a full ensign by the time we docked at our next port-of-call.

"A year later, on my next voyage to the islands, I had him killed ... getting rid of the evidence, you know?

"So, why don't you free yourself and see what awaits?"

"I'm actually quite comfortable, Commander, thank you. So how does your hypnosis work, anyway?" Min'darr asked calmly. Min'darr knew he'd have to challenge him. He suspected that the others were already hypnotized. They would most likely act to defend him. *How best to fight this?*

"Let me give you an example." He snickered as he spoke. "Mah'zan, come here please."

Mah'zan walked to Jak'enge's side. Min'darr looked for any irregularity in his gait, in his stance, in his face. There was nothing evident to be able to say his nephew was or was not hypnotized.

"Mah'zan, who are these people to you?" he asked, pointing.

His nephew answered cordially, pointing to each as he spoke. "She is my mother, Koo'bla. This is Ram'ili, my mother's partner. This is my uncle, Min'darr."

The commander then asked, "Do you love them?"

"Of course I do. They're my family," Mah'zan explained.

The commander pulled a dagger from his belt and handed it him. "Kill the one you love the most."

Mah'zan calmly took the weapon by its handle, then turned to face the two women. They stood stoically as he walked to them. He put his hand on his mother's shoulder to brace her and drove the knife toward her chest.

Min'darr carefully watched the entire thing. When Mah'zan grasped Koo'bla's shoulder, Min'darr acted, changing the dagger into a stalk of celery.

Mah'zan crunched the vegetable against his mother's ribs. They both looked down at the broken stalk, then looked at Jak'enge. The commander laughed. "Enough. Mah'zan, do not kill your mother," he said.

Mah'zan dropped the broken celery piece and faced the commander, standing next to Koo'bla.

"As you can see, Wizard, they are under my complete control. And so you are aware, should you do anything to injure or kill me, they will act on orders I gave them earlier. Orders that they will never tell you about. Following those orders will result in their deaths."

"So, how do you accomplish this?" Min'darr asked. "You have no magic, at least none that I can detect,"

"I would never be willing to give away any secrets. The old witchman would disapprove."

"Just as he disapproved of being murdered, I would imagine," Min'darr added.

"No doubt. However, we know that life will deal us things we aren't happy about, eh?" the commander answered.

In a blast of blue light, Min'darr left the confines of being roped and lying on the floor to standing before the naval commander. "I tire of the small talk. What is it you expect of me?"

"That you would willingly be hypnotized by me."

"To what end? What is it you expect to gain?" Min'darr asked.

"Can we sit down? Standing this long reminds me of my time in the academy."

Min'darr nodded. They sat at the conference table. Jak'enge had the guards stand behind Min'darr.

Min'darr nodded toward his family. "They could sit, too. Maybe get something to eat, if they haven't."

"They're fine right where they are. Nice try."

"What? You said you control them. Say 'Go get something to eat and then come right back.' It doesn't take a genius."

"All right. Unless ... can you do your magic on them while they're gone?"

"No. I am restricted to be in the line of sight to whatever magic I do. Otherwise, it doesn't work." Min'darr flat out lied to keep any edge he could.

"That's good to know. Mah'zan, is your uncle being honest?"

Mah'zan's forehead furrowed in thought. "I'm not really certain, Commander. I've never seen him do any magic from long distance, except for scrying."

"What's that?" the commander asked.

"It's like spying. He can see someplace far away in a magical pool of water," he replied.

"Koo'bla? Ram'ili?"

Both of them shook their heads.

"Okay. Go get something to eat. Then bring it back here to eat. Guards ... you are to follow them. Don't let them out of your sight." They left the room, leaving Min'darr and Jak'enge alone at the table.

"Now, my friend, let's begin," Jak'enge said.

Min'darr interrupted. "One question first," he said. "Why are you doing all of this? What's your goal?"

"That's actually two questions. It's a fair inquiry. Quite simply, for the money. My commission has a retirement amount, a pittance really. I knew I could be the ultimate robber, swindling banks of their entire vaults. Then I realized 'Why take chances getting caught?' So, I began collecting my work force. Wada has been mine for a decade at least. Now, we begin."

He directed him to look at his face, then he began to speak so softly Min'darr had to strain to hear him. He saw the commander's eyes widen. His voice took on a deeper tone, more intimate. He felt his attention drawn to him. He shuddered, deliberately. It covered his casting a spell to lay a magical layer over his ears and eyes. Yet he felt its effect.

This is powerful stuff. He is truly a master at this. I can't dismiss him so easily. He has to release the others. If I stop him now, he'd never do that. They'll be forever under his influence. If I don't, I may risk falling prey to him.

"Drop your magic. You love your sister and nephew. Ram'ili is part of the family too. Drop your magic." His voice ... those eyes ... powerful, entrancing. *Have to fool him.* He persisted. Simple phrases that Min'darr associated with himself. *That's how he gets in.* Min'darr's eyes flashed blue. His face went blank, like the faces he'd seen of the judge and Wada earlier. *Just like mine.*

"You will act as I tell you to. You will not question what I tell you because you trust me, implicitly. I will remember things for you. I will know best. I know best. I know best."

Min'darr concentrated on his magic, pressing it between them. It dulled the voice, dimmed the sharp contrast of his eyes, appearing huge and taking up most of Min'darr's field of vision. The man's voice thrumming in his ears. He could no longer hear his own breathing, his own heartbeat.

"I will be your lord. I am your commander, as my rank indicates. You have known me as nothing else except as your commander. Do for me as you would for yourself. I know best. I know best. Do as I tell you without question. I know best."

This last echoed in his mind. The commander's eyes had conjoined, seeming to spin. *Not magic,* he thought. *Not magic.*

"So, Master Magician, turn yourself into a canary."

A reasonable request, he thought. A flash of blue, and a beautiful blue canary hopped onto Jak'enge's finger.

The others returned with plates of food and sat at the conference table to eat. A guard also brought a plate for the commander. No one asked about Min'darr. No one mentioned the bird, happily singing in its cage. Jak'enge enjoyed this meal like few others.

Lessons Learned

Sunlight brightened the covering of his cage. It seemed right, then again, no. Odd memories filled his head, things a canary should not have reason to know. An entire world lay beyond his cover. A growing resentment for being on this stupid roost quickly rose.

But caution beckoned. He listened. No sounds from near him. He gawked seeing no escape. *I don't need a door,* he thought. "I," he sang. No answer. He looked at himself and preened some of his feathers.

"Nope. This doesn't feel right," he said. His thoughts carried his meaning, his voice, however, trilled. His thoughts swirled. The distinct recollection of burning eyes and a mystically powerful voice surfaced. It caused him to startle. "Jak'enge!"

Still there was an overwhelming sense of caution. *Something isn't right.* Calling on his magic, he looked beyond the cover. On the far side of the room were three ankle/wrist brackets mounted to the wall. *Three prisoners' brackets ... no guessing who those are for.*

Noise from the hall interrupted his thinking. The door opened allowing the commander, the judge, Wada, Koo'bla, and Ram'ili to enter, escorted by four guards. *Where's Mah'zan?*

The commander strode across the room to Min'darr's cage and removed the cover. He looked down at the bird within the cage with a sardonic grin. "Good morning, Master Magician. We have work to do." He carried the cage closer to the others. The guards were finishing cuffing Koo'bla and Ram'ili to the wall.

Commander Jak'enge cleared his throat. Every one of the others stood that much taller, a uniform reaction. *Something hypnotic.* "All of you have served me very well. I am deeply appreciative of the services you have rendered. Unfortunately, one of you must die."

Min'darr watched each but saw no reaction, not even a tic of an eyebrow.

"I have with us our newest partner, Min'darr. I will give him the choice of who this will be." He turned to Min'darr. "Become your human self."

Without thinking about it, he did. He took a moment to rearrange his clothing, then faced the commander. "Are there any specifics I need to use to make this choice?"

"No," the commander responded. "Whatever you think is fair." He then glared deeply at Min'darr, whispering, "I know best. This must be done."

Min'darr felt awash with confusion. He stepped closer to the others to consider who should die. He turned to the commander and asked, "Where is my nephew? Should he not be considered for this as well?"

"He is otherwise occupied. You are to choose from these four."

He looked at them. "Wada," he said.

"Good. Use your magic to destroy him."

Min'darr calmed himself, drawing on his eldritch powers. The head of the Wada Shipping Company stood still, as if he'd merely been told to wait a few minutes. Min'darr's hands and eyes glowed blue. With the simple gesture of extending his palm, a magical bolt shot out, enveloped Wada, sizzling like meat on a hot iron. He dissolved, leaving no trace.

The commander smiled and nodded. "Impressive," he said. "I would have preferred to have a body as proof, however, this is most effective. Thank you, Magician.

"Guard, please cuff Min'darr to the wall." The guard took Min'darr, shackling him. His ankles as well. Min'darr saw no reason to resist, so he cooperated.

The smile broadened on Jak'enge's face. "Guard, would you bring in the nephew, please."

Min'darr had no inkling what the commander had in mind and fought his need to ask questions to find out.

"Commander?" Judge Sar'kat said. "It is most important for me to be on my way back to the capital. My offices in Kim'stwa are booked with cases yet to be heard."

"All right, Your Honor. I hope you have a safe journey. Please remember what happened here today. You are a witness to the murder of Ma'hana Wada."

"As you say, Commander." She curtseyed, then left.

Min'darr twitched, willing to wait no longer. He walked over to Jak'enge. "Excuse me, Commander, a question if I may?"

"What? How did you ..." He looked at the empty handcuffs, then back at Min'darr. "You are going to be a most interesting person to deal with. Back on the cuffs," he said, pointing.

"Really? They are not necessary, I assure you. I need to ask about your comment to the judge."

"What about it?"

"His 'murder'?"

"He is dead, yes?" Commander Jak'enge asked.

"Yes."

"And you made him that way? Dead, I mean."

Min'darr thought a moment. "I did, but it was at your request."

"It is a simple matter of action, Magician. I did nothing to cause his death. It was you who summoned the magic that killed him. Correct?" he asked.

"I see," Min'darr said. "So in this, your words meant nothing. Right?"

"Yes. My words have no legal bearing on your actions. You bear the responsibility for your own actions."

"Even if you control us?" Min'darr asked.

"If I control you? Magician, do to your sister the same thing you did to Wada."

Min'darr turned to face his emotionless sister. His eyes quickly shown blue. A blast of magic shot forth. Koo'bla's chains fell empty.

Jak'enge smirked as he turned away. "Is there anything else you require, Magician?"

"Yes, Commander, there is one thing," Min'darr responded.

With a sigh, Jak'enge faced him again and asked, "And what is that?"

"Your silence." He had not lost the magic aura from his last act. He raised his arm, quickly surrounding the commander in his own aura.

Jak'enge could not move his arms or legs. Everyone could see his mouth moving, although no sound could escape. Min'darr touched the aura, causing it to sparkle. That allowed Min'darr's voice to be heard by Jak'enge.

Min'darr sighed. "You are mine, Lord Commander. You are not being hurt by this so your hypnotic orders to my family need not be carried out. Nor can you be heard now, so you cannot require them to do anything ever again. And ..." Min'darr cast a spell. Before they could blink, Koo'bla, Wada, and the judge reappeared. "... your minions are returned."

They stood aghast to see their commander caged within Min'darr's arcane powers. Min'darr gestured, magically reproducing Jak'enge's voice coming from within the aura reassuring them that he was not being hurt.

"Oh, I can guess what you're thinking. No, I never was truly hypnotized. You got close, I will admit that ... close enough that even I wasn't sure. You yourself gave me the clue to figure that much out.

"When you had me wrapped up, you told me that my magic had protected me from your blades and fire. I believe wholeheartedly that it also protected me from your influence. Still, I had never been a canary before so ... why not? I merely cooperated to keep you convinced I was yours."

He walked across to the others. "Can you see the commander?" he asked all three. They nodded their heads. "Can you sense any messages or instructions from him?"

Each responded no.

"I have given this much thought, Jak'enge. It was your voice with the words you so carefully chose that set all of this into motion. I give you a chance now. Will you remove your influence on each of these individuals?"

The commander violently shook his head no.

"Then you leave me no choice." Min'darr asked the others to wait in the commander's office. Obediently, they left.

Once alone, Min'darr allowed himself to show his anger. He copied the features of the hypnotist's voice and screamed his spell at the man. With each gesture he made, a wave of distortion circled within the aura, sweeping through Jak'enge, causing him to become disoriented. After five of these waves, Jak'enge lost control of himself, throwing up from convulsions.

With a loud conclusion to the spell, Min'darr threw a massive charge of arcane energy at the man. He was physically knocked over. As he rolled, a greenish glob, dripping with blood, burst out from his mouth. With that, the nausea and vomiting ceased.

Min'darr summoned that glob. It floated to him, held within a much smaller aura. He put it up against the magical cage holding Jak'enge. In a quieter voice, he asked, "Do you know what this is?"

Still laying on the floor, Jak'enge could do little else except breathe. Finally, he closed his eyes and shook his head.

"Then I'll tell you because I know you will never say a word to anyone that I took it. In fact, you will never say anything ever again. This is your voice, my friend. That same instrument of destruction you have used to control people to do your bidding all these years. Go ahead, try to say something. Let's hear if it works."

With eyes wide, Jak'enge's mouth moved. He grasped his throat, tugging and massaging it to coax some noise, some sound out of his throat. Nothing came out when he opened his mouth to scream ... even when he sobbed.

"No, I guess it doesn't. At least, not for you. I, on the other hand, am going to take it. I will use it to correct what you have done to ruin the lives of these good people. But to accomplish that, something else must come first."

Min'darr let the voice's aura float, then stepped next to the aura holding Jak'enge. Saturated in his own magic, Min'darr stepped through the shield. Jak'enge was lifted from the floor, still limp, to be eye to eye with him. With eyes flaming a brilliant blue, the magician extended his index fingers to twice their normal length, sinking them into the temples of Jak'enge's head. The commander winced.

"I will have the words you used to hypnotize each of them." A stream of energy ran up Min'darr's arms into Jak'enge's head which shivered for a second. A few moments later, it reversed. When it ceased, he released the commander, who once again dropped to the floor.

"This is going to take a while, Commander. Why don't you sleep 'til dinner," he said as he left the room with the voice's aura floating behind him.

Min'darr spent several hours individually with each of the others, undoing the hypnotic trances and influences established by Jak'enge. He used the commander's hypnotic voice to undo their trances. The judge took the longest as she had been under his influence the longest, thirteen years to be exact. Wada had been his for ten. As each was released, Min'darr asked them to wait in the crew's galley, except for Koo'bla.

Min'darr sent his sister to the base's chart room. That is where his magic indicated Mah'zan could be found. Once returned, Min'darr worked for an hour in order to get him to remember who he was. His complete identity had been buried deep by the commander so as to create the person Jak'enge needed Mah'zan to become. It took great patience to uncover the real Mah'zan.

When he was finally done, Min'darr felt worn out. He knew there was one more thing he had to do. He strolled out to the docks, magically summoning a large predator fish. When it arrived, he threw in what was left of the commander's voice. It was greedily devoured.

He rejoined the others in time for dinner. Ram'ili apologized, interrupting his first bite. "Min'darr, how could Jak'enge lie to us when I pointed the enchanted dagger right at him? I asked about he and Wada."

Min'darr paused, thinking back to the occasion. "As I recall, you asked if he was in league with Wada in any way."

"Yes," she said.

"He twisted the question then. He said he wasn't under Wada's influence. The way he answered it was honest, so the dagger didn't react as it would to a direct lie."

Judge Sar'kat raved about the food. "I wish I knew who the chef was in this kitchen. This is amazing! This dinner is so much better than the lunch was. That had to be the best lunch I'd ever eaten! That soup was so delicate, so flavorful."

Ram'ili blushed a bit. "I made both of the meals, Your Honor. Thank you so much for your kind words."

"That's right. I remember the conversations, now. The two of you... you had a café," she said pointing to Ram'ili. "And you ran an inn," she added, pointing to Koo'bla. "Yes, I recall reading that there had been a fire ... seems to have been set by Wada's minions."

She quickly stood to drag a chair to sit between the two. "I have a proposition for you. There is a building a block from my courthouse in Kim'stwa, about five blocks from the capital building. It is for sale ... has been for some time.

"I propose that you two accompany me home. We will buy that old eyesore. Don't worry, I have plenty of funds of my own ... plus access to so much more ... to create a new hot spot for the capitol's citizens and its visitors. Ram'ili? Of course the kitchen would be yours to run. Whatever food you touch, my dear, will be deliciously profitable.

"Koo'bla, you will become the managing owner of the finest inn in the capitol, if not the country. Dignitaries from other countries will demand rooms for their entourage at your inn! They will sup the grandest cuisine there as well.

"What do you say?" She gazed at them with eyes wide and the most genuine smile either had ever encountered.

Ram'ili captured their shared excitement in her look at her partner. "A dream come true. Absolutely, Your Honor!"

"Okay, enough of that. Now that we're going to be partners, call me Kat." After an enthusiastic hug-fest, Sar'kat excused herself to see to their travel arrangements for the next morning.

"I'm really happy for you both," Min'darr said as he finished his last bite.

"Really? You sound more like you're at a funeral," his sister said.

"Sorry," he mumbled, standing.

"Hey, you don't have to go," Koo'bla said. "What's wrong?"

"I have to attend to Jak'enge."

Ram'ili gave him a hug. "What are your choices?"

"The one thing I know is that it isn't up to me. Gotta catch up with Sar'kat."

He found the judge in a conversation with a naval officer. He stopped and 'Kat, as she insisted on now, introduced the officer as Bri'ark, the acting base commander. When he asked about Jak'enge's possible fate, Bri'ark said, "If you leave him to the navy, he will be executed."

'Kat nodded. "Civil law will stipulate to life imprisonment or a death sentence, assuming his hypnotism can be linked to any deaths," she said.

Simultaneously, she and Min'darr both said, "Gur'ata!"

'Kat asked, "Do you have something in mind, Master Magician?"

Min'darr nodded. "I do. I have a proposal that might satisfy both naval and civil protocols."

Epilogue

Shortly after dawn that next morning, a collection of people gathered in a clearing next to the main gate within the naval base. They stood around a shallow hole dug earlier that morning, lined with rough-hewn lumber. A military guard lined the path from the nearest building to the gathering. Several townspeople, noticing the activity, stayed near the closed gate.

Without any signal, six people emerged from that nearest building. Acting Commander Bri'ark, Judge Sar'kat, Min'darr, with two guards escorted a slumping, barefoot Jak'enge, dressed in green fatigues instead of his uniform. They stopped at the gathering, the naval personnel standing at attention.

Acting Commander Bri'ark stood in front of Jak'enge reading from a paper. "Master Jak'enge, you have been accused of crimes against the Naval Service of Rougahn, of associated criminal charges including manslaughter, kidnapping, forgery, party to fraud, arson, and damage to property. You have pled guilty to all charges.

"According to Rougahn's Naval Code, you are hereby stripped of your rank, commission, pay, along with assorted benefits. You are hereby sentenced to life imprisonment." Bri'ark dropped the paper into the hole. Jak'enge showed no reaction.

Judge Sar'kat stepped up. When she did, Jak'enge licked his dry lips, seeming to mouth some words to her. She ignored his efforts, instead looked down at the paper in her own hands. She read aloud, "Jak'enge, formerly the commander of the naval base at Vila'Borin, you have been convicted of crimes against the Rougahn Navy, its personnel, and to citizens of the port city of Vila'Borin, including crimes in the Southern Sea. It is the sentence of the courts of Rougahn that you are to remain here to serve as a symbol of the consequences of greed."

She continued. "It is further ordered that your form be magically changed to ensure that this sentence be carried out in a manner as humane as possible, contrary to the treatment you have imparted on your victims. That act will be done by Rougahn's national hero, the magician, Min'darr.

Min'darr moved to face the hole. Two guards brought the prisoner to him, stopping on the opposite side of the hole. The magician gestured for him to step down into the hole. He stood as tall as he could muster, refusing to step down.

Min'darr shook his head, sighing. He gestured again. A blue aura surrounded the prisoner. He floated up and forward, then slowly lowered into the knee-deep hole. With another gesture, the dirt from the digging flowed from a nearby pile, filling the hole, firmly packing itself.

"You betrayed your fellows in the navy as well as your fellow human beings. You abused your rank, all for the sake of personal wealth," Min'darr said.

"For the sake of history, your understanding of this sentence is mandated. You stand on lumber from the trees used to make naval ships. They are well-known to be creations of strength and durability. You are hereby sentenced to live out your life as one of them.

"You will not recognize time as you have as a man, nor will you be bothered by any goings-on around you, for you will be, in every sense of the word, a tree. When you die, you shall be cremated, burned on site by those who shall follow us. May the Creator have mercy on you."

Min'darr began chanting loudly, waving his arms more dramatically than he needed to be. Lightning lit the morning. After a minute for showmanship, Min'darr loosed the essence of his spell.

A blue surge hit Jak'enge full on the chest. His eyes shut as he exhaled deeply. His skin tinted darker, thickening to the point of forming cracks. He reached up for the sky, stretching toward the rising sun. As he did, his arms elongated into branches, fingers into clusters of leaves. The sound of wood creaking came from within him as yet another limb extended skyward from what had been his neck.

When it ended, the man was no more. A tree, already ten feet taller than Min'darr, showed signs of some additional branches forming from its upper reaches where, moments before, a human had stood. Min'darr looked at its bark patterns extensively. He found that, from the correct angle in the right light, Jak'enge's human face could be seen looking to the clouds.

*

He stood on the port side opposite the mizzen mast. The aft staysail virtually glowed orange with the light of the setting sun behind it. He breathed deeply, finding the salty air refreshingly calming after a busy day at sea. As tired as he was on this fifth day of sailing, Min'darr had quickly come to value these moments of calm and reflection.

*

Two months had passed since Jak'enge's 'planting.' Min'darr tried hard to soften his heart toward him, without success. Greed had ruled Jak'enge's life, power had held his heart.

Mah'zan had joined the navy, already anxious to complete his basic training so he could set sail again. True to her word, Sar'kat arranged for Koo'bla and Ram'ili to buy the old downtown building in the capitol. He'd gone there with them, agreeing to have lunch with the king and Kordal's ambassador to be officially "thanked" for defeating Magama. Those are the kinds of things that national heroes have to suffer through.

When he'd finally left the capital to return to Vila'Borin, workers were already making lots of noise and dust converting the building's shell into a new life for the two women in his life. They couldn't be happier. Saying their goodbyes was harder for him than he thought it should be. The love of family was the most powerful non-magic thing he could imagine.

It had taken some doing by Sar'kat, but Ma'hana Wada faced no charges. Since he'd been under the hypnotic influence of Jak'enge, the court held him innocent. That didn't make his insurance company very happy. His company was closed. All the ships and equipment were auctioned off, the proceeds going to resolve his legal debts.

He was placed under supervision, though, and was not allowed to be in authority over others. Min'darr had heard that he was considering buying into a cartage company operating between Rougahn's major cities.

Before he left Vila'Borin, he saw to two personal errands. He stopped by the women's magic show venue again. He was delighted with the simple finesse of their act. The younger woman now performed as much as the older one. Nor'lars blushed when she'd recognized him in the audience. They spoke after the act. She'd flirted with him, asking him to show her how magicians liked to be kissed. He'd been tempted. Intent, though, on his pending journey, he gently declined her favor.

The second errand, much less interesting, was not much farther on the wharf. He saw to it that the wharf planking no longer sported the remains of the two mages from the Southern Sea. They'd been chopped at and burned without success. It required him. He magically removed them, doing so after dark to avoid onlookers. After examining the differences of their magic, he destroyed them using his own arcane powers.

What kind of magic existed in the Southern Sea? How had they come to master it? How did the jeweled rings they wore store their power? It was the same region Jak'enge obtained his use of hypnotism. The issue had plagued him since Goat Island. He was determined to find out.

The Southern Sea was his destination. He'd booked passage on this three-masted schooner, the *Wind Snare,* sailing out of Vila'Borin's port. Whoever ... whatever was there, he needed to know. They were magic.

As he drifted off to sleep that first night aboard, he recalled the Mulu's words that magic was a tool. It could be used to build, to heal, or to destroy. Based on his experience, the users of this yellow magic had no qualms of using it to destroy.

The idea of employing magic this way terrified him. He'd have to be prepared to teach them its other uses, with force, if necessary.

III. MAGIC OF THE SOUTHERN SEA

Seaworthy Magic

Min'darr the Magician was desperate.

Two weeks at sea had honed his skill as a seaman, something he never thought he'd possess. Knot tying, however, escaped him. As part of his fare for the voyage to the Southern Sea, Min'darr had agreed to work, to perform tasks usually assigned to the sailing crew. He wanted to broaden his experiences that would make the journey more of an adventure. Besides that, the reduced fare was nice.

His supervising sailor didn't care about any of that. He simply demanded that this landlubber get the jobs assigned him done. Tardin, a twenty-six-year veteran seaman, had run out of patience. Too many times the things Min'darr did became undone for the sake of a poorly tied knot.

"Belaying a running line with a half-hitch or properly anchoring a shroud knot can save your life. But you," he'd lamented, "you're going to kill us all!" Tardin had spent hours reviewing lines, rigging, and especially knot tying to no avail.

Min'darr wanted to rely on his own skills, not the magical ones. Oh, sure, he could use magic. Somehow, though, it felt to him like cheating. Since none of the crew knew he was a magician, he had to confess his plight to Captain Kor'tif. "I believe, sir, that Master Tardin wants to string me up. I've no skill for knots, it seems. I am asking for your help." He then confided his magical ability, providing a private demonstration of some spells.

The captain arranged a demonstration of each knot with his first officer, Hasmu Bucurt, a native of the Isonicus Islands. Min'darr followed magically, casting simple spells for each of the seventeen knots he was expected to use. Both men swore to keep

Min'darr's arcane nature a secret so he would not be hounded by those on board.

The next day, Min'darr's work actually made the old salt Tardin smile.

That night, all hell broke loose.

Min'darr slept in a cabin equipped with hammocks as bedding with two other passengers. Tonight, they tossed about like laundry in a gale. He'd already cast a spell to keep him from getting seasick. A monstrous storm beat their ship unmercifully. Rain, wind, lightning, and waves combined to pummel the ship. On a particularly massive wave, Min'darr was thrown from his hammock.

Before he could steady it enough to climb back in, one of the crew knocked, telling him that the captain requested him to come to his aft cabin. There was no going topside due to the wash from the waves and the high winds. The helmsman was alone on deck. He had to be tied in place else he be swept overboard.

They made their way through the ship's inner passageways. The ship's pitching from the storm resulted in multiple bruises. The ship dipped as Min'darr raised a foot to climb stairs. He found himself standing at the top of those stairs a second later. His sailor escort broke an arm a few feet further down the same hall when he was thrown against a hatchway. Eventually, they arrived at the captain's cabin.

"Thank our Creator, Loy, you are here, Master Min'darr." He dismissed the sailor to the sick bay for his arm to be tended to as First Officer Bucurt entered.

"Is there anything, my good magician, that can be done to help our plight?" the captain asked. "This storm is tearing *Wind Snare* apart."

Min'darr sat at the chart table, strapping himself into one of the anchored stools. "I've created a wind once before. I have never affected any significant control of the weather otherwise," he told them. "Please give me a few moments." Min'darr reached within. It took but a moment for him to feel the familiar warmth of the upwelling of his eldritch powers. Surrounded by the churning waters of an angry sea, his power was stronger than if in quieter seas.

His awareness reached out. Despite the physical movements caused by the storm, the magical energies felt as he expected them to be, albeit with more cohesive force. He found himself drawn to it, wanting to join in the flow. He reminded himself that he was physically strapped in. That thought helped him resist the urge to slide toward the eldritch flow. He magically nudged it, then pushed. Both efforts were spent without any consequence.

He mentally refocused on the physical world's current storm. It battered everything. He tried to calm it. Nothing. He cast a spell to drive the winds upward so to avoid the ship. Nothing. He pushed harder only to find himself pressed back, as if Nature itself was fighting his magic. Shielding the ship proved in vain as well. Too much power was involved in this storm to be stopped or bent by one simple magician.

He brought his consciousness back to Captain Kor'tif's cabin. "I'm sorry, sir. There is too much power, far too much force in the storm for me to affect. One stone alone cannot change the course of a river, I'm afraid."

Kor'tif shook his head. "I thank you, Master Min'darr, for your efforts. You are right, of course, the river will flow around a stone."

First Officer Bucurt's eyes widened. "Then we should abandon being the stone. Let's become part of the river. Or rather, this storm."

Kor'tif scowled. "And how in the name of Loy would we do that?"

The first officer directed his answer to Min'darr. "Before the storm hit us, we had time to furl our sails to avoid them being damaged.

"Is it possible for you to strengthen the sails and masts, magically reinforce them? Then we could truly be the name of this wondrous ship, snaring the wind to ride with the storm instead of being barraged by it." He was enthusiastic, excited with his idea.

Min'darr thought. "I could, to a point," he said. "But, for the sails to work, they have to be flexible, responding to the wind, yes?" They both nodded. "So needing to keep that ability means I can't. Magic would not respond to the winds, so it isn't as flexible as you would need. If I put the sails under magic's control, a change in the wind could splinter the yardarms or the masts before I could adjust the magic. It could even drive the bow down into the ocean. I am sorry."

While they dismissed the idea, a shade of it remained with him. Harnessing such a strong, yet inconsistent, wind would doom the ship.

After a few moments more while the two others conversed, Min'darr spoke up. "There is a possibility here. I could fashion an arcane sail to capture the flow of magical energies produced by the storm. If those forces can be coerced, I could, like the wind, use it to blow the ship away from the danger it faces."

"Oh, would that it could be done?" Captain Kor'tif begged.

Min'darr nodded. "Yes, I believe it can, so long as the physical wind and the magical flow are not going in opposite directions. Those forces working against each other would mean the end of the *Wind Snare* and of us as well."

*

Following his instructions, the crew lashed Min'darr to the main mast below the main decking. He need not be on the deck to work his spell. It would extend from him, so he had to be tied to the ship. Facing the bow, he knew he faced west, the direction the wind blew. In his first contact with the storm's eldritch energies, they flowed more southerly as they naturally circled the storm pattern.

Once alone, he pushed himself again toward connecting with the ocean's eldritch elements. His magic was attracted to it, so he extended an arched swath of his own magical essence toward it. The ocean responded by rising slightly toward his own. Those forces refined to a more distinct flow. They met and meshed. He had to fight hard to keep from being swept away, to keep it acting as a tether, not a tow rope.

Slowly, he pulled his magic closer to the surface to entice the stream closer. The stream also rose. *Good. Time to move.* He thickened his magical swath, making it spread out like a sail. He felt the ship respond, moving more with the magic than the wind.

In so doing, the ship lurched against the storm, buffeting it more, causing the *Wind Snare* to vibrate. *Nature's storm and my magic forces continue to be at odds!* he thought.

The eldritch stream doesn't flow consistently in any recognizable direction to this world. I've ridden within the flow of eldritch energies before, yet I never tried to steer them. Instead of riding the flow, Min'darr directed his eldritch sail, hence the ship, into the path of the flow, keeping Bucurt's phrase about being part of the river, not the rock, in his mind.

Like wishing to move an arm or clench a fist, he tested his control of the connection. Adjusting the angle of his arcane sail, he felt the ship respond.

His main concern at this point was to channel the magical energy to keep the ship upright above the waters. Min'darr strained to tilt his magical sail, bringing the bow up. The ship rose in response until its hull was being slapped by the waves. *Working! Yes!* He pushed himself ever harder to be in sync with the energy flow.

Then, the waves had to reach for the keel. They were above them, literally flying. The crew's cheer resounded throughout the ship, feeling the lessening of the sea's grasp on *Wind Snare*.

In less than an hour, the ship had cleared the southern edge of the storm. Lightning became a light show on the horizon to their aft, no longer a threat, now competing with the dawn's increasing brightness.

The first officer came to Min'darr, who was haggard, sweaty, and semi-conscious. His arms were extended as they'd been while holding the magical sail.

"Magician! Enough!" Bucurt said loudly. "We're safe thanks to you." Min'darr seemed oblivious.

Bucurt then emptied a pail of water over him, drenching him back to awareness. The magician's eyes opened. He nodded, weakly muttering to end his incantation. The first officer had him carried to a bunk in the ship's sick bay to recoup. He was joined by the helmsmen, cut loose from the wheel, also saturated and exhausted.

The crew flooded out onto the decks to begin the cleanup and repairs. The boatswain then ordered the sails unfurled. They set a new course to their original port of call as they were now positioned significantly west of where they should have been.

*

Two days later, they sat still, unmoving, sails limp. There were no waves, per se, just small swells that the *Wind Snare* didn't notice. Doldrums. The mood of the ship fit the term. It is a nautical prison unless you had oars. The *Wind Snare* had none.

"Are you recovered from saving our worthless hides?" Captain Kor'tif asked Min'darr when the magician wandered past him.

"Doing well, Captain, though my arms remain sore from holding my eldritch sail."

"While I am very grateful for your efforts, my friend, I have to scratch me head as to how you do this magic. How can one person—no offense—be powerful enough to pluck a ship out of a savage sea to skim the waves all the way to safety?"

"'Tis nothing I do, Captain. Think of a magician as little more than a sail. That cloth catches the wind which pushes a ship through the waters. 'Tis the same with a magician. There are magical energies afoot across land and sea. Certain individuals can, like a sail, harness those energies to do a task.

"I used those to lift the ship, although it was quite the work to remain so intensely focused for so long, fighting against those winds. Much easier to lift a man," he said as he gestured and the captain rose several inches. "Even if he is a captain."

"Whoa!" the captain called out, grasping the rail they stood at. "Well, looky here. Ha!" he exclaimed as he chuckled. "So, 'tis naught something you make, like ... umm, like spit, eh? Where does this magical energy come from?" he asked, while gawking at his feet above the deck as he wiggled them.

"Nature itself, Captain. Every bit of life from massive whales down to the sea's plankton, wherever there is life there are magical energies."

"So, what happens to it when something dies?" he asked.

Min'darr had to think about that. "I'm not sure, other than there is no longer energy for magic or for life."

"Hmph. Do you have more magic in you than I have in me then since you use it?"

"No, not magic, energy. You have as much energy in you as I have in me," Min'darr explained, lowering the man to the decking. "I am sensitive to it. I know how to control it. That's the magic."

"Wha ...? I have magical energy inside me?" Kor'tif gasped.

"Of course, what do you think I used to lift you?"

"But I'm a big man. You didn't even grunt."

Min'darr smiled. "The magic is in controlling the energy. It does the work."

"Good to know. I think I'll get me a magician to sail with me all the time. Interested in a job?"

Min'darr chuckled. Kor'tif belly laughed, slapping him on the back. Kor'tif continued. "Seriously, if I may be so bold, what brings you to the Southern archipelagos? You coming to study their magic? These regions are famous for their arcane practices."

"Who practices that kind of magic?" Min'darr asked.

A horn sounded above them. Everyone stopped and looked up to the top of the mast. The sailor in the crow's nest called out. "Ahoy, all hands, sea beast starboard astern.

Captain Kor'tif bellowed, "Stations! All hands to stations! Deck crew to arms. Deck crew to arms!"

Reasoning With Fear

The crew of the Wind Snare leaped into action. In an obviously well-rehearsed routine, the bosun blew rapid successions of whistles to order his men to batten the deck hatches, lash the rigging, and secure the bowsprit. The rigging crew flew up the main shroud, then ran across the yardarms to secure the stay lines.

The deck crew clustered amidships to secure their archery weapons from huge chests and a locker fastened to the main mast. Spears and cutlasses were another option. Once equipped, the sailors dispersed to pre-appointed stations. Additional weapons were pulled from storage racks beneath the gunwales, then stored at their stations along the ship's perimeter. Out of nowhere came five small cannons. Two were posted aside the bow, three along the aft gunwale. This entire process happened within two minutes. The passenger/cargo ship had transformed into a fighting vessel.

Captain Kor'tif and Min'darr, already at the rear of the ship, sprinted starboard to peer into the depths. A large, undefined shape slid toward the ship, more visible close up as it passed under the ship's shadow.

A thump reverberated through the vessel. Min'darr felt a slight vibration in his feet. They exchanged a glance. "What?" asked Min'darr.

"The mother of all cephalopods. A giant squid." He grabbed his cone and shouted to his crew, "Squid! Archers, sting it 'til it wants none of us."

The ship rolled a bit as the bow dipped when three long, silvery arms rose up across the railing, then wrapped around each other. The port side bow cannon was snapped off, but the sailors stationed there managed to evade the sea creature's grasp. The tentacled mass writhed, then constricted, pulling the bow down further.

The sailors formed a firing line, loosing a volley into the beast's tentacles. With each strike, the arm twitched. After a second volley, the creature released its grasp, slipping back beneath the surface. A rousing cheer went up from the crew. Sailors hastened to the broken cannon mount to assess repairs.

"That went well, surprisingly quick," Min'darr offered.

Kor'tif's primary attention was on the deck happenings, then he responded, "Just a dumb fish. They come up after big storms like the one we've come through. Figure they probably live deep most of their lives. I remember ... Oh, by Loy!"

Five gigantic squid arms shot up from amidships on the port side. A larger tentacle coming over the gunwale on the starboard side slapped the deck. Two sailors were beneath the arms, kicking to get free. Others of their shipmates rushed in, attacking the nearest squid arm. As they struck them, the arms slashed about, knocking men down, then sliding them across the decking. The suckers on each arm, smaller circles ringed with fine barbs, found many of the sailors, ripping into their flesh. The screams of those men frightened the rest.

The monster thrust itself up against the side of the ship, gnawing at it with its bird-like beak. Captain Kor'tif drew his sabre as he headed for the main deck. He called over his shoulder, "Anything you can do, magician ..."

Min'darr paused, considering his options. He could repel the beast, he could kill it. He could do many things. For an instant, he recalled a moment in his past when he rode his mule along a mountain trail, escorted by a bear, an elk, a cougar, and an eagle. Wild creatures all responding to the presence of his magic. Perhaps ...

Despite the chaos on the deck below him, Min'darr stood calmly while he called forth his magic. The warmth gathered from within him, spreading out into every fiber of his being. He pressed it further until an arcane blue aura surrounded him, a beacon of magical power.

He felt its effect as the noises of battle subdued. He opened his eyes to see sailors standing, weapons at the ready with no target to hit. Some of the injured were being attended to by their shipmates. The beast had withdrawn. Most of the crew's attention was on him, a blue aura shining around him. They failed to cheer for their success, fearing the unknown, fearing who this person could be, what else he could do besides saving the ship from the storm.

Min'darr felt their response, their hesitation. He felt, too, the squid's presence. It was sensitive to him. "It's not over," he called out to the crew just as twin tentacles eased over the aft rail, plucked him up, then withdrew back into the sea.

The cold of the ocean shocked him. He managed to hold his breath as the creature pulled him beneath the ship. It looked odd, seeing the hull of the ship above him, with the giant squid dangling from it. The connection he held with the creature remained strong. It had stopped its attack on the ship and seemed to be waiting. Somehow, he was fairly certain that it involved him. *Time to talk squid.*

With a thought, Min'darr transformed into a squid his own size, significantly smaller than this great beast from the ocean's depths. It was at least as large as the vessel it had attacked, or ... had it? Sensations from the creature already raised questions in Min'darr's mind.

He reached out again, glowing blue, scuttling toward the creature's eye which was the size of the captain's cabin. He circled near it and the squid brought one of its arms up next to him. Min'darr responded by brushing up against it.

He jerked back, unprepared for the wave of terror it was feeling. *Why? Why was this monster so afraid? What did it have to be afraid of?*

Early on, his dad, and later his Uncle Taf, had taught him about animals' behaviors. Some always ran away like a rabbit. Some tended to turn to fight. It was the way of Nature. Could this possibly be the same for something this large? He had to find out. At least his presence here kept it from attacking the ship anymore.

Min'darr reached out one of his own tentacles and entwined it against one of the beast's suckers. It remained outwardly calm, though it shook throughout. He sent his magic out and the blue aura crept onto the beast. The eldritch energy tendril snaked onto the giant squid's tentacle. The beast fluttered its mantle fins. Min'darr lost himself in the beast's mind, a thick and utter blanket of confusion.

*

What is it? What was wrong? Her—the monster was a female—insides hurt. The water felt ... wrong. It moved, pushing against her as it had never done before.

And the light, not the flashes of some fish she'd never seen before. All those ... hurting, not right. Lost. Big fish ahead. Not flashing, too bright.

Min'darr broke their connection. *Not enough. Just getting bits.* Clearly, this beast was not a monster. She was displaced from deeper, darker waters, like the captain said.

She could die if not helped. He filled his vent chamber and puffed, jetting farther up her body, toward the mantle.

He spread all eight of his tentacles against her side, stretching out as far as he could, using his own suckers to hold on. She stayed, bringing one of her arms closer and covering him, pressing him into her. Min'darr took that as acceptance. *So wondrous to be so close to this creature, to learn about her and her world ... sharing thoughts through magic.*

Min'darr again extended his eldritch energy. His aura soaked into a large area of the squid's skin. His consciousness followed, seeking some point of awareness. He found it.

His squid body shuddered as her basic impressions replayed. He distinctly saw the ocean's darkness and felt the heavy, heavy press of deep water against them. *No food. Hungry. Light flashes far above. Food? Shining like the prey she'd fed on in the inky depths, but so far above her. Hungry, have to get!*

Waters moving wrong, doesn't feel right. No pressing. Flashes close and rumbling vibrations. Lost. Hungry. Too bright. Some fish, odd fish, attack. Eat them. No. Big fish ... food? Attack!

Min'darr ended his connection with the giant squid. He had felt everything she was feeling. Being a squid, too, gave him a chance to translate those into something his human self could comprehend.

The glimpses into her perceptions and most recent memories told the story he needed to know. This squid lived in the deepest waters of the ocean and had not been successful finding food of late. The lightning flashes from the storm she mistook as body lights that many deep sea fish have and use to attract prey. Predators like this squid would see them, too, and know it meant something was there that could be eaten.

She'd been desperate enough to rise in order to eat what was making the lights. When she got to the surface waters, the currents and waves confused her. The higher pressures of living in deep water were missing, making her sick and disoriented.

I need to get her to go back into the depths. But how?

So far, he'd let her memories come to him. She started getting fidgety again, twitching and slapping the hull of the *Wind Snare*. He had to get her back to the bottom of the ocean. He had to plant the suggestion to follow him, so he focused his magic and visualized his leading her, repeating it for her several times.

Min'darr then released his hold on the giant squid and jetted away, dropping below her. She didn't move, still attached to the ship's keel. He jetted back up to the beast and swam in circles near one of the eyes. Min'darr then jetted away. Again, no reactions from the giant squid.

He paused to consider what to do next. Her memories had shown her to be hunting when she got lost, moving up during the storm, believing that the lightning was prey. He scanned beneath them seeing nothing that could help. *She won't pay any attention to me either.*

Lightning! Maybe I can mimic the deep sea creatures' little lights on their bodies … use them to attract this massive sea beast.

Min'darr cast another spell and began flashing. The squid twitched, taking notice of him. Min'darr realized that, as prey, he was way too close. Instantly he jetted away, diving down, deeper into the ocean's depths. His squid shape allowed him to pierce the surrounding waters with little effort. The lateral position of his squid eyes let him see both ahead and behind. The squid had released its death grip on the ship and was rocketing toward him.

Yes! She's following! The mass of squid loomed large behind, dwarfing the hull of the ship, looking like a small blob far above them. He scanned ahead, again noting the ever-increasing darkness obscuring what lay below.

Getting closer! He started veering, pulsing his jet as quickly as he could while blinking like the aquatic dinner he needed to look like to keep her attention. She was about two of her lengths behind him when he cast another spell. He rocketed away from the giant, his magic making his natural propulsion more effective. *A different version of the fast walking the Mulu gave the ogre.*

The combination of his speed and depth of the waters pressed against his sides reminding him of trudging through the deep and cold snow as a youth. His human mind noted that his squid body was perfectly comfortable, much more so than when he was under the ship's keel. *Part of her problem too, I'm sure.*

She followed his every move and, despite his arcane boost, edged ever closer. *Umm, I think I'm down far enough. Time to end this.*

Min'darr spewed out a dose of ink. He then stopped his magical blinking and cast an invisibility spell and darted up out of the beast's path. The giant squid blasted through the ink cloud, dispersing it in swirls and trailing behind it, swirling in its tentacles.

It stopped, searching. Min'darr was above and behind it, not wanting to move in the chance it could sense the water's movement. It moved aside and backtracked, now just feet below the invisible magician/squid. He used his magic once more and a flickering light similar to what he'd looked like appeared far below them. A second later, the giant squid jetted down in pursuit of its prey. Min'darr bobbed and swirled in its underwater wake.

Goodbye, your ladyship. I wish you good hunting, but I truly do not wish to ever see you again. Min'darr kept himself invisible and headed back to the surface.

*

He swam up to the ship, which was dragging its anchors. Returning to human form, he hailed the ship. "Ahoy, *Wind Snare.*" Within a few seconds, three heads leaned out over the gunwale. One was Captain Kor'tif.

"Magician! We was about ready to give up your ghost to Loy herself!" He turned and shouted orders. A few heartbeats later, a rope ladder tumbled down to him. As he stepped over the gunwale, Captain Kor'tif slapped him on the back and said, "Glad to have you back, magician."

The winds had returned, explaining why the anchors were down while they hopefully awaited his return. The anchors were drawn up. The sails were set, instantly billowing and the *Wind Snare* plowed a wake toward its destination port.

That night at the captain's mess, Min'darr regaled the crew with his giant squid story, including what he'd learned about it. As much as he hated having his magic be the center of attention, half the crew demanded a show of his arcane skills. The others chose to remain below decks, hesitant, if not openly fearful, of the magician, or at least what he represented.

Min'darr went to talk with them to ease their fears. Too many had experienced the Magic of the Dead, the Southern Sea's infamous form of magic. They refused to witness what they deemed as the wasting of a soul's energy. They resented Min'darr's perceived disrespect toward the value of a life. His explanations of his own magic could not pierce the veil of their prejudices.

Later, with the captain's insistence, he faced the rest of the ship's crew and some of its passengers from the fore poop deck. He explained that his magic did not come from the energies of the dead, instead of the living, and assured them of his respect for all life. "If I was of the Magic of the Dead, I would have benefited from the squid's death, getting her energies. My magic is empowered by life's energies, not death's. That's why I didn't kill the squid. I helped her return to her own part of the sea."

He kept his arcane display simple, enough to entertain his shipmates, without overdoing things. He was accepting their applause when it suddenly ceased. He turned around when a collective "Oow" escaped the crew and followed their pointing to the heavens.

They saw six lights streak across the sky, leaving their trails over the ship, heading westward toward Marsapti, their destination in the Kovasi Islands. He'd heard of meteors, of course, but was not prepared for the crew's reaction. They knelt and waved to them, as if praying. Several murmured "by Loy." The captain, kneeling and looking skyward, said, "Olip bakoy, Monderra," ancient words welcoming back the departed ones.

It lasted a few seconds and then everything returned to normal. The crew and passengers dispersed. Min'darr stopped Kor'tif. "What is it we just witnessed?"

The captain smiled. "It is a blessing from Loy! Six souls have returned. Praise Loy! If you are seeking knowledge of Loy's magic, may you be so blessed as to meet one of these who has returned."

Hinasha's Homecoming

Min'darr loved the sounds of the sea through the open porthole of his cabin. Tonight it helped drown out the snoring of one of his cabinmates, Marsuk, a large, hairy man from the mainland on a vacation who was hoping to find an island wife.

"Min'darr? You awake?" a voice called through the dark.

"Unfortunately," he answered, yawning. "Hinasha, that's your name?"

"Yes." There was a pause. "I'm sorry, I have to ask. How many souls did you use for your magic show tonight after dinner?"

Min'darr sat up, straddling his hammock. "Didn't you hear my explanation?"

Hinasha's tone of voice changed, becoming a bit more coarse. "C'mon, Magician, you can tell me. I grew up on Rac'ken Island. I know all about it. Everything you said was meant to calm the crew. I know better."

Min'darr stared at him, wondering how much he did know. "What is the Fifth Rule?" he asked, the question plaguing him for months since facing the Southern Magic mages in the port city of Vila'Borin.

"I have no idea," Hinasha claimed.

Min'darr used his magic to scan him, finding nothing. *Just like before. Why can't I sense this yellow magic?* He gestured and spun the man into a knot in his hammock.

"What the ... What are you doing to me?" Hinasha blurted.

"What color was the magic I used?" he asked

Hinasha thrashed as much as he could, but was held tight in the wrapped hammock. "It was blue, you freak. Blue!"

234

Min'darr released him. "Blue magic is my strength, not the yellow magic of death you find around here. The magic I have access to is based on life. Living things—people, animals, and plants—all possess an energy and my magic consolidates it for me to use. From what I've heard, this Southern Magic comes from those energies being released when something dies.

"I understand your question about using the energies from souls, but my magic is different. It is why I have come here. I wish to learn." Min'darr finished with a sigh.

"I've seen what you can do ... saving the ship from the storm, then the squid. Did you call the souls to return too?"

Min'darr shook his head. "No. As far as I know, those lights in the sky were meteors, rocks falling from the heavens.

Hinasha said, "All my life, those 'rocks' as you call them, signaled the return of a soul from the dead."

"Have you ever seen one who has returned from the dead?" Min'darr asked.

"That would be only for the Sacred Trio to see, the most holy of their order. I applied to their school. They tested me to see if I could join them, but I had none of the plachum, the essence that's needed to work the magic. I have seen many magical things that they have done while I was within their walls during my testing."

"Please," Min'darr said, "could you tell me? I mean, I know you may not know how they did things. What kinds of magic have you witnessed?"

"Why should I tell you?" he asked.

"It will give me an idea of how they use this Magic of the Dead."

Hinasha's voice became stressed in a harsh whisper. "You have to promise me that no one will ever know how you discovered these things. Swear to it!"

Min'darr, straddling his hammock, solemnly bowed. "I swear."

"I have seen people fly over trees, as if carried by souls. I watched as a group of students were led in a lesson by a talking seagull. Difficult to understand, but speaking nonetheless. And I have seen the consequences of their work. So many, many dead animals, allegedly for the kitchens, all soulless at the hands of instructors and students alike.

"And then, umm ... I remember one night, sneaking out of my berth with one of my roommates ... oh, wow, this is hard to tell, even after so long." Hinasha paused to control his breathing. "We heard lots of noise and knew it was from a gathering. We snuck out and made it to an upper balcony looking down into a huge room with a bowled floor. Students sat on benches that surrounded a massive fire blazing in the center of the room. Masters and Acolytes stood around, chanting, throwing birds and small animals into the inferno.

"Finally, I'd had enough. I was scared. I tugged on my roommate's sleeve to leave. He wanted to stay ... to see what was happening. I stood back behind the corner, pleading with him to come. I peeked around as a figure made of flame stepped out from the fire. The crowd below stilled. I screamed. The fire man rose up toward us. I ran.

He threw flames at us. I ran fast enough to get away. My roommate didn't. I recall hearing a cheer coming from the gathering. I can imagine what happened to his body after I'd run."

"Did they find you?" Min'darr asked.

"Not that night. It was the next night I was told I'd failed and had to leave. They made me leave by walking back to my father's house out through their cemetery. I was chased by spirits rising from their graves. I left the island the next day. That was fifteen years ago. This is my first time back."

"Why are you coming back now?"

"To die. I have an illness and will die very soon, so I wanted to be in my family home on Rac'ken."

"That is most sad, my friend. I have had some success with healing. I mean, I could ..."

"No. No, thank you. You are most kind, but I am resolved. It is Loy's will."

"I wish you then a smooth death," Min'darr said.

"Again, my thanks. May I ask a favor?" Hinasha whispered.

"If it's within me, of course."

"Would you attend my death, maybe help guide my soul to its reward so it can't be used for their absurd rituals?"

"I have never attempted anything like that. The magic I have may not affect their ability to take your soul. I mean, since it is a different kind of magic. I could not make any promises. I am sorry. If it helps to be there, I will," Min'darr said. The two settled back to sleep, after Min'darr magically enveloped Marsuk to silence his snoring.

*

Min'darr's nose wrinkled as he set foot on the dock. After more than seven weeks at sea, it amazed him to be so repelled by the smells of land. Or, more specifically, the smells of people. The ship had docked. Of course it had its own smells, which couldn't compare to the barrage of odors coming from the island's town, market, cafes, and the animals penned nearby. *Hard to imagine that we are so used to these. Sometimes one or two will get noticed, but, argh, so many at once! Whew!*

"Ahoy, Min'darr!" a voice from aboard ship called after him.

He turned to see Captain Kor'tif and his first officer, Bucurt, at the rail. "'Tis tradition for us to feast together at the *Kinsmen's Table*," he said as he pointed passed the ship's bow. "The third building to the left there. I'd be obliged if'n ya were to join us. Ship's treat, after all you be doin' to get us here. What say you?"

"I'd say I'd be a fool to turn down good food and the fellowship of friends. Do they have rooms, too?" Min'darr asked.

"Some of the finest," Bucurt jumped in. "More than mere sailors can afford, though. So you're forewarned! The ale flows at seventeen bells."

Min'darr nodded and waved, then turned toward the row of buildings that included the inn, *Kinsmen's Table*. The market square area was to his right and consisted of roughly a dozen vendors. They were ready for him. Each called to him, begging for attention, waving their wares, be it bakery, leather, or jewelry. Min'darr avoided them, save for the last one.

A hooded, old man sat beside his counter, feet up against its strut, whittling. It appeared to be a well-stocked arsenal, except that each weapon was tagged with a price. Swords and daggers, blades of various sizes with handles of wood, stone, bone, and other materials he couldn't immediately identify. Fancy metallic trim and jeweled insets adorned many.

A withered, tired voice called out to him. "Good sir! A man your age should be wearin' a blade, my friend. No tellin' what manner of vagabond might set upon you. Your money or your clothes may best be your downfall, especially in the less tamed parts of these isles. A good blade will help you keep your soul within you and not floating about." His eyes never lifted from his whittling while he spoke.

"And what, pray tell, sir, would you think the type of dagger be that would best suit my needs?" Min'darr taunted.

"Not the usual kind o' skinsticker, I'd wager. You, my good sir, have an air about you. An aura that defies my explanation, but an aura just the same. An' you best believe me, I've experienced much in my days. A favor ... touch my hand, if you will, so's I can know more ... if I am to recommend the weapon to serve you best." The man blindly raised his arm in Min'darr's direction.

Min'darr smiled, hesitant. The seller had yet to look up at him, so the magician had not seen his full face. *Odd ... almost sage-like from what I can sense.* He extended his hand and rested it on the back of the vendor's. Min'darr felt a spark jump between them, prickling his skin.

The old man jerked back, falling off his chair, onto the ground. "By Loy!" he exclaimed. He rolled to his knees, flailing his arms to find something to grasp. He brushed the side of his vendor stand and holding on hard, pulled himself to his feet, panting.

"Get thee gone, Magician!" he rasped in a forced whisper. "Do not stay! There is nothing for you here save for suffering and death. You are too powerful for them to allow you to live. By all that is good, go!"

He seized Min'darr by the arm, his hooded head bent low. "It is not known except by the Innermost Triune, you are foretold to come and your coming will disrupt the Order for generations. Go back to your boat, change to a bird or a whale, just go. In this version of history, our magic will be your end here." He clung onto Min'darr.

The magician whisked the man's hood back, clearly able to see the old man's face.

He had no eyes. His eyelids looked to be sealed. No scarring was evident. *Must have been done by magic. Why would someone do this to an old man? What did he mean, 'too powerful for them to allow you to live'? Who is 'them'?*

The old vendor's panting was worse, as was his grimace. Min'darr noticed the back of the man's hand was red and blistered where he'd touched him.

"Who are you? How would you know such a secret?" Min'darr asked, holding the man tighter.

"Not who am I, but who was I. Naldalek, the Sodality's founder. I have come back to warn you. It is what I must do to help you."

"Founder of what? The Order? Back from where?" Min'darr asked intently.

The man calmed and raised his hand to touch Min'darr's face. He felt another spark jump from the man's hand to his cheek. His voice was barely a whisper. "From the dead." A breeze came up and the man became like dust which drifted away with the wind.

Min'darr looked about in complete astonishment. The man was gone. His chair and stand ... the weapons ... none of it existed anymore. He struggled to stand, feeling heavy. *Must be using my sea legs. The land never moves.*

Everything else around him remained as before. The ships at dock, their loading and unloading, and the rest of the vendors in the market. No one paid any attention to him or the fact that the old man and his entire cart had dissolved before him.

Had it? How could no one else be aware of what happened? Min'darr felt different, heavier, as if weighed down.

He founded the Magic of the Dead? How is that possible? Why would I be singled out, visited by a spectre of the Order? What did it want? A warning, he'd said. Against what?

Min'darr turned a slow circle, scanning everything in the hope of ... anything. No imprints of the cart or the chair could be seen.

A glint caught his eye in the grass near his feet. He stooped and picked up a stone. A gem, a diamond, about the size of his thumbnail. It glistened in the sunlight. He palmed it. It felt warm in his hand. He put it in his cloak's pocket.

*

Kinsmen's Table was huge and loud. Smaller inns were in a little town a mile down the coast. More respectable travelers rented cabbies to stay there. This was pure seamen's folly. Many tables, each one occupied by a crew of a ship in port, bustled with pitchers of ale and grog. Hens and hams and legs of goat were served steaming and dripping in gravy. Hot potatoes and rice and breads, along with salads of many kinds of greens, carrots, and something red and something else blue. Three fireplaces blazed with warmth and flickering light that made every movement in the room dance across the walls of the dining hall.

Following Captain Kor'tif's prayer of thanks for a safe passage, with a special point of appreciation to the magician who sailed with them, the crew spent nearly two hours in raucous feasting and drinking. At one point, Tardin, the older sailor supervising Min'darr's knot tying, came over with a rope to test him.

After doing six knots, Min'darr tied a buntline hitch, hog-tying the chief petty officer and sending him back to his chair amidst guffaws, back slaps, and much deserved laughter. First Officer Bucurt quickly wiped his face and left the group. Min'darr and Kor'tif shared a smile as Bucurt left the inn with a beautiful, albeit scantily clad, young woman.

"Oh, to be young again," lamented the captain. "There are many more where she came from, Magician, if you're of a mind."

"Thank you, Captain, I will attend to more serious matters." With that, he stood and bid the crew farewell.

"So ya knows, Min'darr the Magician, we will be sailing between the islands in about a week. That should take a month, give or take. We plan to sail north from here in about ten weeks, if you happen to be looking for passage about then. I'd be honored to sail ye anywhere."

"Thank you, sir. I will keep that in mind. Good sailing and stay away from those squid!" They laughed and wished him well.

He stepped out into a dark night, cooler and quieter. Street lanterns flickered with the breeze, a salty one blowing inland across the bay. He walked around the building to its other entrance, the one for rented rooms and climbed three flights of stairs to the room he'd rented earlier.

It was a simple room with a bed, bureau for clothes, chair, table, and a lamp, which he lit with the matches provided. He could have easily ignited the thing with magic, he opted to act 'normal' following this afternoon's ghostly encounter,

Neither his body nor his mind would rest. He'd forgotten how a bed felt, used to a ship's hammock and its perpetual movement. This no longer felt right. His mind also rebelled, musing over the warning the Order's ghost provided. He felt heavy, suspecting it wasn't from being back on dry land. *What could this Naldalek have been warning me of? How is it my appearance here could foretell a disaster for the Order? I have too many questions and nowhere to go to find answers.*

He got up and removed the diamond from his cloak. It instantly warmed to his touch. It also had a slight glow to it. Yellow. He moved across the room to stand before the mirror above the bureau. There was a slight aura around him. Yellow, not the blue he'd come to expect when he showed an aura. Magic of the Dead. *Could it be ... from the ghost? That's when I got this heaviness sensation.*

He looked again at the diamond and thought of Naldalek. The gem brightened. *A magical gift? What is it for? What can it do? The mages in Vila'Borin each had many jeweled rings.* "Well, I guess I'll have to wait to find out." He settled back into bed, allowing both the breezes and the muted din from *Kinsmen's Table* to lull him to sleep.

*

By midmorning, Min'darr had travelled up into the hilly terrain known as Highlands, the main residential area of Marsapti. Despite a restless night, his massive breakfast at the inn promised him enough energy for the day. He found and walked up the pathway to his destination.

An older man opened the door. "What?"

"I am Min'darr, a friend of Hinasha's. We sailed together on the *Wind Snare*," Min'darr said.

The man looked past him and around, then grasped Min'darr's shirt and pulled him in, saying, "Thank you for coming."

Min'darr was escorted to a room on the second floor. In the bed lay Hinasha, markedly thinner and much paler than he'd been the day before when they'd disembarked.

"Go, please," Hinasha said waving to the man. He left and Hinasha pointed to a chair.

Min'darr sat. "How are you feeling? You look ... umm ..."

"Like I'm dying? Yes. This disease is particular to the islands. Natives like me are fine if we stay here. If we leave, the disease becomes active and starts to decimate the body. It takes a long time. Like I told you, I've been gone fifteen years, long enough to make it fatal.

"Returning sooner may have helped, like I said, even though I had to stay away. Once I came back, it has gotten much, much worse. I saw a doctor yesterday. She said I may not see the sun set today. Can you stay?"

Min'darr reached out and took his hand. *Cold.* "I am here for as long as you want me here."

Hinasha managed a weak smile. "Thank you, my friend." His eyelids fluttered and his breathing was shallow. "I need to sleep." He drifted off as quickly as he'd said it.

The older man returned. "He doesn't hurt as much when he sleeps. Good. He was convinced you would not come." He sat in the chair on the other side of the bed. "'Asha told me you are a powerful magician, different from the villains we have here. 'Blue magic?' he said."

"What is this disease he has? I've never heard of one that does this to a person," Min'darr said.

"Disease? Is that what he told you?" The man shook his head and sighed. "My son is cursed. He knows too much of the Order. They cursed him when they kicked him out. Put a spell on him with their death magic, they did.

"He had to run away. Their magic is strongest here, at its source. The further away he got, the less it affected him. Gave him fifteen years to live his life. Otherwise, he would have died within a week. When he got sicker up north, he knew. Prolonging the suffering made no sense to him. So, he came home to die. Damn them! My boy ..." Sobs overtook his words. Min'darr crossed over to hold the man.

Two hours later, Min'darr heard Hinasha's raspy breathing. He looked at his former cabin mate who now appeared as old as any Min'darr could imagine. He woke Hinasha's father, seated in the chair across from him.

Hinasha's eyes were wide and searching. His father held his hands and Min'darr stood at the foot of the bed. Hinasha mouthed words while staring at Min'darr. All he could make of it was "... fifth law ..."

A sudden pain shot through Min'darr's side. He rubbed at his leg and felt the heat from the diamond. He brought it out, glowing brightly. It vibrated and magically elongated, reforming itself into a dagger, a diamond embedded in its handle.

Hinasha pointed at it. His father lunged and, snatching it from Min'darr's hand, drove it into his son's chest. Hinasha exhaled his last breath. The gem changed from yellow to a pulsing green.

His father lifted himself off of his son's body and turned to Min'darr. "Thank you," he said sighing, and left the room.

Min'darr stood speechless. Hinasha's body lay unmoving, the magic dagger still impaled in his chest with the pulsing diamond embedded within a rich wooden handle with a lighter toned inlay. He reached out and removed the knife. He saw the blade, too, was diamond. There was no sign of blood. As he held the dagger, it transformed back into a gemstone, pulsing green.

The Sodality

A near-empty bottle stood atop the kitchen table, a full glass in front of the old man. Min'darr sat down at the table. The man pushed the bottle toward him. He gently pushed it back.

The old man said, "I'm Goytel. Hinasha was my only son, and even though he's been gone so damnably long, I knew ... I knew wherever he was that he was alive. Now, he's finally come home and their accursed magic has finally killed him. My son is dead," he sobbed.

Silence permeated the room. Min'darr cleared his throat. Goytel wiped his nose and looked up at him.

"What can you tell me of the dagger?" he asked.

"You, a magician ... you want to know about a magical artifact from me? How am I to know? How could you have known to have brought it to save my son's soul without knowing what it is? Me? I can tell you nothing."

Min'darr sat back. "You're lying to me. The instant you saw the dagger, you fell over yourself to take it and drive it into your son's heart. Why?"

Goytel squirmed. "I've heard things. It was worth a try."

"A try to what? What does it do to a person's soul? Or did you kill him to prevent their magic from finishing its work? What do you know of the school's set of laws ... the fifth one?"

"I have no idea about any laws they may have," he retorted. "What do you know of my son?" the old man asked.

Min'darr related the story Hinasha had told him while aboard the *Wind Snare.*

"Then you know some." Goytel sighed and emptied the glass in front of him. "Hinasha was our one child. When he was six,

244

he'd been with my wife at the market when a group of students of the Order decided to have some of their brand of fun.

"I'll spare you the grisly details. My wife died two days later, an aftereffect of their magic. Years later, when he was fifteen, old enough to join the Order, he took me by surprise by announcing he would join them. I was livid. I refused to speak to him.

"The day he entered their school, he forcibly hugged me goodbye and whispered in my ear, "I do this for Mother. Knowing how to make them pay has been my life's goal. I will not fail you, Father."

He drained the bottle into his glass. After a long draught, he continued. "About a month later, near dawn, Hinasha showed up at the door, wide-eyed and panting, frightened beyond anything I'd ever seen. He told me of the things that had happened, the same as he told you. He told me he'd been cursed by the Master and was going to die, to keep him silent.

"I forced him out. With little more than a change of clothing and as many coins as I had, we slipped down to the harbor and smuggled him aboard a northbound trading ship leaving that morning.

"He wasn't the first to be cursed. Over the years, those who'd experienced the cult but were rejected, died within days if they stayed here. Those who escaped the islands, getting as far away from here as possible, lived longer, fuller lives. I got a letter from him a month ago. In it he said his life was ending and he needed to come home to see me one last time." Goytel dropped his head to the tabletop and dabbed his eyes.

A minute later he raised his head to face Min'darr. "Is there any way you can help end this evil Order? Thousands of lives will be the better for it. I apologize to you for acting in accordance with my grief.

"I do know some things. In yellow magic, gems save and blades collect souls. Fire will destroy a soul and water holds their magic at bay. And wood ... anything made of wood is immune to their magic. That is what I know."

The two men hugged each other at the door. "Stay strong, Goytel. Better days may come your way. I've come to these islands to learn about them, this Order of yellow magic users. I can promise you nothing except my effort and my will."

*

The roadways and paths were steep in this part of town. Min'darr found himself tiring. He paused to catch his breath in front of a store. He entered and ended up purchasing a walking stick. Next to the store was the *Korbalic Café*. He stepped inside to quench his thirst. The café was empty save for four young men wearing similar tan-colored cloaks seated at a corner table.

Before he could sit down, one of the group, the one with lighter hair, spoke up. "Say, you there. You cannot be in here when we are. Step back outside and wait 'til we leave."

Min'darr glanced at them and sat down. He noticed the woman working in the café kept herself back in the kitchen, repeatedly looking out toward him.

"This won't do," said the same person. "You must be a stranger here. You don't know the rules." He stood up, quickly followed by the other three.

"And do these rules allow you to be rude to strangers?" Min'darr asked.

"Quint, the man obviously knows nothing. Leave him be." The tallest of the others sounded anxious, trying to dissuade his fellow.

"Don't you know, Slakoda, that this is precisely the kind of person we can help educate. He must be taught." Before any response could be made, the blond gestured and the chairs around Min'darr's table flipped away. The chair he sat on didn't move. Min'darr had felt a wave, like the wind, wash over him.

"By Loy, Quint, how could you miss? You need to go back to Master Lyr's tutelage." Slakoda laughed.

The blond, Quint, sneered back at his friends. "Not during this lifetime." He gestured again.

As he did, Min'darr anticipated his move and with a subtle gesture, timed his magic to send Quint's magic back at him. The yellow surge boomeranged, knocking Quint off his feet, into his friends, bowling them over. The tangle of arms, legs, table and chair legs untied themselves amidst jeers and accusations among them.

Min'darr stood, laughing as loudly as he could. "My, my, my ... you gents are certainly a threat. To yourselves more than anyone else, it seems." He turned to face the waitress who kept herself in the kitchen. "Can I have an ade, please. Whatever flavor you have the most of."

He turned to the four who had managed to stand. Min'darr walked to the doorway faster than Quint and stood in his way. "You can't leave yet."

"I can do anything I want to do. Get out of my way." He physically pushed against Min'darr, failing to move him. "Move!" he yelled.

"You are of the Order. Your Masters, I'm certain, would not want you to dishonor them by leaving this delightful café in such chaos. Please go back and straighten the tables and chairs."

The one called Slakoda headed back to do as asked and encouraged the others to do likewise. Quint stood his ground. "No one tells me what to do."

Min'darr tilted his head, looking at him. "I didn't tell you what to do, Quint. I asked.

Your magic failed you. You used it wrongly. It is not something to be toyed with or abused by bullying people. It must be respected. Then you too can be respected."

"Big words coming from someone who knows nothing about magic." Quint shouted at the others over his shoulder. "Come. We're done here."

Min'darr allowed he and his friends to walk past him. Slakoda muttered a quick "sorry" under his breath as he walked by. They continued up the street and out of sight.

Min'darr turned and saw the woman standing next to a table with a glass of pale green juice. He walked to her.

"I know not how you accomplished that, my good sir. It looked like the same magic they have. I thank you for standing up to them. They have demeaned and threatened my customers so much of late that they come here no longer. See?" She swept her arm around the empty room.

"I hope, my lady, that this one called Quint will have a bad taste from his experience here and will leave you alone."

He gave her a copper to pay for his drink, which she refused.

He sat for a while enjoying his beverage, expecting the magic students to come back. They did not. His hostess let him sit in silence, thanking him again when he stood to leave.

"There may be yet one more thing I can do here. Min'darr stood in the doorway and enlarged his magical aura. He was not surprised when it glowed with a yellow tone and not his magic's usual blue. *Something about the heaviness I've felt since my encounter with the ghost, Naldalek. He has to be the source of my yellow magic.*

He sensed no spell or other magic on the café. So he cast a spell placing a magical blanket over the café out as far as across the street. No other magic would work there, absorbed by his conjuring. He turned to her and said simply, "You and your customers are safe here."

*

He ate a light dinner, then returned to his room sitting in the darkness pondering his choices. The one thing he knew, without question, was that he must hide his blue magic. Naldalek's warning about being too powerful weighed heavily on his mind. The yellow magic was different and hard to sense using his own. He tried to use his new yellow magic to sense the blue magic, ending with a headache.

To be certain, he searched his eldritch stream for more than an hour until he found the confirmation he sought. His own magic could be stored in some inanimate object for up to two lunar cycles.

Min'darr sat at the window of his room, the rising moon visible to the east. He worked his spell and drained his own blue magic from him. He'd selected his walking stick as a receptacle. *The wood is from life itself, ancient life, and it is immune to yellow magic, so it's safe from any magical enchantment.* He kept a pinch of his magic after he preserved the stick, making it safe from harm, loss, or destruction.

Min'darr then took the diamond and held it up before the moon. Summoning the magic of Naldalek, he called to the spirit of Hinasha, invoking his magic to release his soul to the heavens and to his god, Loy.

An ethereal fog surrounded the gem. A quick shock stung Min'darr's thumb and a small bolt of light shot upward toward the moon like an arrow.

*

Checking his goods into a locker the next morning, except the clothes on his back, the diamond, and his walking stick, Min'darr walked up to the gated property at the top of the highest hill on the island and rapped on the entrance door.

Within a short time, a woman opened the door's peephole. "What is it you want?"

"I want to learn the ways of yellow magic," he said plainly.

"No, sir, you don't."

"Let me come in. Go, announce me to your headmaster," he insisted.

She shook her head as in despair. The peephole closed and the gate opened. She stepped aside to allow him in. "Only Death lives here, ya know."

Min'darr gave a wry smile. "Maybe up until now."

She escorted him across a large, well-groomed yard and into the house. Without speaking, she continued down a dark hallway. The shadows seemed to watch them as they passed.

*

The headmaster's office was markedly brighter, being on the southeast corner of the building. The early morning sunshine seemed a contradiction to the rest of the place Min'darr had seen. Well-kept and clean, yet naturally old, borderline dismal. Well-worn upholstered chairs and a matching overstuffed settee surrounded a coffee table made from a cross section of a large tree. The wall hangings were either maps or nautical charts, with the one exception of a large portrait of an ancient man above a fireplace. Min'darr noted the fact that he'd met that man's spirit. The founder, Naldalek.

The headmaster stood as Min'darr was ushered in. He extended his hand, each finger adorned with a ring. The metal bands varied in composition and design, and each had a gemstone

249

as a central feature. Min'darr sensed a magical aura surrounding the man, emanating from the rings.

Min'darr shook his hand, expecting some kind of magical charge to jump between them. Nothing happened.

"Welcome to the Sodality. I am Tristian, the magistrate of the Order. What is it we can do for you?"

"I am thankful for your time, Magistrate Tristian. My name is Min'darr. I have heard much of the Order in the northern regions of my homeland. Powerful magicians from the southern islands came our way and impressed many with their skills. I am most interested in learning about your school, and the magic used by your Order."

"Do you wish to work magic, Min'darr?"

"I may have already. I wouldn't know for certain."

During the hours of his voyage, he'd practiced this conversation, unsure if he should use his own name or some other. He'd keep his blue magic hidden, if possible, and work to acquire the other to better understand it. He hadn't anticipated getting yellow magic from Naldalek himself.

"Tell me," the magistrate said.

"Long ago, when I was a child of about five years, two robbers attacked my family, killing my father. They held my mother, sister, and me captive. I was more afraid than ever before. When they started to strip my mother of her clothes to rape her, my fear turned to anger and I wished more than anything that they would die.

"I do not recall specifically what happened. I remember yelling out. The next thing I knew, the two were both dead, lying on the floor, one across my mother's legs. Mother praised the Creator for striking them down. I never told her or anyone this before." Min'darr sat with his head down, hands in his lap.

"And what makes you believe you worked this ... this miracle?" he asked.

"When I yelled out, something else came out of me, a force, an energy ... something.

"Most interesting. History is replete with instances of unexplained phenomena like yours. There may be something of substance to your memory." Tristian stood and came around his desk. "Let me hold your shoulders. I will be able to sense if you have any magic within you."

Min'darr stood to face him. The magistrate touched his shoulders for a few seconds. His left eyebrow rose. 'I do believe, my good man, that you have some sensitivity to magic. I seriously doubt you can exercise any sort of control of it. That is something we instruct our students to do here. We teach, not only about the magic, but how a person, such as yourself, can learn to use it and to make it an integral part of your life. Through us, you could eventually become a magician."

"I would like that, sir, very much." Min'darr smiled as innocently as he could.

"Very good," he said. "How soon would you be able to report here to start your tutelage?"

Min'darr continued smiling. "About ten minutes ago."

The Seven Rules

"The Order requires a minimum of three years of a learner's life. In its early times, new learners came mainly from the more local Southern Islands. Within the last three decades, more and more candidates have come from the northern mainland and the western continent. Of those who enrolled throughout its history, less than two-thirds survive to become full magicians." The words of the magistrate echoed in his head as Tristian orated the school's history.

*

After touring the grounds and buildings, they arrived in the dining room in time for lunch. Magistrate Tristian brought Min'darr to the front table, introducing him to the masters who were present, each one shaking his hand. Each hand he shook was adorned with jewel-studded rings. Min'darr was the spectacle of the room, being watched by about a dozen other students who were seated at three different tables located within the room.

"Oh, they'll get to know you soon enough," Master Lyr said. "Kind of a naturally suspicious lot. I am master of your team, the Blue Team, Min'darr. Welcome. Stay here at this table," he said gesturing. "Your team comes to lunch in about twenty minutes."

Min'darr sat at the round table Master Lyr pointed to. One person at another table was the only one to mutter any kind of greeting. The diamond in his pocket felt warm. *Probably from being in the midst of these workers of magic. More yellow magic around here to react to.* He looked around intently in an attempt to notice anything that seemed significant. In fact, the room, short of the dining tables and chairs, was sparsely furnished. No vases, side tables, or desks could be seen, neither were there any wall hangings.

Within the appointed time, the two groups who had been eating left the dining room and two others came in. The conversation of the group wearing blue tunics ceased when they saw Min'darr seated at their table. A young woman with thin brown hair in a ponytail led them, holding up her hand to stop their walking and talking. Collectively, they then approached in single file. Master Lyr also stepped to the table, arriving simultaneously.

"Good day, Lokina, Blue Team, greetings. I trust your morning has been good. It is my pleasure to introduce you to your new group member, Min'darr. He hails from ... ahh, oh, dear, I've forgotten. Well, from the northern mountain regions, umm ... well north of us, eh, Min'darr?"

"Yes, Master Lyr. The Dreklidal Mountains of Rougahn," he replied.

"Yes, yes. Well and good. I'll let you get acquainted. Lokina, please bring Min'darr to your sessions this afternoon. That is until we can give him his own class schedule. You are expected, as leader, to help assess his current level of proficiency. Your own work will be suspended until his first evaluation in a week." He returned to his table.

Lokina sighed and stared at Min'darr. "How old are you?" she asked.

"Twenty-six," he said.

"Wrong!" she said loudly. "The expected response around here would be, 'It doesn't concern you,' or 'Why do you want to know?' or 'Who cares?' I already know more about you than I'd ever want to know. As workers of magic, the less anyone knows about you the better. What you know about me right this second is as much as you will ever know about me. Got it?"

"Understood, Leader Lokina." Min'darr kept his voice flat and without affect.

"Good," she added. They sat down as wait staff served lunch. Min'darr could not identify anything on his plate, yet he ate as readily as his new team members did. It was palatable. "Introduce yourselves," she told the others.

The boy to his left spoke first. "I am Bikutah, a First Year from ..." He stopped at a stern look from Lokina. He had darker hair and a round face. He didn't seem pudgy at all.

"My name is Demiltarf," said a taller-than-normal young man about Min'darr's age. He had sandy hair and a great nose, enough to fill almost two faces.

After a short pause, the third added, "Mygili" with a nod of her head, her red hair entwined in a ball atop her head. He noticed that she continued to watch him throughout lunch.

Nothing else came from his team members save the sounds of eating. Min'darr finally looked at Lokina and asked, "What class sessions are we scheduled for today?"

With a heavy emphasis on her first word, she replied. "I am scheduled for a session with Master Vukbee. I will be helping train the First Years in understanding the Seven Rules."

"Perfect." Min'darr worked to keep his smile from showing.

"Why would that be 'perfect'?" she asked, head tilting to her right.

"Well, I can't imagine a better place to start my understanding of yellow magic than to be exposed to the rules governing its use. Or am I mistaken?"

"Do you have any idea what yellow magic is?" she asked.

Min'darr nodded. "It is the energies from those who have died and how to manipulate it to perform a desired task." *Not sure where that came from. Sounds pretty good, though.*

Lokina raised an eyebrow. Mygili's eyes widened. "That is the exact wording from the Scrolls," she whispered. "Nicely done, Min'darr."

"So, exactly how much do you know?" Lokina asked. "I'm not interested in wasting my time on stuff you already have learned. How did you get to see the Scrolls?"

"I haven't seen any scrolls." Min'darr looked at his team across the table. The suspicion on their faces told him enough. He turned to Lokina. "I assure you, anything you can tell me and teach me will not be a waste of time. Yours or mine."

*

Half an hour later, they sat in Master Vukbee's suite. The class consisted of about fifteen students of varying ages. Most were younger than Min'darr. Master Vukbee was an attractive middle-aged woman with short, green hair sticking straight out in every direction. She spoke with a northern accent and, like Master Lyr, had gem-studded rings on each finger. She was missing her left thumb.

She went to work with half a dozen Second-Year learners on situational ethics, whether to use magic when other means might work. Lokina pulled Min'darr and seven others aside to work on the Seven Rules. The rest were also like Lokina, Third-Year learners and were debating some point of history and how it may have been altered with a wise dose of magic.

Min'darr was given a scroll containing the Seven Rules. The moment his hand touched it, he felt that same heaviness overwhelm him. He had to take deep, deliberate breaths to keep from slumping over at the table.

Words, spell-making chants, and vague memories swirled through his mind. He looked out and saw another room. He recognized it as the room he was in, despite being furnished differently and occupied by other people. They were dim, not fully there, ghostly in their appearance. He could see they were talking, but he couldn't hear them.

He watched closely. The master's voice did not correspond to the mouthings of the master he saw. *Different words.*

"This was the first class taught through the Seven Rules. No more disasters after that. The magic and the magician had to be protected," it said in his mind.

It took a moment for Min'darr to put things together. The vision showed him the past and the voice speaking to him sounded identical to the old weapons seller, the ghost, *Naldalek! The ancient master was probably one of the authors of the very scroll I have in my hand.* Instantly, a rush of words leaped from the scroll into Min'darr's consciousness. He heard countless voices reciting its contents in unison. He had an immediate knowledge of the contents of the entire scroll.

The vision ended abruptly. Lokina and the other learners were staring at him. Lokina stared hardest. "I asked you a question. Are you or are you not going to open the scroll? If you are interested in learning the Seven Rules, it is best to at least read them. Or ... can't you read?"

Min'darr sat for a heartbeat.

"You must stand out!" the specter's voice screamed within him.

Before he could think to do or say anything, he stood, eyes closed, and began reciting the Seven Rules. He could hear that the voice coming from him was one other than his own. Try as he might, he could not stop it from speaking. "The First Rule is 'Magic is a precious energy and must never be wasted or misused.' The Second Rule is 'Never summon magic you will not use.' The Third Rule is 'Summoned magic must always be used.' The Fourth Rule is 'Magic may not be used for personal profit or enrichment.' The Fifth Rule is 'The sources of your magic must never be revealed to outsiders, under penalty of your own immediate death.' The Sixth Rule is 'Each magician must stand on his/her own in its application.' The Seventh Rule is 'All magic in your possession at the time of your death must accompany you beyond the Veil.'"

Blank stares returned his gaze.

"By Loy, what voice was that?" Lokina gasped.

"You are blessed." Master Vukbee said. "That was a Voice of the Dead. To hear such a voice is a gift from beyond the Veil of Creation." Min'darr was the instant center of attention in the room. "Come here," Vukbee said while gesturing him toward her.

He walked to her and she took him by the shoulders. Closing her eyes, she stood silently, absorbed in examining his aura.

*

Min'darr sat in the magistrate's outer office as they discussed him. He had a vague recollection of what had happened. The masters referred to it as a blessing. Min'darr thought of it more as a haunting. Clearly, the spirit of Naldalek had possessed him, using his body to recite the Seven Rules. That would stay with him, unspoken. *If these masters had any belief that the ghost of one of their founding fathers was empowering me, I will never have a chance to learn their ways. I must be allowed to understand this magic. Why is it so different, so hard for my blue magic to detect?*

His musings were interrupted by the magistrate's secretary. "They will see you now."

He walked into Tristian's office. Seven of them sat round the tree table, which was somehow considerably larger than when he'd been there earlier that morning. Masters Tristian, Lyr, and Vukbee were present, all of whom he'd met, along with Master Piftoren, whom he'd met at lunch. Three others sat at the table who he'd not met.

Magistrate Tristian stood and called for attention, then looked at Min'darr. "Well, Min'darr, you have most certainly had a busy day. Never before in our history has a spirit possessed a First Year, especially considering you have not yet been here a full day. Most curious, yet delightfully so." He sat back down. "Master Vukbee."

She had a different look. From the gentle, although anxious, face of the woman who felt genuine concern for him in her classroom, she appeared as overtly stern, her jaw clenched and lips thinned. She stood, her chair scraping the floor as it pushed back. She came slowly around the table and stopped in front of him.

"Immediately following the voicing, I examined this one and found him to be saturated with yellow magic. He has no gems except for a solitary diamond in his cloak pocket. It is empty, powerless, and could not account for this feat." She paused. Shaking her head, she turned to face the masters.

"I cannot find any way in which Min'darr has perpetrated any kind of ploy or trick on us. It is a most untimely event, being his first day. Suspicions abound." She turned to face Min'darr. "I apologize, for I must join with you to know the truth of how yellow magic fills you as if you were the gem, your own touchstone. Our memories will be one."

"No, Aglagha. You cannot. It goes so far beyond what is acceptable," Master Lyr panted as he leaned forward over the table.

Magistrate Tristian placed a hand on Lyr's arm, restraining him. "No, Lyr. She is correct. Please proceed, Master Vukbee."

Min'darr stood, stunned. He hadn't anticipated any interference in his quest to understand yellow magic. This spirit of Naldalek obviously had some kind of goal and Min'darr was his chosen tool. He recalled the ghost's words to him at the weapons cart.

"Get thee gone! Do not stay! There is nothing for you here but suffering and death. You are too powerful for them to allow you to live."

He could consider that later, however. He hadn't anticipated, let alone prepared for, an intrusion such as this. *No way can I let her into my head ... my memories. She'd know everything! Naldalek, his warning, for certain, also everything about me that was blue magic ... my magic. And she'd learn that I cast the spell that killed the two yellow magic magicians on the pier ... the ones hired by the shipping magnate, Wada, to kill me and my family.*

"No," pleaded Min'darr. "You mustn't do this."

"I promise, you will feel no pain," she said as she clasped her hands together and lowered her gaze. A heartbeat later she looked up. Her eyes radiated yellow light. Her hands glowed and, when separated, were connected with sparkling, yellow streaks. She reached toward him, the eldritch power arching between her palms.

Min'darr became overwhelmed with heaviness, the same he'd first felt with Naldalek at the weapons cart. He found he couldn't move, nor could he protest. No sound came from his mouth, despite his yearning to yell.

Vukbee had told the truth. He felt no pain. He felt nothing at all. Her magic passed over him, shooting out in all directions. It crackled like lightning and bounced off Min'darr, striking the other masters, cracking the table, igniting a fire in the fireplace, and singeing the frame of the founder's portrait.

The masters howled and yelped, screaming for her to stop. She seemed frozen, unmoving with her mouth agape, eyes wide and unblinking. Master Tristian barked an order and the other masters directed their own magical energies, blasting Vukbee aside, landing her in a full stiff sprawl onto the settee.

They surged toward her to assess her condition and offer their aid. Tristian stood next to Min'darr. In a gentle voice, he asked Min'darr, "How have you accomplished this?"

Min'darr stood silently. "I truly had nothing to do with this, Magistrate."

The man looked hard at him. "I believe you, son. I also believe you can shed some light on what is happening around you." He paused a moment to watch as Vukbee sat up, blinking. "You will dine with me tonight. Report to your quarters. I'll summon you when it is time." He then joined the others in tending to their fellow master.

Speaking Truth

"The amount of energy released by the death of this chicken can lift a ten-pound rock and throw it farther than an arrow can fly at a forty-five degree arc," Magistrate Tristian said, holding a piece of fried chicken in his fingers, between bites of potato salad and roast chicken. "It is far more staggering than most people could imagine.

"Life is powerful," he continued. "When a trained individual, sensitive to the arcane applications of those energies uses them adroitly, the results are magical, in every aspect of the word. What do you think, Min'darr?" he asked.

"What of the potato's energies?" he asked without any hesitation.

Tristian chuckled until he shook. "Masterful! I love the fact that you seem to absorb knowledge so readily.

"That, my young friend, brings me to the happenings of today." He glanced at the clock on the mantlepiece. "It has been a span of merely ten hours or so since you first appeared on my doorstep, so to speak. Tell me about yourself."

Min'darr swallowed his food and inhaled deeply. "Well, there truly is little to say. I've told you of my father's death and my experience—I think you used the word arcane?—with his murderers. The rest is fairly plain.

"I worked in the stable of my town and later guided merchants and travelers through the mountain passes until my mother died and I felt I needed to leave. I came down to Vila'Borin and took a position with Wada Shipping and later at a café cleaning tables. Both in my own sailing and at the cafe, I spoke with countless others of their travels. Many of them spoke of seeing people from the Southern Islands doing things impossible to do.

"'Magic' was the word so many of them whispered, whether out of respect or fear, I don't know. The more I heard, the more I wanted to know. And the more I felt it could be somehow connected to my youth and what I did to those murderers.

"So, I decided to find my way here to learn if I had the potential to be a worker of magic. That's about it." He took a long drink of his lemonade, sating both his thirst and his unwillingness to lie any more than he had to.

Tristian wiped his mouth with a napkin and sat back in his chair. "I would say to you as I said earlier. I sensed some magic or magic potential in you when we first met. Raw and uninspired.

"But, since then, you have shown yourself to harbor more power than any combination of two or three First-Year students."

"How is Master Vukbee?" Min'darr interrupted.

"She is recovering, thank you," the magistrate replied. "But before any of that, I must ask you—Purula aba tay sendirka—have you consciously contacted or accessed any source of magical energy since your arrival to the Southern Islands?"

"What was that ... that 'puru aba tasendah' thing you said?" Min'darr asked.

"That was a spell, a magical incantation that requires anyone in this room to speak only the truth," he said.

An upwelling of something surged within Min'darr. He thought for a moment he might be sick. Instead, he became detached, displaced within his own body. He'd lost control. Min'darr felt his lungs fill with air and his lips move. He then heard his own voice saying, "No, Magistrate. I promise you that nothing like that has happened. I am not one to be feared."

Then it was gone. *Naldalek answered so I would not have to lie. I am possessed!*

Magistrate Tristian grinned. "Good. I felt I would have known if anything was different.

"Our quandary remains. What happened when Master Vukbee tried to connect with your memory? How were you able to deflect her magic? Or, I'm sorry, that presumes you had an active role, that potential we have eliminated.

"Still, I have seen her perform that feat numerous times. She knows what she is doing. So, can you lend your perceptions?"

Min'darr thought how to answer. The welling up did not reoccur, and the truth spell was yet in place. "I can say that I felt covered by something heavy. Could someone else place a spell on me to keep her spell from working?" he asked, in part to deflect his deliberately vague answer.

"Yes. Yes, of course. If this cover you speak of was magical in nature, it had to have come from someone else."

"I guess, with so many learners of magic so close ... I mean, it is a possibility."

The Magistrate looked pensive. "Would there be any motive by any of our students?"

Min'darr looked thoughtful, fully knowing what his answer would be. "What if one of your students had acted wrongly, according to your Seven Rules, in my presence and wanted to keep Master Vukbee from discovering his act?"

"The magic you suggest is not complicated, but the level of it ... to be powerful enough to keep a master from breaking it, would suggest that it would violate several rules, on a few levels. Tell me what you are referring to."

"We are under your truth spell. I ask you to ask me to tell you," Min'darr said.

"Understood." He adjusted his position and drank some of his lemonade. "Min'darr, please tell me what you know of any such act by any student in this school."

Min'darr responded with a detailed accounting of the events at the *Korbalic Café* involving the Tan Team, with the exception of his own use of magic. He recounted the actions of Quint against him after he'd tried bullying him out of the room and made sure to give Slakoda credit for his attempts to divert Quint. Finally, he repeated what Dasapti had told him about their history of frightening her customers.

Magistrate Tristian sighed. "I am familiar with this one. Quint is the leader of the Tan Team. Rest assured, we have a process to deal with such infractions. Normally I'd object to it. In this case, I think I will insist on it. Thank you for bringing this to my attention."

*

The quarters for his Blue Team was a suite of five rooms, four bedrooms around a centered sitting room and shared bathroom. His own bedroom ranked as the smallest of the lot with barely enough room to squeeze sideways between the end of the cot and his trunk to open and close the curtains of the old window.

He lay on the cot listening to the winds rustle the leaves of the trees outside his room. A tap on the doorframe broke his concentration. Craning his neck, he saw Mygili. She looked very different with her hair down, flowing over her shoulders.

"Are you all right?" she asked quietly.

Min'darr spun and sat with his legs crossed. "Come in."

She paused a second, then sat on the corner of the trunk. She looked at him expectantly, waiting for him to answer her question.

"I'm fine," he said. "Thank you for asking."

"Rumors are flying throughout the school. Did you kill Vukbee?" she asked.

"No. The magistrate said she'd be fine."

"Good. I don't know you. So, you can be like Lokina, or you can be nice like the rest of us try to be. What happened?"

"Do you want to know because you might be able to help with your understanding, or does knowing give you power over the rest of them?" Min'darr answered.

She stood, her eyes narrowing. "Like Lokina then." She started to leave. Min'darr's outstretched arm across the doorway stopped her.

"Look, I've always believed myself to be a decent person and I don't want that to change. Forgive me, but you might be just like her. I don't know you either or your intentions. Knowing that would help me get to know you," Min'darr said with a smile.

She sat back down. "Don't let her jaded perspective rub off on you, then. If you start off treating people well, more will want to associate with you. Lokina's way is a minority here. She keeps

263

people away from her, doesn't have to deal with personal issues that way. It has something to do with her past."

Min'darr smiled. "Thank you. That does help, makes me more comfortable," he added.

"You're welcome. I like being comfortable around others. So, what happened with Master Vukbee?" she asked again.

"I have no idea. She was trying some kind of spell on me and it, like, blew up. She lost control or something pushed back ... I don't know. I've got nothing to compare it to. I've no idea about this yellow magic or how it works.

"The magistrate was kind enough, but he thinks there is something about me that caused it or contributed to it. I've no clue." Min'darr sat as he spoke, looking sufficiently sheepish.

"I'd offer to help," Mygili said. "But we're not allowed to use any magic on each other. They always know. No matter. This has given me a chance to say hi and, hopefully make a new friend. I like ..."

A voice filled Min'darr's mind. Mygili's too, based on her reaction. "All learners are directed to come to the Weir Chamber immediately."

"By Loy. That's not good. Somebody's going to get spent," she said. "C'mon." She grabbed his hand, leading him out of his room and to the doorway of their suite. She looked at him with a small smile. "I like talking with you. Thanks. I've needed someone like you."

"Thank you, Mygili. It's nice to have a friend." Min'darr smiled back.

They joined the flow of other students heading to the same place.

"What did you mean about someone getting spent? What happens there?" Min'darr asked walking quickly to keep astride.

"It's a magical chamber. A war room of sorts. Magical challenges and conflicts are played out there. Some are punishments." She looked at him more intently. "Have you been completely honest with me?"

"Of course," he responded. "Why?"

"Seeing all you've been through today ... well, never mind."
She walked a bit faster and turned, following the rest into a tall,
darker room. They moved to the right and sat with Bikutah and
Demiltarf on bench-like seating. Torches set into recesses in the
chamber's stone walls gave off a dull, flickering light. The center
of the room was sunken some eight to ten feet beneath them,
remaining shadowed. Above them and to his left was a loft, a
smaller seating area. *That could be the area where Hinasha's ordeal
happened,* he thought.

The room filled and the general whispering faded. Most of the
other students were looking at Min'darr. *Whatever they've heard ...
this would be their first glimpse of "the new guy."* As a team, seventeen
masters entered the room. Five descended steps to the lower floor
area. The rest spread themselves around the room at the top level,
behind the seats.

Mygili sat next to him and took his hand, squeezing it. "I'm
sorry, I hope this is okay with you. I just don't have a very good
feeling about this," she whispered.

He turned to see her looking at him. "What could go wrong?"
Min'darr asked sarcastically.

The Weir Battle

Min'darr glanced around the chamber. *About forty-five, fifty people maybe.* Despite the number of people in the room, it remained surprisingly quiet. *Weird. Ha! Weird in the Weir Chamber.*

Then it got notably darker, but none of the torches had been extinguished. He looked around, clearly seeing each torch. All were lit, each of the flames were the same size, yet their light had greatly diminished. *Why?*

Within the well at the room's center, the magistrate stood bathed in a yellowish glow. Before he even spoke, Min'darr surmised he'd cast a spell directing the torchlight to shine on him.

"Welcome all. You have been summoned here for two reasons. The first is to let you know that Master Vukbee is well. She has suffered a sorg'al, a negative surge of magical energies for you First Years. As a result, she has been cleansed by her fellow masters and will be back in her classroom tomorrow. She thanks you for your concerns.

"Now, this second matter is less palatable for me. This is, of course, due to the need for a magical reprimand. It would appear that one of the Seven Rules has been violated. The Usurper and the Accuser are both present and will be called upon as is our way.

"The rule broken is number four. It has been brought to our attention that a certain team has used magic as an intimidation, thus seeking to enrich their power base. As leader of that team, I hereby summon Quint ... come to the left of the Weir."

The Tan Team stood. Quint sidestepped his way to the steps and came down to stand behind the magistrate and to his left.

"The Tan Team and you specifically are charged with this violation. You have repeatedly used magic to privatize your patronage of the *Korbalic Café* by intimidating its customers, thus driving them out. According to the café's owner, she has lost money due directly to your abuses. How do you plead?"

*

Mygili leaned toward Min'darr. He met her halfway. She whispered while not taking her eyes off the floor area. "Oh, thank Loy. That one is a royal pain. He does nothing except bully everyone in his classes. Oh, he has the magical clout to pull it off, just no sense of what's right. Vicious. The poor Tans, they are the most dominated team members ever. Nobody has ever liked Quint. He and I were First Years together. Even then he was an ass.

"But whoever's accused him has a fight on their hands. He's beaten five others. He likes the Weir. He's a natural predator."

"What is the Weir?" Min'darr asked.

*

Quint stood at a military-esque form of attention. He had a sly smile. "I plead not guilty, Magistrate. I demand to face my accusers."

"It's a magical labyrinth. It catches magical energy and even the souls of combatants," she managed to say before Magistrate Tristian answered Quint's demand.

*

"I hereby summon Min'darr of the Blue Team. Come to the right of the Weir."

Min'darr smirked and, with a half-shrug, stood. Mygili stood, clasped his hand in both of hers. He had to unwrap them to proceed. "I'll be fine," he assured her. Her eyes told him of her concern. It made him smile as he made his way to the steps.

The rest of his team stood as well, agape at their newest member being summoned to the challenge. Each patted his back or shoulder as he passed them. Lokina whispered, "Kick his ass!" as he went by. Min'darr took his position opposite Quint's.

The magistrate's voice again filled the chamber. "No new student, especially on his first day here, should ever be expected to manage the demands and challenges of a Weir competition.

267

However, given what we have experienced with Min'darr, we feel he is magically capable.

"Given the fact that you, Quint, have been called on to endure this discipline for the sixth time, know this. Should you lose this challenge, you will be expelled from our school, stripped of all magic, and banned its use for your lifetime. Should you prevail, however, you will be stripped of your leadership of the Tan Team. Do you understand?"

Quint stared at Min'darr, finally seeming to recognize him. Without taking his eyes from his foe, Quint said, "By my victory here, magic will clear my name of these false charges brought by this ... this nobody."

The magistrate walked over to Min'darr while announcing the rules of the competition. "The Seven Rules must be obeyed at all times. Due to the nature of the competition, we will allow you to direct non-lethal magical energies at each other. Should you enter the Weir, rest assured that your body will be attended and protected. Remember that a soulless body cannot be attacked without dire consequence to the attacker. Lastly, and I say this for Min'darr's sake as Quint is well-versed in this process, the Weir is inhabited by lost souls of previous contestants. There have been many encounters with them in the past, some benign, others more fierce. If one finds you, assume the worst."

He stepped back to the edge of the staging area, raised both his arms in dramatic fashion and, in a louder voice, commanded, "Lower the Weir."

The gathered students applauded as a dark funnel was lowered from the upper reaches of the chamber, centered to descend into the middle of the room's well. It entered the light and Min'darr saw an intricately interwoven cone made of something tubular that flattened with either sections of parallel weavings or of cross-woven strands. Its diameter was easily close to twenty feet. It stopped with a quiver, hanging about three feet off the floor, tapering up beyond the reach of the chamber's torchlight.

Min'darr was tense. The heaviness of the yellow magic had never been greater. He felt as if his hands and feet were iron. *This is so very different from my magic.*

The voice of Naldalek brushed aside his own thoughts. *"Allow me to act, Blue Magician. I could easily obliterate this pup. I will make it look good for your sake."*

"Your guidance is appreciated Spirit. I do have some experience to draw from," Min'darr thought. *"This arrogant one does deserve to be embarrassed."*

"Agreed," said the spirit. *"A blend of blue and yellow, never done before."*

While they waited, he thought back to his brief encounter with Quint at the café. The youth had been cocky in his approach, assuming at the time that he was the more powerful. *Well, he should at least suspect I've got some magical clout, too.* Min'darr braced himself.

Magistrate Tristian again raised his arms. "I call upon the Almighty Loy to guide these combatants in our quest for the truth." He eyed both Quint and Min'darr. He brought his hands together in a magically enhanced clap while shouting "Atka!"

*

At the magistrate's command, both magicians reacted in an instant. Quint surrounded himself with an aura, squatted, and fired a blast of yellow magic at his foe.

Min'darr created a shield, taller than he stood. He stepped quickly to his right to avoid Quint's magic and disappeared. Quint's blast went past where Min'darr had been and dissolved against an eldritch barrier, strategically placed to protect the students attending the combat.

While surrounded by his magic, Min'darr felt a strong force pulling him toward the Weir. *Almost magnetic,* he thought. *I have to be careful based on what the magistrate said.* He could also easily see Quint's magical aura moving around the Weir toward him.

The combatants' magic glowed, auras surrounding each of them. When he stood behind his magical shield, he noted a tendril threaded out from Quint toward the other Tan Team students. When he looked as he changed position aside the shield, he could not see it.

As he moved across the staging area, Min'darr felt the dominant arcane pull from the Weir. Quint's movements also suggested he felt the same draw from the massive inverted funnel.

Another blast from Quint arched around the Weir. Min'darr saw it and deflected it with his shield. It immediately ricocheted toward the Weir which fiercely sucked it in. That confirmed to him that the Weir attracted magic. *Like a whirlpool, drawing in anything around it. Like me, maybe? Or Quint? I wonder ...*

Min'darr's mind took this information and processed it into a new plan of attack. *I have to keep on the opposite side.*

Watching Quint's glow, Min'darr saw it split into three parts. The two outer auras moved away from the center one, both heading toward Min'darr. *He can't be all three ... has to be a ruse.* Min'darr countered by sending three streams of energy out around the Weir. Each struck, adhering to Quint's auras. Min'darr yanked them, trying to drag each into the Weir. Two of them worked, the essence of their magic distorting as they disappeared into the cone of the Weir. The third tugged back against his magical lasso, then rose rapidly into the air, pulling it along and wrapping itself around the upper region of the Weir. Min'darr released his magic and the lasso thread dissolved.

Min'darr looked up to locate Quint and was distracted by the conical Weir's height. It appeared taller than the building they were in.

Quint's next magical blast swept over him. His aim was perfect. The force of the magic went behind Min'darr's shield and washed down, stunning him. He dropped to his knees and the shield he'd been using slammed into the side of the Weir and dissolved.

Min'darr had been using magic for several years, but had never before been struck by a blast of arcane energy. It tingled, stunning his entire body. His hearing and sight no longer made any sense to him. Part of him knew he was on the floor, yet he couldn't be sure which way was up.

Instinct kicked in. Maybe, too, it was the magic. His blue magic had protected him before. *I cleansed myself of blue magic, though. Maybe because it's different?* he wondered.

"Very little blue in you," Naldalek added. *"Time to attack."*

Min'darr surged his magic and his aura brightened, pushing back against the magic of Quint.

Still clinging to the upper part of the Weir, Quint redoubled his effort, sending out another blast. This time his magic bounced off Min'darr's aura.

Regaining his senses, Min'darr rolled aside and stood. In a sweeping motion, Min'darr fired a quick magical volley, knocking Quint from his perch. The youth caught himself with a quick incantation and floated to the floor. The two faced each other. The last time he'd faced another magician, Min'darr recalled, was on the wooden marketplace wharf at Vila'Borin. No such luck here, the flooring was stone.

"I like that spell," Naldalek said, and the power of his yellow magic fired off through Min'darr against their opponent. The spell swirled around Quint several times, deflecting off his aura. Its essence fell to the floor, soaking into it. It then rose into him through his feet.

As the spell took effect, Quint's smirk disappeared. He could no longer walk, his feet fused in place, becoming part of the stone floor. Panic swept across his face as the transformation quickly climbed his legs, stiffening his knees. Then anger. His visage distorted as rage took over. He knew he'd been defeated.

So did Min'darr. He stood and watched as the magic took effect. The battle was won. So Min'darr was not ready when Quint cast a final spell at him. It was a simple spell really. It could have been used to move a heavy cask or chest. Min'darr was knocked onto his back and slid across the floor until he stopped, wedged beneath the Weir.

Min'darr heard himself screaming. He'd no idea having his magic and his soul ripped out of him would be quite this painful.

Within

Nothing worked. Sight, touch, hearing, smell ... nothing. Complete sensory deprivation.

Min'darr had lost any sense of orientation. There was no up or down, over or across. Not far nor near nor in nor out. The one thing he knew was a static. What it was or where it came from he couldn't guess.

Besieged by this confusion, nothing seemed anywhere within his reach. His mind searched frantically for some kind of anchor to fasten onto, anything that might be familiar.

The anguish of being pulled out of his body echoed loudly in his memory. He had to orient himself quickly or he felt he would go mad. This was the one thing he could identify and so, reluctantly, he brought it back. The onslaught of pain resurged through him. He wrapped himself in it, shook from it, until another part of his awareness began tugging at him.

A voice? Distant. Familiar. Not through his ears, though. More like a shared thought.

He concentrated on it, pushing aside the pain memories to make room for this new sensation. Within a few moments, it sharpened. Quickly, he began to recognize the thoughts coming to him, the hint of actual words he could finally recognize, until the voice's scoffing inflections were clear.

"You were warned, Magician. I warned you! So suffer you must. Entering here is fatal for many. Very few can find a way to survive outside their physical forms. Yet, you may be different. It will cost you regardless." The voice rasped, breathy. Min'darr felt a proximity to the speaker.

"Why can't I see?" He reached for his eyes, feeling no movement.

Again the voice. *"Be still. Think of being, not seeing, not moving. Exist. You are no longer in a physical world of mass or space. Only your magic can serve you now."*

With that knowledge, Min'darr forced himself to relax and surrounded himself with the eldritch power he knew he possessed. The remembered pain faded, helping him to further calm himself. He began to sense his surroundings, strands of twisting pathways. *"Where am I?"*

"You are within the Weir," the voice said. *"You are at the threshold to Eternity,"*

"Naldalek, how?" he asked. As he did, an aura became evident to him, pure light. There was no background, no physical sense of position or even of space. His recalled the arcane flow of blue magic he'd experienced many times so long ago. *At least that had some aspects of spatial context. Not this. Not here.* Here he felt completely disembodied.

"It simply is, Magician. Yet, this is not the fate you are destined for. You must work to correct this, for I am not allowed to free you. That is something you must earn.

"Should you have been pure, not contaminated by other magic, you would be better able to free yourself. As it is, Magician, you may face an eternity within this appliance, constrained to exist between realities."

"How can I correct this, this being imprisoned here?" he asked. In his consciousness, he became aware of a swirling within the aura before him. A tendril of which extended toward him.

"Come into me, so you may know what I know," Naldalek commanded.

Min'darr tried, yet whatever form he now existed in failed to act. He pictured raising his arm and reaching out. Again, nothing happened. *"How? How do I move?"* He felt desperate and helpless, like a newborn.

"Alas, Magician, you must learn how to manipulate your essence. The Others ... they may be your impetus. I cannot help, at least with that. You must know how to exist within before I can influence your choices." With that, Naldalek's aura faded away.

Min'darr perceived Naldalek's absence, not that he'd physically seen him, rather sensing a deeper void. *An emptiness. Yes, that described it best.* He had to consider two things. How to move about in whatever form he was in and who these Others were that Naldalek had mentioned.

Min'darr considered his plight. He was trapped within the Weir, a funnel-shaped maze. Yet Naldalek said he had no form, no space. Naldalek seemed cloud-like to him. *Maybe my form is similar?*

If then he had no body, no physical form, he had to imagine himself as a spirit. The times similar to this he'd experienced was when he'd been immersed within the blue magic's flow. But while there, the movement he'd experienced was from the magic itself. He stopped to check around him now. No movement, no flow.

"If all I am is a spirit right now," he conjectured, *"I am the magic, at least according to the teachings of yellow magic. If that's the case, why can't I cast a spell and leave this Weir?*

He did so. Nothing happened. Well, not quite nothing.

Min'darr found he was surrounded by many auras. Seven, at least that he could sense, were crowding him, intermingling with his own essence. *That's hard to do when you have no shape and take up no space,* he reasoned.

But something was happening to him. He felt strange, somehow weaker, smaller, or maybe thinner. The ones closest to him seemed brighter than before. Brighter than the ones further back. *Were these the Others? Hello?* he offered to them. They did not respond.

The auras pressed in, slipping past and between each other to get ever closer to him. A part of him began fighting back, instinctively pushing them away. *What is happening?*

He became aware of a distant sound, a chant. Not verbal certainly, persistent, demanding.

"Magic ... magic!" It was the obvious way to interpret this. *What magic? Where?*

His growing weakness gave him the answer. His.

"No!" he felt like he'd screamed it aloud. A reflex, a magical surge formed and went out through him. He found himself alone. The Others were gone. But, more than that, he somehow knew he'd moved through this maze. It seemed unlike the other place in

the Weir he'd been before. It fit him differently. He must be in a different part of it. The Others were no longer near him. *How long before they find me again?* He also realized he had less magic than before.

They must have tapped into me, draining me of my magic. Maybe my magic attracted them? His thoughts continued and he settled on the idea that they'd been drawn to his magic. Their auras were dim, weaker than his, except when they came closer to him and began drawing off his magical strength. *Like arcane vampires. They have so little of their own magic left. They've got to be trapped here, too weak and cannot escape. How long have they been trapped in here?* The thought brought him a great sadness. *Is that going to be my fate? Naldalek said no. So how do I get out?*

Naldalek isn't here. He must have gotten out, so it is possible. This Weir sucks our magic and souls, too. I guess the teachings of yellow magic are right. There is magical power within a person's soul.

But what happens to it here? Where does it go? Does this Weir use the magic of those it traps somehow? Is this thing somehow alive? Or does it store the magic, maybe for someone else to use?

Min'darr focused again, pushing these unanswerable questions aside. *I have to get out of here. How did I move away from the Others?*

This time he centered on the sensations he'd experienced when he left the Others behind. *Yes, I know how to make it happen again. I have to find a doorway out of here!* He forced his magic to flow to duplicate what happened before. He felt different, yet again. *A new place. Good.*

He took in his surroundings. *What's this? A magical flow?*

He felt a pull, a gentle current to what he'd thought was the static nothingness. *Nothing can't move. What is this?*

A distant aura tugged at the edge of his awareness. *The Others? No, something else. Stronger. It's pulling at me ... or no, my magic. Distant, yet very powerful. Maybe ... maybe this is like the Weir's repository, like its own gemstone.*

Min'darr paused, aware of his magic being coaxed from him. *If I get too close, it might be too dangerous. I'll end up like the Others.*

It seemed like hours, but he felt too weak not to try. *It will be an all-or-nothing attempt. The pull of this is too constant. It will eventually*

suck me dry and I won't have enough magic to do anything, just like them.
He could not shake the impression the Others had left with him.

As Min'darr succumbed to the strain caused by the draining of
his magic, he tried to form a shell to hold his magic back. It
helped until he was magically empty. Virtually helpless, he drifted
along, unable to stop it.

Even at this point from within this flowage, Min'darr became
aware of an aura so different from the Others and his own. It
could be sensed through the twisting filaments of the Weir. While
he had no idea where within the structure he was, he had the
distinct impression he was getting ever nearer to some kind of
narrowing.

The flow increased, becoming rapids careening closer like the
waters of a river entering a narrows or near a waterfall. Min'darr
reasoned that, since it was all about magic, it wasn't because of
gravity. He recalled the shape of the Weir. *It narrowed toward the top,
like a tree or an inverted funnel. Could I be going up toward its top?*

He sensed that he was spinning and twisting through the
interweaving structures of the Weir. His magic shell was giving
way, the pressures of the eldritch energies had stressed his magical
spell to the breaking point.

He had to find a way to protect his power. He reached out to
search the flow. *Sweet mystery! It's yellow magic.* The essence of the
flowage he was in was magic. He had an idea.

Ignoring the arcane battering he suffered, he opened himself
up to the mass surrounding him by cancelling his protective shell.

His trick worked. The magic, as he felt it would, always seeks a
balance. Since there was significantly less magic within him than
outside his shell, it rushed in and filled him, replenishing him.

With more magic, his sense of things increased and he was
immediately aware of the vortex that awaited him. A yellow,
crystalline gem, immense and seeming more powerful than he'd
ever imagined, shaped like a huge star. It drew all the magic within
the Weir toward it, the currents Min'darr was within, bending into
it. Like a leaf riding an ever-swifter current, he neared the massive
yellow sapphire and the vortex it produced, drawn to it as
inevitably as a falling apple is drawn to the ground.

The sense of speed was dizzying, increasingly more difficult for Min'darr to keep his target the center of his attention. Using his replenished magic, he saw the currents around the gem. *I have to keep to the outer flow. It's created a weakness, a flawed spot in the Weir. It could be a way out. If I can push away at the right moment.*

Min'darr kept his attention on the point he hoped he would flow through to escape. The flowage compressed, increasing its speed and swirling within the Weir beyond his expectation. He closed his mind to everything except the flawed wall section. Spinning faster and faster, he pushed. His magic, his essence veered toward the flaw.

He slapped against the wall. All he felt was vibration, rocking and bouncing within the confines of a mere thought. Battling time itself to not progress long enough to escape the arcane vortex without rebounding back into eternity.

He was snatched away.

Reality returned. Min'darr's magical essence hovered next to the sapphire atop the Weir. Within him, he became aware of Naldalek.

"You did it the hard way, Magician. None have ever attempted this."

"You did help me," Min'darr said. *"Thank you for saving me."*

"No such thing, Magician. I merely caught you as a child catches a ball. You did this on your own. Most impressive."

"But you left the Weir before. How did you get out?"

"I did what hundreds have done. I gave the Others my magic. Without magic, you cannot be within the Weir. It will spit you out. Then, your magic in this reality returns to you," Naldalek said. *"Simple. Far simpler than standing on the edge of Eternity and jumping against everything rushing around you, as you did. It is a miracle of Loy that you still exist and are not contained within Caudaric, the gemstone of the Sodality's Weir."*

He paused, paying more attention to Min'darr. He then commented, *"Intriguing. You have come out of the Weir with more magic than when you entered it. Another first, Oh Dangerous One. Come. We must reunite your spirit with your body."*

*

Their two spirits drifted to the floor area. Min'darr saw his body beneath the Weir. Quint was not quite fully consumed by

Min'darr's spell that would change him into a statue. No one moved. It was as if time had stopped.

Min'darr hesitated above his body. *"What is happening?"* he asked.

"Yes, of course, you would not know. It is the first time your spirit has ventured from your physical frame. In spirit-form, there is no thing called time. It does not exist for us for it is a measure of physical things.

"You have exited the Weir perhaps one heartbeat from when you entered it. Your conscience still considered time as real. It is not when you are a spirit. That is the reason why people believe that spirits are eternal. We do not end since time doesn't exist for us.

"Would you like to stay a spirit, Magician?" Naldalek asked.

Min'darr surprised himself by actually considering the prospect. *"Not now, my friend. There is much I must do yet in the time I have left to be in the physical world."*

"There is indeed. I will see you once more before I return to my Eternity." The old spirit gestured and Min'darr's body moved out from under the Weir. *"Until then."* Naldalek vanished.

Min'darr's spirit re-entered his body. It felt refreshing to draw air back into his lungs. Almost as refreshing as feeling his yellow magic return.

A Consequence of Magic

Noise filled his ears. Screams and cries from across the auditorium assaulted his mind. A small group of teachers huddled around Quint. Two of them, Magistrate Tristian and Master Vukbee, were frantically working spells on Quint's unmoving form. Others were comforting each other.

Surprisingly, the students sitting in the section with the other members of the Tan Team were also crying and screaming for the masters' attention. Min'darr looked intently at them, peering through the dim torch light. The three of them sat, unmoving.

He bolted up and ran to them. They sat unresponsive to the crying and prodding, pushing and patting of those who sat near them. They looked just like Quint, pale, stiff, stone-like. Min'darr was closest to Slakoda, the one who had apologized to him when they left the café. His eyes were closed, his face grimacing and looking down, away from the Weir.

Over his shoulder he heard Master Lyr's voice. "Oh, by Loy, Quint, how could you risk this much?"

Min'darr spun, somehow anticipating Quint. It was Master Lyr, standing right behind Min'darr. "This is unforgivable of him. The Sixth Rule states that each magic user must stand on his own. Quint clearly had tied into his team. Your magic, Min'darr, would never have affected them had they not been magically conjoined. This changes things immensely. Come with me, Min'darr." He rose and followed Lyr to the others on the stage, standing next to Quint.

"The entire team ... they were obviously conjoined," Lyr said when they reached the others.

"Shame on him! Well, we will prosecute Quint after Min'darr returns him," Magistrate Tristian said. He looked at Min'darr and beckoned him. "Please, good sir, it was your magic, your spell. Bring them back."

Min'darr stood looking back at him. "I, ahh, umm ... I'm not sure I know how."

Tristian cocked his head. "Do you remember the spell you used?"

"Basically."

"You may or may not know, every spell, every incantation has a reverse spell. Unfortunately, it isn't a simple matter of saying 'not' or 'undo.' Magic is far more complex than that. Even a slight inflection difference in the casting can make the results very divergent from what is intended to be cast.

"I do not wish to pressure you, Min'darr, but if this spell cannot be reversed, Quint and his team are as good as dead," the magistrate said.

He felt guilty. He had intended to stop Quint from attacking him. His recollection of using the spell against the other magicians on the wharf back in Rougahn came back as an action, casting the same spell. *"How can I ...?"*

How can a blue magic spell use yellow magic? Naldalek found the spell interesting. In fact, Naldalek was the one who cast it! How am I going to manage this? I'll have to ask him to reverse the spell, if I can find him.

"Let me try, Masters, to correct my mistake. What of his team?" Min'darr asked. "Am I to be held responsible for them as well?"

"That will have to be addressed later if you are not successful," Magistrate said. "I would prefer we keep reviving them our goal. We masters have been unable to change him back, so it is up to you. We leave you to work it out." They turned and began directing the students out of the theater's seating.

*

Silence filled the room, except for the hissing of the torches. The stage was bare except for him and Quint. The magistrate had ordered the Weir drawn back up into its ceiling recess. Min'darr sat as silent as the statue of Quint, concentrating on the statue spell. He recalled very clearly the spell he used on the wharf. But Naldalek had managed the spell this time and Min'darr had no idea how he'd done it. He summoned the power of the magic he had and called out to Naldalek in his mind. There was no response.

"I'm surprised, Min'darr,"

He turned to see Lokina stepping down from the doorway.

"What? That I haven't reversed this yet?" he asked, turning to face her.

"No. First that you lived to tell the tale. Fighting Quint and surviving the Weir ... if you did that in three years, you'd have bragging rights. Not you! Oh, no, you have to do it all on your first day." She slid into a seat next to the still-petrified Tan Team.

"Secondly, that your magic has confused even the Masters! How did you manage to cast a spell that the Masters can't touch, can't undo? What exactly are you, Magician?"

"Let's see," he mused aloud. "Someone once told me that my history was none of her business."

"It is when their lives are thrust together, despite her wishes."

"Or his," he added. He heard chuckling.

He looked past her and saw the rest of his team sitting there. Bikutah, Demiltarf, and Mygili were sitting behind Lokina. Without meaning to, his gaze rested on Mygili. He sighed a bit when their eyes met. He walked across to join them and sat facing them.

"All right, I have to tell someone. It can't be the masters. They'll see me as a threat. You are the closest thing I have to friends here, so it'd best be you all. Put out your hand," he said putting his own out.

Each stacked their own hand atop his.

"I do, here and now, cast a spell of camaraderie and secrecy. If you agree to what I tell you, you will know about me and be willing to help. If you disagree or are unsure, you will forget everything I say here." He placed his other hand atop the stack and sent a charge of eldritch power through their hands.

Min'darr spent the next half hour telling them of his magical origin in the mountains of Rougahn, his encounter with the yellow magicians, and his sailing to the Southern Islands to learn about yellow magic. He kept Naldalek's part of the story out of his retelling.

He then told them what he'd learned of the Weir ending with the suggestion that it was the most probable source of the masters' powers.

Once done, they rejoined hands and a second jolt of magic sealed the spell.

"Are we good?" he asked.

Each nodded. Mygili pointed past him. "What are we to do about ol' Quint?"

Min'darr shook his head. "I have to reverse the spell. I haven't been able to ... can't remember exactly how I did it. Must have been in the heat of the battle."

Demiltarf spoke up. "I know a memory spell. It may help here." He repositioned himself to sit next to Min'darr. "Please excuse the intrusion," he added as he stuck one finger in Min'darr's ear and another in his opposite nostril.

"No, I really don't ..." Min'darr started to say.

Demiltarf chanted his spell and a thin, misty cloud appeared before them. It showed Min'darr standing, facing Quint. His older memory appeared, showing a fleeting glimpse of the magicians' battle on the wharf and the recasting of the spell against Quint. His words setting the spell in motion were more thought than actually said aloud.

Min'darr thought, *That isn't right, not how it happened. Naldalek must be keeping his own existence secret.*

"That's so wrong. That wasn't yellow magic, must have been your blue magic," Lokina said. "That first memory was before you came here. It had to be your old magic. Min'darr, our yellow magic works so differently from that blue stuff you used. We've got no way to cancel out your blue magic spell."

"But that's the point," Min'darr said, virtually pleading. "I cleaned myself out of blue magic before I came to the school. I didn't want anyone to know. It has to be yellow magic. It has to be."

Mygili shifted in her seat. "Is it possible that, because your memory is of the blue magic spell and you had yellow magic to use, that it somehow mixed together?"

"Girl, you have not been listening!" Lokina said. "They don't mix."

"And you have no imagination, Lokina." Mygili dismissed her team leader with a roll of her eyes and took Min'darr's hand.

"Repeat these words after me," she said.

"What are we doing?" he asked.

"Trust me, hon. Trust me." She took his other hand as well and chanted alternately with him, "Me ah to lia, mark usi ti lati, mah kus um do ol."

Min'darr repeated the spell a second after Mygili and they were both surrounded by auras. Hers was a pure, soft yellow. Min'darr's was a darker, deeper yellow littered with a smattering of blue flecks.

"See? See!" Mygili yelped. "Just as I thought. It has to be parallel spells! Part of the spell on Quint came from yellow magic that you have and the rest from smatterings of the blue magic engrained within you. That's why the masters couldn't reverse it." She sat smiling. Min'darr realized that she continued to hold his hands, rather tightly. The auras faded.

Still gazing at her, he squeezed hers back. "Thank you. That explains a lot. Still, I can't undo the spell."

Lokina asked, "Can you consciously include your blue magic with the yellow magic you have?

"Let's try it," he answered, already heading back to Quint.

Half an hour later they sat together on the floor, Quint and his team remained statues. The dinner chime sounded. Lokina, Bikutah, and Demiltarf rose. Min'darr said he wasn't hungry and would stay here. Mygili said, "You guys go ahead. Save me a spot."

After they left, Min'darr said, "You don't need to stay."

"I want to."

"Thank you," he said softly. "This is so ..."

She leaned over and kissed him. "It kills me to see you have to bear this. Especially over this bully. As harsh as it may sound,

Quint isn't worth this much effort. He was so nasty and rude to everyone. No one liked him, not even them," she said pointing back to what was left of the Tan Team. "He made them share their magic with him. Slakoda told me right after he forced them into it.

"That's against the rules, but you know that," she continued. She stood and walked over to them. "If only we could change things." She looked at him and asked, "Does Blue Magic allow for going into the past?"

"Not that I know of. Never had reason to try ... don't know. I could ..."

"I need to give you a hug." She walked to him, arms extended. They hugged, holding each other for a longer time than he'd expected. Neither wanted to let go, it seemed. "I'm not usually this forward. There's just something about you."

Haven't ever felt like this before. So nice. Min'darr smiled at her, a full head shorter than him. "What do people call you?"

"What?" she asked. "Mygili?"

"All the time? Don't you have a nickname?" he asked.

"Well, there was one my dad used. Gili," she said with a blush. "How about you?"

"My sister and I called each other Bisha." Her furled brow prompted him to expound. "It means stinky."

They laughed and hugged each other again. Then they shared a kiss.

"I've never met anyone like you," Min'darr said. "I've never felt ..."

"No, no, please don't," she interrupted, breaking away. "At least ... well, not now. I've hoped for a long time to find someone I could hope to fall in love with. This isn't the place I imagined. Maybe we could walk down to the pier later ... in the moonlight. I have always been a person maybe too in touch with my emotions. Some days I can see something and it touches me so much. Other days I may not notice it. My dad used to tell me that I ..."

"Wait!" he interrupted. "Do you think that maybe emotions play into this magic? Is it possible my state of mind might have to be considered in reversing this? I was pretty stressed when I cast that spell."

Mygili's eyes widened. "I wouldn't be surprised! It certainly could. I wonder why the masters have never mentioned something like this before."

The answer came from behind them, near the entrance. "Because it isn't something we've ever had to consider." Magistrate Tristian and Master Lyr were coming down the steps toward them. Tristian continued. "I suppose it would be a good idea to research the effect of emotional duress while spell casting. But then again, how many spells are cast that might possibly have to be rescinded? I doubt that study will ever come to pass."

They paused and looked around the room, then continued. "I see nothing has changed. I trust you have been working on correcting your error?" he said while casting a glance at Mygili.

Min'darr paused and took a step closer to him. "I would not call this an error, Magistrate. We were in the middle of a magical battle of the Weir."

Mygili leapt to his defense. "We have discovered two things, Magistrate." She paused and looked at Min'darr, who nodded.

"We have found trace elements of blue magic in the spell Min'darr cast. That explains why you and the masters were unable to reverse it. We also suspect, as you heard coming in, that Min'darr's emotional state, especially given the mix of magics, may have had an unusual effect on the spell. We haven't been able to duplicate his state of mind at the time of its casting in order to effect a reversal."

"Miss Mygili, you have always provided me with untold joy in the way you attack a magical problem. You use your entire being in considering applicable elements and working through myriad combinations to resolve an issue.

"We have come to bear witness to your progress, Min'darr. Given that you have not been able to reverse your spell, we are left with no choice." The two masters simultaneously flung out their arms and wrapped Min'darr and Mygili in arcane yellow shells that raised them from the floor.

Unable to move or speak, Min'darr chose to watch and listen.

"We have no choice. We charge you for the murders of Quint and the members of the Tan Team," Magistrate Tristian said.

Both masters then pointed at the statues. The three members of the Tan Team rose from their seats and hovered across to the area near the Weir. Quint simply slid. When they were together, the Weir lowered.

The masters simultaneously chanted an incantation. The team's stone forms morphed into a fine powder that collapsed into a pile. As the Weir came into position, Min'darr felt its pull across the entire room. He watched intently as the dust that had been the Tan Team was drawn into the Weir.

"You are charged, specifically, for using magical energies in a lethal manner during a governed exercise. Your tribunal begins tomorrow." Tristian gestured again and the diamond in Min'darr's pocket flew into his outstretched hand.

He looked at it and chuckled. "Ha, I'm surprised. It's empty, useless," he said as he turned his hand palm down, dropping Min'darr's gem to the floor. "Since you have no gems, I guess I'll have to figure out where you keep your energies stored."

As the two masters climbed the steps toward the entrance doors, Mygili's prison aura soared above the seating toward the doorway with the magistrate. Min'darr saw her mouth opened in a scream. She beat against the shell as she was carried out of the room.

He strained against his magical bonds. His mind and body told him he was screaming too. The yellow aura surrounding him prevented any from hearing that.

Naldalek's voice whispered to Min'darr. *"They are not meant to survive, Blue Magician. Just like the Tan Team, this entire enclave is destined to die. I invite you, too, to join them and begin your eternity."*

Trust and Truth

It proved difficult for Min'darr to keep his mind focused during that long night, too many things to consider. The prospect of being tried for murder by these people terrified him. He rationalized their reasoning. It allowed them to justify ridding them of him, a new student too powerful with their own magic to be allowed to stay. He'd successfully opposed a master's magic and survived a magic battle with one of their best students, but had also withstood an exposure to the Weir, an arcane appliance Min'darr was convinced acted as the reservoir for the masters' own magical power supply.

Each master wore many rings, some had more rings than fingers. Each ring had a gem set into it. Min'darr surmised that those must serve as their touchstones, accessing both their own magical stores and that of the Weir. The Others, too, the pitiful souls trapped within the Weir ... *Is there a way I could free them? I would probably have to risk entering it again. It would take serious magic to accomplish that and escape a second time, no doubt.* But, Naldalek had said he had emerged from the Weir more powerful than when he'd entered it. The ghost would know.

Then there was Naldalek, the spirit of one of the founders of their academy. One which claimed to have returned from the dead to guide him, warning him of his own impending death. Min'darr had kept its presence his own secret.

And now there was Gili to consider. Damn! He'd avoided attractions before. Even some of the girls in his hometown as he was growing up ... all girls were creepy to him at that age. Then there was Nor'lars, the magic show girl on Vila'Borin's vendors' wharf. She'd showed an interest in him. He'd been curious about her too. Yet, knowing he had to come here first, he wasn't ready to kindle a relationship.

He remembered watching his parents' and his sister, Koo'bla's, relationship battles. Those dissuaded him from pursuing one. Well, up until now. *Mygili just feels right.* Her ability to think things through, to stand up to others and defend her opinion ... and it had started as a simple friendship that blossomed very quickly. Yes, she was pretty, too, especially when she smiled. Moreover, his realization of his own true emotions for her occurred earlier. He felt his heart breaking when she cried being carried out of the Weir room by the magistrate. Despite his own situation, he wanted desperately to save her, protect her, comfort her. He'd never felt this way before. *"I'd bet Koo'bla would have some advice for me,"* he thought.

All was quiet for quite some time. He could not keep the horror from his mind of seeing the magistrate and Master Lyr kill the Tan Team, turning them to dust. *I think I could have brought them back, given time. They didn't give me enough time. They certainly didn't try to help me, either. Actually, all they managed to do was get rid of any evidence and prevent me from working this out. Maybe I can use that in my defense. They killed them, not me.*

The memory of watching their remains drift across the stage, drawn to the Weir also played through his mind repeatedly.

It stopped there with a realization and a question. *It wasn't lowered to the stage floor. Is the Weir always absorbing magic? What about right now?*

Min'darr calmed himself, working to send his magic beyond the master's aura. He concocted a spell and found he was able to move his arms and legs within his magical confines. *That must have been an option of their spell. Gili could move while I couldn't. Or maybe it was simply that the magistrate cast my aura and Master Lyr cast Gili's.*

Very quickly, he felt some flexibility to this shell that confined him. He pushed against it. It bulged. He pushed harder. It responded by moving in that direction. He pushed again and found himself floating gently across the staging area toward the Weir.

Even within the confines of the aura, he could sense the perpetual pull from the Weir, though it was in its raised position. He continued to force it closer. He had an idea.

This feels weird working magic through this shield, like painting with gloves on.

After an hour's efforts, the aura he was trapped in was centered on the stage area directly beneath the Weir. He felt it. So did the aura. At least there seemed to be a physical vibration that had started when he got directly under the Weir.

Knowing that his yellow magic included bits of his blue magic, he reworked and repeated the spell to weaken and chisel away at the magistrate's magic holding him. Bit by bit, first flakes, then strips and chunks of the aura rose from the general mass of it and disappeared above him into the Weir.

The pace of it quickened. Min'darr saw the magic surrounding him defying gravity, literally dripping upward like a gentle rain. As it did, the aura enclosing him rose as well, seeking a closer proximity to the Weir and its gem. It wedged itself into the Weir's narrower webbing.

He felt, too, its pull on the magic within him. Since it was in a raised position, it was nowhere near as powerful as it had been when he'd been sucked into it during his battle. As the Weir absorbed the rest of the aura holding him, he had to reach out to grasp onto its threading structure. Min'darr held on until the magistrate's aura was completely absorbed.

Min'darr hung within the hollow of the device, grasping onto the lower part of the arcane cone. When he no longer felt any significant magical pull, he climbed down about a dozen feet to the stage's surface, free. The room was empty.

*

He walked the hallway and passed an ancient window, the dim gray light from the impending dawn penetrated through the overcast. The sleeping quarters of the Blue Group were vacant. *Why would they have to be gone? And where? Were they taken, or ...?* Again, too many questions. Perhaps the dining room?

Min'darr quickened his pace, assured that his magical cloak of invisibility kept him from being seen. Twice now, he'd pressed against a wall to avoid colliding with other students. Then he stopped a few feet from the entrance to the dining room. Sounds of eating and conversation drifted out to him.

How stupid can I be? Tristian wouldn't have let Gili out to mingle with everyone else. Not after what happened. He'd have her locked away if he hasn't, umm, hasn't already ... Min'darr threw the thought from his mind, unwilling to contemplate the magistrate's ability and willingness to keep her truth silent. *"Gili? Where are you?"*

He felt an arcane surge leave him as his desperation reached out to Gili. A heartbeat later, he felt a response. *Alive! She's alive!*

Heading toward the direction his magic indicated, Min'darr contemplated how he might free her. That he might have to battle Tristian or a combination of masters and other students weighed heavily on him. *I wish I had my blue magic right now. Maybe I should get my staff from my quarters.*

He slowed. Something didn't feel right, like the walls and floor had become too thin to support him. He looked ahead, making out nothing worth noting. *Like looking for a crow's feather in the dark,* he thought. *I need more light, more magic.*

Min'darr returned to the dining room. While in the hallway, Naldalek spoke to him. *"It ends today, Magician. Be prepared for all here must die."*

That caused him to pause. He was tempted to just leave, to flee back to the wharf, go aboard a ship and escape. Yet he knew that would not happen. *Too much at stake. This yellow magic school has evil leaders. Some of the students, too. It cannot be left to continue. Its founder's spirit is here to see to that. Can't leave Gili behind to be killed either.*

In the dining room, he found Lokina, Demiltarf, and Bikutah at their table. He remained invisible, spilling the salt shaker to get their attention.

Bikutah looked at Lokina and asked, "Why'd you do that?"

"I'm too busy trying to figure things out to play a stupid game," she snapped.

"You're not the only one," Min'darr whispered. "Stay calm and pretend everything is normal."

Demiltarf chuckled. "Nothing normal lives here."

"True that, Min'darr." Lokina squinted around the table and looked right at him. "What's going on?" she asked.

"The magistrate and Lyr turned the whole Tan Team into dust and fed them to the Weir. They put Gili and me into auras and took her with them. I got out of mine using the Weir and I'm going to free Gili.

"But look ... there's something you need to know. Everything is going to change here today. I think yellow magic is going to end and not gently. Everyone with that magic may be hurt or possibly killed. Please, get rid of your magic and leave as soon as you can. Actually, I could use it. Help me get Gili free. Please?"

Bikutah started stripping the rings off his fingers right away. Lokina reached out to stop him, casting a narrowed eye at Min'darr.

"What kind of a con artist are you?" Lokina asked. "You blow in here and want our rings and justify it with this story of some sudden upheaval. We aren't stupid."

"I need the extra magic to save Gili," Min'darr pleaded.

"Yeah, c'mon, Lokina. She's your friend, our teammate," Bikutah said.

"You want her saved? I'll save her, then. Everyone, give me your rings." Lokina retorted. "I'm coming with you, Magician." She stood and put out her hands. Within seconds, she had six other rings on her fingers. "All right, Magician, let's go." She stood and headed to the doorway with an invisible Min'darr right behind her.

*

Min'darr guided them in the direction Gili was according to his magic. It showed her in a lower level room at the back of the campus. They couldn't tell if she was alone or with someone.

"I'd bet they're waiting for you, Magician. This seems too easy. Guess they figured that you might escape," Lokina remarked. After a moment of silence, she added, "Yep. A trap." She stopped and turned toward him. "Stop wasting your power being invisible. They know you're coming. I can feel it. They've surrounded her with at least three spells that I can sense. I'd suspect more.

Min'darr dropped the invisibility shield and faced Lokina. "I think we need a plan," he said.

"Idiot," she muttered. "How are you going to plan something against things you don't know about? What spells have they used? Do you know? I don't. Have they sabotaged things so that if you use your magic, you might kill her instead? I'd bet they've got something like that to use.

"Look, Min'darr ... they won't want her alive if, as you say, she knows the truth. What better way to protect themselves and to seal your fate than to have you 'accidentally' kill her when you are fighting them? These people aren't stupid. Yeah, maybe they are afraid of you. Not everyone drops in with a Voice of the Dead attached to them, ya know?"

"Yeah, about that ..." Min'darr muttered. His intent was to tell her about Naldalek's spirit, but then, no, something held him back.

"What?" Lokina asked.

So, he lied. "I, ah, I did that myself. I did a spell to know the scroll's contents as soon as I touched it and I thought a deep, dark, and mysterious voice would impress everyone."

"Did you realize that you were dealing with some of the richest lore of the Sodality?"

"I'd done some research, yeah." Min'darr said, then added, "Look, I, umm, we really need to get to Gili before something bad happens to her. I'll be happy to take my lumps after she's safe. What do you think we should do?"

"Why would you trust me, Magician?" Lokina asked.

"You're right. I know nothing about you," he said. "Maybe you can convince me."

She sighed. "I don't care if you trust me or not. If you want Mygili safe, as I do, you have to at least believe me 'cause you don't know enough. You've been here, what ... two days?"

Min'darr sighed quietly. "Long enough to learn some things. You want me to believe in you? Then give me something that's worthy of belief."

She took off a ring and handed it to him. "I am Lokina Belarna from the Kovasi Island of Raaptulli. That's in the northern archipelago. I am a Fourth-Year tutor. Happy?"

"Thank you," Min'darr said as he accepted the ring. "Now, about that plan ..."

"Well, I think you have to answer this first. Who needs to be saved, you or Mygili?" Lokina asked. "That will guide what we have to do."

"I can take care of myself. Gili gets saved," Min'darr said without hesitation.

Lokina nodded. "All right. Then we have to set this up just right. What if we ..."

*

Min'darr wasn't sold on her plan, but he at least had one of the rings concealed on him. He floated within an aura she'd conjured, like the magistrate's. He could move. For the sake of their ruse, held himself motionless.

Lokina stood alongside him. She knocked on their destination's door, something he hadn't expected her to do. A woman's voice came from within.

"We are too busy to be disturbed, whoever you are," it said. *Master Vukbee's voice.*

Lokina gestured and a slight bit of magic left her fingers and penetrated the door. A few seconds later, it opened. Master Vukbee greeted them, opened the door wide, and stood back as Lokina floated him into the room. Standing in a circle within the room were five other masters, none of whom Min'darr recognized. Their arms were extended, hands clenched. Vukbee's place in the circle was evident by the gap, which she immediately returned to.

"Again," she said.

A low thrumming emanated from the group. Vukbee's voice then raised above them in a chant. Soft and melodic, Min'darr had to forcibly focus on other things to avoid losing himself in her song.

A fiery gemstone slowly appeared, yellow and sparkling, hovering about shoulder's height at their circle's center. It was about the size of a loaf of bread. Tiny filaments of magic reached out from it toward each master, touching their rings and causing those to glow brightly. The masters sighed deeply, soaking in the power being shared with them.

Min'darr stood breathless. *How am I to combat all of them, freshly recharged with yellow magic? Is this gem another in their collection, or is it connected to the one in the Weir?* He concentrated on the gem Lokina had given him. *Weak, not much energy in it.*

He looked around for Gili, finding no sign of her here. He began raising his awareness to locate her when a gasping noise drew his attention to the masters' circle. He looked in disbelief at what he saw.

Master Vukbee's connection to the gem had doubled in size. The streams connecting two of the three others had ceased. They stood unmoving, as if they'd been turned off. The last master connected to the gem, eyes and mouth wide open, gasping for breath and growing rapidly thinner. His magical stream had reversed and now drew energy from him. As he watched, the master was reduced from a vibrant, living man to a virtual skeleton covered with thin and withered skin. He managed one last gasp. Then all that remained of him became dust and was drawn into the gem.

Master Vukbee reached across and collected his rings as they floated in midair. She placed them in a pouch on her belt. "We thank the great Loy for Master Kalindi and his sacrifice," she said. The others repeated her words and their awareness returned. The gem remained, pulsing.

Lokina had moved next to him and got his attention with a quick pulse to the sphere in which she held him.

He looked. She was scanning the room. She then looked at him and mouthed, "Are you ready?"

He glanced around, desperately needing to find Mygili. He had no idea where she could be. He glanced back at Lokina, drew in a deep breath and nodded.

She nodded back and called out, "Master Vukbee!"

She turned to face her.

Lokina gestured toward Min'darr and the aura around him got brighter. He instantly realized he could no longer move. She smiled at him with a slight shaking of her head. "You are far too trusting, Magician." She handed the aura to Vukbee, turned and walked to the door. She paused and looked again at Min'darr. "You'd better be more careful. Trusting the wrong people can get you killed." She left the room laughing.

Vukbee chuckled. "Gotta love that girl," she said. "She'll go far. She's from the Isonicus Archipelago, don't ya know, just like me." She took a few moments to examine the magical aura he was trapped within, admiring her workmanship. "Very nice, no flaws that I can see. You've been caught by one of our best, Min'darr."

"Conned, Lady Vukbee, not caught," Min'darr responded.

"Regardless, my good sir. You are here and within our control. How she managed it matters not. And it is Master, not Lady. If you'll excuse me ..." She turned and directed her attention to the still-floating gem.

Within a few heartbeats, the masters, four in number, reestablished their connections with the gem. The spell Vukbee cast was simpler and was stated, not sung. The gem's pulsing changed, becoming more like the *bump-bump* pattern of a beating heart. Then it swelled, pulsating as it grew, reforming itself into the size and shape of a person. The glow dimmed and the light within its new form darkened, except for the eyes, which remained bright. A minute later, fully transformed, Magistrate Tristian stood in their midst.

He acknowledged their presence and nodded at Master Vukbee.

His face beamed when he looked at Min'darr. "I was afraid I'd lost you to the Weir, Magician. I found remnants of my magic aura within it, but no sign of you. You are to be congratulated. No one I know of has ever escaped a sphere before. It is a shameful waste of your life that it must end without you reaching your magical potential.

"It is not surprising that Mygili pleaded as hard as she did. She even suggested that we could keep you here, study you and your blue magic. It was rather touching. She was more powerful than I'd recalled. The Weir took her gladly."

"You fed her to your power gem?" *He kept his heart from tearing apart by getting Tristian to boast enough to give him information he could use against him.*

"You are a sick, sick band of magic users. I came here in the hopes of learning about yellow magic. To find out how it differed from my own. The one thing you've shown me is that your magic is used by a group of self-serving brigands. You even plot against each other!"

The magistrate grinned. "We are a powerful collection of magicians. We must maintain the strictest protocol to further our own existence. Any who would challenge that, like you, must be removed from the equation."

His visage had lost the gem's glow and looked fully human again. In fact, Min'darr thought he looked a bit older, more drawn than before. "Come everyone, back to the Weir Chamber. It is time for the Blue Magician to die."

A Magician's Death

For the second time in as many days, students packed the Weir Chamber. They had been summoned, once again, to witness a Rite of the Sodality. Yesterday's gathering had been an arcane battle rite when Quint, the leader of the Tan Team, had been accused of improprieties by Min'darr. The Battle of the Weir followed, which Min'darr won. The illegal arcane link between the Tan Team members cost them their lives.

Today's was a criminal proceeding. Its purpose was to "convict" Min'darr of killing the four student magicians of the Tan Team and to suffer the masters' punishment for that crime. There was little physical change to the room. The amphitheater seating gave the room depth, dropping below the hallway level as you went in. Ten rows of seats in an arc covering about two-thirds of the span of the room. Above that, the loft area seating filled with masters. Min'darr counted two dozen.

Before them all, a staging area with full curtain and behind that, the Weir. Min'darr's experience with it showed him that it held enormous power. There were also a few niches that, if he could locate them again, may provide an escape route. The central facet of the coiling cone was the magic-filled gem atop the inverted funnel. Caudaric, they'd called it. It alone channeled all available magical energy into it, storing it for the magistrate's or the masters' uses. He'd gathered power from the Weir in his previous encounter with it, according to what the founder's spirit told him.

He knew this time would not be as simple. Naldalek told him that he'd see Min'darr one more time. The magician didn't know if that would be before or after his death, which had also been predicted by the ancient spirit.

He and the yellow magic aura he'd been trapped in were resting on the stage's floor to the left side. Two rows of six chairs had been set up on the right side. Each chair held a master. Min'darr had not seen Magistrate Tristian since being put on the stage.

A chime sounded and the murmurings of forty-eight mouths ceased. At that same moment, the masters stood and walked off behind the drawn curtain. A harsh rumbling came from behind the curtain and very quickly, the twelve masters magically moved a massive platform out into the view of the students. At its center was a collection of logs arranged for a fire. Also, in a cage at one corner, three chickens squawked and made enough noise to indicate that they didn't want to be there.

Once in place, the masters returned to their seats, except for Master Vukbee. She came to the front of the stage and raised one finger. A single sparkling ember appeared above it. She shook it off, and the ember floated out and began to dart back and forth over the collected student body. It stopped suddenly, hovering above Lokina.

"Blue Group," Vukbee said. The three of them came to the stage area and spaced themselves around the platform. Min'darr watched carefully. He could not guess what role his own team would have in this farcical trial.

They began to chant "Ahl bow auq twa" and repeated it, growing louder each time until the students seated within the room chanted it as well. They got louder and louder, stomping and clapping with their chanting as well. The Blue Team soon glowed brighter and brighter with each repetition.

Min'darr watched, fascinated by the mass spell they were casting. A dim haze spread across the room, emanating from each student. A yellow magic fog, thin though it was, rested on each of them. Their cadence quickened until their chant sounded like a single word, "alboachta." Simultaneously, at their crescendo, they quit.

The abrupt silence was powerful. Lokina and the Blue Team whispered the chant one more time and gestured hard with closed fists toward the preset fire spot at the center.

The entire room seemed to whoosh onto the stage. The auras generated by their chant cascaded onto the platform, creating a spinning column, bathing the Blue Team in its shimmering glow. Min'darr heard it like a gust of wind. Lokina then gestured again and the column transformed into a massive fire, roaring loudly, however giving off no heat.

The Blue Team then retrieved the chicken cage and each took one bird. Holding their chickens by their necks, the birds fluttered and squawked. Each Blue Team member held out a gemmed ring which extended, becoming a dagger like the one Min'darr had at Hinasha's bedside. Without hesitation, they each drove them into their birds. Their blades glowed brightly as the soul of each hen was collected.

"Daggers collect souls. Gems store them," Hinasha's father, Goytel, had told him, Min'darr recalled.

Lokina and the others approached the fire, knelt before it and drove their daggers into the blazing firewood. They offered the chickens' carcasses as well. Within a heartbeat, the blaze doubled in size. Blue Team stood reverently as the students cheered.

The fire roared louder. Bands of flames flailed about, even passing through the Blue Team members. Two then stretched out, entangling Bikutah and Demiltarf. They lifted them and whisked them both into the conflagration. They never had a chance to react. Nonetheless, the student audience cheered ever louder. Lokina then walked across the stage and stood next to Min'darr's aura. He studied her intently and saw her steely and unblinking stare never waver, watching the blaze that had a minute before devoured her teammates. He detected no reaction from her at all.

He looked back at the massive fire and watched as it reformed its wavering arms and finally, on legs of flame, stepped out of the blaze, across, and then off the platform. The fire diminished in size, its flames receding to embers, slowly dimming, becoming more human in its form, appearing like clothing, then skin and hair and beard until it revealed the Sodality's magistrate, Tristian.

He held up his flesh and blood arms and the crowd fell silent. He scanned the group, with his gaze ending looking at Lokina and Min'darr. With an exaggerated gesture, he called them to him. "Bring the murderer to me."

Lokina complied. Min'darr's aura drifted across the stage to him. She walked behind the sphere that held him. "As you have commanded, Magistrate." She then returned to her seat with the rest of the students, oblivious to the gap around her previously occupied by her now-dead team members.

Magistrate Tristian said to him, yet loud enough to be heard by all, "I am very sad for you, Min'darr. You have shown more magical potential within the past two days than most of our students can in a year.

"Yet, you are undisciplined, unable to follow the accepted rules and practices of the Sodality. We are an organized magical discipline and we have existed in practice for over three hundred years. And the reason, young man, that we have existed this long is our dedication to magic through our Seven Rules.

"The very first of those tells us that magic is a precious energy and must never be wasted or misused.

"But you have," interjected Min'darr.

"You will be silent!" Tristian screamed. "The accused is allowed to speak once. This is not your time, fool." The student body remained silent as well. Min'darr was aware of a general unrest in their midst as each tensed from their magistrate's reaction.

"Master Vukbee, present the charges filed against Min'darr," Tristian ordered.

She stood and read from a sheet. "Student Min'darr, you are charged with the following violations of our rules of magic. In the matter of the First Rule, you have misused magic in the debilitation of myself when I reached out to help you. You have misused magic in its application during your Weir Battle causing the deaths of Quint, Slakoda, Barikil, and Fidvar, members of the Tan Team of the Sodality.

"In the matter of the Fourth Rule, you have used magic for your personal profit and enrichment in mimicking a Voice of the

Dead to mislead me and my class, in thwarting my efforts to use my magic to help determine the nature of your abilities and depth of your powers and therein causing me personal injury, and in enchanting Blue Team member Mygili to aid in your plot and in killing her when she refused you, and finally in destroying our Master Kalindi when he found and confronted you after witnessing your murder of Mygili, according to testimony filed by Blue Team leader Lokina. Here ends the charges." She sat down.

Magistrate Tristian said, "Thank you, Master Vukbee. How do you plead, Min'darr of Rougahn?" he then asked.

All the while since Tristian set foot on the stage, Min'darr had been considering his options. Clearly a magical fight was out of the question. Escape was pretty much ruled out. He'd have to pass too many people who saw him as a murderer and would act to stop him. Too, he had very little magic to use. *If they could simply know that these charges are lies. Tristian and the masters have concealed the truth. He hasn't ...*

Of course! The magistrate used it on him when the two of them met in his office. He'd described it as 'a magical incantation that requires anyone in this room to speak the truth.' I probably have enough power to cast that spell. Let's see ... he worked to remember the spell's wording.

That is when Vukbee finished her reading of the charges. Min'darr looked up and out, across the student body and at the masters sitting across the stage from him. He said quietly, "Innocent, Magistrate, of your trumped-up charges."

Tristian smiled at him, as if he was looking forward to a fight. "Perhaps they did not hear your pitiful response. Say it again, louder this time so they will hear you deny what they saw with their own eyes." A magical charge from the magistrate washed over his sphere's aura.

No time like the present, he thought. "Purula aba tay sendirka." He'd felt this yellow magic exit him every time he used any of it. His blue magic flowed more easily. This had seemed more like throwing something as opposed to letting something flow out through him. In any event, he felt what was left of his yellow magical energy flood out and across the theater and wash over the students, the masters, and the magistrate. "Innocent," he said again.

"Truth spell! He cast a truth spell. Then he said he was innocent. How can that be?" Murmurs and whisperings cantered around the students' seating. Min'darr saw a few of the masters look between each other, lips moving.

"Mira ta'ahsh!" Tristian shouted. Four times he called it out. Each time he did, more order was restored until finally, the chamber was silent. "Shall we proceed?"

"Magistrate?" a voice called.

Tristian looked into the crowd and named the speaker. "Have you a question, Mes'derel?"

"I do, sir." A young woman stood, wringing her hands. "How, sir, can the accused cast a truth spell and state his plea if what he says is not true?"

"I understand your doubt, my dear. I fear you do not know this one. He is from the North and has an extensive history of dabbling in blue magic. It is that same blue magic he uses in the hopes of feigning his innocence. Blue magic has no truth spell and cannot be used with our own yellow magic. Simply, he lies, pretending it to be the truth. Now, I ask you, how can I tell you that if he had actually cast a truth spell?"

She nodded as did the others near her.

"He's no fool. He's used a rider spell. When he called for order, what your ears heard was a call to order. Magically, his rider spell was cast because he said the trigger words and cancelled all active spells. An emergency trick used by nefarious leaders. I learned much while within the eldritch stream."

"Naldalek!" Min'darr whispered.

"Shh! I'm in your mind. I've come as I promised, to guide you through your death."

"What do I do?" Min'darr asked.

There was no immediate answer.

Tristian spoke again. "So, we will prove to you the damning truth of his own actions. The charges in the deaths of an entire team of your peers, the Tan Team, hardly needs to be expounded on. Each of you here witnessed the Weir Battle. You saw Min'darr cast his spell that transformed Quint and his team into stone, killing them all.

"Yes, Quint had broken a rule by attaching his magic to that of his team. That, however, is a moot point. It was the same spell from Min'darr that killed them as well. Had they survived the battle, each would be punished for breaking the Sixth Rule. As it is, their indiscretion cost them their lives.

"That is a tragic but poignant reminder to each of you that the Rules are there for your protection.

"Now, Min'darr, as I was saying, you are hereby deemed guilty as charged for the misuse of magic resulting in the deaths of the four members of the Tan Team. For the other charges, I call Lokina, Blue Team leader, to testify before us and Loy, our God and Guide."

Lokina stepped up onto the stage, casting a side glance at Min'darr. She then walked to stand before the seated masters.

"Thank you for this honor in seeking justice for those so horribly taken before their time. Min'darr had come into the dining room under an invisibility cloak wanting all of the Blue Team's rings. He said it was to help him find and free Mygili. He claimed she'd been suspended by Master Lyr, just as you see him. He claimed to fear for her life.

"I gathered our team's rings and offered to help him. I didn't trust someone who'd been here for just a couple of days with our rings. We went into the South Wing and bumped into Mygili walking toward us. That's when he attacked her."

"These are lies, Naldalek. Self-serving lies," Min'darr thought to the spirit.

"I know, Magician. It is destined to be," the spirit said.

Lokina continued. "He used a weird blue magic and pressed my friend against the ceiling. I, umm, I ... I'm sorry, I heard her neck snap when he magically twisted it. She fell to the floor, dead. At that very moment, Master Kalindi came into the hallway. Before I could warn him, Min'darr's magic shot a blue streak through the master, piercing his chest. He shuddered. Then it was like he got sucked into the hole the magic made in him and turned inside out. Then he was just gone. It was the worst thing I could ever have imagined!" She openly wept. "What kind of a horrid, nasty man would so easily murder someone?

"Within a heartbeat he did the same to Mygili's body. That's when I cast the aura and captured him, putting an end to his reign of murderous terror." She nodded to the masters and returned to her seat. She was immediately comforted by those around her.

Magistrate Tristian stepped to the front of the stage. "Thank you, Lokina, for your heart-wrenching testimony. My heart aches for you for the memories you must carry with you. We can talk later."

In a louder voice, he stated, "The testimony is done. The facts speak for themselves. Normally, the accused would be allowed to state their defense. That will not be the case now!"

"I have the right to speak in my defense!" Min'darr hollered.

The magistrate waved his hand. Min'darr knew he'd been muted, that no one could hear him. For the first time in his life, he feared its ending.

"The accused will not testify here. We have his violations of the Rules that speak volumes. We have his disrespectful interruption and his obscene use of his blue magic to influence these proceedings. He has disqualified himself from speaking, from any kind of defense of his defenseless actions." He strode across to the masters. They spoke between themselves for less than a minute. A master from the loft magically sent a paper to the magistrate when he looked up at them. The magistrate looked at it and nodded his approval.

He returned to center stage and raised both arms like a preacher. "It is done," he said loudly. "As Magistrate, it is my duty to announce that the collected masters of the Sodality of Yellow Magic have heard the testimony and find the accused, Min'darr of Rougahn, guilty of violating the Seven Rules resulting in the deaths of six of our fellows. His punishment is his own death."

He looked at Min'darr and continued. "Having been fairly tried by the Sodality, you are sentenced to die. That sentence will be carried out immediately with this multitude as witnesses to our justice. Prepare yourself."

He turned swiftly and walked behind the stage curtain. The masters came to the floating aura holding Min'darr and brought it to the center stage area. The curtain had been moved aside and the Weir was lowering when they stopped.

While being moved, Min'darr called to the spirit. *"Naldalek! Help me! You know this is wrong. Help me, please."*

The spirit responded, making himself known in Min'darr's mind. *"I am here to end them for their crimes. Killing you is one of their worst. For this Sodality to end, you must die. I am to escort your soul beyond the Veil and introduce you to Eternity."*

He paused a second and thought, *"I'm not ready"*.

Naldalek chuckled. *"No one ever is."*

The masters set him in place and stepped back. Tristian reappeared from behind him and declared that justice was at hand. "Know you the fate of those who would defile the Sodality."

Magistrate Tristian raised his arms and twin beams of yellow magic struck Min'darr's aura. A second later, all the other masters directed their magic at the sphere as well. Min'darr sensed no immediate change in the aura.

Tristian spoke a word, "Iyahtol," and the intensity of their magical streams increased. Min'darr felt a slight vibration in the aura holding him in place. It tickled actually, especially his nose and ears. He wished he could move to scratch or rub them.

A static sound emerged from his sphere and progressively got louder. Gradually, miniscule cracks appeared throughout the sphere.

"Iyahtol" again resounded, somewhat muted by the crackling. It grew louder, more pervasive. Then, in a singular snap, it burst. The magic around him was gone, rising up or straight out toward the Weir in countless crystalline beads. The Weir took them all.

The yellow arcane beams from twenty-some sets of magic gems struck Min'darr, driving into him, through him. He wanted to scream for the pain was enough to justify it. He wanted to draw in a breath. Every cell in his body felt like it was exploding. His body was no longer his to command.

"Iyahtol."

His yellow magic was the first thing to go. Drawn out of him by their magic, the searing he felt was as before. Every fiber of his being felt like it was burning. He screamed, not really able to hear it himself. Bits and pieces of him followed the magic. He felt as if he was like smoke, spreading across more and more area every second.

He felt himself being both pulled and pushed. Something within him, it could have been Naldalek, let him know he was losing his body. The pain was not much more than a battering, like falling off a cliff and hitting the rocks below. Whether it was through his eyes or his mind's perception, or even his soul's, he felt he disconnected, like he was drifting away.

Yellow magic was everywhere around him. He could taste it, feel its thick heaviness as it washed over and through him, not quite understanding why he could sense anything at all, Min'darr believed he saw everything about him becoming dust, rising and getting taken up into the Weir. At least that felt familiar.

Then his consciousness rose up and reentered the Weir. *"But wait ..."* And he was gone. Surrounded again by the Weir, he had the distinct impression of being in two places at once.

Naldalek's voice explained. *"That will be gone soon enough. Your soul is here. Your body is too, but not in the same plane of reality. It is a phantom physical memory. To this existence, you are dead."*

The End

Naldalek's presence anchored Min'darr. Once again, as it had following his Weir Battle, Min'darr found himself within the Weir's nothingness. The founder's spirit, however seemed more distant somehow, detached from him and the Weir.

"How are we to defeat them?" Min'darr thought.

"This is not a thing for you to do. The dead linger within this Weir until taken into the gem's collective. I am here to bring them, and you, to Eternity. Before I do that, I am to destroy the Sodality. I will escort the abusers to a separate eternity, one, uhm ... not so pleasant. They must pay for the anguish and suffering they have caused."

Min'darr protested. *"Spirit, I must help. Allow me some magic and I will be at your side to right their wrongs! Please, Naldalek, grant me this."*

Naldalek hesitated. *"Your part in this history has been played. You are a victim of this Sodality, of Tristian and his minions. Rest assured that they will be destroyed. I warned you of your impending death here and yet you remained. I must go about my task. I will drain the gemstone and release its magical energies against them."*

"Wait! Naldalek, wait," Min'darr pleaded. *"What of them? The others! Are they to be destroyed too? They are as much victims of this madness as any are. And Gili! I mean, Mygili. What of her? Is her soul lost here too?"*

"The others you mention will be brought to Eternity as well, Mygili among them. She is within the Weir should you wish to be with her.

To be with her again, even in this form, if for only a second, would be priceless. *"Yes, oh yes, please."*

His consciousness, his soul remained trapped within the Weir, newly deceased. Yet happily, Min'darr awaited her. Within a moment, he felt her presence. Since they took no physical space, had no awareness of temporal measures, their reunion didn't have any real expectations. He'd learned that on his first jaunt within the Weir.

Still within their reality between dimensions, their energies, their souls intermingled. They shared every memory, every hope and fear, every feeling they'd ever felt. For a moment within that sharing, they ceased being two souls.

Then as they drifted apart, Gili shared a final conscious thought. Min'darr recognized it. *"Blue."* What she meant by it, he wasn't sure. An obvious reference to his original magic. To what end he couldn't be sure. Now separated, they had no communication. Neither had any magic. There was no sign of any of the others.

There was no sign of Naldalek either. He thought intensely, calling to him. Nothing happened. *He must be busy with his destruction of the Sodality.* Min'darr wondered how he would do this. *I can't imagine trying to battle a spirit, especially one of the founder's souls who could drain their arcane energy supply.*

If Naldalek is going to put this place to ruins, we've got to get out of here! He spread his awareness. Gili wasn't near him anymore. *Maybe she's figured out how to move in here. That might put her in danger of getting sucked into the gem.*

I have no magic in me, so I can't move against the magic's flow.

A thought came to him. He escaped the first time through outmaneuvering the flow of the magic at the gemstone. Naldalek had said he was stronger because of it, yet lucky to have succeeded. Then he told him that the most common way to escape the Weir was to give it all of your magic, then sink to the bottom and, basically, fall out of it. Since the gemstone attracts magic and he had none, it made sense.

Min'darr had to get out, or risk getting sucked into Caudaric. But if Naldalek drains it, would it continue to draw them up out of the Weir? Would it exist? He didn't know enough about the nature of yellow magic's tendencies to make a valid choice. *Naldalek told me how to get out through the bottom. I'll give that a try first.*

He sought insentience, a psychic coma. He shut out anything close to his awareness, wrapping himself in a self-induced empty cocoon of oblivion. His last thought was to drop out of the Weir.

A sense of touch broke through to him. Awareness revived him. The Weir was shaking, vibrating. He felt he was lying against a floor beneath it. *I'm not solid. What can hold a spirit back? It has to be magic. I have none to give, none to fight back. Damn!*

Another memory. This time from the scroll he'd absorbed that held the Seven Rules. *The essence of yellow magic comes from the soul of the deceased.*

I am my own power, my own source of magical energy. That realization struck him as he became aware of the auditorium, awash with pandemonium. Students were frozen in place. Mouths were open in silent screams. Masters were like statues falling over each other. Time had stopped. Min'darr had to look long and hard at the giant figure leaning out from behind the stage curtain and from the ceiling. The thing was easily ten times the size of a man. Rage was plastered across his face.

My face. It was a monstrous Min'darr with his eyes missing, his lids shut. Naldalek! He had no eyes. Min'darr remembered seeing him when he was the weapons vendor after Min'darr had first came ashore. How many of these masters, or Tristian, would be aware that Naldalek had no eyes? If they did, it would be horrifying for them to see Min'darr's visage as their founder.

Within Min'darr's awareness, Naldalek spoke to him. *"You should not be out, I am using your body to fulfill the prophecy. Your spirit cannot long exist outside the Weir and outside your body. Get to your staff! Take in your blue magic. It will save you! Hurry!"*

In a blink, Min'darr's consciousness was in his dormitory room. He fumbled with his belongings, fighting to open his trunk, but his hands passed through everything. Anxiousness set in, near panic until he remembered *"I am the magic."*

He set himself, calling the trunk out from under the bed and to open. So it happened. He reached for the staff and was filled with a searing pain throughout his being.

What ...? I didn't think this through. Yellow magic can't act on wood. My magic is in wood. Wait! Hinasha's gem is buried within it. As quickly as he could, he knew he had to destroy the staff to free his blue magic.

The gem knows me. The staff knew me before. I have to awaken the gem.

Min'darr concentrated hard on the gemstone he'd embedded into the wooden staff the night before he came to the Sodality. It stirred. He felt it. Still, he needed to push it harder. He dug into the depths of his being, bringing virtually all of his existence to the task. *Will I have enough power to do this? Will there be enough of me left to gather it in or will I be lost, even to Eternity?* He had to chance it,

His arcane surge lit the room. The buried gemstone glowed, seen through the wood in which it was set growing ever brighter, more than a full moon, until it burst.

The shattering of the gem splintered the staff a full quarter of its length, filling the room with shards and splinters. That shattering also freed the magic Min'darr had entrusted to it. From every fiber of wood, blue flashings illuminated their surroundings, swirling about the room in a crescendo of light and power.

With a simple *"To me,"* the magic rushed into him until every atom of energy had been reabsorbed by his spirit. It took his form again. Glancing in wonder at his magic fingers, he startled, remembering the work he had to do. In an instant, the room darkened as he shot through the wall like a lightning bolt. The remnant of the staff followed of its own accord.

*

Min'darr returned to the Weir Chamber to find it empty.

He stood at the base of the Weir. No pull. No draw was felt. *Is this because it is done, broken and dead? Or is this because I am no longer of yellow magic?* He suspected the later, hoping he wasn't too late to rescue Gili. Casting a spell to see, his blue magic bounced off the fibers of the Weir, unable to penetrate it. As a spirit of blue magic, his own efforts to reenter the appliance failed. *It only works with yellow magic.*

The small remnants of Hinasha's gemstone he had absorbed were sensitive to the continuing battles of yellow magic. He sensed their location in or at least near the magistrate's office. His magic took him there.

Naldalek was not to be seen. Tristian was there with Vukbee and four other masters. They looked haggard and fearful. Tristian stood slightly apart from them, yet they were connected by a tether of yellow magic. *Just like Quint. Against their own Seven Rules.*

The magistrate had a long tear across his shirt. The masters looked disheveled as if they'd rolled in the dirt. *Clearly Naldalek is making them work at dying.*

Tristian, with labored breathing, addressed the masters. "It is clear to me that we are fighting someone other than a blue magician. His mastery of yellow magic is pure."

"It is also clear that despite his eyes being sewn shut, he can see everything," Master Vukbee said. "Isn't there some legend about a sightless master, Magistrate?"

"Yes, damn it, yes. In the innermost Triune, the Sodality's founder, Naldalek, sacrificed his eyes to see the energies released at death. There are also documents that warn about a magician arriving with unnatural arcane talents. When this Min'darr arrived, I felt within him more power, more natural magic than in most masters. That's why I had to plan his demise. I had no inkling he would rise the way he did.

"Before Min'darr died, I'd placed another protection spell across Caudaric so he could not touch it. As soon as his soul reached the Weir, he broke through my spell and accessed its power."

Min'darr was about to respond when the door to Tristian's office blazed orange, instantly burning into ash. Min'darr saw himself standing on the opposite side, glowing a brilliant yellow. Tristian instantly covered them with an arcane shield.

Naldalek laughed, no longer sounding like Min'darr at all. "You are feeble. The magic you possess is nothing compared to mine. I command all yellow magic, even yours." With that, Naldalek gestured and the magic surrounding them whisked to Naldalek, absorbed by a massive gem, the pendant of a necklace he wore.

"All of you are mine. Your souls are to be contained within Caudaric. Before you die, though, I wish you to know the truth. I am not who you think I am. I am not who you see. The Blue

Magician Min'darr is there," he said, pointing at the spot
Min'darr's soul was. He became instantly visible, a glowing blue
spirit.

"I took his body when you killed him. A horrible crime, by the
way, adding one more of which you will be held accountable for,
and for which you will pay dearly."

"And who are you that you believe yourself our master and
capable of taking retribution for some imagined wrong?" Tristian
challenged.

Naldalek grinned and looked at Min'darr. "Come here,
Magician, and reclaim what is rightfully yours."

Min'darr approached him and, at Naldalek's gesture, reentered
his own body. As he did so, a bright yellow spirit vacated it,
illuminating the room so much so that the masters and the
magistrate all had to shield their eyes. The visage dimmed and
took the form of an old man, the same one Min'darr met at the
vendors' market. This time, though, he was dressed in a robe-like
uniform, bordered and sequined with impressive regalia.

This time, too, his eyes were sealed.

"Your Triune warns of my coming, disguised as a magician. It
is my spirit you should fear for I am Naldalek, founder of the
Sodality of Yellow Magic. I have watched you bastardize and twist
the Seven Rules to fit your narcissistic needs for power and greed.
I have watched each of you maim and murder, sacrificing decent
souls to fuel your whims. It will be tolerated no more."

Naldalek gestured with his hand and the Gemstone of the
Weir appeared before him.

"No!" Min'darr cried. "Gili isn't out yet! Please."

"It is beyond your reckoning. All will be as it must be," the
spirit said to him. He then turned to face the masters. "As the
messenger of Loy, I summon you home." He held out his arms
and the gem pulsed slowly, sounding like a dissonant old organ in
the process. With each pulsing moan, a master dissolved, whisked
into the gem.

With only Tristian and Vukbee left, the woman sobbed
openly. "Magistrate, Tristian, you must save ..." Tristian stood
alone.

When it would be his turn next, the magistrate buckled to his knees, crying aloud, "I can do better, my Lord Naldalek, I promise you. I can serve you as you would expect me to. I promise to use my talents to foster the Seven Rules, to celebrate our magic. Please, Master, allow me to remain, I pray."

Naldalek lowered his head with a slight sigh. "No, Tristian, I believe you would not. I understand your own reluctance, sir, for you have every right to fear what awaits you." The gem pulsed again. Naldalek and Min'darr stood alone.

In a blink, they stood in the Weir Chamber, Naldalek holding a miniaturized Weir in his hands, the gem repositioned at its peak. Min'darr silently stared, amazed at its intricacy and numb for not having brought Gili from within it.

"I will be going, Min'darr the Magician. I have swept this place clean of the minions of Tristian and those who would abuse magic, save for one.

"Know that this place will live on in legend and that your part in its demise will be heralded. It will be generations before any would dare rekindle the rites of yellow magic. However, mankind being what they are, they will."

"Master Naldalek," Min'darr said softly. "What of Gili? Is her time so finite?"

"Eternity knows not time," he said. "I've shown you that."

Min'darr carefully selected every word he needed to say. "When I first met you, you warned me of my impending death. You said "in this version of history" I would die. I did, but your magic has restored my life. For that, I am most thankful. We have served a common cause, you and me. Please ... my one plea, good ghost, is to save the one I love. Please restore Mygili."

Naldalek raised the Weir above his head. The gem, Caudaric, by name, fired a flow of magical energy into the heavens. When it was spent, Naldalek pressed it between his hands, fracturing it into a pile of dust.

Naldalek set the Weir atop the gem's debris and stepped back. Waving his arms across them, they became a yellow mist, swirling and spreading out into the form of a person. When it settled, Mygili lay before him.

Min'darr dropped to his knees, crying his thanks to Naldalek. "Thank you and bless you my friend, my master, for this most generous gift. I promise I will always ..." He stopped, seeing that she wasn't moving, or even breathing. He sighed, realizing that he was not done here as her life had yet to be restored.

"What must I do to revive her, Master?" he asked.

"There is one more left for you to deal with. From her energies, you will find your love's soul. Lose to her, and all this has been for naught."

Naldalek streaked into the sky as a beam of pure energy. The beams and roof of the building where he'd passed through sparked and blazed into a fire.

A Beginning

'There is one more ... her magic.' It has to be Lokina, he reasoned. He'd watched as Master Vukbee was swallowed by the Weir's gemstone, Caudaric, along with some of the other masters, so the last female had to be her.

Looking down at Gili, he felt the love well up within him. Her sweet face and the quiet peace that shown through her was spellbinding. Even her auburn hair, so still, reflected the light and highlighted a thousand shades of color. Recollections of their joining while within the Weir brought him a knowing peace he'd never known existed.

"I will bring you back," he said to her. "Before I fight Lokina, though, I must protect you." He took his still-enchanted staff, shorter than it was before, about chest high, and laid it on her from her ankles to her chin. He worked to compose a spell, but the words would not come.

"Stupid me. Blue magic works through thoughts and feelings, not words. I don't need to recite a spell. No wonder Quint stayed rock."

He again centered his efforts on his task. The staff glowed a soft, wonderfully familiar blue as he drew his arms across and laid his protection spell over Gili's body. There was something, though, tugging at his arcane awareness, emanating from her. "I'll have to figure that out in a bit," he said aloud.

Another twinge made him nervous. *Lokina! She's close,* he knew. As he turned to face the doorway, a blast of yellow magic struck him, splashing off like a bucket of water. Splatterings of it hit the floor and walls, digging into them like acid.

Min'darr raised a blue shield. Lokina raised a yellow one of her own. They faced each other, ready for battle.

"I guessed you'd show up as your regular size sooner or later. You got your eyes fixed, too, eh?" she said.

"That wasn't me, Lokina. It was the founder's spirit. Naldalek by name. I tried to warn you. I said there'd be a reckoning."

"Really," she spat. "I'm supposed believe a blue magician's prophesy about my world coming to an end? Seriously! What would the Sodality's founder's spirit want with a blue magician?"

"He told me that things around here were no longer acceptable. The masters and students, too few were actually following the Rules. He told me that he needed to destroy the Sodality because it couldn't be fixed. I was the bait."

"I don't know, Magician. Seems like where I'm from, the bait is always eaten." With her last word came another arcane beam. It struck and adhered to his blue shield.

Min'darr countered with his own blast, which hit her yellow shield, ricocheting off.

Lokina moved down the steps toward the stage and waved her arms and shield. Min'darr had seen her do that one other time. When she placed him in the aura sphere to capture him.

He strengthened his shield, but the aura never formed.

She laughed and said, "Second guesses don't count, fool."

From the corner of his eye, he caught the familiar tinge of a yellow aura. He wheeled and saw Gili surrounded by Lokina's sphere.

"Now what are you gonna do?" she chided.

Min'darr knew what he had to do. *She has to be destroyed.*

He sent a charge of his blue magic against the wall and ceiling nearest her. Instantly, the stone buckled and fell. The ceiling section collapsed on top of her. Dust filled the room as the rock and timber pile settled.

Seconds went by with nothing happening. Slowly a yellow light appeared within the pile of debris. It brightened. Some of the debris moved.

Suddenly, strong bright rays broke through the pile. The rock shattered, blowing off the heap and raining down on Min'darr and careening off the aura covering Gili's body.

Lokina stood within the ring of debris, fists clenched. Her rings glared brilliantly.

"Looks like you're cheating. You haven't earned those gems," he teased.

"Oh, you like these? I managed to stop by Caudaric and recharged them in the hopes of taking you down, little man. You haven't seen anything yet." Lokina closed her eyes for a heartbeat to focus her next magical attack.

Min'darr didn't wait. He sent two magical charges into the floor before him to rise up and ensnare Lokina.

She opened her eyes and was immediately surrounded by Min'darr's magic. It washed over her with no effect.

"You see? I told you so! I knew you'd try that one on me. It worked against Quint and some somebodies up north you told us about. Not me! Fool! I'm better than you." She extended both arms, clasped her fingers, and pointed both her fists at him. "Even you won't survive this."

Min'darr stood, a sad expression covering his face. With a flick of his index finger, Min'darr signaled his second charge.

The second blast of blue magic rushed up out of the floor in front of Lokina. This time, as he'd intended, the magic acted as a sword, severing her hands at her wrists. She wailed from the shock of it and fell back, screaming in disbelief, "No! No! You can't … I won't let you. I …"

Min'darr enclosed her in blue magic and lifted her to stand in midair, facing him. "Look on the floor over there, little master. Rings and gems full of amazing power on your lifeless fingers. You have no power. You never did." Min'darr pointed toward Gili, now free of Lokina's magic. "See? Your aura dies with your magic. Therein lies the difference. You can only use yellow magic.

"Blue magic courses through my veins. It is a part of me and I a part of it. I am magic." He set his mind for what he knew had to be done. "And I now use it to send you to Naldalek. I pity your eternity."

Min'darr reached out. His staff rose from Gili's form and arrowed across the room, embedding itself in Lokina's chest, forcing her to fly back and pinning her to the wall. The wood of the staff spread quickly across her, turning every part of her into wood. She managed to move her lips. No words came out. In mere seconds, it was done. She fell to the floor, splintering as she hit.

Min'darr retrieved her rings and gems, laden with yellow magic. The roof continued to burn. Some debris fell into the Weir Room, but they were far enough away. He knelt next to Gili. Recalling Naldalek's words ... "From her energies, you will find your love's soul," he knew Gili's soul existed within one of these stones. He placed them, eleven in all, on her. One at a time, he picked up a gem, cupped it in his palm and placed it against his chest. *I will know,* he told himself.

He could not. None of the gems spoke to him, as he called it in his mind.

Then I have no choice. Min'darr scooped all of the gems into his hands and tossed them up, catching them with his magic. They swirled together in a small cluster, glowing, pulsing. They then compacted into a ball.

As much as he wanted to be done with his own yellow magic, he had to draw on it once more. The gem fragments that had been Hinasha's remained within him. He called on that magic to form a bond with the floating gems. Together then, with the strength of his blue magic, Min'darr clasped his hands around the gems to merge them into one new gem. The brilliance of that magic flared from between his fingers, kindling more fire to whatever contents of the room they touched. The wooden statue that had been Lokina burst ablaze.

Uncupping his hands, a beautiful diamond hovered above Gili, dazzling in reflecting the fires that surrounded them. Min'darr waited and, of its own volition, the gem floated down to rest over Gili's heart. It slipped into her chest, glowing a soft yellow.

Gili gasped a breath and opened her eyes.

*

While yet in the harbor, they stood at the bow of the ship that would take them away the next morning. From there, they could see plumes of smoke and flames of the massive fire still engulfing the buildings of the Sodality. The hillside and streets were replete with animals from the school running about, happily free. Townsfolk stood and watched. The heat was too intense to allow them to battle the inferno, should any be so foolish as to want to. Some sailors and dock workers stopped to pray, thanking Loy for destroying that evil place. He wasn't certain, but he thought he saw Goytel watching the school burn.

They ate at the *Kinsmen's Table* amidst countless conversations speculating on the cause of the school's demise. They returned to the Sodality after using magic to quench the blaze. Ashes puffed with their footfalls. Embers glowed in the increasing darkness. Neither of them could sense any other magic.

They faced each other and Gili's heart visibly glowed. The gem she'd absorbed into her new being carried much yellow magic. She used that to float above a pile of debris and held out her hand. From within the pile, an unburnt shaft of wood rose to her grasp. She returned to Min'darr and handed him his staff. They walked back to the harbor holding hands.

He had to ask, "How could your magic call to my wooden staff?"

She paused, considering. "I believe neither of us are pure yellow or pure blue anymore, my love. We are a part of both."

As they walked the pier later, the full moon's light shown as it rose above the sea. It reminded her of something. "According to yellow magic's tradition, whenever a source gemstone is discovered, it must rightfully be given a name, just like a baby."

"How is this name chosen?" he asked.

"From the one who finds it. Since you magically formed it, you should be the one to name it ... a name that has meaning to you. But, in the language of old, it must include 'ric' as an ending. It means 'source.'"

Min'darr thought for a moment leaned down and kissed the spot it entered her. "It shall be named Gilric."

She smiled and kissed him. "I love you too."

In their room later, Gili and Min'darr had a long, detailed conversation about what truly had happened. The sharing they'd experienced while within the Weir helped foster a calm and deep understanding about who each of them was and what each had endured. Above all else, both of them were grateful at being spared the wrath of Loy and being together to face their future.

That first night out on the water, with Mygili sleeping softly and warm at his side, Min'darr felt comfortable being back at sea. The ship they'd booked passage on was sailing west to the Tan'diali Islands, a land and people unknown to them. Where they went didn't concern either of them. The only thing that mattered was that they were together, ready to make a new life, a new beginning.

***

Don't Miss the Continuing Adventures in
MIN'DARRAN TALES VOL. II
By Steve Rouse

Available mid-2022
Read on for a sneak peek!

MIN'DARRAN TALES VOL. II

IV. THE BLUE KINGDOMS

Cataclysm

It had been a very long time since Min'darr had seen Kim'stwa, the capital city of his home country, Rougahn. Fifteen years had passed since he'd sailed off to the Southern Sea in search of yellow magic.

He'd found it. Died because of it. Then saw its end. Except for Mygili. She still has some. He switched his gaze from the approaching coastline of the capital city to his wife huddled next to him, shuddering from the cool sea breeze. He'd always been attracted to her auburn hair, and with it shining seventeen shades of red while billowing in the wind, he could fall in love with her all over again.

They'd been together since the yellow magic school, the Sodality, had been destroyed, both he and Mygili surviving through the grace of the ghost of its founder, Naldalek. They'd resettled in the Tan'diali Islands, where the peoples lived simpler lives, a lifestyle both of them came to love. They spent their time as physicians, subtly using their magic to heal illnesses and injuries.

Min'darr's blue magic was powered by the life forces of every living thing. The tropical region they lived in provided more than ample life with the forests, people, especially life within the teeming seas surrounding them.

Wherever there is life, there is also the inevitable cessation of life. That was the power for yellow magic. When a tree fell, a shark ate a fish, or an elder's tenure on the planet ended, their life forces were collected, to be used by yellow magic. Mygili had a yellow magic gemstone, a diamond, deep within her. Min'darr revived her with that following the fight with the Sodality. It empowered her own existence. On only three occasions while on the islands did Mygili have to vacate the gem's power when it had absorbed too much energy. Only in the thickest part of the night did they dare release the bright beam of life's energies towards the moon.

The two had wanted children. They found that the gem interfered with conception, absorbing the life forces before any child might have been conceived. It had been a difficult thing to accept, especially since they could not share the real reason of their sterility with their friends.

They adjusted, coming together to love each other all the more.

She looked up at him with that special smile, catching him yet again watching her. She would not have been as happy had that ever stopped. After a quick squeeze, she asked, "Do you feel them yet?" she asked.

"I do," he said. "They seem to be ..." he paused a moment, "... just over in that direction, toward the big reddish building."

"Magenta," she said, used to correcting him on colors he confessed he could not see.

"Yeah, okay." He knew not to disagree. "All three of them seem pretty close together. Probably waiting for us."

*

Two months earlier, Min'darr insisted they go into their island's small town. He'd felt something familiar. He'd long ago described to Mygili how he had placed tiny bits of magic into his sister, her partner, and his nephew so he could always find them. One of them was near.

They went. Walking near the port, they saw that a new ship had docked flying the Rougahn colors. Min'darr didn't need to ask anyone. They followed his magic. As they walked into a shop, they came upon a man in the uniform of a first lieutenant.

"Hello, Mah'zan."

The officer turned with a skewed look on his face. The only ones who knew him here would call him sir, not his first name.

"Uncle!" the officer cried, snatching Min'darr in an instant bear hug, lifting his feet from the floor. "By the gods, it is so good to see you. We haven't heard from you in forever. How are you? What are you doing here?" He set his uncle down and automatically smoothed the front of his uniform.

"Whoa, one thing at a time," Min'darr said, now able to breathe again. "First, I want to introduce you to my wife, Mygili." Turning to her, he said, "Gili, this is our nephew, Mah'zan."

Without any hesitation, Gili invited him to come to dinner. Min'darr smiled, nodding his approval.

*

They exchanged stories into the wee hours of the morning, especially about his time in the Rougahn navy and the destruction of the magic school.

Mah'zan told them of the attempts the three of them made to find him. "Mom, Ram'ili, and I would do our best to scry you. When we'd heard about the destruction of the magic school from other sailors, we learned that you had been there. Since we could feel each other's magic you gave us, we believed you still lived, but we never heard from you.

"That scrying thing you'd taught us ... we really weren't very good at it. But we got enough of a feel for it that we knew you were near water. Every time I set sail, I looked for you, asking others about you ... about a magician."

Mah'zan stayed on their island just short of two weeks, dining with them often. By the time his ship set sail, he had convinced them both that they needed to travel to Kim'stwa to catch up with Min'darr's sister, Koo'bla, and her partner, Ram'ili. He bragged, rambling on about how successful the two had been in their capital city café and inn business. "They've won awards! Seriously, Ram'ili's menu is worth a fortune!"

He took Gili's hands in his. "Mom will fall in love with you right away, Aunt Gili. I can't wait for you guys to meet."

Min'darr was excited at the prospect of seeing them again, more to introduce them to Gili than anything else. On their way to see Mah'zan off, they stopped at the neighboring shipping office to book passage to Kim'stwa for the following month. It would be a four-week journey. Mah'zan would let them know of their coming. The next month, before they left, their friends threw them a lavish bon voyage gala with lots of amazing food and just as many hugs.

*

Now, only an hour from docking, he reassured her of her acceptance by his family. "Mah'zan fell in love with you before we had dessert that first night. I'm certain he's let his mom know how amazing you are," he told her before they'd set sail. He repeated that same observation now.

She grinned. "I like him a lot. He obviously has a strong mother, a good upbringing. I'm looking forward to meeting them."

Mygili had no surviving family. She'd been an only child. Her dad and she were very close, but she never mentioned her mother except to tell Min'darr not to ask. He respected her wishes.

He knew everything, though, from the sharing they had experienced while in the Weir. During the battle to end the school of yellow magic, the Sodality, both Gili's and Min'darr's souls had been captured by a magic absorbing maze called the Weir. During that time, their souls had merged. They had become one, knowing and sharing everything.

Her father's death had been the main reason she had gone to the Sodality. His last words to her were that she had always had 'a special magic' about her.

As they watched the approaching shoreline, a sound arose above that of the ship's prow and sails. They, like others on deck, looked around for its source. The noise continued to grow. As it drew closer, its source became readily visible, a horrific sight.

From high above the ship's wake, a massive orange fireball screamed toward the coast. It looked to be nearly half the size of the city it was about to crash into. Gili stared at Min'darr, holding her breath. Without exchanging a word, they ran to the ship's stern for a clearer view of the meteor. They braced themselves, both of them sending blasts of pure magical energy up to destroy the thing.

Nothing happened. Neither Gili's yellow magic, nor Min'darr's blue magic had any effect on the falling mass. Within a span of mere seconds, the celestial traveler slammed into the heart of the city of Kim'stwa. They watched, horrified, as untold volumes of earth, sea water, buildings—a myriad of pieces of the city were crushed, then thrust upward in an unimaginable upheaval. The sound was deafening. The crash's shock wave could be seen racing across the land, the coastline, as well as far up into the hills inland.

That same impact wave, along with an ever-growing water wave, careened back toward their boat. They focused their magic on it, managing to split the wave. The brunt of it went asides the ship, the mass towering above the ship's sails, yet lifting them a hundred feet or more as it roared past. The ship stayed upright, however, many passengers fell overboard by the force of the blast. Min'darr and Gili managed to hang on to the aft gunwale, but would have been lost too had it not been for their magic.

Min'darr collapsed, exhausted, his magic depleted beyond any level he could recall save just coming out of the Weir. He could barely crawl. Not so for Mygili.

She stood, working to maintain the integrity of their ship, keeping it upright. Min'darr watched, so very proud of her efforts. Her eyes glowed yellow from her magic.

She knelt next to him. "Are you all right?"

"Yes, I just have nothing left. Kinda slow to recover. I love you. You are magnificent," he said.

"I'm not so sure, sweetheart," she replied. "Something's not right."

Min'darr managed to sit up. "By the gods, Gili, your magic ... so many people must be dead from this thing. Can you ...?"

She continued to glow more as he spoke. Now her entire body glowed to the point of casting a shadow on things around her.

"No moon ... have to unload ... Help me, my sweet," she begged.

Min'darr took hold of her shoulders. He couldn't. She was far too hot to touch. "Just point your beam skyward. Release the energy, my sweet love, anywhere ... any way you can! Focus."

At this point she was emitting more light than a large bonfire. Others around them backed away, afraid of what they saw.

"I'll try," she whispered, rising above the deck as high as the crow's nest, splayed out. Min'darr could see the waves of lost souls flowing out toward her from the shore. An endless stream drawn to her through her yellow magic.

"Channel them, sweetest! Open up ... just let them through. Gili!"

She became as bright as a star, a massive energy beam continued to emanate from her heading skyward. The sailors still hanging on in the rigging scrambled down, suffering burns from the energies shooting from her. Min'darr could no longer look at her. She glowed too bright. He could hear her sizzling, yet believed she could do this.

Seconds later, a huge inferno pulsed down onto the decking. The shock wave pushed the ship down, splintering the mast and yardarms. The ship's sails flared, incinerating in a heartbeat. A second later, a diamond dropped onto the deck next to him. The light ... the sizzling ... Mygili ... all gone.

*

Min'darr spent the next day in a small boat at that site, searching for any sign of his love. He floated up to exactly where she had last been, his magic showing him her body's imprint in the physical space she'd last occupied. He could touch that space's aura, but he could not follow. The Gilric, the diamond from inside her, would not respond as none of her arcane self could be found. He could not send his magic through it. This time, death would not be reversed.

He swam, he flew, he used every inkling of experience from his history, including from the archives of the blue magic stream, his concentrated source of magical energy. Nothing could be found in any of it to give him hope that the love of his life had not perished. He seriously contemplated searching for the stream again in order to lose himself within it for eternity.

His time on shore also carried little else besides pain. He had to face the truth that his family was dead. He could no longer sense any magic signal from any of them. That part of Kim'stwa in which they were bore the direct strike from the meteor. They too ... gone forever. Comments from caring individuals that "at least they didn't suffer" did little to alleviate the anguish of their absence. The irony of their journey to reunite with family only to lose them all to this cataclysm quickly became the worst burden he could ever imagine bearing.

The meteor had obliterated the city, its harbor, and the surrounding countryside with its own villages for twenty or more miles out. Death had ridden in on the meteor. An estimate stated that more than a hundred thousand lives had been lost. *No wonder Gili could not handle the surge. The entire Sodality could not have dealt with such a number.*

An idea brewed in his mind that this had been something resulting from Naldalek's influence given their magic's premise of returning souls that arrive on an asteroid. Min'darr summarily dismissed it as fiction. He sensed no yellow magic, even though he still carried shards of Hinasha's gemstone in his chest. Had it been the Sodality's founding spirit, he was certain that he would have been aware of him, given their past encounter.

He felt fated to accept all of this tragedy. It would be most difficult to carry a grudge against a soul that graced them both with a second life despite the devastation. Yellow magic was still dead after all this time. He wished he could be as well.

Three days following the impact, Min'darr wandered toward the massive hole that used to be a thriving municipality. Workers, mourners, scavengers had made their way into the pit looking for collectibles, meteor fragments, mementos of loved ones, even money from the safes of businesses and pockets of individuals lost.

He sat, staring at nothing, yet seeing too much. Eventually, afternoon shadows overtook him, followed by the evening's dimness as the sun set. He didn't move, barely breathing ... to the point that a man came to pick his pocket, thinking him dead.

Min'darr could find no solace. So much had been taken from him. According to the Mulu from the cave of blue magic, he had more than four hundred fifty years yet to live. How could he face that? He'd realized at the outset that he'd lose everyone eventually by simply outliving them. This had only been sixteen years ... and to lose them in such a sudden upheaval.

He knew he couldn't stay here. He didn't want to stay anywhere near Rougahn or, come to think of it, anywhere here.

Min'darr became focused on an escape. The best way he could accomplish that involved an eldritch stream. He knew he'd have to summon one.

He gestured to the depths of the pit, sending a magical strand to stretch the distance. He repeated it countless times. Between each application, he'd send a magical surge deep into the ground to summon a stream. After hours, a sparkling blue shimmer surfaced at the deepest part of the crater in line with his magical tether. Without hesitating, Min'darr, clutching Gili's diamond to his breast, enchanted himself and, like a bolt of lightning, streaked along his tether and disappeared into the comforting river of blue magic.

*

MIN'DARRAN TALES VOL. II
AVAILABLE MID-2022

ABOUT THE AUTHOR

STEVE ROUSE

Rouse has always loved words. He has also always loved stories, from those his grandpa used to tell to those he now tells his own grandchildren. As a middle school teacher in Wisconsin, he worked to instill this same love in his students. He began his own journey as a writer while helping his students concoct stories for an assignment.

As any author will attest, sharing the end product of that writing has its obstacles. Bearing a plethora of rejections slips, Rouse has had some successes. Four short stories have appeared in various anthologies: "The Gilric" – *Mages & Magic* (Walkabout Publishing, 2010), "Hodag" – *Mindscapes Unimagined* (Left Hand Publishers, 2018), "Sailor's Saga" – *Classics Remixed, Vol. 1* (Left Hand Publishers, 2019), and "The Traveler" – *Classics Remixed, Vol. 2* (Left Hand Publishers, 2019)

In addition, Rouse has had published two collections. One is a fantasy genre of short stories including a novella, *Magic's Balance* – (Left Hand Publishers, 2019). The other is a science fiction genre, co-authored with friend and author Paul K. Metheney, *Two Minds, No Waiting* – (Left Hand Publishers, 2020).

Rouse's first novel is *Dragons' Magician* (Left Hand Publishers, 2021). It's a fantasy novel of twin sisters separated at birth. One grows to be a princess, the other a magician. Yes, they find each other and fight to save their father's kingdom. How all that comes to pass makes this a really fun story!

This current novel is a collection of three novellas telling the early life's story of Min'darr the Magician, a character from "The Gilric" short story appearing in the *Magic's Balance* fantasy collection. It will be followed by a second volume detailing the rest of his magical life. A 2022 publication date is planned.

Rouse is currently working on an author's web page/site. More to come! You can reach Rouse via Facebook or at srouse.writer@yahoo.com.

MORE BOOKS FROM LEFT HAND PUBLISHERS

Magic's Balance

By Steve Rouse

Magic's Balance takes you on many journeys of imagination. Some will fill you with trepidation, while others can make you smile. Visit other lands and find new characters who experience their own fantastic lives through magic and the unexpected.

Jonah has known of his family's secret his whole life. One day, a golden apple appears in their orchard and Jonah is whisked into the heart of that mystery ... one that he must now fight to solve. What must he do in order to save himself and restore balance to the world of Magic?

Any story is but a snapshot of the lives of the characters within it. As one of the characters in my stories, the wizard Min'darr has led a full life. You have met him at its end. Did you wonder how he became a wizard? How has he come to be here, at this point in time? What part of his past has led him to want to share his magic? Would you like to know of his adventures? ... his successes? ... his mistakes? ... his love?

"There is an art to writing a short story, and Steve Rouse has mastered it. His collection of prose is lean, no wasted scenes. From the suspenseful 'Hodag,' to the wonderfully magical 'Salt Lick'—and everything in between, Rouse takes you on a delightful ride. Finished this book last night and posted a review this morning. Soooooo fun to read. It is Steve Rouse's first book. Something special about first books. And this one is blessed by fine stories and a beautiful cover."

Jean Rabe
USA Today bestselling author

"Steve Rouse has put together a delightful collection of stories covering a variety of genres. Whether dealing with fantasy battles, science fiction, horror, or odd happenings, you'll find clean, evocative prose, clever characters, humor, danger, twists, turns, and plenty of redemption. Keep this on your nightstand for a quick, fun read before going to bed or load it on your favorite e-reader for an escape from dismal reality during a break at work. You won't be disappointed!"

> **Donald J. Bingle**
> author of the *Writer on Demand*
> series of stories by genre.

"Steven Rouse's writing combines myth with whimsy and contemplation with action - sometimes within one tale! His literary prose has a breezy, familiar style. This collection is sure to please virtually everyone as it ranges from fantasy and SF to classic horror and modern musings. Do yourself a favor and spend an evening (or more!) with Steve's stories!"

> **Stephen D. Sullivan**
> author of the award-winning novelization of
> *Manos: The Hands of Fate* and more than 50 other books.

The book, *Magic's Balance*, contains a collection of stories involving magic, mystery, and worlds beyond imagining.

- Hodag
- Playing Fetch
- Huntress
- Grove of Ancients
- Magic's Balance
- The Note
- Inspiration
- Salt Lick
- The Nothing
- When You Buy an Old House
- The Gilric

Amazon - https://amzn.to/2ZeGKYf
LHP's web site - https://bit.ly/3jm2WGL
Goodreads - https://bit.ly/3aYGIWB

***

Dragon's Magician
By Steve Rouse

Magic powerful enough to reunite a family?

A century ago, Grand Wizard Astik defied his deluded king, magically stealing away all the living dragons to keep them safe from him. Now it is up to Astik to ready that king's great granddaughter, Skylar, who he rescued at birth and raised, to reunite dragons with mankind.

Can dragons and mankind join forces to save each other?

Skylar must also convince her father and twin sister, Myst, that she is their kin, thought to have been stillborn. Will she be able to reunite the dragons and humanity? Is there a magic powerful enough to defeat the evil wizard king in his effort to conquer her father's kingdom?

ABOUT DRAGONS' MAGICIAN

"Rouse masterfully weaves a tale that takes readers of all ages into a world of magic and dragons, and reminds us of the mystical powers of family bonds. *Dragons' Magician* is one of those stories that stays with you long after you've turned the final page."

Karen T. Newman
owner of Newmanuscripts
***

Beautiful Lies, Painful Truths Vol.I

There's an ironic beauty between humanity's love of Life and fear of Death. Life seemingly brings joy, happiness, hope, and love. Death can end sadness, illness, suffering, and pain. We asked writers to "Let the title and quote take your imagination, your story, wherever it wants to go."

Join them now as an international blend of authors, both fresh and seasoned, bring you an exceptional menu of speculative fiction, mystery, realism, horror, and the supernatural. If your palate varies from the macabre to the dramatic, *Beautiful Lies, Painful Truths* provides an assortment of tasty treasures that will chill, delight, and give you food for thought.

Reviews

★★★★★

"An incredibly amazing anthology.
Every author in this anthology should be commended for their work in this collection. Bringing in life and death into a collection of stories, all by different authors, and how their writing varies, but brings to life, this grand collection. I believe there was a lot of thought put into which authors would be contributing their work, and how this work will be displayed."

> **Amy Shannon,** Author. Writer. Poet. Storyteller. Blogger. Book Reviewer.
> **Author Blog:** http://bit.ly/2yLHuFZ
> **Facebook:** http://bit.ly/2ho273i
> **Review Blog:** http://bit.ly/2iPVV4x
> **Amazon Author** Page: http://amzn.to/2ynn2qM

"The quality of the stories read are amazing, with intricate plots in a short story form coming off as so perfect in their construction. The scope of the imagination of the writers just boggles the mind in the executions of stories that make you think. What might be considered 'good' isn't. What is seen as dark and painful is honestly the way it should be. Major kudos to these stories.

"Life is good and beautiful and death is dark and bad. Maybe not. This book presents twenty-four approaches with an amazing array of imagination in the depths of human drama, supernatural, humor, and unexpected twists. These stories will challenge everything you thought you knew—think again.

"*Beautiful Lies, Painful Truths* has stories guaranteed to challenge your view of life and death in mind-boggling ways, taking you down unexpected paths of the serious, humorous, pathos, and the twisted turns of fate. The qualities of the stories are good. The writers are to be commended. An excellent book. Kudos!"
Bruce Blanchard, Book Reviewer
http://bit.ly/2yLBq09

"It's an impressive read. It may be about death, but the mood isn't always dark. This anthology spans several genres including science fiction, horror, mystery, and even some humor. Well-written and well-edited, this book may be long, but it's hard to put down."
David Watson, Book Reviewer

Beautiful Lies, Painful Truths Vol. I

Amazon - http://amzn.to/2reSyIe
YouTube - https://youtu.be/4m1BR6BIBTM
The Reviews on YouTube - https://youtu.be/tTtdf0LQC7Q
LHP's Web Site - http://bit.ly/2FHXzw9
The Reviews on LHP - http://bit.ly/2FHhMlN
Goodreads - http://bit.ly/2BobVCi
***

Realities Perceived

Nothing's more dangerous, or delightful, than invoking a cadre of talented authors to create short stories that defy our perceptions of reality. Do we create our own truth? Or does our view of it shape our world? Neither heroes nor heavens, victims nor villains, may grasp the true nature of our being.

From science fiction, to horror and the supernatural, to dramas about the fabric of our existence, this international fusion of artists will thrill you with an eclectic selection of tales that cross all genres. Sit back and be prepared to have your perception of reality both challenged and distorted.

Reviews

★★★★★

"... it kept me on the edge of my seat and I did not want to put it down even to eat or sleep. You have a great book here."

Lori Kibbey
Book Reviewer

Realities Perceived

Amazon- http://amzn.to/2Dbe1ny
YouTube - https://youtu.be/3SLjzDd9o3Y
LHP's Web Site - http://bit.ly/2Do87SE

***

Beautiful Lies,
Painful Truths Vol.II

Most believe that Life promises light, bliss, and wonder. Death scares most with its shadow of mortality, darkness, and destruction. But what if those may be, if not lies, just facets of the complicated entities that bookend our existence? Life does not mock Death, but feeds it. Death is not the cessation of Life, but an alteration of existence. What would you do if faced with either truth?

An international galley of authors brings us a second repast of tales featuring the complex relationship between Life, Death, and humanity. From the supernatural to the sublime, these writers, both novitiates and accomplished, serve up a banquet of speculative fiction across a wide spectrum of genres. Beautiful Lies, Painful Truths Volume II will continue to feed your craving for the fantastic.

Reviews

"You have to love an anthology that can give you well-written stories no matter what the genre is and it looks at important issues in addition to death such as love, religion, and redemption."
David Watson, Amazon Book Reviewer

"This collection is a recipe for a lost weekend as I found myself wanting to read 'just one more' until by nearly midnight I had finished all sixteen. I will recommend this to my friends and fellow bibliophiles without reservation."
Natalia Corres
Book Reviewer, Twitter.com/Ncorres

"I read the first volume and was more than excited to read a new collection. Life and death is not just black and white, but all the in-betweens and as the title alludes, both are beautiful, but also full of lies and truths."

Amy Shannon, Author. Writer. Poet. Storyteller. Blogger. Book Reviewer.
Author Blog: http://bit.ly/2yLHuFZ
Review Blog: http://bit.ly/2iPVV4x
Amazon Author Page: http://amzn.to/2ynn2qM

Beautiful Lies, Painful Truths Vol. II

Amazon - http://amzn.to/2ngBq0i
YouTube - https://youtu.be/i8dAMSAbkAM
LHP's Web Site - http://bit.ly/2Dxu9n8
Goodreads - http://bit.ly/2slkBpP

***

The Demon's Angel
By Maya Shah

Neha was excited to enter her sophomore year in high school. That was until the boy she went out with sprouted wings, and Lucas, the man who raised her since she was a baby, turned into a demon.

Neha is far from human. She is an angel, the natural enemy of demons. An angel raised by a demon has never been heard of before, which makes some angels see her as a threat. Neha not only has to prove that she does not know anything about demons, she has to prove that she is on the side of the angels.

And she is. So she thinks.

This Young Adult supernatural thriller follows the tribulations of the teenaged Neha as she learns both the truth about her past and herself.

Reviews

★★★★★

"Intensely unique.

The character Neha is something very remarkable, she has depth and grows as a character, especially when she feels she has to prove herself. She thinks she's proving herself a good angel to the other angels, when in fact she's also proving it to herself. Neha is not your typical teenager, nor typical angel."

Amy Shannon, Author. Writer. Poet. Storyteller. Blogger. Book Reviewer. Review Blog: http://bit.ly/2iPVV4x

"This flight of fancy with engrossing plot twists tempts anyone ever dumbfounded by a parental deception."

Wendy Landers, Book Reviewer Author of *Just Let Time Pass* www.wendylanders.com

The Demon's Angel by Maya Shah
Amazon - http://amzn.to/2EVjj7V
YouTube - https://youtu.be/FZuvbiGjMcU
Maya Shah's Web Site - http://mayashahbooks.com/
LHP's Web Site - http://bit.ly/2DuXieD
Goodreads - http://bit.ly/2son5E2

***

A World Unimagined

Beyond what is conceivable to what might be is a universe full of the unexpected and the unexplainable. From science fiction to science fantasy, the location of this realm of creation and the mind is...

A World Unimagined.

An international manifest of authors, both new and experienced, crew this voyage to the other side of the unbelievable with stories unique and thought-provoking. This anthology of science fiction short stories transports us to the future, the past, and to cultures and civilizations undreamed of. Set your imaginations to stunned and your minds to light speed.

Reviews

"An eclectic menagerie of *X-Files* material. My favorite was the alien invasion of the Vietnam War's Hanoi Hilton."

Wendy Landers, Book Reviewer
Author of *Just Let Time Pass*
wendylanders.com

"Science Fiction is the great cosmos governed only by the power of What If. It requires minds seeing beyond our world of limitations and creating through imagination different species and stories boggling anything we ever thought. The stories here prove the writers included have done just that.
"... for the record, science fiction doesn't usually appeal to me. These stories do ... very nice. If these can turn me on, the book is definitely worth reading."

Bruce Blanchard, Book Reviewer
https://www.facebook.com/bruce.blanchard2

YouTube - https://youtu.be/2IO3rl0N_q8
LHP Web Site - https://bit.ly/2IG7Dea
Amazon - https://amzn.to/2yvJ4vS
Goodreads - https://bit.ly/2K7b6zj

***

Drawing From The Well

By Rachel Bollinger

A collection of parables, poems, and anecdotes to enhance your spiritual journey. Author, Rachel Bollinger walks you through her personal challenges and triumphs, referencing scripture and entertaining you as she walks closer to God.

Join her as she draws from her well of experience, faith, and victories on a journey of faith and discovery.

Reviews

"We all journey through dark nights of the soul. In this lovely collection, Rachel shares some of her most challenging life experiences and how she coped and grew in grace through the unchanging Word of God. Rachel's memories, in story and verse, are honest, brave, and witty. I came away understanding that the grief I hold in my heart has a permitted place to live."

Susan V. Smith, Amazon Reviewer
https://amzn.to/2JuDfmz

Drawing from the Well by Rachel A. Bollinger

LHP Web Site - https://bit.ly/2LqIzER
Amazon - https://amzn.to/2th8WGE
Goodreads - https://bit.ly/2M8h57h

***

Mindscapes Unimagined

Open the door to any genre and you will find places where the unimaginable and the unexplained collide with reality. These stories take you far past that point. From the horrifying to the macabre to the edge of real madness, you will travel to ...

Mindscapes Unimagined.

An international bevy of authors, new and experienced, weave tales both fantastic and exciting. This genre-bending collection of short stories blurs the line between what can be and what can be imagined. No monster, dimension, or mortal villain is off limits. When you are ready to risk sanity and sleep, start on the first page.

Reviews

★★★★★

"An adventure in reading
Mindscapes Unimagined is a collection of stories from a grand variety of writers. This collection contains stories stemming from the imagination that blends horror, paranormal and science fiction into one great collection. Most of the authors in this collection, I haven't read before, but I will definitely keep them in mind for future writings. I found the order of the stories very interesting, as one led into another. As Rouse wrote in his story 'Hodag,' 'Did you not just see what joy I brought to these less fortunate? They have broadened their lives, enriched their experiences through my eyes and my story,' it worked perfectly with the concept and collection of the stories. I enjoyed each one, enticing and captivating as the one before it, and yet its own story and imagination of the darkness.

"This collection is definitely a menagerie of stories, from different minds, mixing dark and light, and blending it perfectly. Some are first person, and others are written in third person, and with most stories, it makes a difference and takes a story where it wants to go. I always embrace the anthology that has many different authors, points of views, stories that are shown and not told, and this is no different."

Amy Shannon
Writer. Author. Reviewer.
Amy's Bookshelf Reviews
Facebook: https:// https://bit.ly/2C2YSpS
Blog: https://bit.ly/2mat8sy
Amazon Author Page: https://amzn.to/2ENvyGu
Author Blog: https://bit.ly/2g7KQYn

Mindscapes Unimagined

LHP Web Site - https://bit.ly/2SGN5nf
Amazon - https://amzn.to/2FNVkZ4
Goodreads - https://bit.ly/2ORO1nq

***

Suspense Unimagined

Not all monsters have fangs, fur, or horns. Many times the worst demons are as real as tomorrow's headlines. From criminal suspense to psychological thriller to just plain scary, these short stories of pulse-quickening fear will drive you to ...

Suspense Unimagined

An international fusion of authors, new and experienced, craft tales of terrors unimaginable and thought-provoking. This anthology of suspenseful short stories drags us down paths both inconceivably possible and more horrifying than the supernatural. Unclench your knuckles for a ride to inspire you to think and cringe.

LHP Web Site - https://bit.ly/2P4mvS4
Amazon - https://amzn.to/2UwG7VI
Goodreads - https://bit.ly/2VlHN1x

***

Terrors Unimagined

Far beyond what you can imagine lies a dreamscape full of the unexpected and the unexplainable. The supernatural, the paranormal, monsters, demons, magic, witches, and inconceivable horrors reside
in a world of...

Terrors Unimagined

An international cadre of authors, both new and experienced, lead you down a path to the other side of the unbelievable with stories unique and thought-provoking. This anthology of supernatural and horror-inspiring short stories drags us screaming into a world of creatures and nightmares undreamed of. Prepare to ponder your nights away.
Sleep is no longer an option.

Terrors Unimagined

YouTube - https://youtu.be/ow4XfWt2q7w
LHP Web Site - https://bit.ly/2MSohot
Amazon - https://amzn.to/2OsldAT
Goodreads - https://bit.ly/2LkLO17

***

Classics Remixed Vol. I

An anthology of short stories twisting classic stories and your imagination in all new ways.

Alternate versions of stories you know taking you in new directions.

From much-loved fairy fables to time-honored tales, no genre or classic is off-limits. *Classics ReMixed Vol. I* spins and twists divergent versions of old favorites and stories we all know. Be prepared to have all your ...

Classics ReMixed

LHP Web Site - https://bit.ly/2XLgkY9
Amazon - https://amzn.to/2M0qRLx
Goodreads - https://bit.ly/2LZsIQI

***

Classics Remixed Vol. II

Continuing the anthology of short stories twisting classic stories and your imagination in all new ways.

From much-loved fairy fables to time-honored tales, no genre or classic is off-limits. *Classics ReMixed Vol. II* spins and twists divergent versions of old favorites and stories we all know. Be prepared to have all your ...

Classics ReMixed again

LHP Web Site - https://bit.ly/2IyQGzH
Amazon - https://amzn.to/3aC5aeh
Goodreads - https://bit.ly/2vMBMDm

***

Tower, Sword, Stone and Spell
by Timothy Vincent

What price the cost of immortality, power, glory, or love?

Welcome to Yut. A land of magic, mayhem, and mystery. Follow the personal struggles and triumphs of three unique characters set in a world of mages, cunning thieves, and deadly warriors. If you like your fantasy filled with intrigue, suspense, and realism, this is for you!

The Chain: "Each man is measured for the chain, and the chain takes the measure of each man." A former pit-fighter flees his past only to become an unwilling participant in a deadly march across the red sands.

Awareness: A young mage meets his father for the first time and discovers the darker side of magic.

Heart Scratch: One door opens to the Thaumaturge's Tower. Behind that door lies a terrible secret, a secret that will haunt a young thief and his companion for a lifetime.

Tower, Sword, Stone and Spell
Amazon - https://amzn.to/3e9Y44b
Goodreads - https://bit.ly/3e7TALg
***

Two Minds, No Waiting
By Steve Rouse & Paul Metheney

Take two very disturbed minds. Add the ability to create any worlds or situations they like. And you have the recipe for a collection of science fiction stories like none you have ever tasted.

From alien saviors and attackers, to time travel, to fantastic tales that include unique teachers and hunted mammals. More than just spaceships and phaser beams, this collection contains alternate universes and superheroes. If you're ready to set aside your beliefs in what is or isn't possible, it's time to get your imagination rewired by ...

Two Minds, No Waiting!

LHP Web Site - https://bit.ly/2KOnfi7
Amazon - https://amzn.to/39jAjFm
Goodreads - https://bit.ly/3pkLzH9
***

That Boy Ain't Write in the Head
By Paul K. Metheney

A Collection of Mixed Genre Stories: Sci-Fi, Alternate Universes, Time Travel, Supernatural, & More

A science-fiction author tries to save the world from alien attack, alien visitors that only eat cancer, a man travels back to his past, and a Secret Service Agent must protect his friend, the President, from destroying the White House. These are just a few of the fantastic tales that await you inside.

From sci-fi to stark reality, these short stories will entertain, provoke, and whet your appetite for more. This collection contains not only serves up the best of Paul K. Metheney's short stories, but an all new menu of fresh tales to stimulate your literary palate.

The title of the book derives from a strip bar bouncer in the '80s taking one look at Paul and saying

"That boy ain't right in the head."

Left Hand Publishers' web site - https://bit.ly/3vtMFEo
Amazon - https://amzn.to/3AVTj7v
Youtube - https://youtu.be/zpDkfvbzimw
Goodreads - https://bit.ly/3E02x4z

***

Posse Whipped
By Paul K. Metheney

A novel about a Southern sheriff struggling to save his town from corruption, drug-trafficking, moonshiners, and the economy, all while protecting his most valuable law-enforcement assets... his family and friends. As the sheriff protects his town and family, a villain from his family's past assembles his own eclectic posse of criminals to destroy Sheriff MacDowell and every thing he holds dear.

A down-home journey in to the hills of Kentucky, as author, Paul K. Metheney, brings you a sometimes humorous novel set in a modern day western fight for survival, justice, and family. The spirit of the Wild West meets modern day in an adventure for the John Wayne in us all.

"If you like Craig Johnson's *Walt Longmire Mysteries*, you will LOVE *Posse Whipped*."

"All of C.J. Box's action, but with Metheney's humor and wit."
***

Concepts for Texas Hold'em
By Paul K. Metheney

PLAY FOR PAY!

An easy-to-read pocket guide of concepts, notes, thoughts, and strategies on making more money at the Texas Hold'em Poker tables in casinos. From tactics to use at the table, to money management, to etiquette and terminology, Concepts for Texas Hold'em will steer you toward bigger profits from your poker sessions. Aimed at intermediate to advanced players, we skip over the basics of the game to tricks, tips, and thoughts on how to make the most from your play.

Maximize your wins in your casino cash games of Texas Hold'em Poker. Minimize your losses.

Learn from the superstars ... and Paul.

***

Please Review Our Other Books

If you enjoyed this book, or any of our other books, please feel free to leave reviews at Amazon or Goodreads.com. All of our books are available at Amazon and Left Hand Publishers' site.

Beautiful Lies, Painful Truths I Amazon: http://amzn.to/2reSyIe Goodreads: http://bit.ly/2BobVCi	**Beautiful Lies, Painful Truths II** Amazon: http://amzn.to/2ngBq0i Goodreads: http://bit.ly/2slkBpP
Realities Perceived Amazon: http://amzn.to/2Dbe1ny Goodreads: http://bit.ly/2nU9hvw	**The Demon's Angel** by Maya Shah Amazon: http://amzn.to/2EVjj7V Goodreads: http://bit.ly/2son5E2
Two Minds, No Waiting Amazon - https://amzn.to/39jAjFm Goodreads - https://bit.ly/3pkLzH9	**Terrors Unimagined** Amazon: https://amzn.to/2OsldAT Goodreads: https://bit.ly/2LkLO17
Suspense Unimagined Amazon - https://amzn.to/2UwG7VI Goodreads - https://bit.ly/2VlHN1x	**A World Unimagined** Amazon: https://amzn.to/2yvJ4vS Goodreads: https://bit.ly/2K7b6zj
Mindscapes Unimagined Amazon - https://amzn.to/2FNVkZ4 Goodreads - https://bit.ly/2ORO1nq	**Classics ReMixed** Amazon - https://amzn.to/2M0qRLx Goodreads - https://bit.ly/2LZsIQI
Classics ReMixed II Amazon - https://amzn.to/3aC5aeh Goodreads - https://bit.ly/2vMBMDm	**Magic's Balance** by Steve Rouse Amazon - https://amzn.to/3qJqruG Goodreads - https://bit.ly/3aiLgXp
Magic's Balance by Steve Rouse Amazon - https://amzn.to/2ZeGKYf Goodreads - https://bit.ly/3aYGIWB	**Tower, Sword, Stone and Spell** by Timothy Vincent Amazon - https://amzn.to/3e9Y44b Goodreads - https://bit.ly/3e7TALg
That Boy Ain't Write in the Head By Paul K. Metheney Amazon - https://amzn.to/3AVTj7v Youtube - https://youtu.be/zpDkfvbzimw Goodreads - https://bit.ly/3E02x4z	**Drawing from the Well** By Rachel Bollinger Amazon: https://amzn.to/2th8WGE Goodreads: https://bit.ly/2M8h57h
Dragon's Magician by Steve Rouse Amazon - https://amzn.to/3vxDlj9 Goodreads - https://bit.ly/3AUTZtW	

***

www.ingramcontent.com/pod-product-compliance
Lightning Source LLC
Chambersburg PA
CBHW071214250626
47159CB00001B/305